PRAISE FOR ROBERT ELLIS

City of Echoes

"Ellis keeps everything in focus while building a staggering momentum."
—*Booklist* starred review

"*City of Echoes* is a dark, gritty, one-sit read . . . Ellis' trademark plotting is on full display here."

—Bookreporter.com

"Only really good writers can make you feel so strongly . . . *City of Echoes* is another bravura effort from the talented Robert Ellis."
—*Mystery Scene Magazine*

"*City of Echoes* is an absorbing and entertaining read from first page to last and documents novelist Robert Ellis as a master of the genre."
—Midwest Book Review

City of Fire

"Los Angeles, under a cloud of acrid smoke . . . Robert Ellis's *City of Fire* is a gripping, spooky crime novel."
—*New York Times* Hot List Pick

"*City of Fire* is my kind of crime novel. Gritty, tight and assured. Riding with Detective Lena Gamble through the hills of Los Angeles is something I could get used to. She's tough, smart, and most of all, she's real."

—Michael Connelly

The Lost Witness

"Scorching. Deliciously twisted. Nothing is what it appears to be. Ellis succeeds masterfully in both playing fair and pulling surprise after surprise in a story that feels like a runaway car plunging down a mountain road full of switchbacks."

—*Publishers Weekly*, Starred Review

"Ellis serves up a killer crime tale with riveting characters and relentless twists."

—*Booklist*, Starred Review

Murder Season

"*Murder Season*: a terrific sick-soul-of-LA thriller . . . Before you can say *Chinatown* we are immersed in a tale of mind-boggling corruption where virtually every character in the book—with the exception of Lena—has a hidden agenda. Ellis is a master plotter . . . Along the way we meet wonderful characters."

—*Connecticut Post*, Hearst Media News Group

"Within the space of a few books, Ellis has demonstrated that rare ability to skillfully navigate his readers through a complex plot filled with interesting, dangerous and surprising characters."

—Bookreporter.com

THE LOVE
KILLINGS

ALSO BY ROBERT ELLIS

City of Echoes
Murder Season
The Lost Witness
City of Fire
The Dead Room
Access to Power

THE LOVE KILLINGS
ROBERT ELLIS

THOMAS & MERCER

Published by Thomas & Mercer, Seattle.

www.apub.com

Amazon, the Amazon logo, and Thomas & Mercer are trademarks of Amazon.com Inc. or its affiliates.

ISBN-13: 9781503952744
ISBN-10: 1503952746

Cover design by Marc Cohen

Printed in the United States of America.

For my friend Mark Moskowitz

"It ain't what you don't know that gets you into trouble. It's what you know for sure that just ain't so."

—Mark Twain

AUTHOR'S NOTE

The Love Killings is an experiment for me as a writer in the sense that it's an actual continuation of *City of Echoes*, Detective Matt Jones's first murder case. A lot of loose ends were still in play at the end of that first thriller, and I enjoyed every one of them. But now six weeks of story time have passed—the chase is on—and *The Love Killings* is off and running. While it may not be necessary to have read *City of Echoes* first (and yes, several twists and turns from the first novel are openly discussed in the second), the two novels back-to-back deliver something more than I could have ever wished for or even imagined. I hope you love reading these two novels as much as I loved writing them.

Sleep loose,
Robert Ellis

CHAPTER 1

Matthew Trevor Jones wanted to kill his father . . .

He had been thinking about it every day for the past six weeks of his recovery, just as he was thinking about it now at 2:00 a.m.

Like most nights since the shooting, he had trouble getting to sleep. But tonight he had a reason more palpable than the pain echoing from his wounds or even the ghosts and demons making their late-night visit to his bed.

He was sitting outside on the back deck, keeping an eye on the wildfire climbing up the hill on the south side of Potrero Canyon Park. Firefighters were on the ground, driving the wall of flames upward, while a second crew was on top of the ridge, protecting the homes and pelting the foliage with water the City of Angels could hardly spare.

Holy water. That's all the city had left these days.

On a clear night, Matt's small home on the north peak provided a view that stretched from Santa Monica and Venice Beach all the way east across the basin to the tall buildings downtown. Tonight, the smoke was too thick to see through, just a mushroom cloud billowing into a sky without stars or planets or even a moon.

He looked back at the fire, still thinking about killing his father. He knew in his heart that it was the right thing to do—the only thing to do—and that the longer he waited, the greater the chance his father would hire another lowlife like the late Billy Casper to put a bullet in his head.

Although Matt had kept what he learned about his father's intentions to himself and filed it away as "personal business," although Matt had appeared to be cooperating with the detectives investigating his case, in the end he told them nothing because he didn't need to. The name Billy Casper turned out to be a dead end, a false identity that remained a mystery. Matt knew for a fact that his father had hired the man to kill him. And in a bad moment, a moment when Matt's guard had shut down, Casper almost succeeded with that worn-out .38 of his.

The memory lingered for a moment before Matt pushed it away. It was still too close. Still too painful. Almost yesterday.

He took a swig of beer, the bottle somehow managing to hold its chill. It was the first day of December, still over ninety degrees in the middle of the night, with an endless forecast of blue skies, oppressive heat, and solemn warnings by TV weather people about something they were now calling photochemical smog: a lethal combination of sunlight and exhaust rising from the freeways that smelled like spent jet fuel and didn't do much for anybody's lungs. There was a time, just five years ago, when Matt could actually detect four seasons in Los Angeles. They were subtle, but they were there. Now there was only one season. Wildfire season—mixed with the Santa Ana winds smacking him in the face with dust and sand and saturating his clothing with the smell of burned-down houses and lost dreams.

Paradise redux.

Matt took another swig from the bottle and laughed. It would take more than an endless summer and block after block of dead lawns to sour his mood.

He loved this city. He loved everything about it. LA was the only place he had ever lived where he could feel an actual pulse. He didn't understand where it came from. All he knew was that when he woke up every morning, he could sense its presence. In his chest, his being, in everything he touched, heard, or looked at.

And that's why when he killed his father, when he shot the man dead, he couldn't afford to get caught. His plan, his method, every detail would have to be thought out. Every move, perfectly planned.

Dear old Dad, the King of Wall Street.

A man who lived for appearances' sake, and couldn't afford to let his secret out. His truth. A man who abandoned his young wife and son and knew that if anyone found out now, his reputation would be tainted forever. M. Trevor Jones—chairman, president, and CEO of PSF Bank of New York, one of the five largest banks in the United States.

Matt's cell phone started vibrating. Digging it out of his pocket, he knew that at this hour the caller could be only one of two people. As he read his new supervisor's name on the face, Lt. Howard McKensie from Hollywood Homicide, his heart quickened.

Matt had been cleared for active duty just two days ago by his doctors at USC Medical Center and by an LAPD psychiatrist working out of the Behavioral Science Section in Chinatown.

Matt touched the icon and took the call. "What's going on, Lieutenant? How can I help?"

McKensie cleared his throat, his voice rough and ready. "Why aren't you sleeping, Jones? It's two in the fucking morning and you're not sleeping. This is what worries me about you."

Matt glanced back at the wildfire. "Everybody's up, Lieutenant. The canyon's on fire."

"Your place gonna burn?"

"Doesn't look like it, unless the wind changes."

"Good," McKensie said. "Then I need to see you in my office ASAP."

Matt stood up. "You've got something for me already? A new case?"

"Yeah, Jones. It looks like you've caught a new case."

Something was wrong with McKensie's voice. The gravel was there and so was the punch, but Matt could hear something else going on underneath. Something deep and without form.

"Why aren't we meeting at the crime scene, Lieutenant?"

"I'll explain everything when you get here. And you need to hurry. You need to get here as soon as you can."

Matt leaned against the deck rail, still gazing at the fire. "Who's dead?" he asked in a quieter voice.

"It's not who's dead that we're worried about right now. It's who we're looking for, Jones."

Matt didn't need to ask the question, but did. "Then who is it, Lieutenant? Who are we looking for?"

A moment passed, the clouds of smoke reaching the blank ceiling and rippling across the entire sky until the heavens vanished. Ash began falling through the air like hot snow.

"It's Baylor," McKensie said finally. "The doctor's killing again."

CHAPTER 2

Matt climbed into the car, fired up the V-6, and switched on the air conditioner. Wondering if he'd ever see his house again, he pulled out of the carport into the smoke and falling ash and snaked his way through a set of narrow streets at an even speed. Once he reached the west end of Sunset Boulevard and the smoke began to thin, he powered through the six-speed manual transmission and let the car go.

It was late. Almost three in the morning. Yet as Matt worked the curves and steep hills and kept an eye on his rearview mirror, as he ran through one red light after the next, he realized that his mind was tack sharp.

He was thinking about the concern he'd sensed in McKensie's voice and wondering if it was limited to Dr. Baylor's resurrection as a killer in progress. The crimes Baylor had committed, the innocence of his victims and the harshness of their deaths, his utter lack of humanity, and now his return—all of it would have colored anyone's voice with worry.

But somehow this was different. If Dr. Baylor had murdered another coed anywhere near Los Angeles, Matt would be on his way to a crime scene. Instead, McKensie wanted to meet in his office as soon as possible no matter what the hour.

Instead of action, his lieutenant wanted to talk.

Matt gritted his teeth, made a right onto Wilcox, and pulled into the lot behind the station. As he climbed out of the car, he didn't see his partner's SUV. This seemed odd because Cabrera lived twenty minutes closer to the station than he did. Shrugging it off, Matt hustled toward the building and entered through the back door. Once he reached the squad room, he stepped over to the wall of glass and peered into his supervisor's office.

McKensie wasn't alone. A man in a dark-gray suit was with him. They were standing over the lieutenant's desk, examining a series of photographs. Matt's eyes flicked back to the stranger. No doubt about it, the man in the gray suit was a Fed.

Matt crossed the squad room floor, walking down the hall and catching McKensie's forced smile as he entered the office.

"Thanks for getting here so quickly, Jones. I want you to meet someone from the Department of Justice. Matt Jones, this is Ken Doyle, the assistant US attorney directing the prosecution of Dr. Baylor, if he's captured alive."

Matt held Doyle's gaze as they shook hands, then let his eyes drift down to the eight-by-ten photographs spread across the desk. They were crime-scene photographs of the three coeds who had been murdered in Los Angeles and Kim Bachman, Baylor's fourth victim killed in New Orleans just six weeks ago. They were laid out in four rows and included pictures taken at the coroner's office before the autopsies. Matt noted the girls' swollen faces from their wounds, the cuts from ear to lips and lips to ear, taking on the shape of a hideous smile. A grotesque death mask. What Baylor himself called the "Glasgow smile" or the "Chelsea grin" when he had shown Matt photographs of other victims in one of his medical books.

While it had only been a month and a half in real time, it seemed so long ago. That time when everyone thought Baylor, a highly regarded plastic surgeon, was part of the investigation. That time when everyone thought the doctor was a professional witness trying to help.

Matt turned to McKensie. "Where's my partner?" he said. "Where's Denny?"

McKensie pointed to the chairs in front of his desk. "We'll talk about that later, Jones. Take a seat."

The federal prosecutor started toward the second chair, and Matt sized him up. Doyle was a lean man, forty-five to fifty years old, and just over six feet tall. He had clear brown eyes, a pleasant, even inquisitive way about him, his hair a mix of brown and gray and neatly combed over a chiseled face. But just like McKensie, Doyle had something preying on his mind. Something he was straining to keep hidden from view.

Matt dug his nicotine gum out of his pocket, pushed a piece through the foil, and placed it against his cheek. As the drug began to enter his bloodstream, he sat down with the others and asked the same question he'd asked McKensie over the phone.

"What makes this one different, Lieutenant? Who's the girl? Who's dead?"

Doyle and McKensie glanced at each other. Then the prosecutor slipped on a pair of eyeglasses, turned to Matt, and spoke in a quiet but steady voice.

"Dr. Baylor's interests have changed over the past six weeks, Detective. You might say his methods have evolved. We believe that there are two possible reasons, the first being that he's trying to throw us off and avoid detection by changing gears."

"And the second?" Matt asked.

Doyle kept his eyes on him. "That his insanity is mutating at a ferocious pace."

Matt had predicted it a few days before he was shot. The doctor's behavior was shark-like and required a rising body count. If he wanted to remain hidden, his methodology would have to change.

"Who's the victim? Who's the girl?" Matt repeated, feeling even more anxious now.

Doyle reached for a blue three-ring binder in his briefcase, set it before Matt on the desk, and leafed through the pages until he found a crime-scene photograph.

"It's not a girl, Jones. It's a family. An entire family. Jim and Tammy Stratton, their two daughters, Jennifer and Kaylee, fourteen and seventeen years old, and their son, Jim Jr., who was thirteen. They were well off. They lived in the suburbs outside Philadelphia, a town called Radnor on the Main Line."

Matt could feel his chest tighten, his pulse quicken, the hot load of adrenaline bursting through his veins as he leaned over the photograph for a closer look.

Could he handle it? Was he ready?

The image had been shot with a wide-angle lens and included the entire crime scene. It was a large open space, the image too dark and vast to offer much detail. Matt could see the husband propped against the wall with his two daughters on either side—all three stripped of their clothing and holding hands. On the floor before them, Tammy Stratton's nude body had been left on her back with her legs spread open and her naked son draped on top of her. It seemed clear that the killer had placed the boy on top of his mother after their deaths and with purpose. Even in a wide shot like this one, Matt could see that their genitals were touching.

But what struck Matt most about the photograph was the extraordinary amount of blood coating the bodies and flooding the entire crime scene. As he focused on Stratton and his two daughters, he noticed that the gunshot wounds to their chests were in roughly the same place—far enough away from the heart that it would have continued beating. In spite of the odd shape of the wounds, their placement seemed too deliberate and precise to be a coincidence. Matt's eyes drifted back to all the blood, and he wondered if this was intentional as well. The killer may not have wanted them to die from the actual gunshots. Instead, he may have wanted them to linger until they bled out.

Why?

Matt took a deep breath and exhaled. The nicotine gum wasn't working. When he looked up, he caught McKensie and Doyle measuring his reaction to the photograph. Any questions he might have had as to why either one of them seemed anxious were answered by a single image, a single picture, a single glimpse into Dr. Baylor's demented mind.

"Only six weeks have passed," Matt said. "And this is a long way off from slashing a girl's face. What happened to this family is new territory. How do we know it's Baylor? What makes you so sure?"

Doyle stood up and leaned against the filing cabinet. "The short answer is that he made a mistake on a night that had to be completely chaotic."

"What's the mistake?"

"A fingerprint. A dead match."

"Where? What did Baylor touch?"

"The girl's nipple. Kaylee, the seventeen-year-old. She was home from boarding school for the holidays. She arrived on the afternoon of her death."

Matt sat back in his seat and chewed it over. In Baylor's four previous murders, his wrath had been directed at a parent of the victim. Someone who appeared to be in good standing but had committed a crime or exhibited the will to commit a crime in order to gain personal wealth and power. Most of the doctor's targets, if not all, were narcissists driven by greed who thought the world revolved around them and only them. In Baylor's fractured mind, taking a child away from them, taking away the one thing in their lives they couldn't buy or replace, was his way of punishing them for their hypocrisy. His way of sentencing them to a life of ruin that he felt they deserved. That's why he disfigured each victim's face. He wanted the parent to see the hideous aftermath and carry the image of their dead child with them to their grave.

Baylor reveled in the horror, the punishment. Baylor got off on it.

But this was an entire family, and Matt didn't know what to make of it. As his eyes swept over the image for a third time, it suddenly occurred to him that no one was left behind to grieve or feel any loss or pain. By murdering his audience, Baylor was making the leap from utter darkness into what? The abyss was three miles back. What could be left?

Matt turned to Doyle, his voice barely audible. "Anything else that points directly to Baylor?"

"Mrs. Stratton was raped. There's enough semen for the lab to make a match. And we've got a second fingerprint. Better than the first. It was lifted off the girl's fingernail." Doyle paused a moment, then narrowed his brow. "They were freshly polished."

Matt got up and started pacing, his mind stoked. Baylor got off on painting his victim's nails with polish. He'd seen it with his own eyes.

He shook his head. It all seemed so incredible.

"When did this happen?"

"Just a few days ago," Doyle said.

"I haven't seen or heard anything about it. Something this big, you would think—"

Doyle cut in. "My guess is that you will in about four hours."

"Have you named Baylor as a person of interest?"

"Not yet. Not until we have to. Believe me, Jones, once the details start coming out, well . . . Baylor couldn't have picked a worse place to reappear than Philly. A serial killer worked the city, when was it? Ten, fifteen years ago? He worked it hard. People are still frightened."

Matt knew exactly who and what Doyle was talking about because he had been a teenager living with his aunt in New Jersey at the time. Eddie Trisco and what the media labeled the ET Killings. An estimate of the number of Trisco's victims had changed over the years, but had finally settled in at somewhere between thirty and thirty-five young women. Before leaving for Afghanistan, Matt heard that the house Trisco rented in West Philadelphia had become something of a tourist attraction offering an endless line of curiosity seekers a walk through the basement and what everyone was calling *the dead room*.

Matt let go of the memory and took another look at the photograph. "Who was the doctor after?" he said. "Stratton or his wife?"

"Stratton," Doyle said. "He was an MD and ran half a dozen upscale clinics in the suburbs and around town. Last August two patients came forward claiming they were given chemotherapy and radiation treatments only to find out from another doctor that they never had cancer. Once detectives got a closer look at Stratton's practice, the number of patients receiving chemo and radiation seemed unusually high. When they got a look at his books, the money coming in from Medicare and health insurance companies seemed even higher. Millions and millions of dollars higher. Stratton used his patients as cash cows. Most of them, ninety-nine percent of them, will never recover from what he did to their bodies. When Stratton was confronted with his crimes, he never showed any remorse. All Stratton cared about was Stratton. Until his death he was out on bail waiting for a trial date. It would have been a federal prosecution. His story made the news. He fits Baylor's hit list like a glove."

No one said anything for a while. Except for the sound of the fan straining to push cooler air through the vent in the ceiling, the office had turned quiet. Matt looked at McKensie staring back at him with an odd expression on his face and realized that his lieutenant hadn't said anything since he first sat down.

Doyle checked his watch, then reached into his pocket and pulled out an envelope.

"It's a ticket, Jones. LAX to Philly. The flight takes off at 11:15 this morning. The FBI has formed a special task force in the hunt for Dr. Baylor. I'd like you to consider joining the team. I'd like you to help us hunt down this maniac and put him away for good."

A beat went by. Matt's eyes flicked over to McKensie, then back to Doyle.

"Why me?"

Doyle handed over the envelope. "Because you've got all the right instincts, Jones. The intelligence. The imagination. Because you're the one who broke the case."

"But he got away. He escaped."

Doyle nodded. "And that's why we need you. Inside that envelope with the ticket is a business card for a special agent in charge at the FBI's field office in Westwood. If I were you, I'd go home and pack. At eight sharp make sure you're in Westwood. You'll need federal credentials to join the task force and to get your firearm on the plane. The special agent will swear you in as a deputy US marshal. Your application was submitted yesterday, and you cleared the background check a couple hours ago. After you sign the application and get your picture taken, you'll be issued a new badge and ID. If you're there by eight, you should be able to make that flight without breaking a sweat."

Matt opened the envelope, found the business card, and checked the ticket. LAX to Philly, without a return.

"It's a one-way trip," he said.

Doyle shrugged. "It's an open return, that's all. I'd like you to finish what you started, Detective. I'd like you to be there when we reach the end. We need your help to get there."

CHAPTER 3

Matt tossed his duffel bag onto the bed and walked into the bathroom to pack his shaving kit. Through the mirror he could see McKensie staring at him from the doorway.

"I don't like it," McKensie said.

"Don't like what? You offered to drive."

"I did, Jones. But that doesn't mean that I don't think everything about Doyle's offer is bullshit. I didn't sign off on this."

"Then who did?"

"He spoke to the chief once you passed your background check. The order came from him."

Matt watched McKensie lower his head, then turn away and step out onto the deck. The wildfire was still burning through the south side of the canyon. Although Matt's house had survived the past few hours, he wasn't so sure his luck would last. The winds had picked up, the flames beginning to swirl like a long line of red-hot cyclones. When he and McKensie first arrived, he could see the firefighters retreating down the hill to the sand on the canyon floor. The house on the end had just begun to burn.

Matt tried not to think about it and ripped open a bag of new razors. Glancing into the mirror, he felt a sudden chill wriggling up his spine, and stopped.

McKensie was staring at him with that dark glint in his eyes. He was still on the deck, but he was appraising him again. And he had a certain presence. The shock of his white hair cut against the raw sound of his voice. His heavily lined face and barrel-chested body that reeked of unchecked power and strength.

The man flashed a wicked smile his way and laughed. "You're not ready for this, Jones. You've still got monsters swimming in your head."

Matt turned and gave him a look. "I was cleared," he said. "I'm good."

McKensie laughed again, his voice booming. "No, you're not. Don't you think I can tell? Don't you think I can see it? The last thing you need is a case like this right now. You need something easy. Something that makes sense. A guy kills his wife because she cheated on him. A wife kills her husband because he's a jackass. See what I mean? It's different. It's not messy. You're not chasing some lunatic who gets off on killing kids. You're not chasing a whack job like Baylor."

"This was my case, Lieutenant. It's still my case. Doyle's right about that."

"You really are a dumb fuck, aren't you?"

Matt didn't say anything, turning back to the bag of razors and tossing a couple into his shaving kit. As he thought about it, he had no idea how long he would be away.

"Why you, Jones? Just answer me that. Why you? And why did it sound like the Feds were begging?"

Matt remained quiet. It was the first question that had come to mind when Doyle made the offer, and now, with McKensie beating his chest, Matt still couldn't find an answer that made any sense.

Why him?

He was doing his best to ignore the reality because he wanted to be there. He needed to be there. He had to be part of the end.

"You're a rookie," McKensie went on. "You were shot by a dirty cop less than two months ago. You took three more rounds a couple weeks after that. Tonight an assistant US attorney shows up at your door and says what? You tell me. What do you bring to the table that he can't get ten times better from somewhere else?"

"He looked like a good guy," Matt said.

McKensie narrowed those bright-green eyes of his. "He's Department of Justice, Jones. He's a suit. He'd sell you out for a headline."

"I'll be part of the special task force. Another set of eyes."

"You think anybody has time to teach you on the job? A case like this? A madman like Baylor?"

"But I know him. I know Baylor. And I'm the only one who does."

McKensie flashed another wicked grin from the darkness, the wild-fire burning behind his back like a curtain on the devil's stage.

"Now you see it," he said. "And now you don't."

Matt grimaced. "Now I see what?"

"Don't you get it, Jones? Doyle is using you. He knows Baylor saved your life when you were shot. He's knows Baylor removed the bullet and sewed you back up. He's not sure why. How could he be? But you're the only human being whom we know the doctor spared. He's using that knowledge because he thinks there's a reason. For Doyle, prosecuting Baylor would make his career, so he's all in. He'll do anything and everything it takes to win. Using you, even if it doesn't work out, even if it means losing you, is just the price of doing business on his way to an office on the top floor."

Matt couldn't help thinking how much McKensie sounded like Baylor right now. He took a deep breath and exhaled. He was doing everything he could to overlook his gunshot wounds and the aches and pains his doctor said would take another five or six months to subside. It required effort, and he didn't understand why McKensie was trying to chop him down at the knees. Why McKensie was working so hard at it. He unzipped a pocket in his shaving kit. As he swung the mirror open, he could see McKensie lunging into the small room.

"Look at the fucking meds you're on, Jones."

"I'm good," he said.

"Really?"

Matt gave McKensie a hard look up and down before tossing his prescriptions into the shaving kit and zipping up the pocket. Then he walked out, grabbed his duffel bag off the bed, and lugged it through the living room to the front door. He slipped his shaving kit and meds into his briefcase beside his laptop. When McKensie finally gave up and followed him outside, Matt took a last look at his place, switched off the lights, and locked the door.

He was tired of hearing McKensie list all the reasons why he should stay in Los Angeles. All the reasons why he should park himself on the sidelines and stay out of the chase. Matt didn't hold it against him, and wished that he could have told McKensie why he needed this case so much. All those *other* reasons he couldn't explain or talk about to anyone.

Dr. Baylor was the one who got away. The shadow who had turned his dreams into nightmares ever since his escape. The face he couldn't help seeing when he closed his eyes.

It was 7:30 a.m. The sky was black with smoke, the sun unable to break through the darkness. McKensie's car was parked on the street and covered with ash. The entire atmosphere felt odd and haunting. Matt tossed his bags onto the backseat, climbed into the passenger seat, and checked the envelope for the special agent's business card. As McKensie pulled away from the curb, Matt peered down the hill. Another two homes on the south side of the canyon were engulfed in flames, the fire enormous, even breathtaking. When he glanced up the block, he noticed a handful of cops knocking on doors.

The evacuation had begun on the north slope.

He looked back at his house, his home. It seemed so small and out in the open. It was made of wood and needed a fresh coat of paint. It looked so vulnerable.

He tried to shake it off. He tried to get a grip on himself because he knew there was nothing he could do about it.

McKensie had called it right; the monsters were still swimming inside his head—still alive and kicking. But all of that was okay. Riding on the backs of monsters would give him everything he needed to see this through. Even better, the trip to Philadelphia would put him within a couple hour's reach of his father, the King of Wall Street. Matt needed the monsters in order to settle a debt that had turned grim. He needed the monsters to slay the dragon and find his way back home.

CHAPTER 4

The story of the Stratton family murders broke on national news just as the plane reached airspeed and made the slow, torturous climb over the Pacific. That's when Matt's TV switched on and CNN interrupted their schedule with a special report from Philadelphia.

There was no mention of Baylor. No connection to the serial killings in LA and New Orleans. In fact, Matt was struck by how little information had been released. He switched between the cable news channels, then flipped back again. The stories were thin to none on every network.

But like most attempts to keep something buried, every reporter and news anchor seemed to sense that something was wrong and, whatever it might be, was probably extraordinary.

Matt could hear it in their voices and see it on the screen. He could feel it.

It was in the video images of the Strattons' mansion hidden behind the stone wall and obscured by a carriage house and long row of leafless trees. The patrol units parked along the property line, and the massive blue tarp blocking the narrow driveway. A press release stating that within the first hour of discovery, the case had been passed from local authorities to county detectives, and now, two days later and for reasons that hadn't yet been explained, the FBI and Department of Justice were involved.

Nothing ever moved that quickly. Unless the crime defied the imagination and was extraordinarily vicious like this one.

As Matt looked at pictures of the victims provided by friends and family, a handful of snapshots from happier times released by the FBI's field office in Philadelphia, he wondered how long it would take the media to figure it out. How long it would take them to guess, or when the first leak would occur. But even more, he wondered how much time Doyle and the FBI's task force had before they would be forced to step before the cameras and answer more than a handful of difficult questions.

What exactly happened to Jim and Tammy Stratton and their three children? What is the FBI hiding, and why are they hiding it? Why are you going through so much effort to keep us out of the loop? How bad could the details really be? There's a rumor, Mr. Doyle, that you are overseeing the prosecution of Dr. George Baylor, the serial killer who fled Los Angeles and New Orleans. Is this true, and if so, why are you here in Philadelphia?

Why are you here?

Matt's mind surfaced. The plane was landing in darkness, and he reset his watch ahead three hours to 7:30 p.m. According to the e-mail he'd picked up while waiting to be deputized in Westwood, agent K. Brown would be meeting him once he passed through security. While the message didn't offer a description, Matt guessed by the lack of a first name that he would be greeted by a woman. Curiously, K. Brown shared the same last name as Baylor's first victim, Millie Brown, the daughter of former congressman Jack Brown.

The name was meaningless, but still, it set off a—

Matt let the thought go and got out of his seat to open the carry-on bin overhead. As he turned, he caught a man two rows back staring at him. The stranger appeared nervous and quickly dropped his gaze, but

Matt was still recovering from those four gunshot wounds and couldn't afford to look away. Instead, he did the same thing he'd been doing since he was released from the hospital. He committed the man's face to memory. Something about his appearance seemed familiar, but Matt couldn't place it and quickly sized the man up: late thirties or early forties, three maybe four inches shorter than six feet, a tough call because he was still sitting down. In spite of the belly, he seemed thin and soft and out of shape, with black wavy hair, dark-brown eyes, wire-rimmed glasses, and a complexion so pale and colorless it stood out.

Once Matt had the image locked in his mind—a practice his shrink had called a textbook case of paranoia—he grabbed his briefcase and leather jacket, made his way up the aisle, and exited the plane. The gate was more than halfway down the terminal, and Matt was grateful for the chance to stretch his legs. As he walked past the shops and restaurants, he never looked back for the man he had just seen on the plane. He let it go and breezed past security.

Agent K. Brown turned out to be easy enough to spot, and Matt's guess proved right. She was a she in her late twenties, holding an eight-by-ten card with his last name written across the front and offering a warm, gracious smile as they shook hands.

"Kate Brown," she said. "Good flight?"

"Not bad. The story broke."

She nodded. "Yeah."

She pointed toward the sign to baggage claim, and they started walking.

"We keep an apartment here in the city for long stay over's, but something's come up. I heard from Doyle that you didn't get much sleep last night. I hope you don't mind if we take a short drive."

"I'm fine," he said. "I'm still on California time. What's happened?"

"Dr. Stanley Westbrook, a profiler from the FBI's Behavioral Analysis Unit, wants to brief us first thing in the morning."

Matt winced. They already knew who they were looking for, and he wondered what a profiler could contribute this far into the investigation. The murders didn't begin with the Strattons. They began nineteen months ago with the horrific death of Millie Brown.

"Okay," Matt said. "So where are we going tonight?"

"Doyle and my boss, Wes Rogers, you'll meet him tomorrow, he's the special agent in charge of the Philadelphia office. They want you to walk through the crime scene before the briefing tomorrow with Westbrook. They want you to get a feel for what happened."

Matt didn't say anything. He was anxious to see the Strattons' home, and glad that he wouldn't have to wait until morning.

They reached baggage claim, found Matt's flight on the information monitor, and walked down the line to the carousel on the end. As they waited, Matt gave Brown a quick glance. She was easy to look at—her shoulder-length hair a mix of blond and light brown that was either natural or very well done. Her eyes were a vibrant blue that sparkled even in the harsh fluorescent lights of an airport. Her body, too well drawn to be hidden by her open ski parka or the dark-gray slacks and matching jacket that no doubt was the uniform of the day. But what struck Matt most was Brown's presence, her angular face that broadcasted her obvious strength and intelligence.

She came off true, and his first impression was that he liked her.

He looked away as he heard the first bag hit the conveyor belt with a heavy thud. He wondered what had happened in Brown's life that lured her into law enforcement. Was she following a parent's footsteps? Or was she wounded and looking to heal by spending the rest of her life chasing ghosts and righting wrongs?

After a short wait, Matt's duffel bag slid down the ramp and onto the belt. But as he walked over to grab it, he looked up and caught that man staring at him again. The one he'd seen on the plane just a few minutes ago. Even worse, the man had his cell phone out and was pointing it at him. It seemed clear that he wasn't using the phone. He was faking a conversation while either recording video of Matt or taking his picture.

Matt hoisted the bag over his shoulder and followed Brown toward the exit. He was thinking about the hit man his father had hired to kill him. The man Matt had shot to death on top of Mount Hollywood. Turning back to the baggage carousel, Matt gave the man with the cell phone another hard look. He was still pretending to talk to someone. Still pointing the device at him as if using the camera.

Matt turned away. The read he'd made on the plane felt righteous now. He could depend on it. He had a new shadow, and it had followed him to Philadelphia on a cold night in early December. A man with ultra-pale skin who looked like he spent most of his time in the dark. The shrink in LA could call it paranoia if he liked, but Matt would treat it the way his gut told him to. It was all about survival. All about being the first one to shoot. All about dominoes falling down one after the other.

He checked the .45 holstered beneath his down vest and leather jacket and followed Brown out the door. The air was raw, and the hard wind burned his face. Ready or not, his arrival in the City of Brotherly Love felt like a wake-up call.

CHAPTER 5

The drive to the murder house in Radnor would only take about twenty-five minutes. Brown gave Matt a manila envelope and spent most of the time briefing him on details unrelated to the case. The keys to the apartment he would be staying in were here, along with the password to the Internet, information about parking in the neighborhood, and the access card that would open the security gates and doors to the FBI's field office at 600 Arch Street. When Matt asked about the password to the FBI's website and the chronological record he had been given access to before he was shot, Brown told him that Doyle and Rogers would take care of everything tomorrow morning when they gave him a desk and the keys to a car.

Matt checked the road behind them and saw only darkness. He had been keeping an eye out for the odd-looking man with pale skin ever since they left the airport. No one was following them, and he turned back and gazed through the windshield. They were passing a train station and gliding down a hill. Once they came out of the curve, Brown made a left at the light onto County Line Road.

"It's halfway up the next hill," she said in a quiet voice that shook a little.

Matt could feel his stomach beginning to churn. When he spotted the long line of patrol units parked before the stone wall and all the video cameras and reporters crowded onto a small patch of lawn on the other side of the street, the anticipation was almost overwhelming. Brown pulled into the drive and stopped as three cops dressed in black uniforms stepped forward with flashlights and rifles. They wanted to see Brown's ID, and they asked to see Matt's as well. Matt handed over his new badge and ID and thought he saw something change when the cop read his name. It was in his eyes as he passed the badge back.

It was recognition. Knowledge. Baylor.

They lifted the tarp and waved them through. Brown pulled past the carriage house, continuing down the drive until they reached the Strattons' mansion on the left. She popped open the trunk, and they climbed out of the car. While she unlatched a kit and fished out a pair of vinyl gloves and a flashlight, Matt stopped to take in the building.

"The cop that took your badge," she said. "He knows you. He knows who you are."

It was the flaw in Doyle's plan to hold back Baylor's name in the murder of an entire family. Once they saw Matt's face, once word got out that he was here, everyone would know exactly who they were looking for.

Brown passed over the flashlight and gloves and seemed shaky.

"You okay?" he asked.

She nodded. "Just cold."

The exterior lights were lit up along the drive, yet all the windows in the death house were dark—the Strattons' mansion more than just a bit eerie. Matt took in the property and remembered seeing two mail-boxes on the street by the entrance. Guessing that the carriage house and the mansion were built sometime in the 1800s, both appeared to have been heavily remodeled in the last ten years. The carriage house would have been a horse stable and barn, while the mansion was divided into two sections with four entrances. The first door opened to a small wing and was probably meant for the live-in staff. The more grandiose entrance off the long porch would have been the main entrance just as it was today.

"Where do these two doors in the middle go?" he asked.

"The first opens to a hallway, the kitchen, and a second set of stairs."

"And this one?"

"The house manager's office."

Matt glanced at the carriage house, then turned back to the mansion and took a guess. Two families living in two separate homes, but within close proximity of each other. At least five gunshots had been fired, maybe more. As Doyle said when he first described the crime, it would have been a night of total chaos. A night when Dr. Baylor came to punish another physician and blew his mind.

Matt turned to Brown. "I'm assuming people live in the carriage house, and that they were home, right?"

She nodded. "Yes."

"It's only sixty feet away, Kate. It's hard to believe that they didn't hear anything. The gunshots. The kids screaming and shouting for help. Things got crazy in there. It had to be a loud night."

"No one heard anything," she said.

"How old are they?"

"Early fifties. A middle-aged couple. Empty nesters. The time of death was 11:35 p.m. They were watching TV and didn't hear anything out of the ordinary."

"Eleven thirty-five," he said. "What do you mean?"

"Stratton wore a pacemaker. At 11:35 p.m., the box shut down and he was flat lining. According to the medical examiner, everyone was killed within an hour of Stratton's death."

Matt could almost see the expression on Baylor's face as he shot five innocent people with his gun. The joy and satisfaction. The doctor's sick mind leaking out of every pore.

He let the image pass and switched on the flashlight as he sensed movement in the darkness. There was a large pool and spa on the right side of the house. When he panned the flashlight into the yard beyond, he noticed three more cops in black uniforms, carrying rifles and guarding the perimeter. Deeper into the yard he could see a pond partially iced over and another home he suspected had been part of the original estate. A small gatehouse built of stone and set along a quiet tree-lined road. As Matt spotted the stream and bridge and wrought iron gate, he couldn't help imagining how peaceful the carriage ride would have been as the horses led the way around the pond and up the slope to this beautiful colonial mansion built on top of a plateau halfway up the hill.

"How did Baylor get in?" Matt said.

"There's no sign of forced entry. Either the front door was open—and according to the house manager, it often was—or he waited for someone to come home and followed them in."

"There's no live-in staff?"

Brown shook her head. "Three day workers clean the house and take care of the grounds. The housekeeper doubles as the family chef. Once she makes dinner and cleans up, she's out. Most nights that's around eight thirty or nine."

"Then where does the first door on the end lead to?"

"A one-bedroom guest suite. Same thing on the second and third floors."

"Let's go inside."

Matt started walking toward the main entrance. Brown followed him onto the porch, then stopped as they reached the large glass door.

"What is it?" Matt asked. "What's wrong?"

"I read about you," she said quietly. "The things that happened to you, and the things you did. You received the Medal of Valor."

Matt didn't say anything.

She cleared her throat lightly and seemed nervous. Those blue eyes of hers were all over his face.

"Doyle specifically asked me to wait outside," she said. "County detectives processed this crime scene. Their techs shot enough pictures to fill two murder books, and they recorded everything they saw and everything they did on video. You'll see it all tomorrow. It wasn't until they found Baylor's fingerprints that we became involved. Tonight Doyle wants you to take a walk-through on your own. No one seems to know why Baylor murdered these people where he did. Doyle wants your opinion."

"Where were the bodies found?"

"I've been ordered not to say anything. He's looking for a first impression."

She pointed to the lockbox attached to the door. "The key's in there. One-eight-seven, that's the combination to every lockbox so nobody forgets. I'll be waiting in the car. Take as much time as you need."

He wondered if she realized that one-eight-seven was the penal code for homicide in California, but didn't ask. Instead, he watched her cross the lot as he slipped on the vinyl gloves. A light snow had begun to fall that reminded him of the ash drifting down on his home in LA. He wondered if the house was still standing, and if the coyotes that slept beneath his deck were still alive. Four pups had been born last spring and had survived the grueling heat of summer.

Matt blocked the thought out and took a deep breath, then punched in the combination to the lockbox. Removing the key, he unlocked the door and returned the key to the lockbox. He paused for a moment, trying to quiet his mind and his imagination. Then he turned the handle and pushed open the door. As he stepped over the threshold, he was greeted by the pungent smell of rotting blood. The foul odor seemed to permeate the entire foyer, and he almost choked before covering his nose with his hand. He panned the flashlight across the massive staircase and along the wall. When he spotted the switch panel, he turned on the lights.

CHAPTER 6

Matt pulled his hand away from his nose, forcing himself to get used to the harsh odor. As he moved closer to the staircase, he could tell that the stench was emanating from either the second or third floor and drifting down into the foyer like a toxic cloud of death. And the ghosts were here—lots of them. He could feel their presence in the stillness of the house, the silence, the finality and fate of the five people who had once lived here, but were gone now and never coming back.

The lights to the foyer on the first floor were lit, the rooms dark. Matt didn't bother looking for light switches as he made his first sweep of the layout and searched for anything that might stand out. To his right was a small sitting room with French doors opening to the pool. Directly ahead was a library with an entrance to the living room. Beyond the library he found a sunroom that spanned the length of the house and gave way to a formal terrace. Matt stepped into the living room, noting the high ceilings and another set of French doors that opened to the pool. A rich dusting of fingerprint powder seemed to coat every piece of furniture and doorknob in the room. He gave it a second look, then returned to the foyer and followed the hallway to the very end. The doors on the left opened to the house manager's office and a powder room; on the right, a large dining room and kitchen. Matt shined the flashlight across the dining room table and through the doorway into the kitchen. Every room that he'd seen so far included a fireplace, and he guessed that he would find fireplaces in every room upstairs as well. But what struck Matt most about the building was the extensive woodwork. The paneled walls in the library that continued into the foyer and up the wide staircase. The ornate moldings and the fireplace mantels that were obviously carved by hand.

The woodwork stood out because he had never seen anything like it before and guessed that the art had been lost, and no one knew how to do it anymore.

But even worse, Matt guessed that no one probably cared.

He let the thought fade and tried to shed his disappointment. The first floor was clear. There were no signs of a disturbance. Although Matt's initial walk-through had been brief, he hadn't seen any blood or anything that seemed out of order. As he moved to the staircase and started up the steps, the harsh odor stiffened and became oppressive. When he reached the second-floor landing, he moved the beam of light over the walls and carpet, felt his chest tighten, and froze.

He had reached his destination and needed a moment to get a grip on himself. It wasn't easy. His eyes swept over the pools of dried blood on the floor, the spatter almost completely masking the paint on the walls. A single gunshot to the chest could never account for what he was seeing. For some reason he couldn't explain, he thought of Jackson Pollock, an artist who spattered paint on a canvas to create remarkable works of art that seemed bigger than life. Now, seeing it in blood, breathing the horror and stench into his lungs, he wondered if Baylor was trying to make some sort of demented statement.

A thought buoyed to the surface, then sunk back under before Matt could reach it. The idea felt like it might be important, and he realized that he needed to take a deep breath and settle down.

He remembered the crime-scene photograph Doyle had shown him in Los Angeles and moved closer to the pools of blood. A table and lamp had been dragged across the landing and pushed against the stair railing. Matt understood at a glance that Baylor had chosen this spot to stage the murders. But like Brown had said just ten minutes ago, the question was why? Why in a house this big did the doctor want to murder this family on a second-floor landing?

There had to be a reason, a purpose. With Dr. Baylor there was always a reason and a purpose.

Matt stepped closer and knelt down, panning his flashlight across the wall. There were three holes in the plaster about two feet off the ground. These would've been made by crime-scene techs as they removed the slugs and entered them as evidence. Matt thought about that photograph again. Stratton's corpse, along with his two daughters', had been found leaning against the wall, with their clothing removed and holding hands. Stratton's naked wife had been laid out on the floor directly before them with her legs spread open. Her thirteen-year-old son was draped over her body as if they had been making love.

Their genitals were touching. The photograph may have been dark and shot from a distance to take in the entire crime scene, but Matt could still see it. Still picture it. And then that stray thought buoyed to the surface again, and this time Matt seized it.

If Baylor had been trying to make a statement, it seemed forced. It felt like he was straining. Obviously Baylor's condition had deteriorated over the past month and a half and he'd lost control of himself. He was no longer just a serial killer, but had graduated and become a mass killer. He'd unlocked the door to his demons, and on the night of the murders, they all came running out.

But that still didn't explain why there was so much blood on the walls, nor did it even come close to answering the key question.

Why did Baylor choose to kill these people here on a landing instead of a bedroom? Given the obvious sexual nature of the killings, the crime would seem to have been better orchestrated on a bed.

Why here?

Matt stood up and stepped through the doorway into the master bedroom suite. Like the first floor, fingerprint powder coated every object in the room. But the bed was neatly made, nothing had been disturbed or appeared out of place, and Matt didn't see a single drop of blood. He entered the bathroom, shined his flashlight in the shower and tub, then passed through two dressing rooms and a study and out a second door onto the landing. When he noticed a door at the base of the stairs to the third floor, he swung it open and found what he thought might be a room dedicated to yoga and meditation.

He took the stairs to the third floor two at a time and made a quick inspection of each room; three were bedrooms for the Strattons' children while the fourth had been turned into a rec room for watching TV and playing video games. The tubs and showers in the bathrooms were clean. Except for the fingerprint powder, nothing appeared to be out of order anywhere on the floor, and he didn't see a single drop of blood.

So why the landing? Why do it on a carpet and hardwood floor when a king-sized mattress was right through the door in the Strattons' bedroom?

Matt returned to the second floor. There was a window beside the meditation room, and he could see Brown in the car talking to someone on her cell phone. On the other side of the driveway and garage, a forest of trees covered the steep hill. Matt noted that they were pine trees and guessed that this was the north side of the property. From the forest's size and density, it was a safe bet that the trees had been planted as cover and were as old as the house.

Why here? Why the landing?

He turned and noticed that he'd forgotten to close the door to the study off the master suite. Sidestepping the blood, he shut the door and glanced at the fingerprint powder clinging to his glove. When he noticed another door by the top of the stairs, he opened it to reveal the rear staircase and the door to one of the three guest suites. It was dark. Spooky. He could feel his mind chewing through everything he was seeing. He could feel a certain clarity and vision that he hadn't experienced for a single moment since he'd been shot.

And then it happened—the sudden freeze right between his shoulder blades. This heightened sense of concentration. He could feel the ghosts in the house. They were closer now. They were watching him.

He turned sharply, counting all the closed doors as his eyes rocked through the crime scene.

Why had Baylor staged his killing spree on the landing?

The answer seemed so obvious now.

CHAPTER 7

The snow flurries had stopped with nothing more than a dusting on the frozen ground. As Matt climbed into the passenger seat, Brown switched off her cell phone and gave him a measured look.

"You okay?" she asked.

Matt shrugged. "I'm good."

"Really?" she said in a voice laced with sarcasm. "I've already got you figured out, Jones. When you lie, your left eye twitches."

"How long's it gonna take to get the toxicology reports?"

"A couple of weeks," she said. "You're thinking they were drugged."

"Yeah."

He watched her pull down the drive and give the three cops in black uniforms a nod as they waved them through with their rifles. After making a right turn onto County Line Road, she took a quick glimpse at the media's outpost on the lawn and coasted down the hill. There was a small bridge built over the stream here. Matt read the street sign, searching for the gatehouse he had seen earlier and realizing that it was too far down the road and way too dark. The entire area would have to be explored in daylight, and to Matt, it was important enough that he hoped he could return tomorrow.

Baylor had to have parked his car somewhere, and Matt knew with absolute certainty that it wouldn't have been anywhere near the Strattons' home. He would have parked his car where it wouldn't stand out—maybe the train station—and hiked in through the woods. In a neighborhood like this one, it wouldn't—

His mind switched back to the tox screen. "Were any puncture marks found on the victims during the autopsies?"

"No," Brown said. "And the medical examiner made it a point to look for them. We already had the fingerprint match, so he read your reports and final statement and knew that Baylor had a history of using something to keep his victims docile. Something that works through the system quickly and was never picked up. He didn't find any puncture wounds, but like he said himself, that doesn't mean they weren't there. Baylor's a plastic surgeon and would know where to hide them. We're thinking he's using Pentothal. It works quickly and they would have been helpless."

Matt wanted to get his hands on the murder book. And he wanted in on the FBI's website so that he could read through the chronological record they were keeping online. His mind was back, and he wanted to burn through it while the clarity lasted.

Brown made a left at the light. "I need to know how it went, Jones. Why do you think Baylor killed them on the landing?"

Matt didn't say anything. After thinking it over, he leaned against the door and gave her a look.

"Because he needed to," he said finally.

"What do you mean?"

"He needed to dampen the sound. Like we said before, it would've been a loud night. There would've been shrieks and cries for help, at least until he could get them sedated. How many gunshots were fired?"

"Five," she said. "One for each victim."

"Okay, so Baylor needed to dampen the sound of five gunshots. The landing is surrounded on every side by other rooms. The exterior walls are a foot and a half thick. The only weak spot is the window. When I looked outside, the angle was off and I couldn't see the carriage house. All I saw were pine trees and a steep hill. It was breezy tonight. I could hear the tree branches when we were standing in the drive. If it was like this on the night of the murders, any sound that leaked through the glass would have stayed right where Baylor wanted it."

She turned and met his eyes. "In the wind," she said.

Matt nodded. "In the wind."

It hung there, in the warmth of the Crown Vic on a cold night.

When Brown spoke, her voice was soft and low. "I'll let Doyle and Rogers know."

Matt settled back in his seat and yawned, the sleep he'd lost last night beginning to catch up to him. After a while Brown switched on the radio to KYW, a news station that sounded a lot like KNX, the news station in LA. Headlines began at the top of the hour, with traffic and weather updates recycling every ten minutes. But tonight there was only one story in Philadelphia. Because the media had been given so little information about the murders, the stories and interviews were with retired members of various law enforcement agencies and physicians from local hospitals who had nothing to do with the investigation and could offer little more than speculation.

Most thought that one of Stratton's former patients committed the murders in an act of revenge that got out of hand. Had Matt not been aware of the physical evidence, had he not walked through the crime scene, he might have thought the same thing. Stratton had used his patients as cash cows, administering chemotherapy and radiation treatments even though they were healthy. His vulgar thirst for money and power, his greed, contaminated his entire being. Like most narcissists, Stratton had evolved into a monster. And that's exactly what would have attracted Dr. Baylor. As Matt tossed it over, he couldn't help thinking that the barbaric nature of Stratton's crime was what sent Baylor over the edge. This had to be why Baylor wanted to destroy Stratton's entire bloodline. The fact that Stratton had taken the Hippocratic oath and broken his vows as a physician would have resonated with Baylor in spite of his own personal history and mental decline.

Matt looked over at Brown's face in the soft glow of the dashboard lights. She knew that he was tired and not in the mood to talk right now. And he liked the fact that nothing about his silence felt uncomfortable.

Traffic on the expressway was light, and the drive downtown to the exit at Thirtieth Street Station took less than half an hour. As Brown circled the train station, Matt realized that everything was beginning to look familiar to him again. The FBI's apartment was located in a section of the city called Fitler Square and covered a number of blocks that included the Schuylkill River Park. Brown turned right off Market Street onto Twenty-Third Street, heading south and making the cut over to Twenty-Fourth. A few minutes later she made a left onto Pine Street and pulled to the curb before a pair of four-story apartment buildings that were set directly across the street from the actual square. Matt gazed through the wrought iron fence at the benches and fountain and all the trees that would be leafing out in the spring and providing shade on a hot summer day. When he turned back to the pair of buildings, he noted the same sign, "Fitler Commons," over both entrances.

"You're on the fourth floor of the building on the left. It's a front corner two-bedroom apartment with a view of the square and Center City. The river's only two blocks away, so if this were April or May and you jogged and had any spare time, you'd be in the right place."

She was making a joke and had a look going.

"But this is December," he said. "And so I'm not."

She laughed. "You're in a real nice neighborhood, Jones. Cafés, restaurants, it's quiet here. Not a lot of traffic. You need any help getting your bags upstairs?"

"I'll be fine."

"The elevator's a little shaky."

Matt climbed out of the car, then opened the rear door and grabbed his duffel bag and briefcase. When he looked in on Brown, she was writing something down on the back of a business card.

"It's my home number," she said, "just in case. I live five minutes north of here in the museum district. Call me if you need me. My cell's on the front with our office numbers and the address."

"What about my cell number?"

"Doyle already gave it to me. Oh, and it's supposed to get colder tomorrow. A real deep freeze. The office is on the other side of town. If I were you, I'd take a cab in the morning."

"When's morning?"

"Eight sharp."

Matt thought about what he was wearing: a pair of slacks and a casual dress shirt. He hadn't brought a suit and had forgotten to pack a sports jacket.

"What about the dress code?" he said. "I'm a G-man now."

She gave him a quick look. "A temporary G-man who grew up in Jersey and lives in LA. With that kind of résumé what you're wearing will do just fine."

Matt closed the passenger door, and Brown lowered the window.

"Thanks, Kate," he said. "Thanks for making everything so easy."

She didn't say anything. She didn't need to. She smiled and nodded and pulled away from the curb.

CHAPTER 8

Matt flipped the business card over and glanced at her name and title printed on the front: "Kate Brown, Assistant Agent in Charge." Slipping the card into his pocket, he watched her drive off until she vanished around the corner on Twenty-Second Street. The sidewalks were nearly empty, and he noticed the silhouette of a man walking toward him two blocks away. Matt waited for him to step beneath a streetlight, then grabbed his bags and entered the building.

It wasn't his shadow. It wasn't the man he'd seen on his flight and at the airport. His hair wasn't black, but blond, and he carried a knapsack and had the build, at least from a distance, of someone who worked out in a gym.

Matt found the elevator and listened to the cables creak all the way up to the fourth floor. As he stepped out into a dimly lit hallway, he could hear the sound of someone's TV bleeding through their door. Apartment 4B was just down the way on the left. After unlocking the deadbolt and the handle lock, he switched on the lights and walked inside.

The place was nicer than he expected. Much nicer. Whoever furnished the rooms had taste and seemed to know that the people staying here were away from home. The kitchen was to his right directly behind him. Someone had stocked the fridge with milk and eggs and almost anything he might need for a day or two. He grabbed a beer, twisted off the cap, and took a swig. Then he checked the cabinets and found cereal and coffee. As he walked through the living room, he noted the large bay window and gazed outside at the square across the street. From four stories up, it looked like a very cold and lonely place. Like an arcade on a Jersey boardwalk that was closed for winter and wouldn't open again until spring.

He turned back to the room and took another sip of beer. The art on the walls, the black-and-white photographs, all seemed so familiar. One of the three photographs was by Minor White. It was an incredible shot of a road heading toward the hills and lined with white poplar trees that looked as if they were burning. An actual print of the same photograph hung in the Blackbird Café, one of Matt's homes away from home in LA.

He stepped away from the window. There were no hallways in the apartment, each room opening to the next. He could see that the front bedroom had been converted into a study and shared a bath with the rear bedroom. Matt walked into the room, checked the mattress, then passed through the door into the living room.

Everything felt good, and he was more than grateful to be here instead of a hotel room.

He tossed his duffel bag on the bed. When he came back for his laptop and briefcase, he heard the elevator and looked through the peephole.

It was that man he'd seen on the street. The man with the knapsack. He was walking down the hall, searching for a key on his key ring. Matt watched him unlock the door to the next apartment and announce to someone inside that he was home. When the door closed, Matt got out of his jacket, found the remote, and switched on the TV.

CNN had just cut to a string of commercials. Matt muted the sound and set his laptop up on the coffee table. Then he pulled his shaving kit out of his briefcase and ripped it open. The gunshot wounds were beginning to blister through his chest, the real pain probably an hour off. He sorted through his medications, passing over the Vicodin and opening the bottle of Advil. But as he knocked back two capsules with a swig of beer, he glanced at the TV and thought he might choke.

It was his father, M. Trevor Jones.

Matt grabbed the remote and turned up the sound. It looked like the media had caught up to him as he exited a building in New York and tried to get to the limousine waiting for him in the street. The building was set back from the sidewalk and had an unusually large open-air entrance, so reaching the limo wouldn't be easy.

Within a few seconds, Matt caught the gist of the story and stopped listening. He already knew why his father was being hounded by the media and didn't need to listen to a newsreader from CNN repeat a story that had been in the papers for weeks. His father was negotiating a financial settlement with the Department of Justice, the Office of the Comptroller of the Currency, and the Federal Reserve Bank for an unspecified amount that many believed would exceed one billion dollars. His father's bank had been caught playing games with mortgages to veterans and active members of the military. Overcharges, hidden fees, and improper foreclosure practices had forced thousands of people out of their homes. The investigation had been completed, and now it was time for dear old Dad, the King of Wall Street, to pay up.

But something else was going on here. Matt stepped closer to the TV. The camera was handheld and bouncing up and down in the chaos. Matt looked at his father's face—the man's teeth were clenched, his arms up, his head down—but it wasn't his father making the push through the crowd. It was the two men beside him that were clearing the way. Both of them were wearing suits and appeared hard and tough, the reporters poking his father with their microphones completely outmatched.

Matt took another step closer to the screen.

What concerned him wasn't their appearance or physical strength. It was the fact that both men were armed. Their jackets were open, and Matt could see the pistols strapped to their shoulders.

His father had hired a pair of bodyguards. Armed bodyguards.

This was new, and Matt didn't believe that it had anything to do with his father's financial troubles. His bank could easily afford to pay a billion-dollar fine. This was about Matt. His father knew that he was coming. Matt could sense it. His father had begun to prepare.

CHAPTER 9

The FBI's field office occupied most of the federal building at 600 Arch Street. It was a ten-story low-rise building that shared underground parking with the federal courthouse and had been named after William J. Green Jr., a beloved congressman from Philadelphia who died young and fathered a son who would later become the city's mayor.

Matt breezed through security with his new ID. The special task force was housed on the eighth floor with Violent Crime. Kate Brown was waiting for him and eyed the badge clipped to his belt as he stepped out of the elevator.

"Any trouble downstairs?" she asked.

"No," he said. "It was easy."

"You need to meet someone before Dr. Westbrook gets started."

He nodded and followed her down the hall to a large corner office. Ken Doyle was standing by the desk with a man Matt assumed was Wes Rogers.

Doyle smiled. "Glad you made it, Jones. This is Wes Rogers, special agent in charge. I think you'll like working with him."

Matt met Rogers's even gaze and shook his hand.

"Good to meet you, Jones. Welcome to the task force. We'll get you squared away after the briefing. Sound good?"

Matt nodded. "Thanks."

Doyle rested his hand on Matt's shoulder. "Brown gave us an update on your walk through the crime scene, Jones. You're already paying off dividends, and I'm glad you're here. Now let's get down to the Crisis Room."

Doyle led the way out of the office. As they started down the hall, Matt kept his eyes on Rogers. The truth was that the special agent in charge came off like a forty-five-year-old version of the actor James Earl Jones. His voice was deep and throaty like the actor's, his complexion on the medium side, and he had those steady eyes that seemed to sweep your way and lock in. He was a big man with a firm handshake. Matt couldn't help but be impressed by his demeanor and presence, his confidence.

The Crisis Room was around the next corner at the very end of the hallway. Rogers held the door open, and Matt entered and took a quick look around. His first thought was that the Feds had money. Everything appeared to be ultra-modern and high-tech, including the media wall at the head of the room, which housed three massive video monitors. Below the screens a lectern with a lamp had been set on a low built-in stage. More than twenty members of the task force were sitting in chairs, waiting to be briefed by Dr. Westbrook. Behind them Matt counted twenty-four desks pushed together in pairs so that they faced each other. He looked at the laptop computers on the desktops, the matching desk lamps, and the conference room in back enclosed in walls of glass. Everything appeared to be new and up-to-date. Clearly, he wasn't in an office anywhere near the Hollywood station right now.

"Let's find a seat," Brown said.

Matt followed her over to the last row of chairs, gazing at the monitors as they sat down. The video feeds were different on all three. The first screen was switched to a cable news station and muted. On the far right screen, someone had put together a clip that depicted Dr. Baylor's face as it had been six weeks ago, cut against what he might look like today if he'd made any changes. One shot after the next showed the doctor wearing a moustache, a beard, eyeglasses with different frames, a change in hair color, and a variety of common hats.

Matt found the clip impressive—the Feds had money and they had time—but it was the screen in the middle that grabbed his attention.

The feed was paused and darkened, yet the image still had impact. It was video from the Strattons' second-floor landing, and Matt couldn't take his eyes off it. Last night he could only imagine what had happened on the night of the murders. Now, looking at the victims as they were found, everything changed.

"Their eyes are open," he whispered.

Brown leaned closer. "Wide-open like they're still alive. That's one reason why it went from local to county so quickly. The first responders freaked out."

Matt nodded slightly, his mind fixated on the center screen. He was wondering how he would have responded had he been the first one to enter the Strattons' home and discover the crime scene. How anyone would have responded. He looked at the father sitting between his two daughters. The mother staring at her son, and her son gazing back at her. Matt found the image so disturbing that he could feel his skin crawling. The photograph Doyle had shown him in LA had been a wide shot of the entire landing. The victims' faces had been cast in shadow and stained with blood, the detail lost.

"What's with the bullet holes?" he said. "When I saw the crime-scene photo, they looked like gunshot wounds. Now they don't."

Brown lowered her voice as the overhead lights dimmed. "At some point during the process, Baylor taped over them. We're not sure why."

"What kind of tape?"

"Gaffer tape," she whispered. "They use it in the movies."

Matt took a deep breath and exhaled. Wes Rogers had just stepped behind the lectern and was testing the microphone. He took a sip of water, covered the mike with his palm, and said something to a man standing in the shadows with Doyle who Matt guessed was Dr. Westbrook. After a brief exchange of words, the special agent in charge was back.

"Before we bring out Dr. Westbrook," he said, "I'd like to give everyone a brief update. We have a new member of the task force today, LAPD Homicide Detective Matt Jones. We all know his story and what he's been through. Without Jones's good work, it could have taken months if not years to put these murders together. He should be a reminder to all of us why we're here and what we need to accomplish. Oh, and did I mention that Detective Jones received the Medal of Valor? Matt, why don't you stand up? Everybody, let's give him a hand."

Matt nodded and raised a hand to the applause, but his mind was still focused on the gunshot wounds. Why had Baylor taped over them?

Rogers checked his notes. "We've got news from the Bureau of Forensic Services," he said. "A good portion of the semen sample taken from Mrs. Stratton became contaminated by her son's blood when he was placed on top of her. Everyone at the lab is aware of the problem. A second run is underway as we speak. It's a smaller sample, but thought to be clean. They've promised us a preliminary finding sometime tomorrow. Also, we've got a ballistics report. Of the five shots fired, three were through-and-throughs, the slugs mangled beyond any value when they hit the wall. But the last two were soft-tissue strikes retrieved by the medical examiner. They're in good shape. Details and results will be posted on the web as they come in. Now let's bring out Dr. Westbrook."

Everyone in the room applauded one more time as Westbrook stepped over to the lectern and shook Rogers's hand. Matt had heard about him, but never actually seen him. He wasn't a very tall man and needed to lower the microphone. Matt guessed that the psychiatrist and profiler was in his midfifties. His face was heavily lined, his black hair on the long side and streaked with gray. But what stood out were his eyes. They may have been dark and the glasses he wore may have been thick, but his eyes sparkled like a pair of headlights in the night. Matt still didn't understand why a briefing by a profiler was necessary. They already knew who they were looking for. But here it was—

Westbrook loosened his tie and pointed a remote at the first screen on the media wall. The feed switched from the cable news station to a photograph of Baylor's third known victim, Brooke Anderson, exactly as she had been found on the night of her murder just below the Hollywood sign. Matt had been with the first group on the scene. The girl's clothing had been removed, her body staked to the ground with her face resting on a mirror. Matt could remember the moment he knelt down beside her body with his flashlight and strained to see her face through all the blood. The mutilation had been hideous, her cheeks bloated, her features so deformed that it looked like she was wearing a mask made of pulp. It was an image that he knew he'd never be able to shake.

Dr. Westbrook tapped the mike with his finger and gazed into the audience.

"In my thirty years as a criminal psychiatrist with the FBI, I have never seen anything quite like the work and terror raised by Dr. George Baylor. We all know who we're looking for. But after screening the video of the crime scene shot by the Forensic Services Unit here in Pennsylvania, I thought that it was essential for me to convey to you exactly what's at stake. I thought it was essential that every one of us see the crime scene the way Dr. Baylor wanted it to be seen."

Westbrook picked up another remote and pointed it at the second video monitor towering over his head. Once the images brightened and began playing, Matt could feel the air in the room deaden.

The victims' eyes were open, but it was more than that. Worse than that. Just as Brown had said a few minutes ago, the Strattons didn't look like they were dead. Instead, they appeared dazed and exhausted. Looking at each other. Watching each other.

The horror of Baylor's act seemed to reach a fever pitch.

Matt heard Dr. Westbrook begin speaking again. He tried to look at the man, but his eyes rocked back to the video monitor. The camera had moved in and isolated Stratton leaning against the wall with his two daughters. After about ten seconds, the image widened to include Stratton's wife and son.

"None of us were at the crime scene," the psychiatrist said in a voice filled with dread. "None of us were there, but let me tell you something—Dr. Baylor won't stop killing until we lock him up for the end of time, or until he's dead. Look at these images. Look at the crime scene the way the doctor left it. The way the doctor wanted us to find it. He won't stop killing because he likes it. The act of raping a victim gives him power. And the act of murder gives him even more power. Now he's graduated to mass murder. It gives his life purpose. Compare what you're seeing on the first two screens. Compare and remember that only a few months have gone by between these two murders. The doctor's lost his precision in favor of size and scope, but he's still creating a spectacle. The spectacle is as important to him as the kill. He's using the same theme, going after and punishing an identical target. But now he's wiping out the target's entire family. My guess is that he started killing a long time before the murder of Millie Brown. What Detective Jones discovered in LA was what Baylor wanted him to discover. But there are others—there have to be others—a string of murders that no doubt began in his teens. A string of murders we will never hear about.

Never know about. But here's what you need to understand. Except for the fingerprints he left, he doesn't make mistakes. This man does not panic. He's methodical. Steady. He wants what he gets, and gets what he wants. What you're seeing isn't a meltdown on Baylor's part. It's an evolution. A monster, becoming."

The dread in Westbrook's voice turned to doom and had a certain shake to it. When he switched off the video, no one moved or said anything. Everyone just sat there with the lights dimmed. Matt glanced at Kate Brown. Her eyes had lost their focus and were turned inward.

CHAPTER 10

Rogers glanced at Matt, then walked around his desk and sat down.

"Close the door, Jones. Take a seat."

Matt watched the special agent in charge empty the contents from a manila envelope onto his desk.

"Here's the key to your car. The space number is on the tag. You'll have to sign this form." Rogers slid the sheet of paper over and handed Matt a pen. "You're gonna need the access card Brown gave you last night to get through the gate at street level. You'll use it again to open the security doors between the garage and the elevators."

Matt sat back in his seat and watched Rogers slip the paper he'd just signed into a file folder. After setting the folder down, Rogers checked his credenza, spotted a blue three-ring binder, and picked it up.

"You can use the desk across from Brown's in the Crisis Room. She'll give you the password to the website. County detectives are keeping a murder book, which is online as well. Here's a hard copy of what we've got so far. It's up-to-date as of an hour ago."

Matt took charge of the binder. "I met two agents in LA," he said. "Jeff Kaplin and Steve Vega. I was wondering where they are."

Rogers's eyes rose from the desk and settled on his face. It was a hard look, a dead look that seemed out of place and came without warning.

"Listen, Jones. We need to get something straight. Okay?"

Matt nodded carefully. Something was wrong.

"Your background check," Rogers said. "You passed, but I'm not sure why. Had it been up to me, you'd still be in LA, and you wouldn't be wearing that badge."

"What happened?" he asked. "What's wrong?"

"The woman you call your mother, Julie Clemens. That was her maiden name, right?"

Matt nodded again, still confused, still trying to get a read on a man he barely knew.

"The special agent in Westwood found her death certificate, Jones, but couldn't locate her birth certificate."

"That would have been a long time ago. More than fifty years."

Rogers's eyes were still drilling him, still searching his face. "The woman you call your aunt, the woman who raised you. Abigail Clemens."

"Aunt Abby."

"The same thing is going on with her. We've got a death certificate, but no record of her birth. Their pasts aren't documented, Jones. There's no history or record that your mother and aunt even existed until they reached the age of twenty-one. We can't say with any certainty that they were related to each other. We can't find their parents' names or anything that comes close to a family tree. On your father's side, things get even worse. There are two hundred and eleven men in the United States who share your name, one of them quite famous. Have you ever heard of M. Trevor Jones, the New York banker?"

Matt paused a moment, then shook his head slowly. "No," he said finally.

"Well, he hasn't heard of you either," Rogers said. "None of them have, at least the ones we've been able to reach. Are you still claiming that you don't know who your father is?"

Claiming?

Matt became very still, not wanting to show anything on his face. When he spoke, his voice was low, but steady.

"I was a boy when he left. My mother was sick. I don't understand where this is going."

"Where it's going, Jones, is that when I see loose ends like this in someone's past, I begin to think I'm looking at bullshit. It's got that vibe of being manufactured and overprocessed."

"But what you're talking about happened a long time ago. Records could have been destroyed or misplaced."

Rogers flashed a mean smile. "Yeah, sure, Jones. Somehow everybody around you winds up getting misplaced. You know, I said those things about you at the briefing because I run this place and that's what I was expected to say. But you're Doyle's project, not mine. I don't want you here. From the very beginning I thought it was a bad idea. After reviewing your background check this morning, I don't know who you are or where you came from, and I sure as hell don't trust you. Do we understand each other, Jones?"

Matt didn't say anything. He knew that if he spoke, the things he'd say would get him thrown off the case. He still wanted Baylor, no matter how difficult the circumstances might be.

"Do we understand each other?" Rogers repeated.

Matt got up from the chair with the murder book. "What do you want me to say?"

"That you'll stay out of my way. That if you have anything to contribute, you'll work through Brown. That if you screw up, you'll go away."

Matt gave Rogers a grim look and exhaled. The special agent noticed.

"The last thing I need is attitude, Jones, so wipe it off your face. As far as I'm concerned, your background check is a work in progress. I intend to keep digging until I find out what you're hiding. Now take the murder book and get out of my office."

Matt walked out of the room dazed and confused and trying to understand what just happened. His first impression of Wes Rogers, the image he'd formed when they met and shook hands, had been the wrong one. Wes Rogers, special agent in charge of the FBI's field office in the City of Brotherly Love, was a shithead.

CHAPTER 11

Matt pulled himself together and tried to think it through. He knew full well that the shock he'd just endured had nothing to do with who Rogers turned out to be. It was more about the thoughts he'd dredged to the surface. The memories.

Matt entered the Crisis Room and spotted Brown seated at her desk, typing something on a laptop. Doyle seemed to have taken over the conference room. Matt could see him standing over the long table while leafing through an array of files and speaking with someone on the phone. A TV mounted to the wall at the head of the table was switched to CNN.

Matt crossed the room and sat down at the desk that had been paired off with Brown's. When she looked at him, her eyes widened.

"What happened to you?" she asked.

"Nothing."

She smiled at him. "Were you with Rogers?"

Matt noticed that the laptop on his desk had already been powered up. He could feel Brown's eyes still on his face.

"What's the password?" he said. "Rogers told me to ask."

"You know, he's not as bad as you might be thinking he is. He gives everybody a hard time. Once you get to know him, he's a pretty good guy."

"I'll bet he is. You got that password?"

She flashed another sarcastic smile his way, then wrote a series of letters and numbers on a pad, ripped the sheet off, and pushed it over. Matt found the FBI's website and logged in. Then he took a moment and tried to clear his mind and ignore what had just happened in Rogers's office. It wasn't easy, but he needed to catch up on the case as quickly as he could.

He found Dr. Baylor's file, then clicked through the screens until he reached what was essentially a live, digital version of the chronological record in a murder book. When any member of the task force learned something new or had a thought or question that seemed relevant to the investigation, it was added to the record beside the time and date, then stamped with the agent's electronic signature. For all intents and purposes, this area of the site worked like every other blog on the Internet. Everything about it was fluid, everything current, except in this case, everything was validated and a matter of record.

Matt skimmed through the timeline, surprised by the lack of progress that had been made over the past month and a half. He read through an entry made by Jeff Kaplin and realized that he and Steve Vega had just left New Orleans and were heading back to LA. A tip that Baylor had been staying at Le Pavillon Hotel in the French Quarter had proved fruitless. The doctor had covered his tracks, his trail ice-cold until the Strattons had been found murdered in their home.

A small window popped up on his screen, announcing that someone had posted a new message. Matt scrolled forward on the timeline and started reading. Apparently there was something wrong with the two slugs that struck Stratton's wife and son. Although they had been found in soft tissue and recovered by the medical examiner, there were marks that the Bureau of Forensic Services in Montgomery County couldn't account for. Close-up photographs of the slugs were included in the post, and Matt studied them carefully. Each slug appeared to have been lightly scratched all the way around. And there were gashes running lengthwise as if each bullet had hit a hard edge. The forensic scientist who examined the evidence and posted his findings had more than twenty years on the job. In spite of his experience, he had never seen anything like it before and was sending both slugs to the FBI's Firearms and Toolmarks Unit at Quantico.

Matt looked up. Brown had left her desk, and he hadn't noticed. He turned and saw her talking to Doyle in the conference room with the door closed. She was holding a file folder and showing him something inside.

Matt checked his watch. It was almost noon. He glanced at the murder book sitting on his desk and tried to clear his mind again. Concentrating on anything seemed difficult right now.

Wishing for a Marlboro and a cup of strong coffee, he reached inside his jacket and slipped a piece of nicotine gum into his mouth.

He could no longer block it out. No longer ignore the things Rogers had said to him in his office. At the time he had tried to keep cool and not let his thoughts and emotions show on his face. But now he was sitting here wondering why the FBI couldn't find his mother's and aunt's birth certificates. Why their history had suddenly become so vague. It seemed odd, peculiar, even corrupt, and he didn't know what to make of it. As much as he despised Rogers, he couldn't fault him for being suspicious. Had Matt been wearing the special agent's shoes, he would have said and done exactly the same thing.

There were holes in Matt's past. And they stood out.

Although his early years had been tough, Matt used to be able to count on the fact that everything was at least self-evident and true. But all of that had burned up in Rogers's office thirty minutes ago. As Rogers said himself, when he sees loose ends like this in someone's past, he begins to think he's looking at bullshit. It's got that vibe of being manufactured and overprocessed.

Matt bit into the nicotine gum, feeling the drug rush through his head. When the wave subsided, he grabbed his leather jacket and walked out.

CHAPTER 12

The air had a raw feel to it, and Matt wished that he hadn't left his down vest at the apartment. He headed south on Sixth Street, passing Independence Hall. When he reached Walnut Street at Washington Square, he made a right and started walking toward city hall. He was looking for a café. Something small and quiet where he could sip hot coffee and collect his thoughts. He had a vague impression of a place he'd been to in his teens and looked up and down the street. When his eyes landed on Rogers half a block ahead, he stepped to the side and stopped.

Rogers was speaking to someone on his cell phone and so distracted that he bumped into the man ahead of him. They were entering a sushi restaurant, but it didn't seem like they were together. Matt waited until the special agent disappeared behind the glass door, then walked by without letting it get to him. Two blocks up he spotted the Walnut Street Theater, and everything started to become more familiar. Across the street he noticed a hospital. The building appeared new and had been set halfway into the block to accommodate a drive-up entrance and a work of sculpture that rose several stories into the air. As Matt took in the sculpture, he couldn't help thinking how much it reminded him of Marcel Duchamp. The design of both the building and the sculpture, the mix of different materials and all the curved lines, was stunning.

Matt had forgotten that Philadelphia was different than other cities. It felt like Europe here. It looked like Europe. He could remember his aunt taking him to a van Gogh exhibition at the Museum of Art. They had just walked out and were standing at the top of the steps overlooking the city. She was younger then, all jazzed up after seeing so many paintings by one of her favorite artists. She was saying that what made this city different was its relationship to art. Art was everywhere here. Not just in the museums, but on every street.

Why couldn't the FBI find her birth certificate?

Matt tried to shake it off, but the string of memories just kept pounding back one after the next. He crossed Broad Street and the Avenue of the Arts. A few blocks later he glanced around the corner and saw a brick building with awnings, sidewalk tables, and gas heaters. This was the place. Benny's Café Blue.

Matt walked in, ordered a large cup of the house blend, and found an empty booth by the window. As he stirred sugar into the piping-hot brew, enjoying the sounds of people talking and laughing, he realized that the café had changed since his last visit. The place seemed brighter, cleaner, warmer than he remembered. The Formica tables had been replaced with beautifully grained woods, and logs were burning in the fireplace. Sipping through the steam, he sat back and gazed out the window. Across the street was a gym, and he could see a pair of young women working out on StairMasters. He took another sip of coffee, letting the hot java soothe his stomach. One of the women had just ended her workout and was wiping off the machine with a towel.

His eyes drifted down to the sidewalk, sorting through the people waiting for the light to change. And that's when he spotted him. He was standing on the corner, staring back at him. The man with the ultra-pale skin. The man he'd seen on the plane and at the airport. His shadow.

Matt tried to keep cool, but heard the café go quiet and realized that he'd shifted over to automatic pilot; he'd drawn his gun and had already rocked back the slide. He pushed the door open and burst onto the street, his expression fierce and determined as he started sprinting. The man had his cell phone out, no doubt shooting video again. But now it was different. He seemed frightened. He turned away and started running.

Matt chased him down the street. When the man ducked into a dress shop, Matt reached out and got a piece of his jacket before he slipped away. The man was yelping and trying to flee through the racks of clothing. But he was too soft and too slow, and Matt lunged forward, tackling him to the floor.

He rolled the man over, stuffing the .45 into his mouth. The man started weeping and appeared to be panic-stricken. He was struggling to catch his breath. As the sales staff rushed behind the counter, a woman at the cash register reached for the phone. Then Matt held up his badge and shouted, "Police business. Put down that phone."

She backed away, and Matt seized the man by his hair and banged his head on the floor. He felt a breeze behind his back and heard the door.

"Why are you following me?"

The man tried to speak, but couldn't get the words out. Matt removed the gun from his mouth and jammed the muzzle into the side of his head.

"Why are you following me?" Matt repeated. "Give it up, or I'll blow your head off right in front of these people."

The man met his eyes, still trying to catch his breath. "I'm doing a story."

Matt didn't believe him. "A story," he said in a voice filled with sarcasm. "A story about what?"

"You and your father. I think I know who he is. I'm gonna prove it."

"Who are you?"

The man let out a sigh. "You've seen me on TV. I'm on every night."

Matt shook his head. The woman by the register was staring at the man, and Matt could see recognition beginning to bloom in her eyes.

"That's Ryan Day," she said. "He's the star of *Get Buzzed*. Oh my God. It's Ryan Day."

A thought flashed through Matt's mind. He'd never watched the show, but had seen the commercials. *Get Buzzed* was a popular celebrity gossip program that followed the network news five nights a week. He looked the man over—he seemed familiar—then began patting him down just in case.

"How did you know I'd be on that plane?" he said.

"I got a tip. I took a chance, and you were there."

"A tip from who?"

The man shrugged. "I don't know. A voice left on my service. Is M. Trevor Jones your father?"

Matt clenched his jaw, but didn't say anything. He found the man's wallet and opened it to check his ID.

"Why are you afraid to answer the question, Jones? What are you hiding?"

The driver's license confirmed his shadow's identity. The man he'd tackled to the floor and almost shot was Ryan Day.

"I'm a reporter," Day said as he thought it through. "But you didn't know that. What did you think I was here to do?"

Matt remained quiet. He could see Day putting it together in his head.

"Your father's trying to keep tabs on you, or is it something more than that?" Day's eyes lit up. "My God. You thought I'd come to—who shot you in LA, Jones?"

Matt holstered his pistol. Day looked at someone behind him. When Matt turned, he saw a man with a video camera on his shoulder.

"You get it?" Day asked.

THE LOVE KILLINGS

The man with the camera nodded. "I got everything. We're still shooting."

Matt stood up, then helped the gossip reporter to his feet. "Why me?" he said.

Day was flashing a big grin as well now and offered to shake Matt's hand. "Why not you?" he said. "It'll make a great story. Tonight's segment will probably be pretty good, too. I guess I should thank you, Jones. No harm, no foul. My producer will pay for any damage you may have done here, so don't worry about it. We still win."

Matt shook Day's hand, but only reluctantly, then started toward the door. He could hear Day calling after him.

"I know the reason why you're here in Philly, Jones. After tonight, everybody's gonna know."

Matt yanked the door open and walked out into the blast of cold air. He was in trouble. He'd blown it. Now Rogers could act with a clear conscience. Matt would be thrown off the case and shipped back to LA. He hadn't even made it through his first day.

CHAPTER 13

He found Doyle in Rogers's office. They were watching a video on a desktop computer with a large screen. When Doyle saw Matt in the hallway, he waved him into the room and around Rogers's desk for a look.

It was the video the gossip reporter had shot on the plane and at the airport with his cell phone. Day had posted it on his show's website, along with the words "Why is LAPD Detective Matt Jones in Philly?"

Doyle gave Matt a look. "Did you know you were being photographed?"

"I saw him with his phone, but I wasn't sure."

"Who?"

"The gossip reporter. Ryan Day."

Doyle seemed surprised. "Do you know him?"

A moment passed as Matt tried to think of the right words. When he noticed Rogers staring at him, he turned back to Doyle.

"We've met," he said finally.

Rogers got to his feet and walked over to the window, shaking his head. Doyle sat on the end of Rogers's desk.

"I thought we'd catch a break and keep Baylor's name out of it for a few more days," Doyle said. "But now the media knows you're here and they're pretty good at connecting the dots. Rogers, you'll need to hold a press conference this afternoon."

Rogers gave Doyle a look over his shoulder, then turned back to the view through his window. The Ben Franklin Bridge was just seven blocks away.

Matt stepped over to a chair, but remained standing. "Something just happened that you guys need to know about. None of it's good."

Rogers turned to face him, the distrust and suspicion in his eyes easy enough to read. Matt spent the next five minutes telling them exactly what had happened with Ryan Day and warning them that everything had been recorded and would be aired on tonight's show. When he finished, he held on to the back of the chair and braced himself.

Rogers turned to Doyle. "This is exactly what I was afraid of. He's jeopardizing the case. He could scare off Baylor."

"You need to hold a press conference, Rogers."

Rogers shook his head and pointed a finger at Matt. "Everything's different now, Doyle. You're the one who needs to hold the press conference. He's your boy."

Doyle turned to Matt, measuring him. "What do you have to say for yourself, Detective?"

"I thought he was trying to kill me. He followed me on the plane and at the airport. When I caught him on the street, I knew it wasn't by chance. I didn't know who he was, so I confronted him."

Rogers narrowed his eyes. "Sounds like it was more than that, Jones. It sounds like it got physical."

"It ended as soon as he identified himself," Matt said. "It ended quickly."

"What the hell's that going to look like on national TV?"

Matt didn't say anything. He could pack his bags in fifteen minutes and make it to the airport inside of an hour. He turned back to Doyle. The federal prosecutor was staring at the floor the way a chess player sits over a game board and decides on his next three moves. After a long moment, Doyle seemed to snap out of it and met Matt's gaze.

"I think Rogers is right, Jones. I'll take care of the press conference. Then we'll let this gossip reporter air his dirty laundry and see what happens next. A word of warning, Detective. If this Ryan Day makes us look like fools, you're the world's next fall guy. If it looks like we're taking on water, you're going over the side."

CHAPTER 14

Matt had the Crisis Room to himself and didn't understand why. Given the lack of any plausible leads on Baylor's whereabouts, he wondered how anyone calling themselves a special agent with the FBI could have packed it in and gone home. It was just 6:45 p.m. The only one still working was Brown, and she had walked up to a market on Walnut Street for coffee.

Matt glanced at his laptop and turned up the volume. He had been waiting for Ryan Day's *Get Buzzed* to begin, but the network news had picked up on the Stratton murders. An eerie shot of the mansion hit the screen first, followed by pictures of the family. After a few seconds they cut to footage of Matt at the airport lifted off the *Get Buzzed* website, and then the money shot, the killer, Dr. George Baylor. After they set up the story, they cut to the press conference Doyle held this afternoon.

Matt studied the reporters' faces. It was more than a story now. Everyone asking those tough questions looked frightened. Everyone knew Baylor's history and the gruesome things he'd done to four innocent girls.

What exactly happened to Jim and Tammy Stratton and their three children? What is the FBI hiding, and why are they hiding it? Why are you going through so much effort to keep us out of the loop? How bad could the details really be? LAPD Detective Matt Jones was one of the lead detectives in the hunt for Dr. George Baylor, the serial killer who fled Los Angeles and New Orleans. Baylor's first victim was the daughter of a United States congressman. There are rumors that the Department of Justice will be supervising the prosecution of the doctor in at least two trials if he's captured alive. Why are you and Detective Jones in Philadelphia? Did Dr. Baylor murder the Strattons? Why are you here, Mr. Doyle?

Why are you here?

The segment ended. It seemed obvious to Matt that Doyle had a knack for speaking to the media. He'd remained calm, seemed to answer every question as best he could, and, in the end, had given the reporters what they really wanted. He admitted that Dr. Baylor was a person of interest in the Stratton murder case, and that LAPD Detective Matt Jones had recovered from his gunshot wounds and was joining the FBI's special task force.

The only question Matt had was why Doyle used his name. Doyle knew that Matt was about to be smeared on a gossip show airing on national television later that night. So why did the federal prosecutor stick his neck out? He didn't just mention Matt's name, he underlined it.

Why?

Matt let the thought go and looked back at the murder book. He'd spent the last two hours reading the medical examiner's report and studying what must have been more than one hundred photographs taken at the crime scene. It seemed clear to him that Baylor had planned the night the same way a film director might stage a scene in a movie. There had to be an order to things. With Stratton as his target, Matt had no doubt that Baylor would have saved him for last. The medical examiner confirmed that Stratton wore a pacemaker and that the device shut down at 11:35 p.m., so it was a safe bet that everyone else would have been killed prior to Stratton's death.

Matt leafed through the photographs until he found a shot that included all five victims. Stratton was leaning against the wall between his two daughters. Their eyes appeared fixed on Stratton's wife and son. They were Baylor's audience—they had to be Baylor's audience—which would mean that the two girls would have been murdered just before Stratton. That left Tammy Stratton and her son. One of them had to be the first to go.

He flipped the page over, then glanced at his laptop just as *Get Buzzed* faded up from black. Brown entered the room, placing two cups of coffee on Matt's desk and staring at the screen. They were opening the show with footage of Matt chasing Day down the street. It turned out that the man with the video camera had been running behind them the moment Matt hit the corner. As Matt watched, his stomach churning, he realized that they were maximizing the drama by leaving the announcer out and letting the sound from the street carry the moment. Every bounce the camera made amplified the emotional context. Matt glanced at Brown, then turned back to his laptop. He could see himself tackling the reporter onto the floor, jamming his gun into the innocent man's mouth. Then Ryan Day, fearing for his life, began stammering. Worse still, the gossip reporter was asking Matt if M. Trevor Jones, the King of Wall Street, was his father.

Matt stood up, pried the lid off one of the coffee cups, stirred a pack of sugar into the brew, and took a first sip. He couldn't watch anymore. He knew what it looked like because he'd seen the same shot so many times in so many cities over the past couple of years.

It came off like police brutality. The chase and takedown had occurred over a period of three or four minutes. But the clip had been cut down to include only the worst moments. Everything about it came off harsh and overdone.

He took another sip of coffee, watching Brown get out of her coat and sit down in his seat with her eyes still glued to the screen. He felt his cell phone vibrate in his pocket. When he slid the lock open, he

read the text message. It was from Wes Rogers, special agent in charge
of the FBI's field office in Philadelphia.

We need to talk, the message said. *Now.*

Rogers had included his address in the suburbs, and Matt committed it to memory. As he slipped his cell phone into his pocket, Brown
gave him a look.

"What's going on?" she said.

"Rogers. He wants to see me. Guess I'm toast."

She shook her head. "That's not his style, Jones. If you were toast,
he would have said so. Rogers doesn't keep people waiting."

CHAPTER 15

Matt knew something was wrong the moment he saw the house number on the mailbox and gazed up the long drive. He pulled over and killed the lights and engine. When he fished through the glove box, he was glad the Crown Vic he'd been issued came equipped with a flashlight.

But he didn't switch it on. Not yet.

Instead, he got out of the car and gazed at the silhouette of a large mansion on Fairfield Road. The windows were dark, and from where Matt stood on the frozen ground, all the exterior lights had been shut down as well. He noticed the wind finally, a hard wind whistling through the trees and knocking all the branches together.

Matt dug his cell phone out of his pocket and double-checked Rogers's text message. The house numbers matched, and so did the directions. He could see a school on the other side of Sugartown Road exactly where it was supposed to be. Wishing for a Marlboro, he pushed a piece of nicotine gum against his cheek and tried to process what he was seeing.

Rogers didn't live here, that much was clear. No one in law enforcement lived here. He was looking at an estate—a building so massive that it dwarfed the Strattons' mansion on County Line Road. Matt took in the open gate and guessed that the six-foot-high wrought iron fence circled the entire property. As he scanned the grounds in the darkness, the length of the fence from the corner to the property's end on Fairfield Road, the depth and proportion of the house, it felt like a lot of land— maybe ten acres, maybe even more. And the neighborhood was quiet. He hadn't seen or heard a single car on either road since he arrived.

He turned back to the mansion. His eyes had adjusted to the darkness, and he could make out four three-story-high columns supporting the roof over a formal entrance.

Everything about the place looked like trouble. Everything about what he was seeing felt wrong.

He wondered who had sent him the text message. Who wanted him to be here? Who knew enough about what went down today to put Rogers's name on it?

He slipped the flashlight into his back pocket, drew his .45, and chambered a round. Then he started up the drive, slowly and carefully, hoping the moon would stay behind the clouds for another five minutes or so. There was a second building here, a two-story carriage house with five of its six garage doors open. In spite of the darkness, Matt could see a handful of vintage cars inside, along with a Land Rover, a Jaguar, and a Lexus SUV parked in the drive. He turned back to the mansion. It may have been below freezing tonight, the wind may have been howl-ing, but none of that was on Matt's mind right now. All he could feel as he reached the entrance and started up the granite steps was his heart beating heavy and hard in the center of his chest.

One of the two glass doors was cracked open. Matt slid into an entryway that had to be three times the size of the FBI's apartment on Pine Street. The ceiling was two stories up, the extra-wide staircase ris-ing to a pair of French doors set above the entrance and finally making the turn with ten more steps up to the second floor.

Matt didn't move. Clearing his mind, he quieted his breathing and spent several minutes listening to the house. Moonlight suddenly flashed through the entryway, and Matt glanced at the French doors above his head. Then he lowered his eyes and composed himself with his gun still raised.

He knew in his gut that he was listening to the sound of the dead. He'd heard it before, and it was always the same. A silence that seemed too silent. A stillness that appeared frozen and absolute. The house was beyond quiet. Not a clock ticking. Not a refrigerator stirring. Not even the fan from the building's heating system. Just that eerie sound of the dead cascading through time.

Matt pulled the flashlight out of his pocket, switched it on, and pressed it against the barrel of his gun. Working his way from front to back, he cleared the living room, a den, another sitting room, a library with a false wall that had been left open, an office, a room that looked just like an English pub, a game room, a powder room and two full baths, a gym with a steam room and sauna attached, a dining room, a washroom, and finally the kitchen and pantry. The entire back of the house appeared to be lined with windows that ran all the way up to the ceiling. Matt walked over to the door and peeked outside at an Olympic-sized swimming pool. Through a row of trees at the rear of the property line, he could see lights from another home or building. Still, they were a long way off. If Matt could trust his instincts, and he thought that he could, the doctor would have had no concerns about the sound of gunshots or his victims shrieking at the top of their lungs.

He tried to shake off the image, the sounds of innocent women and children shrieking, but couldn't. He knew where the dead bodies would be found. He realized that he'd known it all along.

He found his way back to the front of the mansion and started up the staircase. When he reached the second-floor landing, he panned his light and gun across a sitting area that included a sofa and two reading chairs. There was a fireplace here, with a handful of small logs still burning. Matt moved to the center of the landing and turned around—

And that's when he saw them.

Three were leaning against the far wall, a carbon copy of the crime scene on County Line Road. A father with his two daughters, stripped of their clothing, eyes open, and a small piece of gray-colored tape covering their chest wounds. All eyes were pointed at the woman on the floor with her son draped over her body. It looked like they were in the middle of making love. The only difference Matt could detect between the two crime scenes was the age of the son. In this case, the boy looked a few years older, fifteen or sixteen years old.

Matt took a deep breath and exhaled. As he gazed at the horror, it felt like his stomach was in his throat. He checked his hands and was surprised to find them so steady. He tried to pull himself together. It was difficult because his imagination always seemed to take over when the shock hit him this hard. He could never understand how anyone, no matter what their psychological issues might be, no matter what ordeal they may have faced, could take another human being's life. Now he was standing before five corpses. Standing in the aftermath of a mass killing committed by a maniac.

A memory surfaced. And while it had been more than five years since Matt was overseas, he could remember watching someone he'd shot take his last breath. A fifteen-year-old boy with a grenade launcher. He went out like a fish gasping for air, his mouth opening and closing, his eyes glazed. That's when Matt heard the sound of death for the first time. A silence and stillness that had weight to it and wouldn't go away. When memories like this flared up, he tried not to linger on them. If he could shut them down fast enough, they seemed to fade back into that pool of experiences that slept in the gloom. But tonight, looking at the woman with her arms around her son, their eyes meeting somewhere in the middle of a thousand-yard stare, he didn't think he stood a chance.

He tilted the flashlight down, the pools of wet blood glistening before his eyes. He moved closer, stepping around the puddles and streams until he reached the woman embracing her son. He didn't have a pair of vinyl gloves with him, so when he knelt down and touched her forehead, he used the back of his wrist.

She was still warm, still fresh. Minutes had gone by, not hours. He reached for his cell phone and slid the lock open.

And that's when he felt the muzzle of a gun poke him in the spine.

He flinched, nearly jumping out of his skin. He could feel the hairs on the back of his neck standing on end.

"Hello, Matthew," the doctor said in a calm and pleasant voice. "I see you've met the Holloways. They look like they used to be nice people, don't you think? A nice family. And how 'bout this house?"

Matt didn't say anything.

Baylor nudged him with the pistol and lowered his voice. "I'm gonna have to ask you for your gun," he said. "And I'm afraid I'll need your cell phone as well. No worries. You'll have them back when I leave."

Matt wondered what kind of pistol Baylor was pressing into his spine, then figured that at point-blank range, it didn't really matter, and the doctor couldn't really miss. He passed back his .45, then turned around and handed over his cell phone.

Baylor smiled at him, his blue eyes sparkling in the moonlight streaming in through the row of windows set above the staircase. Matt noted the chiseled face, the brown hair that had been lightened by the sun and appeared spiked, the energy still radiating from the man's being. He had to remind himself that Baylor had been shot six weeks ago as well. He had to remind himself that Baylor was in his midfifties. He came off younger than that, stronger and better fit.

Matt glanced down at the gun.

The doctor was pointing a Glock 17 at him. The semiautomatic pistol seemed to have become a favorite in law enforcement these days, no doubt because of the nine-by-nineteen load it carried and the magazine's capacity to hold seventeen rounds. Matt remembered reading about the pistol on the manufacturer's website not too long ago. *Safe, easy, and quick*, the description said. *Just what you need in high-pressure situations.*

Matt struggled to find a steady voice as he watched Baylor slip his phone into a jacket pocket.

"Why don't you let me bring you in, Doctor? Why keep doing this? What meaning could there possibly be in killing an entire family?"

Baylor switched on a flashlight and shined it in Matt's face, then smiled again like he hadn't heard him. "Someone's shut off the power, Matthew. I was looking for the circuit breakers when you arrived. My guess is that the box is somewhere near the kitchen. Why don't you lead the way?"

CHAPTER 16

Matt switched on the circuit breakers, and the mansion came back to life as if hit with a defibrillator. Wires replaced veins as lamps snapped on, and the hum of the heating system took over the building.

As Matt led the way back to the front entrance, he couldn't help noticing how bizarrely the mansion was furnished. Every room they passed seemed showy and forced, and there was a certain ignorance to the way everything had been put together. Matt assumed that price was no object, yet the feel of room after room came off cheap and overdone. But it was the art on the walls that really stood out. The paintings were modern, mostly portraits rather than landscapes, and decidedly angry. It looked like most of the paintings came from the same artist, and that his or her psychological issues were a decade or two past neurotic. It was the choice of only using primary colors and the raw brushstrokes that gave the artist away. Every painting Matt looked at reminded him of a concrete wall he'd seen by Thirtieth Street Station last night. Every painting in the house came off like graffiti with no meaning, no subtlety, and no soul.

Matt wondered how anyone could be comfortable living in a place like this. He couldn't imagine waking up every day and thinking that he was still asleep and trapped in a nightmare. A world reduced to visual noise.

They reached the entryway, and Baylor waved the Glock 17 toward the staircase. When the doctor spoke, his voice was riddled with sarcasm.

"Nice art, don't you think? You can't buy taste, Matthew. That's one of life's secrets. You can't buy class either."

Matt caught the wicked glint in the man's eyes, the look of curiosity and amusement that wouldn't go away, then started up the staircase. The power was back on, and his view of the crime scene would no longer be limited to the narrow beam of a flashlight. The second-floor landing would be just as it had been when the Holloways were murdered. The horror elements would be amped up. They had just passed the French doors. Matt counted ten more steps, and knew that he needed to prepare himself.

The first thing he noticed was the lights on a large Christmas tree that stood between the fireplace and the five dead bodies. The second thing he noticed was the heads mounted on the wall. Big game heads. They were hanging right above the victims, and Matt couldn't believe that he had missed them.

Baylor must have noticed him gazing at Holloway's trophies. When he spoke, his voice was muted.

"They're known as the *big five*," he said. "The African lion, the elephant, a Cape buffalo, a leopard, and the rhinoceros. They call them the big five because these are the five most difficult animals to hunt on foot."

"Is that why you killed the Holloways, Doctor? Because this man shoots big game and you've got a problem with it?"

Baylor laughed, then moved in for a closer look at the bodies. He seemed so fascinated by the horror, his eyes wagging back and forth through the corpses. He pointed his pistol at Holloway leaning against the wall with his two daughters. Beneath the coating of blood, they were naked and holding hands just like the Strattons had been found.

"His name's David Holloway, Matthew. He runs a software company, and before tonight, he was doing quite well. That's his wife, Mimi, holding their son, Nicholas. He's sixteen. The two girls are Sophie, age twelve, and Victoria, who's nineteen. And yes, I have a real problem with people who shoot big game. They're cowards."

"That's why you killed them?"

Baylor flashed a faint smile that came and went. "David didn't hunt animals on foot. That would have been too risky. Too dangerous. And it would have made things difficult for the film crew he used to take with him. David had self-esteem issues and always seemed to need proof that he was on top. With every kill there was a video and a head, even if it had to be smuggled out. I was told by one of his macho friends that he used to wear makeup and a costume when he moved in for the kill."

"He fits your list, Doctor. He fits it like a well-tailored suit."

"He does, doesn't he. David Holloway was a real shithead."

Baylor took a step closer to the nineteen-year-old girl and knelt down to take in her body.

"How did Holloway ever come up on your radar?" Matt said.

The doctor's eyes were still pinned on the naked girl. "He shot a lion a few years back. Not the one over his head. He shot a special lion. A tourist attraction that made money for an entire village. Holloway lured the animal off the reserve and then shot it and claimed he didn't do anything wrong. Apparently, the lion experienced a tortured death. It ran off, wounded. They found its remains two days later. A pack of hyenas had dragged the lion into the brush and were feeding on it. It's a real jungle out there, Matthew. And David Holloway was a lot more than a coward. Look at the size of the diamond he's wearing in his right ear. The world's better off without him. I'm glad he's dead."

Matt's eyes flicked down from the head mounted on the wall to Holloway's pierced ear. The diamond was almost the size of a grape and appeared stupid and crass, even embarrassing. When he turned back to Baylor, it looked like the doctor was examining the girl's teeth.

"They were your audience, Doctor. You murdered the Holloways here because of the animal heads. Look at their eyes. It feels like they're watching us."

"I think you're right about that, Matthew. The Holloways were murdered here because of the animal heads. They witnessed the spectacle along with Holloway and his two daughters. It's worth noting that the landing is out in the open. There's no door. No expectation of privacy. No doubt, murdering them in an almost public space heightens the thrill."

Baylor's words about the need for an audience struck a nerve. Matt had been thinking the same thing. It was about the order of the deaths. Holloway would be last because he needed to be punished. The two girls would go next to last because they were needed as witnesses. But who would've been murdered first?

His eyes moved back to Mimi Holloway and her son, Nicholas. The answer seemed so obvious that he didn't know why it had taken him so long to see it. It was in the way the mother was holding her son. It was a death embrace. The boy's corpse had been draped over his mother's body while she was still alive. She was cradling him in a fit of despair and hopelessness as she died.

"Ah," Baylor said. "Victoria's got a secret."

Matt ignored the pun, then stepped over a pool of blood and knelt down beside the doctor. "What is it?"

"She's pregnant."

"How can you tell?"

"See these small red growths on her gums?"

Matt moved in for a closer look. They were there, on her gums and between her teeth.

"They're called pregnancy tumors," Baylor said. "They only show up in about five percent of pregnant women. They're not dangerous, but I'll bet she experienced some degree of discomfort."

"They know that you're not who you say you are, Doctor."

Baylor gave him a thoughtful look, but remained quiet.

"Before I was shot the FBI gave me access to the chronological record they keep on the Internet. They think you murdered the real George Baylor. He was jogging and you ran over him with your car fifteen years ago. The man lived in Chicago and graduated from medical school. Six months before his death, he'd completed his internship and residency at the University of Chicago Medical Center. The FBI thinks you met there, or somewhere along the way. That you were running from something in your past and needed a new identity. Someone who shared your medical background. Someone who fit."

Baylor bowed his head and lowered his voice, still amused. "Everybody needs a new identity from time to time. A new outlook on life."

"They found out that you traveled to the East Coast, and that you did it every year. They have receipts from your visits to Princeton and Greenwich and your hotel in New York. They think that's where your history is. That you grew up somewhere on the East Coast."

"That was a long time ago, Matthew." The doctor stood up with the gun in his hand. "It's getting late. I want you to unbutton your shirt. I want a look at your wounds."

"Why?"

"Open your shirt," Baylor said. "Do it quickly. Do as I say."

Matt got to his feet and unbuttoned his shirt. Slowly. Reluctantly. Once he pulled it open, Baylor switched on his flashlight and began his examination of the four gunshot wounds. The one the doctor, a former plastic surgeon, had mended himself in Matt's shoulder, and the three shots in the gut that had nearly killed him.

"Sloppy work," the doctor said. "I can fix those if you like. It would take time to heal, but after a year or two, the scars would go away."

Matt looked at Baylor's eyes still fixed on the four wounds. "Why won't you let me take you in, Doctor?"

"Because you need me."

Matt shook his head. "But I don't need you. Let's drive into the city. Let's end this before anyone else gets hurt. I know there's something inside you that's worth saving. You wouldn't have saved my life if there wasn't. You did it twice. You mended this wound, and you saved me from the fire."

The doctor met Matt's eyes finally, his voice almost a whisper. "You still need me. You just don't know it yet."

"You murdered these people. You murdered the Strattons. Even by your own standards, you're out of control. If they find you, they won't waste time fooling around. They'll shoot you. It's easier that way. It's safer."

Matt watched as Baylor's gaze turned inward. It looked like he was sifting through his past. It seemed like he had become lost in the darkness.

"Jim Stratton, MD," the doctor said with another faint smile. "Can you imagine a doctor using chemotherapy and radiation treatments on patients who were perfectly healthy?"

"Nothing surprises me anymore. It's the world we live in. Generation *Me*."

"The world we live in," Baylor repeated pointedly. "And now Jim Stratton, MD, is finally dead, and again the world is a better place. I knew his daughter was home for the holidays, Matthew. I'd done my research, I'd made my plans, and I went to the house a couple of hours after midnight to scout the location and make my final preparations. When I got there, the front door was unlocked. I walked in and found them on the second-floor landing. They were already dead."

Matt paused a moment to think it over. "If they were already dead, then why did you touch the bodies, Doctor? Why didn't you just leave?"

"But I didn't touch the bodies."

"Yes, you did. The FBI has your fingerprint."

"From where?"

"The girl's nipple. I read about it in the murder book this afternoon. They examined her entire body. You touched the girl's nipple. And you painted her fingernails. You left a print there, too."

Baylor was inside himself again, that odd glint burning in his vibrant blue eyes.

"So maybe I did," he said finally in a softer voice. "Maybe I left those prints for you, Matthew. The truth is that I left a total of five."

Matt shook his head. "You left five fingerprints, and now you're saying that you left them on purpose and want me to believe you. If you're ever questioned, you'll need to do better than that, Doctor. A lot better."

"I like to think of them as calling cards. I wanted you here. I wanted to make sure you got the call."

"Where are the other three?"

"In the library you'll find something hanging on the wall. It's a page from the *Philadelphia Inquirer*'s society section. Jim Stratton, MD, poisoned his patients and got rich hurting them and killing them, but he liked to think of himself as a kind and generous human being. Don't they all? He sponsored a charity event for one of the hospitals in Center City. A golf match at his country club for, of all things, kids with cancer. It made the society page. He had the story framed. I touched the glass with one finger, and the lower right corner of the frame with another when I straightened it on the wall."

"Where did you leave the third?"

"The most obvious place of all. The kitchen sink. I washed my hands and touched the faucet."

Matt gave him a hard look. "Why are you doing this? What do you expect to gain by playing let's pretend? You're saying that you just happened to show up at the Strattons' house on the night they were murdered? And now I find you here, and the bodies are still warm? Really? You just happen to be here tonight?"

"It's a coincidence."

Matt frowned. "A coincidence?"

"A striking occurrence of two or more events all at once, and apparently by mere chance, Matthew. We call it a coincidence. Three thousand years ago, they called it magic. Two thousand years ago, it was called a miracle. Words change over time."

Matt laughed sarcastically. "Call it anything you like, Doctor. Call it anything you want, anytime you want. It doesn't make any difference that Jim Stratton, MD, and David Holloway were whores or even monsters—it doesn't matter what they did or who they were. You murdered these people. If I'd been here any sooner, I would have caught you in the act."

Baylor met his eyes. "You're here because I sent you an invitation."

A beat went by. And then another.

Matt remembered the text message he'd received. It seemed so long ago.

Baylor cleared his throat. "You're working with people who have their heads in the sand, Matthew. It's the corporate way, you know. Special Agent Rogers and Assistant US Attorney Ken Doyle have blinders on and can't see who and what they're really dealing with here. They want it to be me. They need it to be me. They get more stuff if it's me. Bigger headlines and better jobs. That's why I left my fingerprints. That's why I sent you that text message tonight."

Matt let it settle in as he buttoned his shirt. All of it. Everything Baylor had just said. The five corpses at his feet. The five animal heads mounted on the wall. The diamond in the dead macho man's ear that was so big it looked cheap and crude. The twenty-foot-high Christmas tree with its bright lights and decorations, even the gifts already wrapped with bows and ribbons.

The word *nightmare* didn't cover it. He wished he could call it a hallucination, but that wouldn't work either. It felt like he was trapped in something more potent, more terrifying, more everything.

"You know what, Doctor?" he said finally.

Baylor narrowed his brow but remained quiet.

"I saw what you did to the four girls in Los Angeles and New Orleans. I know what you're capable of. Your methods have changed. That was my first thought when I saw the crime-scene photographs from the Strattons'. And it was the first thought I had when I climbed those stairs tonight. You're in a state of decay. You need to hand over your gun. You need to come with me so I can help you. You need medical help. Psychiatric help. The killing has to end."

"You're disappointing me."

"You need help, Doctor. Before anyone else gets hurt."

"May I ask you a question?" Baylor said in a particularly quiet voice.

"Why not."

The doctor turned and gazed at the victims. "The killer is obviously selecting his victims from the same pool I am. But when you see something like this, when you add everything up, when you concentrate on the whole, and not the meaning of any single part, what are you left with, Matthew? What need was the killer trying to fulfill?"

Matt remained quiet as he took in the horror one more time. A father with his two daughters. A mother with her son. Then he felt Baylor poke him in the back with his pistol.

"It's getting late," the doctor said. "And I have another stop to make tonight. We're leaving. We're off to the kitchen, and you're leading the way."

Matt gave the doctor a look and noticed that odd glint blooming in the man's eyes again. He appeared disappointed and irritated and, all of a sudden, was in a rush to leave. Matt glanced back at the landing as he started down the staircase. His mind was reeling, and he held on to the rail all the way down to the entryway.

There was too much information here—and he couldn't get a grip on any one piece to even begin sorting things out.

They started walking toward the back of the house. Baylor remained quiet as they passed all those rooms with all those lousy paintings. At least now Matt had a sense of who Holloway had been before his death. The paintings worked like a mirror and revealed who Holloway had really been.

Matt turned and watched the doctor following him into the kitchen. Baylor crossed the room, swung open the glass door, and pointed at the property line in the distance. He was still in a hurry. Still disappointed and abrupt.

"You can't see it from here," he said. "But there's a stone wall about four feet high behind those trees. That's where you'll find your things when I'm gone. If you make any attempt to follow me, I'll shoot you. Good luck, Matthew. I think you're going to need it. Whoever murdered these people is someone special. I wouldn't waste too much time thinking about how you'll pay your father back right now. The last time you became distracted, you took three shots in the gut, remember?"

Matt could feel Baylor's eyes on him, and then he was off—crossing the backyard at a brisk and steady pace. Matt stepped outside and listened to the doctor's footsteps break through the frozen ground in the howling wind. Once Baylor disappeared behind the trees, Matt hit the lawn in a full sprint. It took longer than he expected, the actual size of the property lost in the gloom, but when he finally reached the stone wall, he found his pistol and cell phone waiting for him. There was a rear gate here, and a condominium on the other side of the wrought iron fence. A car had just pulled out of the lot onto Sugartown Road. Matt strained to focus his eyes through the darkness, but the car was too far away to make out any detail.

He noticed his breath in the air, thick as smoke. He couldn't catch it. He couldn't think. The world seemed like all of a sudden it was floating through space upside down.

CHAPTER 17

It felt more like an interrogation than anything else. A violation of some kind. Matt was seated at a reading table in the Holloways' library. A bright desk lamp had been pushed into his face. On the other side of the table, he could make out Doyle's figure in the shadows, along with Special Agent Rogers and Dr. Stanley Westbrook. Agent Brown was listening from a chair by the window.

"You're sure it was Baylor?" Rogers asked in a loud voice. "You're sure it was him?"

Matt remained quiet, taking a deep breath and exhaling. He could see Doyle uncapping a bottle of water and taking a quick sip. After he set the bottle down, the federal prosecutor leaned over the table.

"Let's start from the beginning," he said. "Let's go through it one more time, Jones. You said that he left five fingerprints at the Strattons' mansion. That he wanted us to find them because he thought it might bring you to Philadelphia. Where are they? Where are the fingerprints?"

Matt winced. The bright light hurt his eyes.

"Why is this light in my face?"

"Where did Baylor leave the fingerprints?" Doyle repeated.

Matt shrugged. "I didn't believe him when he said it."

"Of course you didn't, Jones. Where did he say he left them?"

"There's a page from a newspaper that Stratton had framed. Baylor said it's hanging in the library. He said he touched the glass and the frame itself. He left a third print on the kitchen faucet when he washed his hands."

Matt could see Rogers leafing through the sections in a three-ring binder and realized that they had pulled the murder book from the passenger seat of Matt's car. It felt like another violation. He watched Rogers find the page he was looking for, his indignation rising. He watched the man skim through the copy and look up at Doyle.

"All three were located," he said finally. "They were smudged. There was no probative value. They could have been anyone's fingerprints. They could have been there for weeks."

Rogers had become defensive the moment Matt told them that Baylor had found a way to send him a text message using the special agent's name and phone number. Matt gave the man another hard look. The gunshot wounds had begun burning in his gut, and he could feel a headache coming on from the bright light in his eyes. It was time for this one-way conversation to end. He grabbed the desk lamp, got to his feet, and turned the bright light on his interrogators.

"Hey, hey, hey," Rogers said. "What do you think you're doing?"

Matt glared back at him. "You want to talk about what happened, Rogers, then I'm more than happy to do that. But this is bullshit, and I don't like you."

Matt smashed the lamp on the floor, then started around the desk toward the special agent. When Rogers took a step back, Doyle grabbed Matt by the shoulders.

"It's been a long night. Why don't we all calm down? You, too, Rogers."

"I'm in charge here," Rogers said under his breath. "He's not qualified to be here. Nobody talks to me that way."

Doyle smiled. "Yes, he is, and he just did. Now find a seat and sit down. Both of you."

Matt glanced at Kate Brown as he took the chair beside her and turned back to Doyle. The federal prosecutor had started pacing up and down the long room and appeared to be thinking something over. After another quick sip of water, he finally spoke.

"This is exactly what we thought would happen. Jones is here, and tonight Dr. Baylor made contact. It's a step forward. A huge step forward. Tell us again, Jones. What did the doctor say?"

Matt leaned forward in the chair. "He claims that he didn't kill these people. And he didn't murder the Strattons. He wanted to, he'd done his research, but someone got to them first. Someone who's picking his victims from the same group."

Doyle glanced his way, then lowered his eyes back to the floor. "That's what the guilty always say. He didn't expect you to believe him, did he?"

"I think he did. He was disappointed when I didn't."

The truth was that Matt thought the doctor had been trying to play him the same way he played the detectives investigating the murder cases in LA. Baylor had done everything he could to make everyone involved think that another man, Jamie Taladyne, was responsible for the three women he murdered in Hollywood and the Valley. Taladyne died at the hands of the police before Matt was able to see through the doctor and single him out.

Matt had reached this conclusion six hours ago after watching the doctor's car vanish down Sugartown Road. He'd made two calls, first to 911, and then to Kate Brown. It had taken less than ten minutes for the township's first response units to arrive. But it had taken almost an hour before anyone from the city made it to the Holloways' mansion in the suburbs. An hour Matt had used to reexamine the crime scene on his own and process what he thought had happened here tonight.

He looked up and caught Dr. Westbrook staring at him through those thick glasses of his. He could see suspicion showing on the man's face, and wasn't sure if he liked him any more than Rogers. The two men seemed to have a great deal in common.

Matt turned back to Doyle, still pacing, still tossing something over in his mind.

"After Baylor tried to persuade you that his connection to both murders was a coincidence, what happened next?"

"I tried to convince the doctor to turn himself in."

"How?" Doyle asked. "What did you say?"

"He wanted to see my gunshot wounds. He wanted to see how they were healing."

Westbrook broke in. "Any show of concern or kindness is an act," he said. "Dr. Baylor is a psychopath. Showing concern is just another tool in the madman's bag of tricks."

Matt didn't think so, but kept his mouth shut.

Doyle stopped and turned and shot the psychiatrist an odd look. "It seems to me that this is more than a trick, Westbrook. How do you explain the fact that Dr. Baylor saved Jones's life in LA?"

Dr. Westbrook shook his head. "I can't," he said. "But I've never met a psychopath who wasn't a manipulator. I've never met one who wasn't a great role player. They know how to push buttons to get what they want, and they're good at it."

Doyle nodded. "Point taken," he said as he turned back to Matt and started pacing again. "Okay, Jones. Baylor examined your gunshot wounds. What did you say that you hoped might convince him to turn himself in?"

"I told him that there had to be something left inside him because he *did* save me. He saved me twice."

"Anything else?"

Matt stood up and leaned against the windowsill. "I told him that his story defied the imagination. No one would ever believe that he just happened to show up at the Strattons' on the night they were murdered, and then again tonight at the Holloways' with the bodies still warm. I told him that time was running out. That ever since his escape, the FBI has known that he's not who he says he is. That everyone believes he murdered the real Dr. George Baylor fifteen years ago in Chicago. That the two of them may have met while attending medical school. That he was from somewhere on the East Coast and obviously running from something in his past that required a new identity."

"Where did you learn all that?" Doyle asked.

"I was given access to the website before I was shot."

"How did Baylor react?"

Matt paused a moment. He could still see the expression on the doctor's face. He could still hear his voice.

"He said that I needed him."

Doyle turned and gasped incredulously. "He what?"

Matt reached into his pocket and opened a fresh pack of nicotine gum. Everyone in the room was staring at him.

"He said that I still needed him. I just didn't know it yet."

CHAPTER 18

Matt wasn't exactly sure, but he thought that he'd lost his footing. He thought that he'd missed something while talking to Dr. Baylor and that it was important.

He hadn't been afraid. That was the trigger.

Once Baylor jabbed him in the back with the gun, once the shock wore off from being startled, only the horror of the actual crime remained.

Matt knew from his experience as a soldier in Afghanistan that fear was an instinctual response. Fear wasn't something he could control. Fear couldn't be switched on or switched off. Fear was an automatic response to danger and went side by side with his will to live.

Matt understood exactly who Baylor was and what he'd done to four innocent young women. Baylor had the Glock 17 and had taken charge of Matt's weapon and cell phone. Matt had every reason to be frightened of the man.

So why didn't his body perform the way it should have? What had overridden his natural response to being held by a madman?

Matt had always relied on his instincts and his imagination to survive, and he didn't understand what was going on. Either he'd lost his touch or he'd missed a key component that he should have seen.

As Matt played it back in his mind, as he considered all the innocent people Baylor had terrorized, ruined, or killed, he realized that he hadn't responded to the doctor as a threat.

And this worried him.

Matt zipped up his leather jacket and walked out of the Holloways' mansion. For whatever reason, probably at Doyle's urging, Rogers had returned the murder book to him. There were two trucks from the county crime lab still here, along with an almost endless line of patrol units parked on the grass along the drive. It was just after five in the morning. The murder victims had been removed by a team from the coroner's office a few hours ago. Rogers and Brown had left around the same time, but Matt could see Doyle holding an impromptu press conference with the media on the other side of the street.

He could hear the federal prosecutor acknowledging the murders and making a preliminary statement for the morning news. He could hear a reporter shouting Baylor's name and noted the anxiety in the man's voice.

Why did Baylor pick Philadelphia? Why is he here?

Matt stopped listening. He was just grateful that the crowd of reporters and their camera people were far enough away that he hadn't been noticed and could make a clean break for his car.

But then he stepped through the gate onto the street and was hit by the sudden shock of light from a video camera. It was Ryan Day, the celebrity gossip reporter, in Matt's face with his microphone and backstepping his way beside his camera operator. When the reporter spoke, the drama in his voice sounded over-the-top.

"What's it like inside, Detective Jones? Five more murders by the infamous Dr. Baylor. Another entire family dead. What are you feeling right now?"

Matt wouldn't make the same mistake twice. Flashing an affable smile that died off quickly, he ignored the question, kept his eyes away from the camera, and walked past both men. Then he got in his car and drove off. He could see them in the rearview mirror. They were still shooting until he reached the corner and made a left onto Sugartown Road. That's when the camera light finally went dark.

Matt reached into his pocket, then stopped. Nicotine gum was useless. He needed a cigarette, and he needed one now.

On the drive to the Holloways' mansion, he had seen a Wawa food market just off Sugartown this side of Route 30. Matt remembered reading a sign that said the store was open twenty-four hours. As he glided down the hill, he spotted the lights in the winter gloom and felt the pangs in his gut lessen some. The lot was empty. Matt nearly ripped the door off its hinges and climbed out of the car. Inside the market he could smell fresh-brewed coffee and counted ten glass pots filled to the brim. He poured a large cup and added two sugars. Walking over to the register, he noticed a basket of soft pretzels wrapped in plastic. He grabbed two and asked for a pack of Marlboros, a disposable lighter, and two packets of Advil.

He couldn't move fast enough as he exited the market. He slammed the car door shut, got the engine started, and lit up. The cigarette tasted like shit and smelled even worse, and within a few seconds he remembered all five reasons why he'd quit. Still, he shook those reasons off one by one, then ripped open both packets of Advil and downed four caplets with his coffee. He took another drag on the cigarette, cracked the window open, and turned up the heat. He didn't care how rank the cigarette smelled or tasted. His body was already beginning to relax, his mind sharpening. Within an hour, the pain from the wounds in his gut would fade away. If he followed up with two Tylenol caplets in a couple of hours and went back to a normal dosage of Advil two hours after that, he might make it through the day without having to open that bottle of Vicodin.

He pulled out of the lot, following the road into the valley and picking up the expressway into the city. Early morning traffic was still a long way off, and Matt made the drive with his foot on the floor in less than half an hour. By 6:30 a.m. he'd showered and shaved and was out the door, heading for Benny's Café Blue.

He walked in with the murder book, ordered a cup of the house blend, and sat at the booth by the window. The sun still hadn't risen, and he could see two young women and a middle-aged man working out on those StairMasters across the street.

He sat back and let his eyes wander down to the sidewalk. The trees were bending in the cold wind, the lights on the branches hypnotic after a night without sleep. He turned back, took a first sip of coffee, and gazed at the logs burning in the café's fireplace.

He'd missed things. Important things. He knew it now.

It had been showing on Baylor's face when they switched on the lights and returned to the second-floor landing. The expression on his face as the doctor moved closer and gazed at the Holloways. The curiosity in his eyes, that strange glint moving from one dead body to the next. Matt had noticed it at the time, but couldn't fathom what it meant. Now he was ready to make a wild guess that didn't feel so wild.

Baylor had been seeing the crime scene for the first time.

The first time.

Matt's heart almost stopped. What if this really was different than LA? What if the doctor wasn't looking for a scapegoat? What if he had told Matt the truth? What if someone else was out there? Someone off the grid. Someone the doctor had called *special*.

Matt let the idea settle in.

It would explain why he hadn't seen Baylor as a threat. It would explain why he never felt like he was in danger and had no sensation of fear. His gut instincts had seen it from the beginning, even though it had taken until this very moment for his mind to catch up and cross the finish line.

Matt thought about the text message the doctor had sent him. Could Baylor have committed the murders and sent the message as a ploy in order to confuse the issue? Yes, but Matt imagined that human behavior, even in the case of a psychopath, wasn't so complicated.

The more likely explanation was that the doctor had been telling him the truth. As Matt considered this concept, he could feel the main wheel in his gut click forward like the clock on the wall striking 7:00 a.m.

It felt so odd. So outrageous. So possibly righteous.

The doctor could be innocent.

He opened the Strattons' murder book, checked who was sitting nearby, then began leafing through the crime-scene photos. He was thinking about something Baylor had said at the Holloways'. A question he'd posed just before leaving.

When you add everything up, what need was the killer trying to fulfill?

Matt's eyes drifted from body to body until they came to rest on Tammy Stratton holding her thirteen-year-old son, Jim Jr. She was cradling the boy exactly the way Mimi Holloway had been holding her son, Nicholas. It suddenly occurred to Matt that these murders might not have anything to do with either Jim Stratton, MD, or David Holloway. Nothing to do with Stratton's crime of giving his healthy patients chemotherapy or Holloway's habitual acts of cowardice in killing big game. Matt had no doubt that both men were complete shitheads, but there was a chance, an emerging possibility, that these murders had nothing to do with them.

He looked back at the photo of Tammy Stratton. The death embrace. He thought about the order of things. Jim Jr. would've been the first to die. His mother holding him in her arms would have gone next.

These murders weren't about greed. Matt was certain of it now. This was about a killer with a different issue. A killer with an entirely different motive.

Matt noticed that his fingers were trembling slightly as he made
the revelation. This wasn't about money or greed or even power. This
was about *Mommy*.

A thought surfaced. Matt rushed through the set of photographs
until he found a copy of the one Doyle had shown him in McKensie's
office at the Hollywood station. The image may have been dark, but it
was shot from a distance and took in the entire crime scene. He focused
on the mother holding her son, noting once again that their genitals
were touching.

This was about *Mommy*.

But something else was going on here. That stray thought he'd had
when he first examined the Strattons' second-floor landing on his own.
He had thought about the way the bodies were posed, the blood spattered all over the walls—he'd known it all along. His first impression of
the crime scene had been the right one.

*If Baylor had been trying to make a statement like he did in LA and
New Orleans, this one seemed forced. It felt like he was straining.*

The reason it felt different was the most obvious reason of them all.
It confirmed everything in Matt's mind.

There really was someone else out there. Someone *special*.

Matt saw a man approaching him out of the corner of his eye
and slammed the murder book shut. When he looked up, Ryan Day
was taking a seat on the other side of the booth and sipping a cup of
coffee. His eyes through his wire-rimmed glasses were big and wild,
and Matt guessed that the gossip reporter had caught a glimpse of the
photograph.

Day set his coffee cup on the table. "We could help each other,
you know."

"We could what?"

"Help each other," the reporter said. "I have information."

Matt tried to reel in his exasperation. "About what?"

"About everything."

Matt pushed his coffee aside, then checked the café and glanced out the window. When he didn't see Day's camera operator, he turned back. "Give me a sample," he said. "Tell me something that will help me."

Day leaned on the table, his brown eyes sparkling. "Okay," he said. "Your father has hired two bodyguards. Both are former Navy SEALs and licensed to carry firearms. Apparently, your father thinks someone is out to get him. That wouldn't be you, would it?"

Matt didn't say anything for a long time. He sat back and stared at Day and let his mind roll out line. He already knew about the bodyguards. He'd seen them walking his father through the crowd of reporters on TV. When Matt finally spoke, his voice wasn't much more than a whisper.

"I thought you hadn't confirmed who my father was. That's what you said yesterday."

"He has to be your father, Jones."

Matt shook his head slowly. "That's all you've got?"

The reporter paused a moment, then leaned forward. "Do you know how many corporate-created, bitchy, no-talent celebrities I've had to push on my show to keep the ratings up and pay the bills? How many times I've wanted to lose my lunch after interviewing one of these low-rent reality stars? You have no idea how great it is to be working on a real story."

"That's the part I don't get, Day. What's the story?"

"Who your father is. Who shot you on Mount Hollywood. Who you really are, and why did Dr. Baylor save your life. That's the story, and it's a great story. I can't believe you wouldn't want to help me tell it."

Day's voice shook with emotion and more drama. The gossip reporter came off so sleazy that Matt thought about driving back to the apartment and taking another shower.

"I don't think you can help me," Matt said.

He picked up the murder book and got to his feet. Day grabbed his forearm.

"Please, I can help you," he said. "Here's something to get you started."

"I'm not interested."

Day narrowed his eyes. "Your mother's maiden name," he said quickly. "It's not Clemens. It's Stewart. Julie Stewart. That was your mother's real name. It was changed in her early teens. Same with your aunt Abby."

Matt clenched his teeth and gave the man with black hair and ultra-pale skin a long, hard look. Then he ripped his arm free, and walked out.

CHAPTER 19

Matt stepped off the elevator and hustled down the hall to the Crisis Room, wrestling with his emotions. He resented being led on by someone like Day whom he didn't trust or even respect. He couldn't afford to waste time chasing phantoms right now. Especially after making what he considered a significant step forward in his understanding of the Stratton and Holloway murders.

He burst through the door and cut across the room to the desk he'd been assigned. It was 7:30 a.m. Fifteen to twenty people were already here, but he didn't know or recognize anyone.

Matt opened his laptop and switched on the power. As he waited for the machine to boot, he tossed over the idea of coming forward with his revelation about the doctor. He wondered how Doyle and Rogers would take it given the fact that he had no tangible evidence. Just thoughts and guesses and personal observations made before the crime lab had a chance to process their findings and file their reports.

The truth was that Matt wished he could talk to Dr. Baylor about his revelation. He wished that he had some way of making contact with the surgeon.

That, too, worried him.

Deciding that his best bet was to keep his thoughts to himself, to remain cautious until he found something so real even Rogers would be convinced, Matt pulled his laptop closer and typed a name into the search engine.

Julie Stewart.

He didn't expect to get a hit. He wasn't sure he even wanted one. But then he clicked the Search key with his cursor, and something strange happened.

Hundreds of links to articles were assembling on the screen. Julie Stewart was mentioned in books and newspapers. As Matt scrolled down, he spotted his aunt's name as well. Photographs were included. The two sisters appeared very young—eight or nine years old—and were posted with two siblings Matt didn't know existed, Joseph and Eleanor. But it was the names and photographs of his mother's parents, Howard and Michelle Stewart, that dominated the listings. Matt had never met either one of his grandparents, nor did he know anything about them. He was only a boy when his mother died of cancer, and he was sent to New Jersey to live with his aunt. He clicked through the photo gallery, comparing their features with the vague memory of his mother's face. When he couldn't find a single image of anyone in the family that wasn't at least four decades old, he guessed that something catastrophic had happened and recalled how his aunt never seemed to want to talk about her past.

Matt sensed movement close by and looked up. Doyle had just entered the conference room, closed the door, and picked up the phone. Kate Brown was looking his way as she sat down at her desk with a cup of takeout coffee and a bagel.

"Everything okay?" she said.

Matt nodded. "Just catching up."

Her phone rang. When she took the call, Matt's eyes rocked back to his laptop. Something catastrophic had happened to this family. His mother's family. Something no one wanted to talk about.

Matt sorted the listings by the most recent and found an article that had been published in the business section of the *New York Times* just a few years ago. It was a historical piece for the column Throwback Thursday on Wall Street. Another photograph of his grandfather was featured, along with his business partner, Robert Kay. Once Matt got a feel for where the story was headed, he checked on Kate Brown again, then turned back to his laptop and started eating up the words in huge bites.

Four decades ago Matt's grandfather, Howard Stewart, had run a Ponzi scheme on Wall Street that burned down and caused a recession. Investigators estimated the size of the fraud to be in the neighborhood of thirty-two billion dollars. World markets before China's rise, particularly in New York, London, Berlin, and Tokyo, crashed. Nearly five thousand investors in Howard Stewart Investment Securities LLC lost everything they had, including their homes and cars, their futures, their retirement accounts, their pensions, their savings. All of it gone in a single day, their lives ruined.

Yet Stewart and his business partner and many of the top executives at their investment firm had lost nothing.

The target of the investigation had always been centered on Matt's grandfather. But after a few weeks, his business partner's frequent claims that he was innocent and had no knowledge of the financial scheme began to fall on deaf ears. The two men had begun to argue as the net tightened. And one night, as Matt's grandparents slept in their home in Maplewood, New Jersey, they were shot dead.

Matt's heart skipped a beat. All he could think about was his aunt and his mother and what they'd gone through. According to the article, the four children had heard someone break into the house and sought refuge in the attic. When they heard gunshots, they waited until dawn, then the boy snuck downstairs and called for help.

In spite of the darkness, one of the children caught a glimpse of the killer and thought that he looked a lot like their father's business partner, Robert Kay. Kay had been over that night, and there had been another argument—this one so loud that the neighbors noticed. When questioned by local detectives, Kay admitted that he and Stewart fought, but claimed once again that he was innocent. Unfortunately for Kay, he had no alibi and couldn't prove where he was at the time of the murders.

Kay was found guilty on two counts of murder in the first degree and sentenced to 150 years with no possibility of parole. After one week in prison, he tried to hang himself in his cell. Ten days after that his body was found in the showers with a bar of soap stuffed down his throat.

Matt stopped reading so quickly. He could guess what happened next. The four children would have been carted off to parts unknown and raised by a family member. Once the four siblings came of age, the umbilical cords to their pasts would need to be severed once and for all. That would have been when their names were changed from Stewart to Clemens.

Julie and Abby Clemens, Matt's mother and aunt.

Somehow Ryan Day had found this. Somehow the gossip reporter had unearthed a huge chunk of Matt's family history. No wonder the special agent at the FBI's office in Westwood hit a black hole when he ran his mother and aunt through the system.

Matt needed a cigarette and looked up when he heard someone slap their hand on his desk. It was Special Agent in Charge Wes Rogers, glancing at Matt and then Brown, who'd just hung up the phone.

"Listen up, you two," he said quickly. "The Holloway autopsies have been moved up to 10:00 a.m. this morning."

"Where?" Brown asked.

Rogers handed her a three-by-five card with an address jotted down on its face. "Chester County Hospital," he said. "It will probably take you guys an hour to get there. You better head out."

Rogers started to walk off, then seemed to remember something and turned back. "Oh, and Jones," he said. "I spoke with your supervisor in Hollywood last night, Lieutenant Howard McKensie."

Matt met Rogers's gaze but didn't say anything. For some unknown reason, the special agent had shed his anger and smiled at him.

"It's your lucky day, Jones. McKensie wanted you to know that the fire's been contained. Your house survived. It's still standing."

CHAPTER 20

Andrew Penchant sat at a table in the arcade, sipping from a bottle of mango-extremo-flavored Gatorade that he'd stolen while on the job at the Walmart Supercenter. He was skimming through the newspaper, shaking his head, and trying to ward off that weird feeling again. That odd sensation that seemed to have inhabited his body and mind over the past several years, and controlled his entire being now.

He didn't know if his condition had a name, but after the past few weeks, he'd started to call it dream walking.

It was like he'd stepped out of his skin and couldn't find his way back in. It was like he was standing on the other side of that idiotic pinball machine, watching himself read this lousy newspaper.

He could see his lean body, his long blond hair braided into corn-rows, his light-brown eyes the color of wheat, his angular face, and clear complexion. But with his summer tan erased by an early winter, he thought he looked pale, and despite his strength, even a bit unhealthy.

His mind surfaced. Some asshole kid playing the pinball machine was staring at him.

He tried to shake it off, glanced at the last page in the city section, then flipped the paper over in disgust. The people he'd been reading about today were so fucking boring that he had to fight off a yawn. Half of them were so stupid that they ate three meals a day with their hands. The other half were so full of themselves that they had to be hand-fed on silver spoons or they'd die of starvation.

What the fuck happened to normal? Where did all *those* people go?

Andrew felt a blast of cold air and looked up just as a blonde entered the arcade. He figured she was somewhere in her late teens and could tell that she had a hot body going on underneath her parka. With girls like her, the untouchable ones, he could always tell without really seeing. He dug her gray eyes, her soft and gentle face. She looked naive and shy, and he liked that, too. He picked up his Canon digital SLR, zoomed in on her face, then focused the lens and snapped the shot.

The camera flashed, and those bright-gray eyes turned his way like a pair of headlights. He read her lips as she made a goofy smile and mouthed the words *What are you doing?*

She walked over. Girls like her never walked over. She was gazing at him, staring at him, taking in everything on the table. He didn't like the feeling of being measured. She really was naive.

"You just took my picture," she said.

"So what?"

"It's my picture. I want it back."

He liked her. He could tell that she liked him, too, but he didn't know why. He flashed a lazy smile at her and shook his head.

"You can't have it back," he said. "It's mine."

"Ha—"

She laughed and unzipped her parka. He'd guessed right. She had a killer body. Lots of curves and a better-than-decent, even perky, set of tits. He liked perky, even though he knew they never lasted long. Gravity and time always won when it came down to tits. Not that the result was necessarily bad. It was just an observation he'd made over time.

His eyes rose up to the girl's face. She was gazing at the newspaper on the table, then giving him a suspicious look, her eyes shimmering.

"No offense," she said, "but you don't look like someone who spends a lot of time reading newspapers."

He laughed. "I like headlines," he said. "I'm on my way to becoming a headline. A living legend. Right now I'm only a man of mystery."

"A man of mystery—oh my God. At least you've got nice hair. Who ties your braids for you?"

Andrew thought it over. He didn't want to tell her that his mother braided his hair.

"A friend," he said in a quieter voice. "How come I haven't seen you here before? What's your name?"

"Avery Cooper.'

"How old are you?"

"Nineteen. What's your name?"

"Andrew Penchant, and I just turned twenty-one."

She thrust her hand out. He gazed at her for a moment. She reminded him of someone, but he wasn't sure who. Then he stood up, took her hand, and gave it a soft squeeze.

"Glad to meet you," he said. "Want to have some fun?"

"What kind of fun?"

He flashed another smile and glanced at the storage closet door. The padlock was hanging open from the clasp, the arcade manager outside emptying the trash.

"Let's go in there for a little while," Andrew said.

She still had that suspicious smile going on. Maybe it was even a naughty smile because those big gray eyes of hers were starting to burn a little. All Penchant knew was that she started marching toward the storage closet without being pushed or even dragged. Once she stepped inside, he slammed the door on her and jammed the open lock shackle through the clasp.

She was locked inside the closet. Locked in complete darkness. Locked in a small and incredibly disgusting place, and he couldn't stop laughing. He could hear her fists banging on the door. She was making the climb to panic mode, and doing it quickly, and he loved everything about it.

"Is this a joke?" she was saying through the door. "What are you doing? Let me out, you asshole. Let me out right now."

He pulled the lock out of the clasp and swung the door open. As the light struck her face, he saw the fear showing in her eyes, but still couldn't stop laughing.

"Very funny," she said. "You're already a legend, Andrew."

"I had you, though. Didn't I?"

She didn't say anything.

"Ah, come on. It was just a joke. Why can't you take a joke?"

"Let's go back to the table," she said finally.

"You want something to drink?"

She grabbed his bottle of Gatorade as she sat down. "I like mangos. I'm drinking yours. If you want something, go buy it yourself."

She was still stewing. Still pissed off. He tried to pull himself together and sat down.

"Tell me about your family," he said.

She sipped from the bottle. "What do you want to know?"

"You look like you come from money. You've got that refined look goin' on."

"Nobody who lives in Northeast Philadelphia is refined, Andrew."

He shrugged as he thought it over. She might be right.

"Guess not," he said. "Is your mother pretty?"

"What?"

"Is she pretty?"

"I don't know. I guess so."

"How many brothers and sisters have you got?"

"Two brothers."

"Do they make you have sex with them?"

She gave him a look, but remained quiet. The fear and anger had faded away, but he'd struck a nerve.

"No," she said finally.

"What about your father?"

She was eyeing him carefully, and then a wicked smile flashed across her face. "Andrew Penchant, you are the single most disgusting person I have ever met in my life."

He nodded and smiled back at her.

"What about your family?" she said.

He shrugged. "I don't really have one."

She seemed delighted and laughed. "Oh, that's right. You're a man of mystery. An international man of mystery."

"Not yet, but I like the way you say the word *international*. It's got a ring to it."

She leaned across the table and lowered her throaty voice. "You look like trouble, Andrew Penchant. You look like a real project. My dad would never let me go out with you. He'd look you up and down and call you a loser boy."

He sat back in his seat and took it all in. He could feel his stomach stirring. He could feel joy coming to a boil inside his body. He'd just met a hot-looking bitch named Avery Cooper, and she wasn't running away. This girl was falling for him. He didn't know what to make of it. It had never happened before.

CHAPTER 21

Matt spotted the Ford SUV as Brown rolled off the expressway in King of Prussia and brought the car back up to speed on Route 202, heading south toward West Chester. Lots of cars, if not most, were doing the same thing, yet something about the Ford SUV behind them stood out.

Matt checked the speedometer. Brown was doing seventy-five miles per hour in a fifty-five-mile-per-hour zone. He turned and took another look through the rear window. The SUV appeared to be doing exactly the same speed about ten car lengths back.

"Slow down," he said. "Bring it to fifty and stay there."

"Why? We'll be late."

"We won't be late. Just do it."

She looked at him with concern, then checked the rearview mirror. "What's going on, Jones?"

"Maybe nothing."

Matt watched her slow the car down and set the cruise control to maintain an even speed. When he gazed back at the SUV, he noticed that the driver had slowed down as well and was keeping his distance. No doubt about it, they had a shadow.

"It's that black Ford," Brown said, her eyes pinned to the rearview mirror.

Matt nodded. "Yeah, but I can't see who's behind the wheel. Bring the car back up to seventy-five. Let's see how much time we've got when we get closer to West Chester."

In spite of road construction along the 202 corridor, they made the drive from King of Prussia to the Paoli Pike exit in fifteen minutes. According to the navigation system on the dashboard, they were less than five minutes away from the hospital, and it was still only 9:20 a.m. The black SUV had just reached the exit and was starting down the hill toward the traffic light.

Matt watched the vehicle disappear in the trees and spotted a shopping center on the right. "Pull into the lot," he said. "Hurry. Before he reaches the light and sees us."

Brown made a hard right and floored it. Hiding behind a bank, she found an empty parking spot with a view of the street. The SUV was just passing the lot, but the identity of their follower remained hidden behind tinted glass. Matt watched as the driver suddenly hit the brakes and swerved into the lot. In all probability, the driver hadn't seen them on the street and made a guess. He'd lost them and was idling by the stores, heading in the wrong direction. There were well over two hundred cars parked in long rows. There was a gym here, a grocery store, a liquor store, and a bookshop that looked more than inviting called Chester County Book Company.

Brown shifted into Drive and started easing the car forward. Matt looked back at their follower still searching for them and still heading in the wrong direction. When the SUV started down another aisle of parked cars, Brown used the bank for cover and pulled back onto the street. She brought the car up to speed in a quick thrust. After Brown made a right on Montgomery Avenue, Matt turned and gazed out the rear window.

The road behind them was completely empty. Brown had shaken their tail.

He gave her a look. She turned to him, her eyes bright and alive.

CHAPTER 22

Matt had never witnessed an autopsy before. While he and Brown got into their hazardous material suits, what one of the medical examiners called a hazmat suit, Brown admitted that she had attended only three and each one had been difficult to deal with. Matt's expectations were bleak, particularly after learning that the autopsies for all five victims would be occurring simultaneously.

Matt followed Brown through the doorway into a large operating room. The entire Holloway family was already here. Five naked corpses on five stainless steel tables. Less than a day had passed since their deaths, yet time hadn't been very kind to them. Matt noticed that the diamond had been removed from Holloway's ear, the lobe stretched to the point of appearing deformed. But even worse, Holloway's mouth was wide-open, his eyes glazed over and milky. The macho man didn't seem so macho anymore.

Matt looked away. But even with a respirator, he couldn't escape the smell of rotting flesh and human waste that permeated the entire room.

He turned and saw Brown standing over the twelve-year-old girl, Sophie Holloway. Somehow seeing a child in this state, this condition, brought everything into sharp focus.

Matt took a step back, his mind going.

Dr. Baylor was obviously a psychopath and a killer of four young women. He was a sick man—an insane man—and in spite of the things Matt had said, too far gone to be helped or brought back.

But the doctor didn't do this. He didn't kill this little girl, or her sister or her brother. He didn't murder Mimi Holloway or her asshole husband. Matt felt sure of it now. Baylor couldn't have murdered these people. The look on the doctor's face when they switched on the lights and climbed the stairs had been one of fascination. Someone wrestling with a horrific situation and trying to understand it.

There had to be someone else out there. A monster who defied the imagination. Someone even more insane than Baylor.

The autopsies were underway—ten times more brutal than an operating room or any field hospital Matt had seen during the war. No matter how difficult the experience, he had learned something. He'd learned that he would have to trust the feeling in his gut. His thoughts were wild, and he'd still need to keep them to himself for a while. He had his family situation to deal with, his deadbeat father and his mother's mysterious past. He would have to avoid Ryan Day. He would have to be careful. But he thought that he'd reached the point where he could move forward with confidence again. The truth was, he didn't think he had much choice.

He felt someone touch him, and his mind surfaced. It was Kate Brown, standing before him, holding his gloved hands. And she was standing close. He could feel her legs brushing against his legs, her mask and respirator touching his own. She gave his hands a squeeze, her eyes burning with emotion.

"I can't do this," she whispered. "I can't stay here, Matt. I can't be in this room."

"It's okay," he said. "Everything's okay."

She shook her head. "No, it's not. I'm paid to be here. I'm supposed to be here, but I can't handle it. They'll be at it for hours, and I don't want to see them cut up the kids."

"Don't worry about it," he said. "I'll cover for you. Wait outside for me."

She dropped one of his hands and touched his chest. It seemed intimate, but he didn't take it that way. Brown was in distress, and it seemed like they'd known each other for more than a few days.

"Are you sure?" she said. "You'll be on your own."

He nodded. "I'll be fine. Wait for me outside."

"Thanks, Jones."

He watched her cross the operating room. When she stepped out and closed the door, he turned back and saw the medical examiner working on Holloway pick up his skull saw. The view had turned even more harsh. He straightened his mask and exhaled through the respirator. No one could see him clench his teeth. No one could see him grimace.

CHAPTER 23

Andrew Penchant spotted Reggie Cook's beat-up Chevy in the driveway and pulled to the curb, debating whether or not he should go inside. Cook was a big, hairy slob, an obvious piece of white Northeast Philly trash, whom his mother had started seeing again. Andrew hated the man more than anyone he had ever met, and for good reason. Somehow Cook had found out that his mother, Sarah Penchant, had been raped by her best friend's father when she was fourteen years old. Some religious asshole dude who hung framed pictures of Jesus Christ on his walls and was wrapped too tight. Cook knew that his mother hadn't aborted the pregnancy and that Andrew was a rape baby. He liked to tease Andrew when they were alone. He liked to call him a devil's child, and often asked if he'd been born with horns and a tail.

Andrew had to eat it—for the sake of his mother, he had to deal with the bully—but the whole thing was wearing him out.

He opened the ashtray, searching for what was left of a joint he'd rolled before going to work this morning. It looked like there were two, maybe three hits left. Striking a lighter, he held the charred end over the flame and took a deep hit. As he exhaled and started coughing, he noticed their neighbor Mr. Andolini sweeping his front steps. He was an old man, a crackpot who thought he ran the neighborhood, and Andrew didn't like him much either. Why would anyone sweep their steps on a day this cold? What fool wouldn't wait for the wind to die down?

The only good thing about Mr. Andolini was that he grew Concord grapes and was a generous old fuck. Andrew had to give him that. It was Mr. Andolini who had taught him how to eat a Concord grape, how to squeeze the inside out with his tongue and swallow it whole, then spit the sour skin onto the lawn. Mr. Andolini's Concord grapes were the best grapes that he had ever tasted.

Andrew turned and looked at the steel plant behind the rundown houses across the street. At the end of the block, he could see the Delaware River. There was a small park here that included two benches and a narrow dock. The city of Philadelphia was just ten miles downstream. Andrew liked to get high at night and gaze at the lights and tall buildings and dream about the way things could have been. The way things would never be, except in his mind, except when he was stoned.

In spite of the frigid air, he had sat there last night for the better part of an hour. He'd smoked an entire joint and tried to pull himself together. Tried to understand what happened during his field trip to the suburbs and another visit with the rich and famous. Tried to focus on who he'd been and what he was now becoming. Tried to stop the rage and the anger and the shaking and the dream walking. Tried to slow everything down.

He could still see them. Still see the terror in their eyes. Still hear them whimpering and begging. Still hear their faint moans and weak attempts to cry for help as they bled out.

A headline.

A living legend.

What he wanted, and what he was becoming.

Those stupid fucking animal heads. He could still see them on the wall watching him do what had to be done.

Andrew took a last hit on the joint, scorching his fingertips as he flicked it out the window. Then he turned back to Reggie Cook's car and gazed at his mother's cedar-shake house. It was more of a cottage than a real house. It was small, the walls too thin to give anyone any privacy.

He could feel his mind buzzing from the weed, his empty stomach growling. Only two hits and he was stoned and hungry.

He felt a draft from the window and shivered. He had to go inside, he decided finally. He might freeze to death out here.

He locked the car, hiked up the steps to the porch, and pushed the front door open. He found them in the kitchen. Cook was seated at the table with a shit-eating, I-just-fucked-your-mother kind of grin seared onto his stupid face. Andrew's mother, Sarah, was standing beside the slob, wearing a completely transparent baby-doll top, a bare midriff, and a pair of low-riding, skintight jeans.

Andrew glanced at his mother's full breasts, her puffy nipples and supersized areolas, then lifted his gaze to her face. She was only thirty-five, with golden-brown eyes and light-brown hair that she liked to have highlighted. She was only thirty-five and still hot in a trashy, Northeast Philly sort of way. Still dirty hot and messing with his head.

"What's he doing here?" Andrew said.

His mother smiled at him. "He came over to visit, Andrew. Reggie was just leaving."

"Good," he said.

Andrew could smell his mother's sex lingering over the table and guessed that Cook hadn't washed his face. He could feel the man's eyeballs on him. When he turned to give him a look, Cook slapped the table and howled.

"You're weird, kid," he said, his voice booming. "Goddamn it, you're weird. You give new meaning to the phrase *odd man out*."

Cook's eyes got big and lit up as he roared with laughter. Andrew's mother frowned.

"Stop it, Reggie. It's time to go."

He nodded and got up from the table with his fly undone. Zipping it up, he gave Andrew a wink and a hideous smile, and walked out still laughing. Andrew watched his mother follow the man into the living room. They were whispering, and he could hear them kissing. Then the front door opened and closed and his mother strolled into the kitchen with a warm smile on her face.

Andrew looked at her tits again. The transparent top. He could feel his dick getting hard. He couldn't help it.

"Why do you dress this way in front of me?" he said in a quiet voice.

She moved closer and ran her hand through his braided hair. "I do it for you," she said. "Everything I do is for you, Andrew."

"For me? It's not proper to dress this way in front of your son."

She met his eyes and smiled again. "But you like it."

"I don't. I really don't like it."

"Yes, you do. You've liked it ever since you were a little boy. Since you were a baby. You like looking at them. You like looking at me. You like the time we spend together."

The time we spend together.

Andrew gazed at her face, wondering if someone had slipped LSD into his weed. It felt like he was tripping. He knew from experience that it wasn't safe to trip alone.

His mother brushed her nose over his cornrows and kissed him above the ear. "Did you bring anything home tonight, honey?"

Andrew nodded and pulled two partially frozen New York strip steaks out of his jacket pocket. Like the Gatorade he'd stolen from the Walmart Supercenter, dinner would be on the house tonight, just as it was most nights.

His mother looked at the steaks and seemed pleased. Andrew lifted the camera strapped to his shoulder over his head and set it on the table.

"You could do better than working at Walmart, Andrew. You were given a gift. A real talent. You should be making a living with that camera. Photography shouldn't be something you do part-time."

He didn't say anything. He looked at her bare shoulders and back, her hips and ass as she turned on the stove. His dick was still hard, and he felt stupid. Mortified. He hated her, even though he loved her. He hated her.

CHAPTER 24

Andrew switched on the lights and TV, then sat down at his worktable by the window and woke up his laptop and printer. As he attached a cable to his camera, he glanced at the TV and then the clock radio by the bed. His favorite show, an animated comedy called *Olive Kills Her Neighbor's Cat*, wouldn't begin for another fifteen minutes. Until then, he'd have to endure this ignorant show that pandered to the weirdos who got off on gossip magazines.

Get Buzzed with Ryan Day.

He had caught glimpses of the show many times in the past. It was a carbon copy of every other gossip show he'd seen on TV, and just as difficult to avoid. The segments almost always involved young celebrities, especially but not always young female celebrities who were in some sort of trouble. Picked up for drugs or drunk driving, failing to attend a court hearing, a return trip to rehab on a beach in paradise, weight loss and a new bikini, a young female climbing out of her car with her panties in her purse, or even the well-tested and overdone "wardrobe malfunction" at a public event that usually involved a young female celebrity showing off her tits accidently on purpose.

The one constant was that none of these people had anything else going on. Their careers, if they even had one, were short and sweet and over. They were washed up and circling the drain, and so desperate to be noticed that Andrew thought he could see it on their faces.

He turned back to his laptop and snickered. It didn't make any difference. An appearance on a show like *Get Buzzed* worked like a signal, a warning beacon, a eulogy given at a funeral. It was like getting your ass kicked with millions of viewers laughing at you. The big good-bye.

Andrew let the thought go as he downloaded thirty-seven new images from his camera. When the photo library opened, he skimmed through the portraits he'd taken until he reached the photograph of Avery Cooper. Without protesting, Avery had let him take a handful of close-ups before leaving the arcade. He caught a whiff of his mother's perfume on his skin as he examined each image, then clicked backward until he found the picture he thought might be his favorite. His stomach was stirring again—glowing—and this surprised him.

Avery Cooper was the first girl to ever come on to him. He wondered if he could trust her. If she wasn't playing with him. Messing with him the same way his mother messed with him.

He thought about his mother, and after a few moments, managed to shake it off. Things happen for a reason, he reminded himself. There had to be a reason why he and Avery Cooper met this afternoon. A purpose. A meaning. He'd given her his cell phone number. Now he wondered why he hadn't asked for hers.

He heard someone say something and glanced at the TV. It was Ryan Day poking his microphone into some guy's face on the street outside the Holloways' mansion on the Main Line.

Andrew rolled his desk chair closer, mesmerized. They were doing the story on a national TV show. Who cared if the show sucked?

What's it like inside, Detective Jones? Five more murders by the infamous Dr. Baylor. Another entire family dead. What are you feeling right now?

Who were these people? What were they talking about?

Andrew got up and closed his bedroom door, then rushed back to his seat and watched the detective push his way past the camera and drive off. Then Day moved over to the driveway and finished his segment with the Holloways' mansion just visible in the darkness behind him.

The image was haunting and creepy, and Andrew felt a chill crawl up his spine. It was almost as if he'd never been there. Almost as if he were hearing about the five murders, an entire family savagely killed, for the first time.

But even more, Day was recapping the story. He was introducing Andrew to a detective from Los Angeles named Matt Jones and a psychopath, someone Day kept calling the *real* killer, a Dr. George Baylor. What a great name for a mad scientist. Dr. Baylor. What a great name for the *real* killer.

The story ended with a photograph of Dr. Baylor and video of Matt Jones chasing someone down a street in Philadelphia with his pistol out. When the segment ended and they cut to a commercial, Andrew took a deep breath and exhaled. Then he grabbed his bong and a lighter and rolled his chair back to the computer. He wanted to see who he was dealing with. He wanted to have some more fun.

He clicked open the search engine and typed a name into the window as quickly as he could. The one he'd seen on TV. That detective who'd come all the way from Hollywood to investigate the mass killings here in the City of Brotherly Love.

Matt Jones.

CHAPTER 25

Matt found Brown sitting at a table by the window in the cafeteria. It looked like all she had was a glass of ice water. She gave him a look as he walked over. She was still wearing the same emotions on her face that he'd seen in the operating room. He could tell that she was disappointed in herself.

"It's okay, Kate," he said. "It's over."

She shook her head. "No, it's not. It's not okay, and it's not over. How did it go?"

He reached out for her hand. "Let's get out of here. Let's go someplace quieter."

She got to her feet, and they walked out into the hall, heading for the lobby.

"We can do that later," she said. "Rogers wants us downtown. Something's come up."

Matt checked his watch. It was 7:30 p.m.

"Did he say what happened?"

"No. He just said that he wanted us to drive straight back once the autopsies were over. He said that it's important."

They reached the hospital's main entrance, walked outside into the frigid air and down the steps to the parking lot.

Brown gave him a look. "You never answered my question. How did it go in there? What's the official cause of death?"

"If the tox screens come back clean and there aren't any surprises, then it's the gunshot wounds. The ME said that it would have been a slow death. An hour, maybe even longer. He thinks that's why the wounds were taped over. The killer was regulating their blood loss."

"Baylor," she said in a dark voice.

Matt remained quiet. He wanted to tell her what he was thinking, but knew that holding back was the right move for now.

"What about puncture wounds?" she said.

"They didn't find any. Not on any of them. They think the tox screens could come back clean, Kate. That the loss of blood from the gunshots would have been enough to keep them docile."

More evidence that Baylor really wasn't the killer, Matt thought. More evidence that a ghost was out there. An alien working in the dark with no one even looking for him. Baylor had used a drug that still hadn't been identified to keep his victims in a vegetative state for days while he sexually abused them. Matt had seen the doctor inject something into Anna Marie Genet, an eighteen-year-old college freshman, who was the only known victim to survive.

They reached the car. Brown clicked open the door locks, then turned and stepped in front of Matt. She was standing close to him again. He could feel her left arm find its way around his waist, her right hand on his chest exactly the way she had held him in the operating room. Her eyes were smoked out and hot.

"I'm sorry I wasn't with you," she said in a quiet voice. "I'm sorry you had to go through that alone."

"Everything's good, Kate. You're covered. I'm glad I was here to help."

She didn't say anything. She stood there holding him and looking at him. Matt could feel her thighs brushing against his thighs, her warm belly pressing into his belly. In the operating room, they had been wearing their hazmat suits. Now they were wearing street clothes and their jackets were open. The moment was decidedly sensual, even erotic.

And then it passed. And then Brown let go, opened the car door, and climbed in behind the wheel as if nothing had happened. Matt didn't know what to make of it. As he got in the car and fastened his seatbelt, he wondered if he should say something. In the end, he decided to let it go. The last woman he'd been with, the way it played out and ended, was still too close. He had spent the last month and a half working through it with his psychiatrist from the LAPD's Behavioral Science Section. Over and over and over again. It was essential to his recovery that he let go of his feelings for her, make a clean break, and move forward. On most days he was fine. On others, not so lucky.

But tonight he'd felt something.

He looked over at Brown as she pulled the car out of the lot. He wondered if she wasn't exactly what he needed. He could remember his shrink saying that the sooner he had sex, the better off he'd be.

Matt watched her switch on the radio, then settled into the passenger seat. He'd missed another night's sleep, but was afraid that if he closed his eyes, he'd replay the last eight hours in his head. All those horrific images of the Holloway family being cut into pieces and then sewn back up with a heavy black twine. All those hideous memories that he knew would never go away.

CHAPTER 26

Matt followed Brown past their desks and across the floor to the conference room. He could see them through the glass. Rogers and Dr. Westbrook were seated at the table, while Doyle paced back and forth along the far wall.

Rogers swung the door open and waved them in. "There's been a development," he said.

Matt could tell by looking at the somber expressions on everyone's face that whatever happened wasn't good. Once he closed the door, Rogers returned to his seat and shook his head.

"A development," Doyle repeated. "That's one way of looking at it, I guess."

Matt leaned against the credenza and watched Doyle walk the length of the room, then turn back.

"What happened?" Matt said. "What is it?"

Doyle clasped his hands behind his back and shrugged. "The lab report came back, and this time it's definitive. The semen found in Tammy Stratton doesn't match Baylor's DNA."

It hung there. Matt couldn't believe it. Definitive proof. Finally.

"No," Rogers said in a low voice. "The DNA doesn't match the doctor's. It's worse than that. As bad as it gets."

Matt turned to the special agent. "What could be worse?"

Rogers met his eyes. "The semen came from the boy, Jim Jr.," he said. "He was only thirteen."

Doyle nodded. "They had intercourse, Jones. The way the boy was draped over his mother, we thought the semen had been contaminated by his blood. Now we know that there was no contamination at all. Baylor forced the boy to have sex with his mother. It's a safe bet that the Holloway boy was forced to do the same thing. Forced to have sex with his mother while his sisters and father watched."

The idea, the image, the thought and all the darkness that came with it, settled into the room like nerve gas. No one said anything for a long time.

But Matt's mind was spinning. He looked at Doyle and Rogers, then Westbrook and Brown. He looked at their faces and knew that he had to say something.

"I don't think it's Baylor," he said quietly.

Doyle jerked his head up, aghast. "What?"

"I don't think that Dr. Baylor is responsible for these murders. I think there's someone else out there."

Rogers slammed the table with his fist and got to his feet. "You're young, Jones. You've been a homicide detective for what? Is it two months or is it two and a half? I told you before what I thought about you being here. But this is different. What you're saying, what you're thinking, could get you into a lot of trouble."

Doyle stepped forward, measuring Matt carefully with a brutal expression on his face. "What makes you think it's not Baylor, Jones? Give me something that would stand up in court."

"I can't do that. But from everything I've seen, especially tonight with the lab report, these murders wouldn't seem to relate to what we know Baylor did in LA and New Orleans. All four of those murders were about greed."

Doyle cocked his head, his voice loud and angry. "But these murders *are* about greed. Stratton treated his healthy patients for cancer so that he could steal a fortune from the insurance companies. Holloway stole the lives of animals on the endangered species list for his personal pleasure. My God, the two match up like twins."

"I know who they are and what they did," Matt said. "There's no doubt that they're from the same pool. I'm just saying that this time around I don't think the motive is greed. I don't believe that either one of them were the targets."

"Then who was?" Doyle shot back.

Matt realized that he'd made a mistake. He shouldn't have said anything. Everyone in the conference room was visibly outraged. Doyle's face had turned beet red, his jugular vein pulsating on the side of his neck. Rogers and Westbrook reminded him of a pair of rattlesnakes all coiled up and ready to strike. But it was the disappointment he saw in Kate Brown's eyes that really got to him. She was staring at him like he'd just committed treason. He could remember the things Baylor had said to him as they stood on the Holloway's second-floor landing and gazed at the victims and what had been done to them. He could hear Baylor making his final argument so clearly that the doctor might have been standing right beside him at this very moment.

You're working with people who have their heads in the sand, Matthew. It's the corporate way, you know. Special Agent Rogers and Assistant US Attorney Ken Doyle have blinders on and can't see who and what they're really dealing with here. They want it to be me. They need it to be me. They get more stuff if it's me. Bigger headlines and better jobs. That's why I left my fingerprints. That's why I sent you that text message tonight.

Doyle shouted at him. "If you don't believe Stratton and Holloway were the targets, then what's the goddamn motive, Jones?"

Matt grimaced. "Their wives," he said.

Doyle's eyes almost popped out of his head. "Their wives?"

"The killer's got a problem with Mommy."

Dr. Westbrook cleared his throat, looked at Matt like he was the world's biggest loser, and spoke in a low voice that had a certain shake to it. "Detective Jones, did it ever occur to you that Dr. Baylor might have a problem with his mother? Most serial killers have issues with their parents and their childhoods. At this point, it's a cliché, and I'm surprised by the lack of originality you've shown tonight. I think Special Agent Rogers put his finger on something important here. You're playing with fire, Detective. What you're saying could derail the investigation and spin it off in an entirely different direction. What you're thinking could destroy your career."

Matt tried to control his anger. He was afraid that he might hurt Westbrook. Afraid that he might grab the man by his head and smash it through the glass wall. He turned to Doyle.

"How do you explain the text message Baylor sent me? If he'd just killed these people, why would he call a cop?"

"I have no idea," Doyle said. "Psychopaths aren't usually known for being very logical. They do just what you're doing, Jones. They do all sorts of things that make no sense."

Matt clenched his teeth, his heart pounding. Baylor had been right. They wanted him to be the killer. They needed him to be the killer. And if they had to, they'd *make* him the killer. Doyle wanted the headlines and the media attention that went with a nationwide manhunt. Doyle wanted to move up the food chain.

Matt had seen it before and knew that he would see it again. Any piece of evidence that pointed to Dr. Baylor would go into the file. Anything that pointed in another direction or raised doubts would be left out.

It's the corporate way, you know.

Matt heard Doyle say something but missed it. Then the federal prosecutor grabbed Matt by the shoulder. Matt gave him a long, dark look—a dangerous look—then pushed Doyle's hand away. When Doyle spoke finally, his tone of voice sounded offensive, like an angry father talking down to his son.

"How do you explain the one piece of hard evidence that we've got, Jones? How do explain the fingerprints? Are you so naive that you really did believe Baylor when he told you that he left them on purpose? That he thought it might bring you into the case? Why would his fingerprints bring you into the case? Why would he leave a fingerprint, knowing that it would irrevocably link him directly to the murders of an entire family? Why would he want to lock himself into two crime scenes as horrific as these? How could you not see through his explanation that his presence at the Strattons' and the Holloways' was a series of coincidences? I'm not going to be as hard on you as these guys. You've missed two nights' sleep in almost as many days. But when you walk away tonight, please understand two things. Dr. Baylor is a psychopath. And a fingerprint isn't a feeling. It's a lead. It's a fact. It's something that a prosecutor can go to trial with, and everyone in the courtroom understands exactly what it means, including the jury."

CHAPTER 27

A sudden wave of doubt shook Matt's soul as he walked back to his desk and sat down. On top of the argument Doyle had made was an errant memory that surfaced. It was something the medical examiner had said about halfway through the autopsies this afternoon.

The killer knew something about human anatomy.

The gunshots had been carefully placed to avoid a quick death. No major organs had been violated. The arteries in each victim were intact. Baylor was a skilled surgeon who would have known where to fire his weapon so that he could regulate blood loss and keep his victims conscious, but easily managed.

The doubt only lasted for a second or two. When Matt glanced back at the conference room and saw Rogers and Doyle shouting at each other with the door closed, his skepticism vanished.

He could remember something his favorite instructor at the LAPD Police Academy had told him on the firing range one day. Crimes were solved in exactly the same place they were created. That place was the imagination, the human mind. He could recall his instructor saying that a homicide investigation was more like a journey, and that most of the trip would occur in utter darkness. Crimes were solved by someone who could rely on their instincts to lead them through that darkness. Someone who soaked in evidence without bias or rushing to an early judgment. Doyle could make his argument about the value of a fingerprint in the courtroom. But Matt knew that a fingerprint was just a fingerprint until they made the case. In order to solve these murders, they would need to know what the fingerprint really meant.

Matt felt certain now that the doctor had been telling him the truth. In this case, the fingerprint wasn't an error, but a call for help.

He should have kept his mouth shut. He should have kept his thoughts to himself.

But even worse, Baylor had been right about something else. The man who had murdered these people was completely depraved. The killer was truly someone *special*. Matt glanced out the window at the lights to the city, wondering where he might be. The idea that he had no real need to hide, no need to cover his tracks, the idea that the entire task force refused to believe that he even existed, cut to the bone.

An image surfaced—the one he couldn't get out of his mind. The two boys forced to have sex with their mothers while their families watched. Their sisters and fathers. The image was more horrific than anything he'd dealt with in LA. More devastating. More radioactive. He knew that he would be living with this gruesome reality for the rest of time, and it made him angry.

Someone tapped him on the shoulder. He looked up and saw Kate Brown getting into her jacket.

"Let's get out of here," she said. "Let's get something to eat and call it a day."

He was surprised. The disappointment he had seen on her face in the conference room was completely gone. He nodded, packed up his things, and grabbed his jacket. Kate Brown was a tough read.

As they exited the building and headed south on Sixth Street, Matt slung his briefcase over his shoulder and lit a Marlboro. When Brown tapped her first two fingers together, he handed over the cigarette and watched her take a drag.

"Where do you want to go?" he said.

"I know a quiet place off Walnut."

They walked the next block and a half sharing the cigarette but not speaking. When they reached Walnut, Matt checked the light at the corner and spotted Dr. Westbrook scurrying across the street. He gave Brown a nudge with his elbow and picked up the pace.

"Hey, Westbrook," he called out. "Wait up."

Dr. Westbrook turned and didn't seem very pleased to see them.

"I want to ask you something," Matt said.

"What is it?" he said in an impatient voice. "I'm meeting someone."

"I want to know what a profile would look like if we didn't already know that Dr. Baylor was the one."

Westbrook glanced at Brown, then gave Matt a long look without saying anything.

Matt took a step closer. "What would the profile look like, Doctor? You must have considered the possibility. With your reputation, I can't believe that you'd take anything at face value."

Matt followed Dr. Westbrook's eyes to all the people walking up and down the sidewalk. They were standing at one of the entrances to Washington Square.

"Let's go into the park," Westbrook said in a lower voice.

Matt traded looks with Brown as they followed the profiler into the square. He could tell that Brown was nervous. That this wasn't the corporate way. That if either Doyle or Rogers found out that Matt was continuing to pursue an alternate line in the murder cases, there would be more trouble.

Westbrook stopped at the first bench, looked around, and seemed okay with the surroundings. Matt checked the shadows and didn't see anyone within earshot.

"What is it, Dr. Westbrook? If Baylor was out of the picture, what would the profile look like?"

Westbrook glanced at Brown again—tossing something over in his mind—then gave Matt a hard look. "If Baylor was out of the picture, if his fingerprints hadn't turned up, I'd be looking for a white male in his twenties. A white male still living with his mother, probably abused by her in some fundamental way and for a long period of time. I'd say that he was probably abused from as far back as he can remember. Based on who his victims are, I'd be looking for someone without much money, someone feeding a fantasy of a happier, richer life that's out of reach and impossible to obtain."

Pay dirt. And Dr. Westbrook was no idiot. Matt lit another Marlboro.

"So what you're saying, Doctor, is that if Baylor wasn't on the map, we'd be looking for a sexually abused white male who's seeking a way out of his despair by selecting victims and then punishing them for his situation, a private hell, a world he can't seem to escape."

Dr. Westbrook was measuring him, his eyes shimmering through his thick glasses. "I didn't say that, Jones, but you're quite right. He's punishing his victims for the hand he was dealt. That's what makes him so dangerous. So vicious. For him, there's no end here. There's no way out." Dr. Westbrook raised his eyebrows and seemed amused. "But there's no real need for a profile, is there, Jones? It's Dr. Baylor. We already know who we're looking for. We're all moving down the same track."

Matt took it in without reacting. "Because of the fingerprint."

Dr. Westbrook hesitated for a moment, then nodded.

"Any surprises, Doctor?"

Matt watched Dr. Westbrook's face change as he thought it over. That odd look was back in his eyes.

"Now that you mention it, Jones, I am surprised."

"By what?"

"I'm going to make an assumption. The semen found in Mimi Holloway will turn out to be her son's just like the semen found in

Tammy Stratton belonged to her son. We won't know for a day or two, but let's just say for the sake of argument that the lab confirms they match."

"Okay," Matt said. "Okay. But what's the surprise?"

"Both boys were forced to have sex with their mothers. Now that we know this, there's no indication that Baylor sexually abused anyone. Other than the one fingerprint found on Kaylee Stratton's nipple, there's no evidence of a sexual component here. Kaylee and her mother weren't raped. You were at the autopsy today. I know that we don't have the results from the rape kits yet, but what did the medical examiner say about the Holloways?"

Matt shook his head, trying to ward off the memory. "The girls weren't touched," he said. "No one was raped or violated in any way."

Dr. Westbrook zipped up his coat. "You'll recall that in LA and New Orleans, the sexual component was even stronger than the actual motive. No semen was ever found, but evidence of rape was loud and clear. Kaylee Stratton was seventeen. Victoria Holloway was nineteen. Both of them shared the same look and style as his first four victims. Young and normal from wealthy families with a parent who went out of their way to screw everybody. It just seems odd to me that Baylor left the girls alone."

Matt took another hit on that Marlboro as the idea settled in. Dr. Westbrook pulled his coat tighter and turned to leave.

"I've gotta go," he said. "I won't mention our conversation to Rogers or Doyle. It's probably best for all concerned if we pretend it never happened."

Matt shrugged. He didn't care either way. He watched Dr. Westbrook walk off and vanish into the crowd moving up and down Walnut Street. When he turned back to Kate Brown, she motioned for his cigarette and took another deep pull.

Trouble ahead. Matt could feel it in the darkness, the raw air.

CHAPTER 28

"He believed you," Brown said. "I had my eyes on him. Westbrook isn't sure what to think. You're pushing his buttons."

"In the conference room it looked like you were disappointed in me."

She shook her head. A smile leaked out, then faded.

"Shocked is more like it, Jones. You're here two days and you just told everybody that they're wrong. They're chasing the wrong man. Oh my God, you know what I mean?"

She took a sip of wine and shook her head, still gazing at him. The quiet restaurant off Walnut had been packed and didn't work out. When they tried another place on Chestnut, they were told a table wouldn't open up before 11:00 p.m. That's when Brown suggested that they buy a pizza and go back to her place.

Matt was more than curious and had agreed. It turned out that Brown lived two blocks away from the Philadelphia Art Museum on the corner of Twenty-Third and Mount Vernon Street—a large red-brick Georgian townhouse that the previous owner had completely restored. High ceilings, ornate moldings from the 1880s, and hardwood floors.

The rooms were big and deep and uncluttered, the walls painted in warm colors, with most of the art unframed. Matt's first thought as he walked through the double set of front doors was that Brown's home was exceedingly comfortable.

He took a sip of wine and watched her throw another log on the fire, then sit down beside him on a large Oriental carpet. Her hesitation was back again. She'd start to get close, then back away just as she had in the parking lot at the hospital. Something was going on in her head, but Matt wasn't really paying attention to it. The wine was starting to get to him. They had opened a second bottle, and he could feel the weight of the pizza in his stomach after losing another night's sleep.

She turned and looked at him. "What if it's true?" she said in an uneasy voice. "What if you're right, and there's someone else out there?"

"What did you think of Westbrook's profile?"

"It made me think of that guy who walked into Sandy Hook Elementary School and shot all those kids."

"Adam Lanza," Matt said. "Newtown, Connecticut."

Brown nodded. "He shot his mother while she slept in bed. He shot her in the face, Jones. Then he got into his car, drove over to the elementary school, and slaughtered twenty-six innocent teachers and kids with a Bushmaster assault rifle."

"I remember. When he was finished, he killed himself the way they always do. They're cowards. It's in their nature."

"Do you know what a bullet from a rifle like that does to the human body?"

Unfortunately, Matt knew exactly what a round from a Bushmaster did when it struck the human body. The Bushmaster was a redesign of the commercially available AR-15, which fired a .222 Remington cartridge. The upgrade was an attempt by the gun designer to meet the standards set by the US Army for the battlefield. In order to pass the test, a round had to be able to penetrate a steel helmet from five hundred yards away. The Bushmaster fired an amped-up .223 round that traveled at almost three times the speed of sound and easily met the army's standards for a military assault weapon. The round didn't put neat holes into people's bodies. Instead, it ripped and tore and broke everything up as it exploded through them.

Brown gave him a look. "I'm sorry, Jones. I forgot that you served overseas."

Matt took a deep breath and exhaled, trying to void out his thoughts. "That's okay," he said. "I've got a pretty good idea of what Adam Lanza did with his Bushmaster."

"Westbrook's profile made me think about it," she said. "If it's not Baylor, then the man Westbrook described has to have something in common with Lanza."

She was right. They were born from similar molds. If you could get past the catastrophic details—the killing of an elementary school principal and a psychologist, four heroic teachers, and twenty young children in the first grade—if you could climb over the details and make the leap to metaphor, then it seemed to fit with the mass killings of two families here in the suburbs of Philadelphia. It was only a hunch, but in both cases it seemed like they were killing what they wanted most. Hope for a new life and a bright future. Matt could remember reading about Lanza in the newspaper. His relationship with his mother seemed particularly odd. According to the journalist who wrote the story, they lived in the same house, but never spoke and only communicated through e-mails. Matt wondered if this was true. Lanza had killed his mother first. The act was brutal and over the top. There had to be a reason why. Something no one had written or spoken about.

An image surfaced. A photograph of Adam Lanza's bedroom that had been published in the same newspaper article. There were no sheets on the bed, just a bare mattress. The windows were covered with dark-green trash bags taped to the walls, and every inch of the room was littered with debris, garbage, and dirty clothing.

Lanza had been twenty years old at the time of the murders, and that fit Westbrook's profile as well.

Matt looked over at Brown, but she'd left the room. He took another sip of wine and gazed at the fire. When he heard footsteps, he turned and watched Brown enter from the hallway by the stairs. It seemed more than obvious that whatever hesitation she might have exhibited toward him in the past had come to a final resolution.

Her slacks were gone, her blouse open to reveal a white bra and a pair of muted-red panties. She moved closer, almost in slow motion, straddling his body and coming to a rest on his legs with a certain animal elegance. Matt eased back onto the carpet and looked at her lazy smile and smoldering eyes. He could smell her skin, her person, the shampoo in her hair. He touched her bare thighs and gazed up at her. She was removing her blouse, taking hold of his hands and pushing them into her breasts. As he smoothed his hands over them, her eyes became glassy, and he thought he heard her moan.

Matt reached around her back, unclasped her bra, and tossed it on the floor. Then Brown lowered her face to his, her lips and tongue, and kissed him through her smile.

"You know that you can't stay, right?" she whispered in a throaty voice.

"Why not?"

She met his eyes. Everything felt good. His psychologist had been right—the sooner the better. The details weren't important. The hows and whys, irrelevant.

"Because I'm a female agent," she said. "I work for the FBI, and I'm a professional. I can't take the risk of someone seeing you in the morning."

She kissed him again, and he kissed her back.

"But I'm from out of town," he whispered. "I'll be gone soon. I'm only a rental."

She laughed. "If you're a rental, Jones, then that means I'm a conquest."

That smile was still going, the fire in her eyes all stoked up. He pulled her closer. Everything about the moment felt true.

CHAPTER 29

Andrew Penchant pushed the newspaper away and looked at the live video call from Avery Cooper on his laptop. She was on her bed, wearing a peach-colored tank top over a black bra and a pair of old jeans. She was stretched out on her stomach, the camera on her computer only a few feet away. Andrew couldn't believe that she'd called tonight. When she'd asked if he wanted to hook up on the web, he began to wonder what she might be up to.

It seemed so fast. So peculiar. So in his face.

And he had things to do. He had spent the past two hours on the Internet reading everything he could find about that detective from Los Angeles. He knew Jones's story, his dark past, and the people he had killed—a corrupt detective and a man who shot Jones on top of Mount Hollywood but still hadn't been identified. He felt a kinship with Jones because they shared painful histories. He wanted to see him and watch him. But even better, Andrew had found more video clips by Ryan Day on the *Get Buzzed* website. It seemed like Day had been working the story for a long time, and the idiot reporter had a way of uncovering secrets. A clip from earlier in the day, a website exclusive, was shot at Fitler Square with an apartment building in the background.

Day had found out that the FBI kept an apartment here, and while he didn't say it outright, Andrew guessed that he would find Matt Jones staying there.

He wanted to watch him. He wanted to see who he was in person. Maybe even exchange pleasantries. After all, they were chasing a mad scientist, Dr. George Baylor, a serial killer on the run who had brutally murdered the Strattons and the Holloways. Andrew could get close to Jones because they were so stupid they didn't even know he existed.

"Take off your shirt."

Andrew's mind crashed through his high, and he looked at Avery Cooper on his laptop.

"What?" he said.

"Take off your shirt."

"Why?"

She laughed. "Because I want to see your chest."

"Why don't you take off your shirt?" he said.

"Okay."

She got up on her knees, slipped off the tank top, then plopped back down on her belly and looked into the lens. It happened so fast Andrew couldn't really see anything. Just her cleavage and the black bra and the devious smile on her face.

"Your turn, Andrew Penchant. And since I went first, I want more than just a shirt. Now you've gotta get out of those pants." She made a goofy face, looked off camera, then turned back and spoke in a whisper. "My parents just came home. I need to lock my door."

She got off the bed and walked out of the shot. But Andrew kept his eyes on the screen. He was looking at Cooper's things, the quality of the bed and comforter, the stack of pillows, the walls painted in a color that demonstrated class and style, the side table with a modern lamp that looked expensive, and books by authors he had never heard of because he didn't read books. Books were boring. More boring than newspapers.

Why read a book when he could play a video game or watch TV for free on the Internet?

Cooper dove back into the shot and bounced on the mattress. "I'm waiting," she said, batting her eyelids.

He could see through her bra. There were flowers in the lace, and he could see through them. When he looked at her face, his dick got hard and his stomach began to light up again. He didn't understand these feelings, but thought he liked them.

"Ready or not," he said.

He pulled off his T-shirt. When he climbed out of his jeans, he heard Cooper burst out in laughter. He looked at his computer screen, confused and completely stoned. She was staring at his boxer shorts, her smile now a big grin.

"Hey, what's going on down there, dude?"

He looked at his shorts, his erection pushing the fabric straight out. He smiled at Cooper. He liked this. He needed this. Cooper started getting out of her jeans. But then his mother knocked on the door.

"What's going on in there?" she said. "Is someone with you, Andrew?"

"No," he said in a lame voice that cracked. "I'm alone. Everything's fine."

His mother paused a moment, then spoke in a whisper. "I'm gonna take my shower, honey."

Andrew didn't say anything. He listened to the silence, weighing it carefully. When he heard her close her bedroom door, he turned back to his laptop. Cooper had witnessed everything and seemed to think it was funny.

"That was embarrassing," she said, teasing him and mocking him. "I thought you told me you didn't have a family. You called yourself a man of mystery."

Andrew sat down before his worktable. The moment was lost. Everything black.

"I've gotta go," he said. "I'll talk to you later."

"Are you okay?"

"I'll talk to you later, Cooper."

"Maybe we could hook up and—"

Andrew closed the program on his laptop and shut down the power. He could hear his mother turn on the shower. After a few minutes, he heard the shower door close. His mother liked to get high, drink a little wine, and take long showers when she was alone. Andrew loaded his bong with a hit, struck his lighter, and sucked in the smoke. Holding his breath for as long as he could, he exhaled slowly and noticed that his erection was still there. He could feel his head buzzing as he peeled off his shorts, walked out, and opened his mother's bedroom door.

Dream walking.

The bed was turned down, her clothing on the chair. The only light in the room came from two battery-powered candles by the bed, and two more on his mother's chest of drawers. When he gazed through the open bathroom door, he saw another two candles burning by the sink and mirror and his mother's glass of red wine.

His heart was pounding as he stepped into the room and moved out of the flickering light into the corner. He looked at his mother on the other side of the glass door. His dick felt like a lamppost as he took in her naked body. She was only thirty-five, he thought to himself. Only thirty-five.

"Is that you, honey?"

He froze. He locked up.

She opened the shower door and was gazing at him in the shadows. Her eyes drifted down from his face to his bare chest, then kept going until they reached his hand and penis. She had a certain glow about her. A certain something as she stood there with the water dripping off her breasts.

Oh my God.

"Let's be friends tonight," she said quietly. "Get in the shower with me, and we'll be friends."

He didn't move. He dropped his hand away and felt even more naked. More crazy.

"Come on, honey. Before we run out of hot water. It's not like it's the first time."

He paused but couldn't think it over, his mind blurred out from the strong weed. After several moments he stepped out of the shadows and into the dim candlelight. As he entered the shower, he could feel his mother's body brush against his body. She closed the shower door. Then she turned back and looked at him with a sensuous, even hungry smile, moving closer, and closer still.

CHAPTER 30

Andrew Penchant sat before his laptop and skimmed through the portraits he'd taken of the family. One image appeared to stand out, and he made a copy and moved it into his photo library. The Christmas tree in the background seemed fine, but it was December, and everyone in the shot looked pale.

He clicked open his effects package, highlighted the Correct Skin Tone option, and double-checked the levels. The tan and blush were off, but only slightly. Once the effect rendered on the screen, he gave the image another look and thought the color correction helped. But something was wrong with their eyes. It might have been subtle, but it was there. He zoomed in and noticed the woman's left eye was glowing slightly. When he checked her husband and their children, he found the same thing going on in everyone's eyes.

He checked his watch. It was 7:30 a.m., and if he didn't hurry, he'd be late for work.

He opened his red-eye effect, marked his range and targets, and clicked Done. Then he zoomed out and checked the result. His mother had been right. He had talent, and this photograph was way better than just a plain old everyday family portrait. If he added a spark to their eyes and enhanced the gleam, the picture would be even better. He zoomed in so close that the image was reduced to pixels, then opened his paint package and added white specs to each eye. Once he was finished, he zoomed back out and checked the result.

They looked perfect. They looked like they'd just come back from a vacation in the Caribbean.

He powered up his printer, added photo paper to the tray, and hit Print. As he grabbed his backpack, he could hear his mother stirring in her bedroom. He didn't want to see her. He didn't want to remember what happened last night or where he'd woken up or what he hadn't been wearing. He slid the print into a manila envelope and placed it in his pack. When he zipped up the pocket, he turned and felt his chest tighten. His mother was standing in the doorway, gazing at him as if nothing were wrong when everything was wrong. At least she was dressed. At least the air was cold enough in the house that she was wearing a sweater and jeans.

"What's going on, honey?" she said.

"I'm late for work."

"Thank you."

"For what?"

She smiled and gave him a submissive look. "You know . . ."

He thought he might get sick. He frowned at her and threw the pack over his shoulder.

"It has to stop," he said in a sullen voice.

"But you enjoyed it."

"I'm seeing someone. It has to stop."

She made a face like she didn't believe him. "Who are you seeing? Who is she? I'll bet she's a slut."

"She's a girl from a decent family. They don't act the way you do."

She gave him another look. "Come here, honey."

He shook his head, walking past her and hitting the stairs. "I hate you," he said in a louder voice. "Don't you understand? I hate everything about you. Don't bother waiting up tonight. I'm gonna be late."

He slammed the front door shut and groaned. Then he bounced down the porch steps and hurried up the sidewalk to his car. The air was so cold it burned his face. As he ripped the car door open and climbed in, he realized that he just couldn't get past the anger. The horror and the rage. He hadn't chosen this sick woman to be his mother. Why did she have to get pregnant? Why did she have to bring a rape baby into the world? A devil child, with horns and a tail? Why did she have to screw up his life? Why didn't she just get rid of it and move on? She'd only been fourteen years old. She had no business being a mother.

Andrew started the car and pulled into the street, promising himself that if he ever met the freak who had raped his mother, he'd cut his balls off and stuff them down his throat, then wait until the child molester bled to death.

And that was only if he was in a good mood. Only if he had been properly medicated with decent reefer and was feeling gracious.

He checked his pocket, then almost lost it when he realized that he hadn't rolled a joint. Stopping at a red light, he combed through the ashtray, searching for a roach or burnt end. There weren't any. He'd smoked the last one yesterday afternoon. He'd have to score some weed somewhere else. He couldn't go back home.

The drive to the Walmart Supercenter at the Franklin Mills Mall took less than ten minutes. Circling the building, he parked in back and entered through the loading docks. After checking his watch, Andrew hurried down the hallway to the employee lounge, punched in his time card, then burst through the doors into the store. The home furnishings department was in the rear corner, the picture frames in aisle two.

He wanted something special for the family portrait he'd taken. Something that would evoke the holiday spirit and went with the Christmas tree in the background. He found it beside the plain silver frames. This one was made of molded plastic, but everything about it seemed to fit, especially the raised depiction of Frosty the Snowman in the upper-left corner of the frame. Centered beside Frosty were the words "Happy Holidays to You." At the bottom it just said "Frosty the Snowman." Andrew didn't think it was necessary to write Frosty's name on the frame, but the raised mold made up for the designer's lack of discretion and taste.

He turned and noticed an employee restocking shelves farther down the aisle. It was an older woman, Maria Flores, whom he spoke with once in a while during his lunch break. He held the frame up to get her attention.

"This one's broken," he said.

"Bring it here, hon, and I'll take it back to the warehouse."

"How 'bout I do it for you?"

"That's even better."

Andrew hurried across the floor, through the doors, and down the hall to the employee bathroom. After removing the price tag, he opened the picture frame and cleaned the glass with a paper towel. He could hear people talking outside and moved into a stall just in case. As he found the envelope in his pack and slid out the photo, the bathroom door opened and someone entered. He could hear the guy unzip his fly and begin peeing in one of the two urinals.

"Is that you, Andrew?"

It was his boss. Andrew placed the photograph in the frame, attached the back, and tightened the clasps.

"Yeah, Mr. Trotter," he said. "It's me."

"How you doing?"

"Actually, I'm not feeling so great this morning."

Mr. Trotter couldn't have been more than five or six years older than Andrew, but insisted that no one call him by his first name. Andrew never held it against him. If his mother had named him *Emile*, he would have felt the same way. Mr. Trotter wasn't a bad guy.

"You want to take the day off?" Mr. Trotter said. "If you're coming down with something, it might be better for everyone."

Andrew flipped the picture frame over and gave it a good look. The frame with Frosty the Snowman on it was perfect. Even inspired.

"Thanks, Mr. Trotter. I think you're right. No sense getting everybody sick."

Mr. Trotter finally stopped peeing and zipped up his fly. Andrew heard him flush the urinal, then rinse his hands in the sink.

"Get some rest, Andrew. See you tomorrow morning."

"Thanks."

The bathroom door opened and closed, and he was alone again. He stuffed the picture frame in his pack and zipped it up. He wanted to drive over to that apartment building across the street from Fitler Square. Before that, he thought he'd hit Love Park and score some weed. He needed his medication. He needed to chill.

CHAPTER 31

Matt checked the time on the cable box, then walked through the den into the bathroom. The Strattons' funeral at St. David's Episcopal Church was set for eleven. Brown had called this morning to give him a heads-up that she would be driving out to the suburbs with Rogers, Doyle, and Dr. Westbrook. There was no need for him to come to the office. If he left the city by nine thirty, traffic would be headed in the other direction, and he'd make it early enough to be briefed and help scout the churchyard along with her and ten undercover agents. They wanted to see who attended the service. They wanted pictures and video. Matt already knew that the FBI had been working with both the *Inquirer* and the *Daily News* to ensure that the announcement in the obituary pages wouldn't be missed. But also that the time and place of the Strattons' funeral made the news yesterday on every TV and radio station in the city.

Brown was all business, and despite the early hour, Matt assumed that she made the call from her desk in the Crisis Room.

Matt smiled as he turned on the shower. He could still smell her sex on his skin, and it felt wonderful. It felt like physical therapy. It felt like healing. He was surprised and even grateful that he hadn't been distracted by his past, his history. More than grateful. And he completely understood why Brown had seemed so tentative in the beginning, and why she wanted to keep whatever they had under wraps. Brown wanted to be seen as the professional that she was. Nothing less would do.

For anyone, Matt thought.

It occurred to him that he really was a rental. And that Brown's decision to come forward last night might have had something to do with the fact that Matt lived in another city and would eventually be going away.

He smiled again as he stepped into the shower, letting the hot water rain down on him and thinking about the progress he thought he'd made earlier this morning. He'd left Brown's townhouse around 1:30 a.m. In spite of the late hour, he'd set the alarm for seven and brewed a pot of strong coffee as soon as he got out of bed.

He couldn't get Dr. Westbrook's second profile out of his mind and had wanted to get back on his laptop. But even more, the possibility that the man he was looking for shared something with Adam Lanza, a mass killer, seemed white-hot. As he drank coffee and yearned for a cigarette, he typed Lanza's name into the search engine and tried to bring himself up to speed as quickly as he could. After an hour or so, he spotted a link on the list and clicked it.

It wasn't an article about the Newtown shooting. Instead, he'd found a related story from the *New York Times* about Dylann Roof, the twenty-one-year-old who had shot six women and three men at the Emanuel AME Church in Charleston, South Carolina.

Matt stepped out of the shower and dressed as quickly as he could. After pouring another cup of coffee, he slipped a piece of nicotine gum against his cheek and sat on the couch before his laptop.

Dylann Roof had gunned down nine people. Nine innocents. A group of pastors and Bible study members gathered peacefully for a prayer service. Nine African Americans from all walks of life, ranging from twenty-six years old to eighty-seven years young. Like the elementary school in Newtown, the crime scene at the church had been a blood bath. Multiple gunshots with a Glock .45 semiautomatic pistol from close range. Eight magazines loaded with hollow-point bullets to maximize damage. Like the teachers and children at Sandy Hook Elementary School, the Bible study members at the Emanuel AME Church didn't stand a chance.

Matt kept reading. The Bible study group had invited Roof to pray with them. Roof thanked them and sat with them, then waited until they closed their eyes before he opened fire and slaughtered them.

Matt clenched his jaws and narrowed his brow.

What struck him as he read the article a second time wasn't the fact that Dylann Roof was an obvious racist. He was a racist and would be indicted for hate crimes on top of the nine murders. But what stood out for Matt was the role he seemed to share with Adam Lanza as a mass killer. The fact that they were almost the same age. The fact that they both lived troubled lives. The fact that they didn't just kill people, they slaughtered them. And then the final blow. The fact that when he downloaded their photographs and examined them side by side, they could have been brothers.

The presence Roof seemed to share with Lanza was difficult to pin down. It was somewhere in the photographs. Somewhere between the lines. Not the shapes of their faces, but their blank expressions. Their attitude. They came from a similar place. A dark corner. Matt could see the hate showing on their faces, the hopelessness and rage. But nowhere was the physical match more telling than in their eyes.

Matt took a sip of coffee and pulled his laptop closer.

Their eyes, he thought. That's where it was coming from. Both of them had the eyes of a predator—ultra-intense, completely riveting, and over-the-top psychotic. It was almost as if their eyes were no longer a window to their minds and emotions. It was almost as if the line had been snapped and their souls died off and vanished. The photograph of

Dylann Roof had been taken during his arrest. Because of the number of death threats, he was wearing a bulletproof vest over his white T-shirt. The crowd was hostile, his life in the balance, and he should have been nervous and frightened. Yet his face appeared empty, devoid of any expression at all, just those dead eyes drilling through the camera lenses. When Matt took another look at the photograph of Adam Lanza, he found the same thing. The kid looked like a zombie. An alien. The kind of reptile that lives in the mud beneath rocks or behind glass in a zoo. It seemed so unbelievable, so unfathomable, even outlandish, that no one looked at these two kids and didn't know in an instant that something was incredibly wrong with both of them.

Dead eyes and the psychopathic stare. Both Roof and Lanza were a long way past being odd. Why didn't anyone see it? Why did anyone have to die before they did see it?

Matt bookmarked the pages and saved the photographs. As he packed up his laptop, he wondered if the man he was looking for, the man who killed the Strattons and the Holloways, might not possess this same look. These same eyes. He wondered if the killer would show up at the funeral, and if he might not seem familiar enough to stand out.

Matt holstered his .45, grabbed his scarf, and got into his jacket. Slinging his briefcase over his shoulder, he walked out and locked the front door. A woman was just exiting the apartment next door. On the night he arrived, he had seen a man in his thirties with blond hair and a knapsack enter the apartment and announce to someone that he was home. This woman was at least fifty and dressed immaculately in a business suit.

Matt stepped over to the elevator and pressed the button. He could feel the woman behind him and, when he turned, caught her looking away. The elevator doors opened. After following her in, he pressed the button to the lobby, stepped to the back, and gave her another look up and down.

"My name's Matt Jones," he said finally. "I'll be staying here for a while."

She didn't say anything and seemed anxious.

He cleared his throat. "Was that your husband I saw the other night?"

"I don't live here," she said quickly. "I was just dropping something off."

The elevator reached the first floor, and she hurried out. Matt watched her burst through the lobby and out the doors. People who live in cities, particularly on the East Coast, often become uncomfortable around strangers. Matt had been raised in the East and spent time here in Philadelphia, and even more time in New York City. But this seemed different than that. This woman appeared to be frightened when she looked at him.

He checked his pistol. It was hidden beneath his jacket. She couldn't have seen it. He wondered if he wasn't projecting his baggage on her. He probably could have used another couple of hours' sleep.

He stepped into the lobby and stopped before the mailboxes. When he found the box that matched the apartment number the woman had walked out of, he read the name.

Dick and Donna Martino.

He thought about the man he'd seen walking into the apartment the other night. He had blond hair and wore it on the long side. The name Martino didn't exactly fit.

CHAPTER 32

Andrew Penchant flinched as he saw Matt Jones in the lobby from a bench in the park across the street. The detective was jotting something down on a pad as he spoke on his cell phone. Directions maybe? An address? Or was it a lead in his hunt for Dr. Baylor, the *real* killer. A woman had just walked out of the apartment building. It seemed like she was in a hurry as she hailed a cab and raced off.

Andrew couldn't believe his luck. Instead of copping some weed at Love Park, he'd had a feeling that maybe he should put that off and swing by Fitler Square first. It was after nine, and he had no expectation of crossing paths with the homicide detective from Los Angeles.

But here he was.

Andrew smiled as he adjusted his shades in the bright sunlight. He felt his pulse quickening, his heart beating, as the glass doors opened and Matt Jones stepped outside.

He watched him check the street, then start down the sidewalk heading east on Pine. Andrew pulled himself together, grabbed his knapsack, and exited the park. After crossing at the light on Twenty-Third Street, he caught up to Jones and stepped in right behind him. He was close—so close—his eyes all over him.

Jones was taller than he had guessed. Stronger and more formidable than he thought he'd be. Andrew could remember reading that Jones had been shot once and survived, then three more times atop Mount Hollywood, where he should have probably bled to death but didn't.

Andrew stepped closer, measuring the side of the detective's chiseled face. His strong chin and prominent cheekbones. He tried not to laugh. Jones might be formidable, but he couldn't be too smart. He was chasing a phantom. He was chasing the wrong man.

I'm over here, dude. I'm right behind you. I'm your shadow, man.

Jones stopped at the corner, and Andrew missed it and almost plowed into the man. He'd been fooling around in his head and hadn't been paying attention. When Jones turned, Andrew tried to absorb the shock. The detective was looking right at him, and it wasn't a glance. It was a long look, almost as if he was trying to commit Andrew's image to memory. He could feel Jones checking out his cornrows, his blond hair and milky-white skin. He could see him making note of his Ray-Bans and trying to see through the dark glass.

The adrenaline rush was awesome. It had been a long time since Andrew didn't need reefer to get this stoked. Oh my God. He could feel Jones measuring him.

Andrew nodded at the detective like everything was copasetic, then dug his cell phone out of his pocket like he'd just received a call, or even better and way more cool, like he'd just received a text message from one of his countless friends. His *social network*, man. His *crew*. Jones bought it and finally looked away. When the light turned green, Andrew hesitated a moment and let Jones lead the way across Pine Street. He could see where the detective was heading now. He could see a parking garage around the corner on Twenty-Second Street.

Andrew watched him enter the garage, then looked directly across the street and saw a place called the Good Karma Café.

He slipped his cell phone into his pocket and laughed out loud at the name. It seemed so perfect, so in the moment that he couldn't make it up. He walked in, glanced at the menu, and ordered a Popeye bagel with a scrambled egg, spinach, and American cheese. After seeing Jones in person, after taking into account his demeanor, his persona, even his posture, it occurred to Andrew that strength might make the difference someday in the future, and the Popeye bagel with spinach seemed like the way to go.

Andrew walked his coffee over to the window bar and pulled a stool away while they made up his bagel. Then he dug his Canon digital SLR out of the knapsack, removed his shades, and waited.

Patiently. In the Good Karma Café.

It only took a couple of minutes. As Jones wheeled his Crown Vic down the ramp and out the doors, Andrew snapped the picture. He didn't really care about the government-issued license plates. He had zoomed in and didn't include them in the frame. It was more about getting a close-up shot of the detective who didn't know he existed and wasn't even looking for him. More about getting a shot of Matt Jones chasing a phantom. More about the fact that within a single day, he'd figured out who Jones was and where he was staying.

He knew the building. The high-end neighborhood.

He watched the detective race down Twenty-Second Street and vanish. When Andrew turned, the woman behind the counter smiled at him. His Popeye bagel with a scrambled egg, spinach, and American cheese was ready, and it smelled good.

CHAPTER 33

Matt stood in the churchyard, staring at the five new graves waiting to be filled in. He could smell the earth below the frost line, the frozen ground below his feet crunching as he shifted his weight. His eyes rose to the headstone. When he first arrived, three men had been setting it in place.

The funeral service for Jim and Tammy Stratton and their three children had begun about half an hour ago. It wasn't being held across the street in the modern building on the hill. Instead, the service was here in old St. David's Episcopal Church, a modest sanctuary built in 1715 of wood and stone and set in the middle of the churchyard beneath a forest of tall trees.

Matt could hear what he guessed was a pair of violins playing Bach's "Jesu, Joy of Man's Desiring." The music was leaking out of the church into the graveyard and drifting over the headstones.

It seemed so still out here. In spite of the music, it seemed so quiet and grim.

He looked through the trees and saw the media camped out on the south lawn this side of the stream. One of the video cameras appeared to be from a TV station in Baltimore, but like the couple paying their respects before a grave closer to the church, the groundskeeper trimming bushes by the fence, and a pair of mourners attending the service inside, the man and woman with press credentials and a video camera were special agents with the FBI recruited directly out of Washington.

Matt walked up the steps and opened the door without making any sound. As he entered the church, he saw Doyle and Rogers standing against the rear wall with Dr. Westbrook. Kate Brown had taken a seat in the last pew just ahead of him.

After a few moments, Matt could feel someone move in behind him. When he heard Doyle's voice, he pricked up his ears.

"Remember, Jones. We're looking for Dr. Baylor, not some asshole kid that has issues with his *mommy*."

Matt turned and gave him a look. Doyle's eyes were drilling him, his jaw clenched. It seemed more than clear that the federal prosecutor was still incensed by the things Matt had said last night. He watched Doyle step away and glance at Rogers. He saw the two men exchange nods.

They have blinders on. It's the corporate way, you know.

But not Dr. Westbrook. He was looking at Matt as well, but no longer appeared to be judging him. Instead, it was an even, measured gaze. The look of genuine curiosity.

Matt wished that he could have read Westbrook's mind, but shrugged it off and turned back to the church. He slipped a piece of nicotine gum into his mouth and let his eyes drift from face to face. Baylor hadn't shown up. Nor had anyone even close to Dr. Westbrook's alternate profile. As Matt counted heads and subtracted the two special agents, only thirty-one people were here for the funeral, and not one of them was a single male in his twenties.

Matt looked at the five caskets lined up before the altar. When the music came to an end, the church rector, Reverend Lillian Brey, began to speak in a gentle but clear voice. Because of the egregious crimes Jim Stratton had committed, there was an awkward feeling to the service that seemed more than palpable. Brey spent several moments speaking about forgiveness before concluding that William Penn had named their city Philadelphia for good reason. Penn was a Quaker and had experienced religious persecution, people trying to force other people to believe what they believed. People thinking that they were right and everyone who didn't agree with them was wrong. Penn wanted his colony to be different than that. He wanted his colony to be a place where anyone could worship freely no matter what their beliefs. And that's where the word *Philadelphia* came from. *Philos* meaning love or friendship, and *adelphos* meaning brother. It was Greek for the words *brotherly love*, she said, and today it was time for us to forgive.

While Brey led the mourners in prayer, Matt turned and glanced at the funeral director standing on the other side of the church behind the last pew. His name was Lester Snow, and Matt had met him at the briefing before the service. He looked like he was about seventy, and he had told Matt that his funeral home had been operating for forty-five years.

So why did the funeral director seem so anxious? Why did he look so spooked?

Matt followed Snow's gaze to the five caskets, then looked back at the man. Something was on his mind. The worry showing on his face appeared out of place, almost as if this were his first funeral.

After the prayer ended and the music began, the service moved into the churchyard. It seemed strange, but there were no pallbearers. Just ten men in black suits who ferried the caskets out into the yard and positioned them on the nylon straps stretched over the five graves.

Matt checked the graveyard, but didn't spot anyone new. To the north he could see a steep hill and, set on top, a home that, like the church, might have been built three centuries ago. But through the final moments of the service, he kept his eyes on the undertaker, Lester Snow.

It occurred to Matt that Snow could have been worried about logistics. Jim Stratton, MD, didn't appear to have many friends left. Not after giving his healthy patients chemotherapy and radiation treatments.

The poor turnout and the lack of people willing to serve as pallbearers might have put a strain on Lester Snow's services. But once the coffins were lowered into the ground, once the mourners walked away, nothing had changed on Lester Snow's face.

The man was worried. Matt knew in his gut that there had to be a reason.

Kate Brown walked over. "We should get going," she said.

He gave her a look. He wanted to stay and talk to Snow but knew that it would require subtlety and wanted to do it alone.

"Why don't you go with Rogers and Doyle?" he said. "I'll meet you at the office."

"You want to stay? Why?"

"I have something I want to do."

"What?"

He lowered his voice. "Did you say anything to Doyle about Westbrook giving us that profile?"

She seemed surprised, and narrowed her brow. "No," she said. "Why would I?"

"I don't know. Something Doyle said inside the church."

"I didn't say anything. Maybe Westbrook did."

"Maybe," Matt said. "Why don't you go with them?"

"I'm not leaving until you tell me what's going on. I sure hope it doesn't have anything to do with last night."

He gave her a long look as he thought it over. He wanted to talk to Snow on his own. He didn't want it to seem official.

He lowered his voice. "Come on, Kate. It has nothing to do with last night. You're the best thing that's happened to me in a long time. I've got something I need to take care of, that's all. It's personal, and it's on the way. I'll see you downtown. Wait up for me, and we'll grab something to eat."

She didn't buy it. She gave him a suspicious look and marched off.

CHAPTER 34

Lester Snow had vanished. The ten men in black suits who worked for the funeral home were still here in the graveyard and inside the church, cleaning up. But Snow was gone.

Matt looked through the large pane glass windows in the church and saw a hearse heading north on Valley Forge Road. Exiting the building, he ran into the parking lot and climbed into the Crown Vic. The camera crews were here, milling about and packing up their gear. Matt eased the car through the crowd as quickly as he could. When he finally reached the street, he made a left and gunned it up the hill.

The hearse was about two hundred yards ahead, making a right onto another narrow country road. Within a quarter mile, Matt had closed the distance and began riding his tail. Once he confirmed that Snow was behind the wheel, once he saw the undertaker's face in the side mirror, he slowed down and followed at a distance of twenty car lengths or so.

These were quiet neighborhoods and tree-lined roads in the middle of the day. There was no reason to not ease off the gas and give the undertaker some room. Matt lowered the window a few inches, lit a cigarette, and settled into the driver's seat. He didn't know the area very

well. Still, he had a decent feel for where the church was located in rela-
tion to the Holloways' mansion and the Wawa Market off Sugartown
Road. He knew all three were very close, within a few square miles,
and that Snow was working his way toward Route 30, a.k.a. Lancaster
Avenue, the strip of highway that followed the railroad tracks and
snaked through the entire Main Line.

Matt noted the Wayne Library as Snow finally reached Lancaster
Avenue and made a right at the light. A few blocks later, he pulled into
the lot at the Lester Snow Funeral Home. Matt followed him around
back and parked before the loading docks as Snow climbed out of the
hearse.

"Mr. Snow," he said. "May I have a word with you?"

Snow gave him an odd look, but finally nodded. "Sure," he said
quietly. "But let's do it inside, okay?"

"Okay," Matt said.

The undertaker smoothed back his white hair, then led the way up
the steps and to the rear entrance. They passed through a room that
was dimly lit and appeared to be refrigerated. When Snow opened a
thick door and flooded the room with light, Matt saw ten coffins set on
wheeled gurneys against the far wall. He noted the ID tags and followed
Snow into the hall.

It was warm in here, and he was grateful for it. He could hear music
in the building. Snow held a bony finger to his lips, calling for silence
as he spoke in a voice that was barely audible.

"There's a memorial service underway. We need to be quiet."

They walked down the hallway, the carpet thick and plush and
absorbing any sound of their footsteps. They passed a display room
filled with coffins varying in style and, Matt guessed, price. When they
reached the source of the music, Matt peeked inside the large room
before Snow could get the set of double doors closed. There were at least
seventy-five people seated in the room, and the memorial service had a
theme to it like he'd read about in LA.

The casket was open, and the middle-aged man inside had the look and feel of a wooden mannequin with marbles in his eyes. He was dressed in a golf shirt and pants, his casket designed to mimic a golf cart. Beside the casket, a set of old golf clubs stood on a spread of artificial grass.

Snow finally got the doors closed, then gave Matt a nervous look and showed him into the room next door. It was about the same size as the room they'd just passed, and there were a large number of folding chairs set in rows here as well. Matt glanced around. The walls were painted gold. When he turned he noticed a Christmas tree with lights and decorations and wrapped gifts standing beside an electric fireplace with fake logs.

Snow turned and looked at him as he shut the door. The worry was still there, and seemed to have intensified over the past few minutes.

The undertaker cleared his throat. "Your name again," he said in a quiet voice that quivered. "I'm sorry."

"Matt Jones."

"What can I do for you, Detective?"

Matt shrugged like it was nothing, moved over to a seat, and sat down. "I couldn't help noticing how worried you looked during the service. I figured there had to be a reason and wanted to ask you about it."

"Why does there have to be a reason?"

"Because this wasn't your first funeral service. You've been in business for forty-five years. I'd like to know what's wrong."

Snow's eyes got big as he considered the situation. He took a deep breath and sat down on a chair across the aisle. Snow couldn't seem to look him in the eye anymore, and Matt sensed that his hunch was about to pay out.

"Nothing's wrong, Detective."

"I've got eyes, Mr. Snow. Something's bothering you. Something's going on."

The undertaker gave him a quick look before his gaze dropped down to the carpet. "It's an internal matter," he said.

"I wish it could be an internal matter, Mr. Snow. I really do. But this is a homicide investigation. A mass killing. There's no such thing as an internal matter. I need to know what's going on, sir."

The man shook his head, still eyeing the carpet. "But you see, I'm not sure that it was anything at all."

It hung there for a while. Matt glanced at the Christmas tree, noticed the natural scent of pine in the air, then turned back.

"You just said that you're not sure if it was anything at all. It's the word *it* that concerns me, Mr. Snow."

The undertaker appeared upset. Matt could see him trying to reel it all in, his eyes wagging back and forth across the carpet like a dog's tail. He let out a sigh and lowered his voice.

"I just had the feeling that the Strattons had been disturbed in some way."

A long moment passed, the scent of the Christmas tree vanishing in its wake.

"Tell me what you mean by disturbed."

The undertaker finally met his gaze. "It's just a feeling," he said. "I have no evidence. I'm just glad it's over. I'm glad they're in their final resting places and hope that the entire family is finally at peace. That's a beautiful churchyard, don't you think?"

A feeling. A hunch. The possibility that the Strattons' corpses had been disturbed in some way.

"You called it an internal matter. What about your employees?"

"I was just trying to avoid your questions. Everyone who works here has been with me for a long time. Like I said, I can't put my finger on it. It's just a feeling I had."

Matt didn't know how far to pursue this right now. The details of both crime scenes were still confidential.

"Let me ask you something, Mr. Snow."

"Anything, Detective."

All of a sudden the undertaker seemed eager to please, like the weight he'd been carrying had finally been cast off his shoulders.

"You've been in the funeral business for a long time."

"Yes, I have."

"How many times have you worked on someone who was murdered?"

The undertaker thought it over for a moment. "Now that you mention it, not many."

"What's that mean?"

"To tell you the truth, the Strattons might be the first."

"What about car wrecks, anybody who died in a violent accident or house fire?"

"Too many to count, Detective."

Matt stood up and thanked the undertaker for his time. The only thing he knew for certain was that Lester Snow hadn't been influenced by the way the Strattons had died, and that he was lying. Blood and gore wasn't an issue here. The issue was limited to the worry showing on the undertaker's face at the funeral service. And now the relief he was exhibiting as he thought he'd succeeded in deceiving Matt and ending the conversation.

Matt stepped outside and started around the building to his car. He had asked Snow a direct question and the man had lied to him and wasn't about to give it up. Not today anyway. Not without something more to force his hand.

Matt shook his head. Someone had done something to the Strattons' corpses, and it left a really bad taste in his mouth.

CHAPTER 35

Matt cruised down the hill on Matsonford Road and made a left when he reached County Line. As he backed off the gas, he glanced at the clock on the dash. It was only four thirty, but already dark.

He spotted the Stratton mansion on the other side of the stone wall, idled down the drive, and parked beneath the trees. The media had pulled out, which didn't surprise him. But so had the men in black uniforms carrying rifles, and this did. He didn't see any sign of law enforcement on the property. No one was keeping an eye on things anymore.

He got out of the car and gazed at the death house, all those dark windows. When his cell phone rang, he saw Kate Brown's name on the face.

"What's up, Kate?"

"Where are you?"

"At the Strattons'."

"Why?"

Matt gazed into the backyard. "I wanted another look."

She didn't say anything for several moments. When she finally spoke, her voice had changed and become softer.

"Is this what you had to take care of? Is this why you wanted to be alone?"

Matt started to nod, then caught himself. "Sort of."

"I'm sorry, Jones. I should've guessed."

"There's nothing to be sorry about, Kate. Let's hook up later."

"Okay," she said. "Sounds good."

She hung up. Matt slipped the phone into his pocket. He wasn't thinking about Brown, or even the undertaker. As he stood before the death house, his mind was fixed on the sight of the Strattons' new graves and the sound of those two violins wafting through the churchyard. That grim feeling of stillness.

That was the moment Matt knew that he had to forget about the crimes Jim Stratton had committed, the things he had done to his patients for the sake of money. Seeing those five fresh graves cut into the earth was the moment Matt had signed a personal contract with each one of the five victims. The contract covered the Strattons as well as the Holloways, no matter what kind of man David Holloway had been. No matter how much Stratton and Holloway deserved to pay for their crimes. But even more, the contract no longer required Rogers's or Doyle's approval or even permission. If the FBI and the Department of Justice wanted to drive up the wrong road, so be it.

Matt didn't care anymore. He was in the hunt for the duration, no matter how things turned out.

He stepped onto the porch, punched in the combination on the lockbox, the California penal code for murder, one-eight-seven, and plucked out the brass key. He was in, and after he pushed the door open, he returned the key to the box and switched on the foyer lights.

The Strattons might be buried in the ground at old St. David's Church, but their ghosts were still here. And the haunting stillness of the graveyard couldn't compare to the weight of the silence permeating the Strattons' home. Matt noted the smell of rotting blood still

cascading down the staircase from the second-floor landing. The harsh
odor seemed to have backed off some, but was still very much here.

He walked into the library, looking for the framed picture Dr.
Baylor had said he touched. He found it hanging over a long, narrow table on a wall beside the fireplace. Slipping into a pair of vinyl
gloves, he switched on the lamp, glanced at the magazines and art books
on the table, then checked the picture frame for fingerprint powder.
Rogers's report had been correct, the frame dusted. And Dr. Baylor had
been right as well. Behind the glass was a sheet of newspaper from the
Philadelphia Inquirer's society page. Jim Stratton, MD, had sponsored
a charity event for one of the hospitals in Center City—a golf match at
his country club for kids with cancer. But the article that filled page one
and continued on page three was really focused on Stratton's generosity
and his life as a well-regarded physician, a husband and father. There
were photographs of the family in the backyard and by the pool, along
with a shot of their Georgian mansion here in the heart of Radnor.

In spite of the contract Matt had made standing before their open
graves—his personal commitment and mission—he found the article
difficult to read and finally stopped.

Jim Stratton, MD, was a piece of human garbage, and dwelling on
it couldn't be good for the case.

"Interesting reading, isn't it?"

Matt froze. It was Dr. Baylor, and he sounded close—within ten
feet right behind his back.

Baylor chuckled. "My first thought when I read that piece was that
Jim Stratton, MD, might be the son of God making his return to earth
after more than two thousand years. Sweet Jesus, he's back."

Matt turned. The doctor was standing in the living room cloaked in
darkness. His Glock 17 appeared to be up and ready, the muzzle poking
through the gloom into the light and pointed directly at Matt's heart.

The doctor stepped out of the shadows and through the doorway,
the light from the table lamp raking across his body. "It's unbelievable,

isn't it? The games people play in order to hide who they really are. I'm afraid I'm going to need your pistol, Matthew. I'd appreciate it if you'd turn around and lean against the mantel for a moment or two."

Matt nodded without saying anything. As he leaned forward and grabbed hold of the mantelpiece, he could feel the doctor lifting his .45 out of its holster and quickly patting him down. It was a textbook body search, so well done that Matt had a hard time believing that the doctor hadn't been a cop in one of his many identities.

"What are you doing here?" Matt said.

"I thought it might be a good time to catch up."

"But how did you know I'd be here?"

The doctor cleared his throat. "Let's just say that I've got eyes here and at the Holloways'. It's the only safe way I have of making contact with you. In this case, I followed you from the funeral home. Thanks," he said in a lower voice. "I'm finished."

Matt turned and watched Baylor slip the .45 into his coat pocket and take a few steps back, the Glock still pointed his way.

"Do I really need to hold you at gunpoint, Matthew?"

Matt shook his head. "No," he said. "Not anymore."

Matt could tell that his response had surprised Baylor. The doctor smiled and gave Matt a long look as he lowered the Glock 17 to his side.

"Something's happened," the doctor said. "What is it?"

Matt sat down on the couch. "The semen found in Tammy Stratton wasn't yours."

"I'm well aware of that," he said. "But you've got DNA. You've got a match. Whose semen is it?"

Matt met the doctor's gaze. "Her son's."

"The thirteen-year-old boy?"

Matt nodded and settled into the couch, measuring Baylor as the doctor sat down on the arm of a leather chair and appeared to be thinking it over. Matt couldn't believe that he was dealing with a monster, that he was using a monster, that he needed a monster. A memory surfaced. He had been packing his bags for the trip to Philadelphia and his supervisor, Lieutenant Howard McKensie, had been mocking him. How did McKensie put it?

You're not ready for a case like this, Jones. You've still got monsters swimming in your head.

Baylor got up and walked over to the window. "The way the boy had been draped over his mother's body, I was afraid this would be the case. When you get the results from the Holloways, it'll be the same."

"I think so, too," Matt said. "And you were right about Rogers and Doyle."

"Right about what?"

"They want it to be you. Anything that points in another direction will never make the file."

"You confronted them?"

"I thought I had to when the DNA results came in."

The doctor shook his head, the glint his eyes bright and wild. "Matthew Trevor Jones," he said. "What happened?"

"Exactly what you'd expect. But later that night, I confronted Dr. Westbrook on his own."

"The profiler from the FBI. I read about him in the newspaper."

"I cornered him on the street. I asked him what a profile would look like if you weren't in the picture."

"I already know what it looks like. That's why I tried to warn you at the Holloways'."

"How could you know?"

"Look at the crime scene, Matthew. What need was the killer trying to fulfill? Look at the boys. The mothers. Dad and his daughters stripped of their clothing and holding hands as they watched. Let me guess what Westbrook told you. If it's not me, then you'd be looking for a young man in his twenties. A young man who probably still lives with his mother and doesn't have much money. That's why he's taking bigger risks and picking on the wealthy. He's a young man who undoubtedly spent his entire life as a victim of sexual abuse. And don't kid yourself, Matthew, it has to be sexual abuse because he's forcing the boys to have sex with their mothers. Like I said before, this one's different."

The doctor met his gaze and smiled. Matt flinched, but managed to catch himself halfway through. It wasn't Baylor's smile. It was his eyes. For one short moment, the doctor had the look of a predator. For ten, maybe fifteen seconds, his eyes had gone dead. Matt could remember the photographs of Adam Lanza and Dylann Roof that he'd found on the Internet this morning. The doctor seemed to share the same psychotic look, but somehow had the ability to turn it on and off at will.

Matt took a deep breath. When he glanced at his hands, his fingers were trembling slightly. It was the unpredictability of the man, he thought. The idea that at any moment—

Matt cleared his throat. "It gets worse," he said.

Baylor was staring at him, and Matt guessed that he'd noticed his reaction.

"Worse?" the doctor said carefully.

"I just came from the funeral home. Someone's messing with the corpses."

"Did the undertaker say that?"

"He mentioned it, then wrote it off."

"Did you believe him?"

Matt shook his head. "Not when he tried to back away. Someone messed with the Strattons' bodies. Whether or not it's the killer is another story."

"Oh, it's him, Matthew. Trust me on this. It's him and it fits."

"How?"

"I'll let you figure that out."

The doctor glanced at Matt's hands, then met his eyes again. When he spoke his voice was dark and frightening.

"Are you better now?"

He'd noticed. "You mind if I smoke?"

"Would it matter?"

Matt dug his cigarettes out of his pocket, lit one, and crossed the room to the fireplace. The doctor was staring at him again, his eyes focused and glistening in the light.

"You know he'll never stop, don't you, Matthew. He'll keep going until he's either captured or killed or blows up like a shooting star. And it's not what I read in the newspapers. It's not that he likes it. It's that he can't control himself anymore. He's playing out his own life. He's dreaming about his escape to a better life. And somewhere deep inside he knows with absolute certainty that he'll never make it. He'll never get there. He'll never have the life he wants and needs. That's where the anger's coming from. The rage."

Matt couldn't tell if Baylor was talking about the killer or himself. Either way, he wanted to get out of here. He tapped the ash from the head of the cigarette into the fireplace and took a quick hit. When he finally checked on Baylor, he caught the doctor eyeing him again and realized that the dread had returned, but was stronger now. It suddenly occurred to Matt that the reason he hadn't been afraid of the doctor on the night the Holloways were murdered was probably due to the shock of the crime itself. The sight of a mass killing, an entire family. The blowback had dulled his consciousness, his senses. But not tonight. Not with the doctor glaring at him like a leopard eyeing prey. Yet Baylor was the only person in the world whom he could talk to. The only person who understood that someone else was out there. The only human being he knew who had an *insider's view* of committing an actual murder.

Matt took another hit on the Marlboro. "May I ask you a question?"

"Of course."

"I found out something about my family. My mother."

The doctor nodded slowly. "What did you find out?"

"Her father was a big guy on Wall Street, just like my father. He was running a Ponzi scheme with his business partner and it fell apart. A lot of people lost everything they had. A lot of people got hurt."

"What's his name?"

"Howard Stewart. He's dead. His business partner shot him after an argument. He waited until my grandparents fell asleep, then broke into the house and murdered them in bed. I couldn't find my past because my mother's name had been changed to protect her and her brother and sisters from the scandal."

"When did this happen?"

"A long time ago. My mother was just a girl."

Dr. Baylor moved back to the chair, sat down, and crossed his legs. "What's your question, Matthew?"

Matt turned and looked at him. The doctor's face was in shadow, masking his eyes.

"You know who my father is," Matt said.

"I knew the minute you walked into my office."

Matt took another drag on the Marlboro. "Why didn't you go after him? Why didn't you do to me what you did to those four girls?"

The doctor shrugged. "That's easy. Those girls were loved by their parents. They were the only real thing their parents ever had. Take them away, and what are their parents left with? The money they stole. Some faint memory of a time when they cared about something more than themselves." Baylor leaned forward, the light from the lamp striking his face. "Your situation is entirely different, Matthew. Your father, M. Trevor Jones, the King of Wall Street, wouldn't mourn your death. He'd celebrate your passing. That's the only explanation for why you were shot by that man on top of Mount Hollywood. Your father is trying to keep a secret. You're working a headline case, your name's out there, your picture's in the newspaper, on TV and the

Internet, and he's getting nervous. His best option, his only option, is to have you killed before anyone figures out what he did to you and your mother."

Matt flicked the butt into the fireplace. "Maybe," he said. "But my father's a bigger symbol of greed than anyone you hurt. He might even be the most self-centered person in the world. He's a textbook narcissist. I spoke with an LAPD psychiatrist during my recovery. I never mentioned anything about my family, but we talked about narcissism because everyone you hurt was a narcissist. He said that it's reached the point of becoming an epidemic. Everyone is out for themselves and couldn't care less who they hurt or what it takes to get what they want. It's something short of being a human being. It's a mental illness that wipes out evolution in favor of the knuckle dragger. He said that most shrinks won't even take them as patients because their disease can't be cured. They like being animals. They enjoy it. That's why I wonder why you spared my father. Why didn't you do everybody a favor and just kill him?"

A moment passed. When the doctor finally spoke, his voice had changed and become gentle and warm.

"Because I thought that the honor belonged to you, Matthew. The only thing that will give your father's death meaning is if it comes from you, and only you. But even more important to your personal recovery, he has to see you. He has to know that his death came from you. And you have to witness his revelation. You have to see your father's face as he experiences fear and terror. You need to see him take his last breath. You need to watch him pass."

Matt let the thought linger. Those monsters were swimming in his head again. And then he heard a noise. The loud banging of footsteps. Someone with heavy feet was racing down the rear staircase. Matt traded looks with Baylor, then bolted through the foyer and out the front door.

A figure was sprinting around the house and into the backyard. Matt gave chase but lost him in the darkness as he cleared the pool and spa. He stopped and listened, but the ice-cold air was as dead as a vacuum.

He didn't get a decent look, but guessed that it was a man. Because the intruder was so fast on his feet, he had to be young. Matt rushed back to the house and through the foyer into the library. His .45 had been left on the coffee table, and Dr. Baylor was gone.

CHAPTER 36

Andrew Penchant had hit the skids and become more than irritated.

Jones had been sitting on that stupid wall by the pool for a good twenty minutes. Andrew was hiding beneath a pine tree just thirty yards away, and didn't dare move. The moon wasn't out, the sky black. Still, he knew that after five minutes, Jones's eyes would have adjusted to the darkness. He also realized that the stories about Jones as a soldier had to be true.

Jones was sitting there in the cold with his pistol, sitting still as a statue and gazing into the backyard. He was waiting for Andrew to screw up. He didn't look like a detective wanting to make an arrest. As Andrew peered through the branches, he thought Jones came off more like a local yokel who couldn't wait to fire his gun and make the kill.

Jones had to know that he was out here. He had to know that he was hiding. If Andrew had continued to run across the lawn and down the hill, he would have been seen before he reached the pond. Jones must have realized that he had disappeared too quickly to have escaped.

But even more, even worse, Andrew had heard Jones talking to the mad scientist inside the house. Jones wasn't following the program. He wasn't looking for Dr. Baylor like everybody else was. All those people in the newspaper and on TV.

Instead, Jones was looking for *him*.

Andrew had heard everything. He'd been in the house when Jones entered the foyer and switched on the lights. He'd been in Tammy Stratton's dressing room when he heard the front door open. He'd been cataloging the contents of her drawers, examining her bras and panties and comparing them with what he'd already collected from her hamper.

When he realized that Jones wasn't alone, he'd moved out onto the landing and listened from the top of the stairs. He heard the detective use the doctor's name, and didn't understand how they could have teamed up. According to the newspaper, Baylor was a psychopath who had brutally murdered four coeds. It didn't make any sense that he and Jones could know each other, none of it did, and so Andrew sat down and followed the conversation and tried to think it through. They seemed to know everything about him, and he found this unnerving. They had a rough idea of his age. They knew his story. His background. And somehow they'd found out about his mother and the things they did when they were together. The things they did when his mother got stoned and drunk and wanted her son to be a friend.

If Andrew hadn't left his pistol underneath his bed, he would have shot Jones here and now. But after another five minutes, he reconsidered.

Jones and the doctor only possessed a rough idea of what Andrew might be. A rough sketch. But there was still no direct link between the idea and the man. They didn't have a name and they had no clue what he looked like. They didn't even have any physical evidence. No fingerprints or body fluids or DNA. Even better, from what Andrew could tell, no one that Jones worked with was on board. The two people Jones mentioned, Rogers and Doyle, the two big shots Andrew had heard Ryan Day mention on his gossip show, *Get Buzzed*, were still chasing the mad scientist. Andrew could walk right up to Jones exactly the way he did this morning and the detective would never get it.

He was still safe. Still not compromised. Still an international man of mystery.

He smiled. Jones was finally getting off his ass and walking toward the mansion. Andrew watched him vanish around the corner, but didn't move. Instead, he watched and listened and made sure Jones wasn't trying to trick him. When the lights switched on in the Strattons' bedroom, he shouldered his knapsack filled with the silk and lacy spoils of a life in crime and walked out onto the lawn. From the shadows he could see Jones examining the room with great care. Andrew imagined that he was trying to piece together why someone had been in the house.

He shook his head and gave Jones a last look. Then he hiked through the yard down to the gatehouse on Gulf Creek Road. Just up the hill in the woods, Andrew had found a place to park his car without worry. It was a large old house on a huge piece of property that had been converted into a night school for adults. He looked at the lighted windows, the grand porches, the lot filled with cars. Street lights led the way through a maze of paths carved through the forest of extraordinarily tall trees. He took in the dead gardens and ice-covered lawns and dreamed about what it must have been like to live in a house like this before it was ruined and became a school.

He dreamed about what life must have been like before everything became crowded and people didn't matter anymore.

Schools of minnows, he thought. Who cared if they lived or died?

He climbed in behind the wheel, idled down the winding drive, and made a right onto Gulf Creek Road. Switching off his headlights, he pulled past the gatehouse and gazed up the hill at the Strattons' mansion. After five minutes or so, he saw the lighted windows on the first floor go dark, then pulled the car down to the stop sign and waited.

He didn't need to guess what Jones's car might look like. He'd seen it this morning and knew the exact make and model. When Jones cruised by, heading up the hill on County Line Road, Andrew waited a beat, then switched on his headlights and began to follow.

He needed to keep his eyes on the man. He wanted to know where Jones was going and why he seemed to be in a hurry. But even more, he needed to know why Jones wanted to kill his father.

That was the bright spot in the detective's conversation with the mad scientist; for reasons unknown, Jones wanted to see his father dead. Andrew found the idea more than intriguing, and realized that he and Jones shared the same goal. They had something in common. Something profound.

Jones made a left at the light, heading for the expressway into the city. Andrew turned as well, but hung back like everything was cool.

He wished he'd had enough time to roll another joint. The reefer he'd scored in the city this morning turned out to be awesome. He shivered in the cold air, wishing the heater worked better and dreaming of buying his first Mercedes. He'd look good in a Benz, he decided. He'd look like the man he was born to be. A living legend.

CHAPTER 37

Matt crossed the floor, saw Brown's empty desk, and knew that she had left for the day. He took a moment and looked around. The lights in the conference room were shut down, and he didn't see Doyle anywhere in the room. As it turned out, most of the desks paired and pushed together were empty tonight.

Matt popped the lid on a cup of takeout coffee and stirred in a single packet of sugar. After a quick first sip, he sat down at his desk.

He had spent a half hour sitting on that wall by the pool, studying the lawn and field that stretched down to the frozen pond and gatehouse. He had sensed that he was being watched and felt certain that the intruder was still out there hiding in the darkness. He was hoping that the man would make a mistake. A cough or sneeze, an errant footstep—any sound that might rise above the peaceful din of the stream running this side of Gulf Creek Road.

But after half an hour, Matt had started to worry about time. He walked through the entire mansion, searched every room, and found nothing out of the ordinary. No clue or reason that would explain why someone had broken into the house. And it wasn't exactly a break-in. He hadn't found a single open window or unlocked door.

How had the intruder managed to get in? How had Baylor gotten in?

Matt took another sip of coffee, wondering if the intruder had been listening to his conversation with the doctor. He wondered if the man understood the magnitude of their meeting.

He wondered if the intruder was the actual killer making a return trip to the crime scene once the men with rifles went away. It made sense that it would be him. It made a lot of sense. It had been Matt's first thought as he ran past the pool and lost sight of the man in the darkness.

He let the thought go, dug his cell phone out of his pocket, and called Brown. The phone rang four times before bumping him over to her voice mail. After leaving a short message, he grabbed his briefcase and coffee and walked out of the Crisis Room. It was almost seven, and every office he passed was dark. Matt couldn't help thinking about the way the Feds ran their business. It felt so slow. So hands off.

And then he passed Special Agent Wes Rogers's office.

"Where you been?" Rogers said in a loud voice.

Matt stopped and looked through the doorway. Rogers was seated at his desk with his sleeves rolled up and his collar loosened. He had a pair of reading glasses on, a pen in his hand, and appeared to be signing papers.

"I was out at the Strattons' place," Matt said.

"I already know that. Brown said you wanted another look. What's going on?"

Matt stepped into the office. "We need to exhume the bodies."

Rogers smiled like it hurt. "We need to what?" he said quietly.

"Exhume the Strattons' bodies."

Rogers sat back in his chair, shaking his head. Matt assumed that the special agent wouldn't listen, but pressed forward nonetheless. It was part of doing the right thing. Doing a good job. He gave the special agent a quick but detailed briefing on his conversation with the under-taker, Lester Snow, and his encounter with the intruder he'd chased at the Strattons' mansion. He gave him everything without mentioning that he'd spent more than a half hour with Dr. Baylor, the man Rogers and Doyle and the FBI's special task force were looking for. At a certain point, Rogers raised his right hand like he'd heard enough.

"Let me see if I get it, Jones. The undertaker says that he thought the bodies might have been disturbed in some way, but in the end, it turned out to be nothing. You say he's lying. Someone is messing with the corpses. Do you really think that you can convince a judge to sign off on disturbing a gravesite because it's your belief that Lester Snow is a liar? Is this how they do business in Hollywood? Give me a break, Jones. It doesn't matter what you think. You can't dig up five graves on a hunch. My God, can you imagine what the media would do with that? Can you imagine what we would look like?"

Matt didn't say anything. He didn't care what the media would think or what the FBI might look like. If they had a chance to examine the bodies after they'd passed through Lester Snow's funeral home, they'd have a definitive answer.

Rogers glanced at the paperwork on his desk, then back at Matt. "You know you'd be doing everybody a real big favor if you'd just get on a plane and fly back to La-La Land. A real big favor, Jones. I'd even drive you to the airport. It would be a pleasure seeing you off."

Matt looked at Rogers's hands. They were soft and smooth and didn't show the wear or tear Matt would have expected for a man his age. Even a woman for that matter. He looked back at Rogers's face. His attitude. His apparent ignorance. It seemed obvious that the special agent couldn't think outside the box. He wondered how he made it this far up the food chain.

But then he shook if off. Wes Rogers was exactly the kind of person who made it up the food chain. Matt guessed that the special agent had spent his entire life in neutral. Not forward or in reverse, but neutral. If Rogers never took a stand, he'd never be seen as wrong, and those bonus checks would keep coming in the mail.

"What about the intruder, Rogers? What about the man I chased?"

"You know what happens at crime scenes when the cops go away. Everybody in the neighborhood gets curious. You said he was young."

Matt nodded. "He was fast. He had to be young."

Rogers tossed his pen on the desk and gave Matt a long look. "That doesn't sound like Dr. Baylor to me. How 'bout you?"

Matt would have liked to have said that the man he chased might have been the same man who murdered the Strattons and the Holloways. The real killer. He would have liked to have told Rogers how much sense it made that the real killer would come back for a second look once the cops were gone and he felt safe. He could have been looking for trophies. He would have had time to think things over. He could have made a return trip for a long list of reasons.

But Matt kept his mouth shut. He watched the special agent wave his hand toward the door, pick up his pen, and get back to signing papers. In the grand scheme of things, Matt imagined that Rogers was pretty good at signing papers.

You're working with people who have their heads in the sand, Matthew. It's the corporate way, you know.

Matt turned around and walked out. The finish line seemed so far away.

CHAPTER 38

Andrew looked at Jones seated on the park bench, checked on that cop by the steps, then tried to steady his hands in the cold air and roll a joint without shivering.

He had followed Jones from his office to Love Park on the JKF Plaza in Center City. It looked like Jones had picked a bench that gave him a view of the Love sculpture, the huge Christmas tree standing atop the shutdown fountain, and the art museum at the other end of the Benjamin Franklin Parkway. He wasn't doing anything, really. Just sitting there sipping coffee and smoking cigarettes. Every once in a while, he'd pull out his cell phone, make a call, and hang up without saying anything.

Andrew guessed that Jones was trying to reach someone who wasn't home.

He licked the paper and rolled the flap to finish off the joint, then checked on that loser cop again. Unfortunately, this was one of the worst places to smoke weed in the entire city. A great place to score, but not to light up. Andrew knew everything about Love Park because at the age of twelve, he used to come here two or three times a week. He used to come here to get away from his mother and think pure thoughts. He'd take the bus into the city, buy a hotdog, a Coke, and a pack of Reese's Peanut Butter Cups, then find an empty bench and watch the *show*.

Andrew pulled his wool cap over his cornrows but still couldn't handle the frigid air. After tightening his scarf, he looked around to see who was close by. The woman on the next bench was staring at him until their eyes met, then she got up and hurried off. Andrew was used to getting that look, especially from women, and let the moment pass with just a bit of indignation. When he turned back to the cop and saw him step behind the trees, he lit up and took a deep hit.

While the official name for the square used to be JFK Plaza, everyone called it Love Park now because of the Love sculpture by Robert Indiana. And while even Andrew had to admit that he liked the artwork, it was the architect who designed the plaza itself that made the place famous.

Love Park was a skateboarder's paradise, and that was the *show* he liked to watch so much as a boy. The steps, the smooth surfaces, the dips and rises—all of it made this plaza the most important single block to skateboarding culture in the world. The list of professionals who made their names here, an international list, was too long to count.

The *show* lasted for ten years or so, and Andrew had only caught the last two summers. He could remember when he heard the news that skateboarding was now illegal on this sacred ground. He could remember sitting on the very bench that Jones was using. He could remember watching the construction workers giving Love Park its facelift. Although the park had been deemed "unskateable," people still showed up with their boards. When city officials realized that their facelift had been a failure, cops were posted on the plaza twenty-four hours a day.

And that was the problem. The shithead cop on the other side of the fountain.

Andrew turned and snuck a quick second hit, then palmed the joint and glanced back at Jones.

He was standing up and beginning to walk away. He could see Jones moving down the steps onto the sidewalk and heading up the block toward Market Street.

Andrew pressed the head of the joint between his fingers and doused it with his tongue. After jogging down to street level, he fell into line behind Jones and slipped the joint into his pocket. The detective didn't seem like he was in a hurry anymore. He was taking his time, looking at the people he passed on the extra-wide sidewalks here. Andrew could feel those same people looking at his face, but tried to ignore it the way he always did. He could feel them judging him, he could see them shunning him, he could tell that they knew something was wrong with him and were afraid. He turned and gazed at city hall on his left. When he checked on Jones, he realized that the detective had beaten the red light on Market Street.

Andrew stood back and waited for the light to change. He could see Jones racing across Fifteenth Street and finally entering a building at the other end of the block on the Avenue of the Arts. Once the light changed, Andrew legged it down the sidewalk and gazed through the glass doors.

It was a bar. An elegant bar that Andrew could tell was more than pricey. And it looked like it was attached to the lobby of the Ritz-Carlton hotel. He moved closer to the doors, watching Jones order something then pull out his cell phone and make another call. After a short moment, the detective lowered his phone to the bar without saying anything.

Whomever he was trying to reach still wasn't picking up.

Andrew stepped away from the entrance and leaned against the building. He wished that he could just approach Jones and ask him why he wanted to kill his father. He wished that they could share their notes. He wanted to know what the mad scientist meant when he called Jones's father the King of Wall Street. What did those words mean? King of Wall Street.

All these questions with no answers. He needed someone he could talk with. He was tired of living his life in secret. Tired of always being alone.

Andrew felt his cell phone begin pulsating in his pocket. He pulled it out and turned away from the people on the sidewalk. He was stoned, and entertaining the idea that the caller might be Jones seemed funny in a depressing sort of way.

He unlocked the screen. It turned out that the call wasn't coming from Jones, but Avery Cooper instead, and she was requesting a video call. Andrew accepted the offer and watched Avery's image render on his phone. He could see her on her bed again, only this time she was removing her bra. He looked at her tits standing straight out from her chest like a pair of rockets. The weed was really good.

"Hi, you," she said in a cheery voice.

Andrew giggled. "Yes, I am," he said. "Hi, you, too."

CHAPTER 39

Matt took a first sip from his glass, savoring the bourbon as it warmed his throat and stomach. After setting the glass down, he watched the bartender mix three vodka martinis for two young women seated at the other end of the bar with an older man.

On most nights, Matt would have looked at the three of them and tried to guess what their story might be. Was the man their father? Their boss? Or just a sugar daddy?

On most nights he would have enjoyed sipping bourbon, collecting visual evidence, and trying to put a story together. But not tonight.

He let his eyes wander through the large room, taking in the three-story-high columns carved out of marble, the rich woods framing the windows, the sitting areas with tables surrounded by chairs and couches, and the vibrant color from the three massive water frames hanging on the wall behind the bar. It was the kind of lounge that only a five-star hotel could provide. And in spite of the size of the room and the ultra-high ceiling, the place was quiet and easy and just right.

The bartender walked over. "You okay?" he said.

"I'm good, thanks."

The man nodded and Matt watched him walk off. He had a certain confidence in the way he handled himself. Matt guessed that he was in his midfifties and had been serving drinks for a long time.

He took another sip of bourbon.

This was the right place to be tonight, and the bourbon seemed like the perfect drink, but he still couldn't let himself relax. He'd gone to the park to think things over, and he'd come to a few conclusions.

Rogers and Doyle would never be convinced. Matt could make his case with words or even hard evidence, and neither one of them would see what now appeared to be plain as day. In their way, Rogers and Doyle were every bit as bad as the three detectives Matt had outed in LA. Three LAPD homicide detectives who got caught up in a rush to judgment until their worlds came crashing down. Six weeks ago all three of them had been alive. But not now. Not ever again.

Matt let the memory pass, then got back on point as he thought about the Holloways' bodies. Even though their autopsies had been completed, he didn't think the medical examiner would release them until more results came back from the lab. The tox screens could be weeks off, but enough samples would have been harvested by the ME to deal with any result. Matt's best guess was that he wouldn't have more than a day or two to figure out which undertaker would be handling the bodies and managing the funeral service, and get someone to agree to put eyes in the room.

What he didn't understand about Rogers was that even if what Lester Snow had said this afternoon seemed hollow, any decent investigator had to assume that the undertaker's initial response was the truth. To be safe, Rogers should have erred on the side of too much knowledge.

Someone was messing with the corpses. It should have been considered true until proven false.

Instead, Rogers was concerned about the way things looked.

Matt took another sip of bourbon, picked up his cell phone, and tried Brown's number again. When his call bounced over to voice mail, he switched off the phone and looked up. The bartender was staring at the entrance with concern, his brow narrowing.

Matt turned and saw a young man breezing into the lounge and heading toward the bar. He noted the wool cap pulled over his head, the worn-out jeans, the unusually light-brown eyes that were glazed over and fixed on his cell phone. The man was bobbing his head and giggling at whatever he was watching on his phone.

Matt glanced at the bartender, then lowered his glass and turned back.

The man was headed in his direction. And the closer he got, the more his fixation on the phone came off like an act.

Matt watched him grab a stool two seats away and sit down, then knock on the bar as if it were someone's front door.

"Barkeep," he said in a loud, blusterous voice. "Barkeep."

The strong smell of reefer emanated from the man's body and clothing. It seemed obvious that he was wasted. That there was something false about his presence. That his act was some sort of play.

The bartender walked over and, from the way his face changed, smelled the weed, too. Matt watched his eyes get hard, like he was used to dealing with situations like this and had lost his patience.

"You need to get out of here, pal. You're in the wrong place."

The man with the wool cap glanced at Matt without meeting his eyes, then made an exaggerated face like he was hurt. "Oh, Barkeep. We were so close to having a good time."

He held out his cell phone and turned it so that Matt could see the display. It was a young blonde on a bed with her top off. She was getting out of her jeans and seemed horrified because Matt's face was now on her monitor.

The man giggled again, like he couldn't control himself. "My new bitch," he said. "You believe this shit?"

Matt could hear the girl squealing over the phone. Apparently, the bartender could as well.

In a flash, he jumped over the bar, grabbed the man with the wool cap by his coat, and ran him out of the lounge. When they spilled onto the sidewalk, and the bartender started back and entered the lounge, everyone clapped and cheered.

He shot Matt a look as he slipped behind the bar. "You get a whiff of that guy?"

Matt nodded. "Have you ever seen him before?"

"No," the bartender said. "But you never know these days. He could be staying in the penthouse, and I could be out of a job."

CHAPTER 40

Andrew Penchant looked at all the faces passing his way, then grabbed his cell phone and picked himself up off the sidewalk. The screen hadn't been damaged, the phone appeared to be working, but Avery Cooper had ended their video call.

Just the thought of her big bare tits got his dick hard.

He looked at the people moving by him on the sidewalk and felt the wrath surging through his chest. If he'd been a dog, he would've barked at them. Maybe sunk his teeth into them. How about a thigh, or some arrogant bitch's tight little ass? He was about to open the door and re-enter the bar, maybe give that shitty bartender a good long look at what act two would play like, but he saw something remarkable through the glass and stopped.

It was Ryan Day, the gossip reporter from *Get Buzzed*, hiding behind a plant in the lobby, trying to act casual while spying on Jones. He had his cell phone out and, from what Andrew could tell, was shooting "hidden camera" video for his show.

Goddamn it, this weed was good.

Andrew gave the reporter another look. Within a few seconds he was certain that he hadn't been hallucinating. Ryan Day was pretending to use his cell phone while shooting video of Matt Jones.

The idea of it, the audacity and overt rudeness, the in-your-face bullshit, took some of the sting off his anger. But as he thought about it, there was plenty of steam left. Ryan Day was a Hollywood sleazebag.

Andrew felt someone touch his shoulder and turned. A man was trying to come between him and the glass doors in order to enter the hotel. Andrew grabbed him by the shoulders and reeled him in nice and close so he could see who he was pushing around.

He gritted his teeth, his fangs, imagining that he was a dog again. "The main entrance is around the corner, asshole."

He could see fear welling up in the man's eyes. A wild overdose of terror. The man was trying to pull himself away, but Andrew's claws were digging into his coat. After several moments, he shoved the man away and let out another bark.

"Get the fuck out of here."

He watched the man run down the block and vanish around the corner. People on the sidewalk were staring at him and going out of their way to avoid him. As he pulled himself together, he thought about what had just happened and decided that this was probably a good time to leave.

He turned back to the glass doors for one last look. Someone was walking over to Day, a teenage girl and no doubt a fan of his TV show. The reporter seemed startled by the intrusion, his cover blown, but somehow managed to find a gracious smile for her. He let a bellhop snap a picture with the girl's cell phone—the two of them together— then shook her hand. After a wave and another smile, Ryan Day hurried out of the lobby.

Andrew stepped away from the doors and watched him exit the building. He had never been this close to anyone so famous, and he could feel his heart fluttering in his chest. As Day ignored him and started down the sidewalk, Andrew waited a few moments, then began following the celebrity reporter. Day had already returned his cell phone to his pocket, but Andrew gazed at the briefcase thrown over his shoulder and thought it looked a lot like candy.

The reporter was heading east, breezing down the sidewalk across the street from city hall. He seemed to be admiring the way the building was lighted for the holiday season. Macy's was on the corner, and Day started down Market Street, gazing at the window displays. For one brief moment, Andrew could hear a Christmas carol in his head. Some song that his boss had started playing over the PA system at the Walmart Supercenter two weeks before Halloween this year. Some old jazz singer who had probably been dead for half a century.

He could hear it—the music and the lyrics—and it felt like torture.

Andrew's mind surfaced. Day hadn't waited to cross Market Street at the corner. Instead, he'd scurried through heavy traffic in the middle of the block and was heading toward the Marriott Downtown hotel. Andrew knew that he'd have to risk being noticed. There was no way around it, and he stepped into the street. Ignoring the people blasting their horns, he rushed between the cars and caught up to Day before the reporter reached the hotel's rear entrance.

Day must have been in the zone because he never looked back and didn't seem to notice. Andrew entered the hotel and glanced around the lobby. It seemed obvious that there were too many people here to grab Day's briefcase and make a run for it. Instead, he followed the reporter across the room and into an elevator. He watched Day press the button to the nineteenth floor, then turn to him and ask what floor he'd like. But when the doors closed and Andrew said something like *nineteen sounds pretty good*, the expression on the reporter's face changed.

Their eyes had met, and for one brief moment, Day had been able to look inside.

Andrew smiled and turned away as if he'd lost interest in the man. He guessed that there would be a camera in the ceiling and another somewhere on the rear wall. He found Day's image in the mirror and saw the panic showing on the man's face. Andrew couldn't tell for sure, but it looked like the reporter might be trembling.

They reached the nineteenth floor. Andrew held the doors open with a pleasant smile and followed Day down the hall. They were passing suites, one after another until they reached the second door from the end.

And that's when Ryan Day suddenly turned around with a small canister in his hand. Andrew didn't get it at first, but then realized that Day was too nervous to work the sprayer. His hands were shaking and his fingers appeared soft and rubbery.

Andrew flashed another pleasant smile, then smashed Day in the face with his right fist. It was a hard, crushing blow, and the gossip reporter collapsed onto the floor like a tree hit by lightning. Andrew glared at Day's body, incensed by what the man had tried to do to him. And then he felt something deep inside him snap.

He started kicking Day in the face and in the stomach, over and over again until he finally gave the man one last shot in the ass. Blood was streaming down the reporter's face, his nose bent in such a way that it appeared broken. Andrew didn't give a shit. When he spotted the canister on the carpet beside the reporter's eyeglasses, he knelt down and snatched it up. It was pepper spray.

Andrew shook his head as he felt the fury exploding through his body. He grimaced and groaned and painted Day's face with coat after coat of pepper spray. Ignoring the toxic gas hovering in the air, he pried the reporter's jaw open and emptied the canister in his mouth. Satisfied that Day had been neutralized, Andrew grabbed the reporter's briefcase and ran down the hall back to the elevators.

His hair was soaked through with sweat. He was hyperventilating and couldn't catch his breath. The night had been so thrilling. So entertaining. He didn't understand why he couldn't stop shaking.

CHAPTER 41

Matt's cell phone was vibrating on the bar. He saw Kate Brown's name on the face and unlocked the phone.

"Sorry," she said. "I couldn't pick up."

"What's going on?"

"Doyle did a TV interview. I went with him to the studio. The story's getting bigger, Jones."

"Where are you?"

"Home," she said. "The studio's just a few blocks from my house. It's still early. You want to come over?"

"I'm at the Ritz. See you soon."

Matt cashed out his tab, left the bartender a decent tip, and walked out. His car was parked on a street close to Love Park, and within ten minutes he was knocking on Brown's front door. A moment passed, and then another. When the door finally opened, he saw Brown's sleepy smile and the gleam in her eye. She stepped aside to let him pass, then closed the door.

She was wearing a short robe. And it was open so that Matt could see her bare chest and lavender-colored panties.

"You got any bourbon?" he said.

Her smile broadened while she thought it over. "As a matter of fact, I do. You want it on the rocks or straight up?"

He could tell that she was playing a game. It felt good.

"You decide," he said.

"Okay. How about a kiss first?"

He moved closer and pulled her into his arms. He kissed her, and she kissed him back. He could feel his soul healing. He could see himself making a clean comeback.

"Let's get those drinks," she said.

"We need to talk about something."

"Okay."

He followed her into the kitchen. Brown kept a small bar in an antique wooden chest and grabbed the bourbon, then poured two glasses a couple of fingers high.

"Let's go straight up," she said.

"Sounds good to me," he said with his eyes on her. "I met with Dr. Baylor this afternoon."

She flinched. "You what?"

"We spoke this afternoon. We spent about a half hour together."

"At the Strattons' mansion."

He nodded. He could see the worry showing on her face.

"Why didn't you arrest him?"

"Because he had my gun."

"How did he know you were there?"

He shrugged. "He followed me."

She passed over a glass, then tapped his with her own. Matt took a short sip, then walked with her into the living room. He stood and watched her curl her legs beneath her body on the couch. Matt took another sip and decided to sit in the chair.

"He's not good for these murders, Kate. He's not even close to being good for them. I spoke with the undertaker today. Someone messed with the bodies while they were there. I told Rogers about it, not that

I spoke with Baylor again, just the undertaker. He couldn't care less. But I need your help. At some point the medical examiner will sign off on the Holloways and release their bodies. We need eyes on them, twenty-four seven. We need to know what's going on, and we need to be there when it does."

She seemed confused—too much information, too fast.

"You see where I'm going, Kate? We've got a chance to catch this guy. The real killer. We finally have something he wants. We've got a chance to end this, but we'll be on our own."

She still seemed troubled. "What do you mean, messed with the bodies, Jones?"

"The undertaker told me that he thought that the Strattons' bodies had been disturbed. When I pressed him on it, he recanted. I think he got scared and lied, hoping it would go away."

She paused a moment, her wheels turning. When she finally spoke, her voice was quieter.

"Come sit with me on the couch," she said.

Matt stepped around the coffee table and sat down close enough to put his arm around her. He watched her sip her drink and lean back.

"You should've seen Doyle tonight," she said. "The way he handled himself. The way he handled the news anchor."

"What are you saying?"

She turned and gazed at him for a long time. "The story broke open tonight, Jones. With the funeral today, and the Holloways being murdered a week after the Strattons, it's a bigger story now. A story that feels like it has a life of its own."

CHAPTER 42

Andrew Penchant closed his bedroom door, ripped open Ryan Day's briefcase, and dumped the contents on his worktable.

He spread the file folders out and stared at them. They were paper files, not digital, and this surprised him. He didn't find a laptop in the briefcase. And when he searched through the pockets, he didn't see a calendar, an appointment book, or even an address book.

Just a pair of shades, a pack of breath mints, and a small makeup kit.

Day must have done most of his business with his cell phone and a computer tucked away in his hotel room. Andrew wondered why he hadn't taken a moment to search for the gossip reporter's cell phone. How much time would it have taken to frisk the idiot and grab his phone?

He let the moment play in his head. He could see himself punching the man and kicking him after he went down. He could remember seeing all the blood spewing out of Day's broken nose, then running down to the elevator. He liked seeing the blood. He liked the rush. But he'd had trouble catching his breath, and he didn't understand why his perspiration was so profuse, or why he couldn't stop shaking. It may have been the cloud of pepper spray hovering in the stagnant air, but he thought it might be more than that.

Andrew shook off the memory, picked up the file folders, and checked the tabs. There were only three. One for the Strattons, another for the Holloways, and a third file dedicated to LAPD Detective Matt Jones.

He grabbed Ryan Day's file on Jones, sat down in his desk chair, and hit the switch on his surge protector, powering up his laptop, the lights, and the TV all at once. After checking the time, he muted the sound on the TV and started reading the file.

It became clear from the dates that Ryan Day had been working on the story of Matt Jones's life since the detective was shot six weeks ago. He was trying to solve the crime. He was searching for a motive to the shooting, as well as the identity of the man Jones had killed at the scene. Along the way, the gossip reporter sensed something was wrong with Jones's background information and began digging.

Jones shared his full name with three people of interest, but only one stood out. Andrew remembered overhearing the mad scientist call Matt's father the King of Wall Street. According to Day's file, he agreed with Dr. Baylor and had narrowed down his search to a power broker from New York City by the name of M. Trevor Jones. Day had put together side-by-side photographs of the detective with the banker. The likeness was indisputable, yet the banker claimed that he only had two children and both still lived with him and his wife at home.

Andrew lowered the file to his worktable and settled back in the chair as he considered what he'd just read.

Jones was the son of one of the wealthiest men on earth. He could have lived a good life in a good world, but his father had stolen his identity from him when he wouldn't even admit that the detective was his son.

If Jones needed a reason to murder his father, that sounded like a good one. But what if it worked in reverse as well? What if the things he'd heard Dr. Baylor say were true? What if Jones's father wanted to keep his past buried, and was trying to kill his own son?

Andrew tossed it over as he thought about his own father. The pervert who had raped his mother when she was only fourteen. The man-devil whom he shared half his biological life with. He wondered if his father had ever thought about killing *him*. He wondered if a shot might not ring out when he least expected it. He could see himself falling to the ground. He could see himself bleeding out and dying like an animal at the hands of a child molester.

This had to be the reason why Jones wanted to kill his father. M. Trevor Jones was a rich man living in a rich land and needed to be punished. The King of Wall Street needed to be stopped.

It occurred to Andrew that he and Jones were brothers after all.

He heard his mother tap on his bedroom door, and he pricked up his ears. She didn't say anything, and after several moments, he heard her bedroom door close.

That feeling in his stomach was back. All the churning. He dug the half-smoked joint out of his pocket. Then he lit up, took a hit, and held his breath until he started coughing. He heard his mother turn on the shower, and took a second hit. The eleven o'clock news had started on TV, but there was no mention of finding the gossip reporter on the nineteenth floor outside his hotel room.

Andrew stood up and steadied himself against the worktable, the reefer storming his brain all at once. He sensed from the way the walls of his room appeared to blow out like sheets on a clothesline that the weed had been cut with something. When he had smoked opiated hash a few months ago, he experienced the same kind of hallucinations. Still, he couldn't figure out how opium could possibly be blended with reefer. It had to be something else.

He listened to the shower running and imagined his mother standing beneath the warm spill. He thought about her body, and the idea that she was still so young. Still so hot in that Northeast Philly kind of way.

Andrew heard another tap and was surprised when the door opened. His mother walked in, dressed in a robe that was loosely tied around her waist and didn't hide much skin.

"I'm feeling lonely tonight," she said in a quiet voice. "I could use a little TLC, honey."

He didn't say anything. His mother's eyes were burning, and she looked hungry again.

"I need company," she went on. "I need to be with someone right now."

He watched her gaze rise from his crotch to his face.

"I hate you, Mother. I hate everything about you."

"I know you do," she said. "I've hated you since before you were even born. But that doesn't mean that we can't be friends tonight."

She took him by the hand and led him into her bedroom. The battery-powered candles were burning, the bed turned down. He could feel her undressing him as if he had become a little boy again. He watched her toss his shirt on the chair and unzip his jeans as if he were still a child.

The weed had to be cut with something. Everything about his mother's body seemed fresh and new, like just maybe she wasn't his mother at all. Like tonight would be easier than ever to pretend. She smiled at him as she helped him out of his jeans.

"That's my boy," she said. "Mommy's so proud of you."

CHAPTER 43

Matt heard something in the hallway and peered through the peephole while sipping his second mug of coffee of the day. The door was open to the apartment next door. A man was on his hands and knees collecting items he'd dropped and returning them to a canvas tote bag. The distance was too great, the lens too scratched, and Matt couldn't tell what he was tossing into the bag.

Curiously, this was someone new. Not the blond man in his late twenties or early thirties with a knapsack thrown over his shoulder, and not the middle-aged woman in the business suit who claimed she didn't live here and was just dropping something off. Instead, this appeared to be a man of slight build in his midforties who wore eyeglasses and had shaved his head. But even more, once he got everything picked up, he closed the door to the apartment and locked it with a key. The man with blond hair had used a key as well.

Matt realized that if he pulled his eye away right now, the man might notice the peephole change from dark to light, so he watched until the elevator arrived. When the man vanished inside and he heard the doors close, he turned away and took another sip of coffee.

It was early. He couldn't seem to sleep anymore. He'd left Brown's place just after one in the morning. When he finally got in bed, he fell asleep quickly, but woke up an hour later. He fell asleep again, then woke up an hour after that. By 5:30 a.m., getting back to sleep seemed like a long shot, so he showered and shaved and got dressed.

The TV was on in the living room, and a journalist was reporting from the Middle East. We'd already been at war for sixteen years, and it didn't sound like anyone in the White House or on Capitol Hill had a plan to bring the troops home very soon. Matt didn't care for politicians or their views about much these days. But more specifically, he didn't like to hear them talk about war. Most of them had no idea what it was like to be at war. They never served and they possessed no knowledge or experience. Instead, they'd show up at hospitals with the cameras rolling, flash a phony smile, pretend to be concerned, and say thank you. After more than sixteen years, Matt didn't think hearing a politician say *thank you* was good enough. Not nearly good enough.

He stopped listening and tried to let his frustration subside as he topped off his coffee. And then the story on the news changed. The video feed switched from Kabul to Philadelphia.

Matt walked into the living room.

According to a reporter from CBS News, Ryan Day, the celebrity gossip reporter and host of the popular TV show *Get Buzzed*, had been attacked and robbed at his hotel in Philadelphia last night. Details were still sketchy, but detectives from the Philadelphia Police Department's Major Crimes Section had gone through video from the hotel's security system overnight. Several shots had been pulled of someone they described as a person of extreme interest.

Matt moved closer to the TV for a better look. The first shot captured a man entering the hotel and following Day through the lobby. A second shot covered Day in the elevator with the same man. Although it was a close-up shot, detectives believed that the suspect had been aware of the camera's location and deliberately kept his head down. But the third shot appeared to be the most telling. The suspect had returned to the lobby and was rushing toward the Market Street entrance with Ryan Day's briefcase slung over his shoulder.

Matt didn't need three video shots to know what was going on. All he needed to see was a single image of the wool cap pulled over the man's head.

He set his coffee mug down on the table and waited for the reporter to end his piece, hoping that he was at the hospital and not the hotel. When they cut back to a live shot, the reporter was standing in front of the emergency room. Matt grabbed his jacket and scarf. The EMTs had taken Day to Jefferson University Hospital over on Tenth Street.

Within fifteen minutes Matt had parked his car in the garage across the street and badged his way through security. The receptionist at the front desk was an elderly woman who came off like a volunteer and pointed out that visiting hours wouldn't begin for two hours. When Matt identified himself as a deputy US marshal, she seemed more than pleased to help. Once Matt hit the elevators, he was free and clear.

Day's room was at the end of the hallway on the right. But once he reached the door, he caught a glimpse of the patient and thought he'd been given the wrong room number. Someone he couldn't see was in the room as well, a woman, and she was saying something. Matt moved to the other side of the door and realized that it was a doctor. She was giving her patient an update on his condition.

Matt looked back at the man in the bed and tried to see through the gauze wrapped around his skull, the purple bruises tattooing his entire face, the swollen cheeks, and the fresh stitching that ran from the corner of his upper lip to the base of his nose. When he noticed the pair of wire-rimmed glasses on the tray, his eyes flicked back to the patient's face.

It had to be Ryan Day. Ryan Day after a brutal beating.

Matt took a deep breath and exhaled. He might not have a name, but he knew that the man with the wool cap pulled over his head was more than a person of interest. He was certain of it now.

A memory surfaced. It happened yesterday morning while he had been on his way to the Strattons' funeral. He had been walking from his apartment to the parking garage when he turned and saw a man wearing dark shades waiting for the light to change. The man had blond cornrows. Last night, the man at the bar had been wearing a wool cap over his hair and had avoided eye contact.

They were the same man. They had to be the same man.

Matt guessed that the morning encounter had something to do with curiosity. But somehow the man with blond cornrows had skipped ahead and, for reasons unknown, returned to the death house in Radnor that afternoon. Even worse, the intruder had to have overheard his conversation with Dr. Baylor. He'd made a discovery, and learned that they had some idea of who he was. Some understanding of his background and plight.

He had overheard Matt talking to Dr. Baylor and realized that they had a profile. They were looking for him now.

It was the only explanation that made sense. The man with blond cornrows had been following Matt since he left the Strattons' mansion because he had to keep tabs in order to stay safe. He had to keep tabs on Matt because he'd become the target of the hunt.

He was no longer invisible. No longer on his own. And he needed information. Knowledge. He needed to know what they knew. He needed Ryan Day's briefcase.

Matt heard the woman begin speaking again and took a step closer to listen. According to the doctor, Day was a lucky man. The amount of pepper spray he'd endured could have killed him all by itself. The fact that her examination found no internal bleeding had to be considered remarkable. While he might be experiencing a great deal of pain, other than a broken nose, his injuries were limited to soft tissue, and she predicted that his recovery would be quick and certain.

Matt stepped over to the water fountain and waited until the doctor left. He watched her walk down the hall. She was Asian, probably in her late thirties, and appeared exceedingly gentle and easy to look at. When she vanished around the corner, Matt slipped into Day's room.

Day gave him an even, almost helpless look. Matt moved closer, taking his hand as the reporter began weeping in silence. After several moments, Day pulled himself together.

"What are you doing here?" he said in a weak voice.

"I saw it on the news this morning. I overheard your doctor. She said you'll be okay, but I've gotta tell you, Day. I wouldn't spend too much time in front of a mirror. You really look like shit."

Day started laughing, raising his hand and mouthing the words *Stop, it hurts.*

"The doctor called you lucky," Matt said.

"Lucky that I don't remember much, and somehow he didn't knock out any teeth. What are you doing here?"

"How did you put it at the café?"

Day tossed it over, then found the memory. "We could help each other."

"And I owe you one for giving me my mother's real name."

Matt could see the change in Day's eyes—the glint sharpening like he was beginning to come back to life. Day checked the door, then turned back to Matt.

"What's going on?"

"The guy with the wool cap. The guy who did this to you."

Day nodded. "Yeah," he said. "Who is he?"

"The short answer is that he was following me last night, and I missed it. I was having a drink at another hotel, and he walked in and got himself tossed out. Somehow he picked up on you."

Day shut his eyes for a moment. "The Ritz. I was in the lobby."

"Doing what?"

He shook his head and sighed. "The usual," he whispered. "I didn't see him either. But when he stepped into the elevator, Jones, one look and I knew I was in trouble."

A nurse walked into the room, surprised to find someone with her patient. "Visiting hours don't start for another two hours," she said. "Who are you?"

"His priest. I just need a few minutes."

She crossed her arms over her chest like a traffic cop. "You don't look like a priest."

"Everybody says that. I'll be out in a few minutes."

She thought it over for a while. Then without a word she walked out.

Matt glanced out the window at the city, then turned back and leaned against the sill. "What did he get?"

"What?"

"What was in your briefcase?"

Day shook his head. "Not much. When I'm done for the day, my laptop and everything else gets locked up in the hotel safe. I can't afford to leave anything like that in my room."

"But there was something in your briefcase," Matt said.

"Files. Hard copies. Research."

"Research on who?"

"The Strattons, the Holloways."

"Who else?"

Day paused and suddenly appeared uneasy, then met his gaze. "You," he said finally.

A moment passed, and it had a corrosive burn to it. Matt pushed a piece of nicotine gum through the foil and slid it against his cheek.

"How much about me?"

"Not a lot," Day said. "Side-by-side pictures of you and the man you won't admit is your father. A little background on him, but not much detail. Like I said, I keep everything on my computer. I had those files with me because you got me going the other day and I wanted to take another look."

Matt didn't say anything. He could feel the nicotine beginning to light up his body. His mind was becoming clearer, sharper. He saw Day staring at him as he adjusted his pillow. Then the reporter pushed the tray away and finally spoke.

"You know what, Jones?"

Matt nodded, but didn't say anything.

"A few minutes ago I asked you who he was. You gave me the short answer and said that he followed you last night. I've been a reporter for a long time, Jones. A real long time. And so I'm gonna make a wild guess that the long answer has something to do with *why* he was following you."

Matt gave Day a hard look, weighing how much it might cost him if he gave the gossip reporter a small piece of the truth.

CHAPTER 44

Matt entered the Crisis Room and did a double take as he walked over to his desk and glanced at Brown. The entire floor had been turned into a movie set. Two chairs were positioned in the center using the video wall as a background. Three different photographs of Dr. Baylor were up on the huge monitors. In front of the chairs were a pair of digital video cameras on tripods. Banks of movie lights on stands flanked the cameras and chairs on both sides as a handful of video and lighting techs made adjustments.

Matt turned to Brown. "What's going on?"

"Doyle's doing a series of interviews. He wants to talk to you."

She didn't take her eyes off her laptop as she spoke. It seemed odd.

"Where is he?"

"In the conference room, but don't bother him right now. A girl's doing his makeup."

She still hadn't glanced his way. Matt turned toward the conference room, but his view was blocked by a grip rigging a four-by-eight sheet of white foam core to a light stand. When the man finished up and walked the foam core onto the set, Matt got a look at the federal prosecutor. He was seated at the conference table while a young woman applied makeup and Rogers watched. Doyle seemed to be enjoying the attention and looked like he was in heaven. All three were laughing.

Something about seeing Doyle with his tail up and a big grin on his face knocked Matt down. He sat at his desk, eyeing the cameras and chairs and a video wall that pointed to Dr. Baylor and only Dr. Baylor.

Case closed.

Why did the man with blond cornrows make a return visit to the Strattons' mansion? What was the real killer doing in the death house?

That's all that really mattered, yet Matt had difficulty keeping his mind focused while a federal prosecutor and a special agent with the FBI flew at light speed into the void. Eventually they'd crash and burn, and like most weasels, run for cover by blaming somebody else.

It didn't take a degree in screenwriting to understand that, most likely, Matt would be playing the role of *somebody else.*

Matt settled back in his chair to watch. He had given Ryan Day an unofficial rough sketch of what he was thinking and underlined the possibility that the FBI's investigation was on the wrong track. He mentioned that Dr. Westbrook had been the profiler who helped hunt down the ET killer, Eddie Trisco, in Philadelphia fifteen years ago and that an alternate profile of the man who murdered the Strattons and Holloways had never been made public or even discussed. When Day asked why, Matt told him: the second profile pointed to someone younger than Dr. Baylor, someone who had been sexually abused. While Matt had no information on the man who attacked Day in the hotel, no knowledge of his background, he pointed out that there was only one connection between Day and himself. Only one line could be drawn from Matt to the celebrity reporter from *Get Buzzed*—a single thread that joined both of them to the mass killings of two families on the Main Line.

Matt heard Doyle call out his name and turned to the conference room. The federal prosecutor was marching across the floor with Rogers, the makeup artist, and a man Matt guessed was the producer in tow. Matt measured them as they gathered around his desk and

Brown's. Doyle wasn't laughing anymore. But even worse, the man had an audience.

"Listen here, Jones," he said in a voice loud enough and self-righteous enough to be heard in a courtroom. "Brown told me about your meeting yesterday at the Strattons'. When all this is over, we need to talk."

Matt searched for a calm voice and found one. "With all due respect, sir, don't do these interviews. You're making a mistake. A big one."

The silence was stunning. The look on Doyle's face worth whatever it might have cost.

The producer stepped closer, hitting Matt with a barrage of questions. "Are you Matt Jones?" he was saying. "Are you the detective from LA? Is there a problem here? Would you sit down with us after we interview the prosecutor?"

Doyle's face had turned a bright red in spite of his makeup. And that vein in his neck had popped out again and looked like it might explode. When he finally spoke, his voice was quiet and dead and hard as stone.

"The only one Detective Jones will be speaking with is me, and that's an order."

The producer didn't get the vibe in the room and still seemed cheery and excited. "But it would be great," he said. "Jones is the key to this story."

The producer's words settled into the room. No one said anything for a while. Matt stood up. After glancing at Rogers and ignoring his venom, he turned back to Doyle. He wanted Doyle to do the right thing. He didn't want to watch the prosecutor do something that he would never be able to recover from.

Matt met his eyes. "You're making a mistake, sir. Don't do this."

The words bounced off Doyle's body armor, and he appeared to be seething and unable to think straight.

"Get out," he said finally. "But make damn sure you're back by one, Jones. Make damn sure you're back by one."

Doyle stormed off, heading for the conference room. Matt checked on Brown, realized that she was horrified, and headed for the door. As he ran down the hall, he could feel her giving chase. He hit the lobby and grabbed an open elevator. Just as the doors snapped shut, he heard her call out his name.

He didn't want to talk to her. He needed a break. He needed to settle down.

The doors opened in the garage, and he breezed past security. As he hustled toward his car, he turned and saw Brown running toward him. He clicked open the locks, but not before Brown reached him. He turned and took a moment to size her up and reel in his emotions.

"What's going on, Kate? Why the hell did you tell Doyle about Baylor?"

She shook her head, trying to catch her breath. "I had to, Jones. This is too big a case. You told me that you spent a half hour with Baylor. Doyle deserves to know what was said."

"What part of 'Baylor didn't do it' don't you get, Kate? It's a big case no matter who gets indicted."

She gave him a nervous, uneasy look. Matt couldn't believe how far down the rabbit hole these people were.

"You're ruining your career," she said. "You're not a team player, Jones."

"I guess it depends on the team you're playing for."

Her faced hardened. "You screw up here, and you'll never bounce back," she said. "Doyle's going places."

Matt stared at her for a long time.

Doyle's going places.

He couldn't believe that she'd said it. But even more, he couldn't believe that she could think it. He couldn't believe how far away she was from his first impression of her. It almost seemed like the water these people were drinking had become tainted with lead.

Matt glanced at his car and noticed a copy of the *Daily News* he'd picked up at the hospital. A large photo of the man with the wool cap was on the front page—a wide, blurry shot taken from a security camera in the lobby—along with the story of a celebrity gossip reporter who had been beaten and robbed in a Center City hotel last night. Matt yanked the door open, grabbed the paper, and pushed it in Brown's face.

"Did you see this in the paper this morning, Kate? It was on TV as well. It's the story of the day. Do you have any interest in it? Do you know anything about it?"

She gazed at the newspaper, but apparently didn't like his tone of voice and remained silent.

"How about Doyle?" Matt went on. "He's going places. You think he knows anything about it? Look at the goddamn picture."

She raised her hands to her face and appeared to shudder. "Why are you taking this so personally?"

He let out a sarcastic laugh that faded sharply and shook his head. "Why am I taking this so personally?" He paused a moment, reflecting. "A reporter was beaten up and robbed last night. Are you following the story or not, Kate?"

"No," she said. "Why should I?"

Matt could feel a river of pain flowing through his body. He stabbed the photo with his index finger. He looked at her in utter disbelief and grimaced. He'd lost his patience and was drowning in disappointment.

"Because he's the one, Kate. He's the killer. He's the one who murdered the Strattons. He's the one who killed the Holloways. Now go upstairs and stick your head up Doyle's ass. The two of you deserve each other. You're going places, all right. The first stop's a town called *nowhere*."

She didn't move, and she didn't say anything.

He tossed the newspaper into the car, then climbed in behind the wheel. When the engine flooded and the Crown Vic wouldn't start, he punched the dashboard with his fists and swore. He was enraged and incensed and electrified with fury. The engine finally lit up, and he could hear the tires screeching on the concrete floor as he sped off. When he hit the exit ramp and checked the rearview mirror, Kate Brown was still standing there. She hadn't moved. He punched the dashboard again, then hit the street and sped off.

CHAPTER 45

Andrew Penchant unlocked the front door, walked into the kitchen, and found Reggie Cook sitting at the breakfast table in his boxer shorts. He had another one of those shit-eating, I-just-fucked-your-mother kind of grins seared onto his stupid face. And he was sipping a glass of Southern Comfort on the rocks at 11:00 a.m., the bottle on the table.

"What are you doing home this early?" Cook asked, still grinning. "It's not even lunchtime."

Andrew didn't say anything, noting the man's body hair on his chest and back, even his arms and legs. The hair was so thick that it looked more like fur—the kind of fur you might find on a hoofed animal.

He crossed the room, digging two steaks and a bag of frozen french fries out of his jacket pocket and tossing them into the refrigerator and freezer. Cook smacked his hand on the table and laughed.

"Thanks for bringing home dinner, devil child. But what are you gonna eat? I'm staying over tonight. I'm bedding down with Mommy."

Andrew tried to bury the anxious feeling in his gut. He tried to override it, but he could feel the slob's eyes on him. After a few moments, he turned and gave his mother's hairy lover a careful look.

"Where's your car?" he said. "I didn't see it in the driveway."

"I took the bus, devil child. You really need to do something about your eyes, kid."

"What's wrong with my eyes?"

"They're weird, just like you're weird. You're an oddball. A freak of nature. A rape baby born with horns and a tail."

"I don't have to talk to you. And I don't have to listen to you either."

Cook winked at him and grinned again. "I know your secret, devil child. I know what you do with your mother. You're a pervert, kid. That's why she called and wanted me to come over. That's why she wants me to stay. I did her three times this morning. I did her hard. Once in a while she needs to know what it's like to get laid by a real man, and not her fucked-up little boy. I'll bet you don't even have a cock, oddball. Sounds to me like your little-boy noodle gets lost in there, and you've got no idea what to even do."

He slapped the table again, laughing so hard that he began coughing when he took a sip of Southern Comfort from his glass.

Andrew felt the dam break inside his head, the rush of anger flooding over the banks and out of control. He started shaking and bolted out of the room. He could hear Cook taunting him and insulting him as he fled upstairs to his bedroom. He couldn't take it anymore. He couldn't hold it all in.

He needed it to be over. He needed it to end.

He reached under the bed for his Glock 22, a .40 caliber semiautomatic that carried fifteen rounds in the mag. The pistol was lighter than a .45, but still packed a heavyweight punch. Andrew liked the way it felt in his hand. He also really liked the way it scared people when he turned his G-22 into *Dirty Diane*.

He slid the top drawer open beneath his worktable, fingered through a tray of spare change and paper clips until he found the adapter and screwed it onto the muzzle of his pistol. It was a small round metal disk he'd bought from a gun manufacturer on the Internet that allowed him to attach an STP oil filter to the barrel of his handgun. For seventy-five dollars plus ten dollars shipping, and another two hundred dollars to register the adapter with the Bureau of Alcohol, Tobacco, Firearms, and Explosives, it all seemed worth it. His G-22 no longer made any noise when he fired the weapon. His .40 caliber semiautomatic was transformed into Dirty Diane, and when she sang, the only words she knew were click, click, click.

Andrew opened his closet, grabbed a fresh oil filter—the one he'd used at the Holloways' had caught fire—and screwed it onto the adapter. It wasn't easy, because of all the raw energy coursing through his being. He could feel himself coming apart at the seams, his fingers trembling. But after a couple of tries, he felt the oil filter mate with his pistol and reached for his spy glasses. He switched on the wireless camera set in the frames. Fitting them carefully over his ears and nose, he ran out of the room.

This was another moment worth recording for later viewing. Another memorable moment like so many he had experienced in recent weeks.

Reggie Cook was still sitting at the breakfast table, drinking Southern Comfort at just after eleven in the morning. Still wearing the scent of his mother's perfume on his hairy skin.

Andrew raised the pistol, surprised that the shaking had nearly vanished and his hands were almost steady. He laughed when Cook looked at him the way they all had looked at him. The confusion on their faces as they gazed at the oil filter, and then the sudden shock of dread when they spotted the gun and figured out what was really going on. Andrew was glad that he'd decided to record the moment. He never wanted to forget the look on Reggie Cook's face. Never ever.

Reggie's eyes locked on the bright-blue oil filter. Dirty Diane.

"Goddamn it, you're weird, kid. What the fuck is that?"

Andrew waited a beat for the dread to hit. Then he pulled the trigger twice and slammed Reggie with a center shot to the forehead, and a through-and-through in the hairy slob's neck. After the two clicks,

Reggie's head snapped back, then bounced forward, smashing against the breakfast table. Andrew watched Reggie flop onto the floor like a dead fish. Then he pushed the body over with his foot and double-checked the gunshot wounds. No question about it, Reggie Cook was a corpse.

Andrew ran upstairs, his mind finding a narrow lane through the jumbled fog and darkness. He found his mother sleeping in bed. Moving closer, he tried to pull himself together. He was hyperventilating now—seeing himself from a distance—in the moment, and dream walking again.

He lifted the sheet away and knelt down to gaze at his mother's naked body. Her smooth legs and round hips, her trimmed pussy and full tits. He looked at her face in wonder. Something happened in the moment. Something even better than the fear showing on Reggie Cook's face. He began to forget about his mother's body, and looked at her face the way a son would. The way he'd never looked at her before. He listened to her light breathing. She seemed so peaceful. So beautiful in a cheap sort of way.

He raised the pistol to her chest, heard a light click, and felt the blood spray him in the face. After a few moments, he stood up and gave her another long look.

She was gone finally. No more Mommy. He was free.

CHAPTER 46

Why did the man with blond cornrows make a return visit to the Strattons'
mansion?

What was the real killer doing in the death house?

Matt had arrived at the mansion on County Line Road about an
hour ago. He'd scoured the third floor, avoiding the fingerprint powder
as best he could but searching through every closet and examining the
contents of every drawer. He didn't sense that anything was wrong until
he reached Kaylee's room and realized that the seventeen-year-old girl
didn't seem to have any underwear. He couldn't find a single bra or
panty. While it may have been true that she went to boarding school
and had only returned for the holidays, Matt couldn't believe that she
hadn't packed clothing for the trip.

He sat down on her bed to think it over. It seemed bizarre. He
could feel the answer in his gut, but didn't want to rush it, didn't want
to go there until he made sure.

After a few moments, he got up and went through the girl's dresser
again. The second drawer seemed thin; a few tank tops and a handful
of tees. Based on the contents of the remaining three drawers, if this

had been Matt's room at seventeen, his underwear would have been in the second.

He walked over to the closet and dumped the contents of Kaylee's hamper onto the floor. Sorting through the pile, he found two changes of clothing. Two pairs of jeans, a top, and a pair of socks, but not a single bra or panty.

Matt headed downstairs, ignoring the smell of rotten blood and stepping into the master bedroom. Both Jim and Tammy Stratton had separate dressing rooms. Matt found Tammy's and went through her chest of drawers. When he didn't find any lingerie at all, he dumped her hamper on the floor and sorted through the pile of clothing. Within a matter of seconds, he stepped out of the dressing room, sat down on the bed, and gazed at the room.

The killer had come back for trophies.

Like Dr. Westbrook's alternate profile, like Dr. Baylor had said himself, they were looking for a man who had been sexually abused for a long time. He was more than just a mass killer. He was a sexual deviant who had come back for the lingerie.

Matt wondered why the killer hadn't collected his trophies and taken them with him on the night of the murders. Why risk exposure by making a return visit to a high-profile crime scene?

He let the thought go. He had this uneasy feeling in his stomach. Something was wrong in here, and he got off the bed and studied the room. When he turned back to the bed, he noticed the rumpled-up spread. The pillows were mussed as well.

He pulled the spread down and gazed at an unmade bed.

The answer to his questions now seemed obvious. The killer had come back for the lingerie, but he wanted to spend time here as well. He wanted to savor the moment. He had slept in their bed.

Matt suddenly became aware of the bedside table. Something seemed out of place here as well, but he couldn't put his finger on it.

He stepped closer, taking an inventory of the objects before him. A modern lamp, an e-book reader, a charging cable for either a cell phone or a tablet, a clock radio, and then, finally, the family portrait. It was the photograph that didn't belong here. As Matt took a second look, it was the frame the picture had been set in that didn't fit.

Matt picked up the picture frame and examined it carefully. It was a cheap frame. A frame molded out of plastic. Frosty the Snowman was depicted in the upper-left corner. Centered beside Frosty were the words "Happy Holidays to You." At the bottom it just said "Frosty the Snowman."

Matt gazed at the furniture in the bedroom. On the fireplace mantel he found several family photographs set in sterling silver frames.

He looked back at the cheap plastic frame in his hands. The photograph was a family portrait. The Strattons were posed before a Christmas tree that had been decorated with lights and ornaments. Matt didn't remember seeing a Christmas tree in the mansion. As he thought it over, he didn't remember seeing any holiday decorations anywhere at all.

His eyes flicked back to the photograph. Why did it seem so familiar? So overwhelmingly familiar. It almost felt as if he had been standing in the room when the picture was snapped. He took another look at the Strattons' faces, the gold wall in the background.

And then everything went black. In a split second everything began spinning. He staggered over to the bed. He needed to sit down. He needed to catch his breath.

He saw Dr. Baylor enter the room and give him an odd look.

"What is it?" the doctor said. "What's happened? Are you all right?"

"The killer," Matt said in a winded voice. "He was the one in the mansion. He overheard us talking. He knows we're on to him."

"That's not why you look so pale. Your hands are shaking."

"I know," he said. "I know. Take a look at this photograph, but don't touch it."

Matt set the picture frame on the fireplace mantel, took a deep breath, and exhaled. Steadying himself, he crossed the room and sat on the wide windowsill as he checked his vinyl gloves.

Baylor shrugged, still eyeing the photograph. "I don't get it."

"Take another look."

As Matt watched the doctor study the image, he brought him up to speed on his confrontation at the hotel bar and the brutal beating and robbery that Ryan Day had endured. He described the man with blond cornrows as best he could and discussed his fascination for lingerie. Along the way he mentioned Ken Doyle's series of TV interviews with the media today and the federal prosecutor's inability to see past his own nose.

It occurred to Matt that the doctor had entered the room without the Glock 17 in his hand. Baylor must have seen him checking him out and read his mind.

"It's in my pocket," the doctor said. "Don't get any funny ideas, Matthew. And you'll have to give me a hint with this photograph."

Matt walked over and pointed at the Strattons' faces. "You ready?" he said.

"Of course."

Matt nodded. "They're dead."

"What?"

"The photograph was taken at the Lester Snow Funeral Home. That's the Christmas tree in one of the reception rooms. Everyone in the picture is dead."

Matt watched Baylor take the shock as his words settled into the room, the idea astounding. He could still feel the chills tingling up his spine, the back of his neck ice-cold.

The Strattons' bodies had been disturbed. Played with. Photographed.

That was the killer's real trophy.

Baylor eyed the picture more closely. "I see it now," he said in an excited voice. "He's processed the image, and done something to make their eyes seem more alive. Now we know why he shot them in the chest. He's trying to preserve their faces for the photograph. It's important to him."

"Why do you think he brought it here and placed it on the table? Why not keep it by his own bed?"

"It's unprecedented," the doctor said. "The way his mind works."

Matt picked up the picture frame and gave the photograph another look. "We already know that he wants to be part of this world. He's putting a piece of himself here because he likes it."

Baylor nodded. "And he doesn't care if anyone notices or not. It's about him knowing that the portrait he took of the people he killed sits right beside their bed. That the picture he took of the people he murdered is right in front of the police and the FBI and they're never going to figure it out. They're never going to catch him. I'll bet you're right, Matthew. I'll bet he keeps a copy by his own bed as well."

CHAPTER 47

The lot was full at the Lester Snow Funeral Home. Matt pulled behind the building and parked by the loading dock. He tried the back door. When he found it locked, he hustled past the parked cars and entered through the main entrance. He had the Strattons' family portrait with him, only now it was inside a Ziploc freezer bag that he'd taken from their kitchen.

He stepped into the lobby and could hear a recording of the Beach Boys' "Good Vibrations" coming from one of the large reception rooms down the hall. An easel was here with a poster that included a photograph of the deceased during better days. On the table Matt saw a copy of the obituary page from the *Philadelphia Inquirer*. When he flipped it over, he stopped and eyed the section underneath very carefully.

It was the society page.

A moment passed, whatever was on his mind slipping away before he could snatch it up. He thought that the idea might have been important, and this concerned him. He started down the hallway, walking in the direction of the music. When he found the room with the Christmas tree empty, he stepped down to the next doorway and peeked inside.

It was another viewing with forty to fifty people in the seats. The coffin that looked like a golf cart had been replaced with a casket designed to mimic a surfboard. Sand had been spread on the stage with a large picture of Venice Beach in Los Angeles projected on the far wall. The man in the surfboard casket appeared ravaged, too young to die and very difficult to look at.

Matt felt someone tug on his arm.

"What are you doing here?" the undertaker whispered.

Matt turned and met his gaze. "We need to talk."

"But I'm busy right now."

"I am, too, Mr. Snow. We can talk in the next room, or we can go to my place. It's your choice."

Matt was pointing at the room with the Christmas tree. The undertaker shook his head, but finally led the way. This time, Matt closed the door.

"What is it?" the undertaker said impatiently. "Why are you here?"

Matt walked between the rows of folding chairs and turned. "Why don't you have a seat?"

"I want to get back to our service."

"You heard me, Mr. Snow. Take a seat."

The undertaker shuddered in protest, but finally sat down. Matt handed him the picture frame in the plastic bag.

"What is it?" Snow said.

"Take a look."

His eyes met the photograph and immediately bounced back. "It's the Strattons," he said without adding *so what?*, though it seemed implied.

Matt frowned. The undertaker wasn't going to make it easy. When the man tried to hand over the picture frame, Matt pushed it back.

"Take another look, Mr. Snow. A long look. Your fate depends on it."

"What's the problem?"

"I want you to explain to me how this photograph was taken."

"I have no idea, Detective."

"But you agree that the photograph was taken in this room. This is your Christmas tree. The fireplace and the color of the walls in the background match."

The undertaker shrugged. "I don't understand."

Matt took a step closer. He was losing his patience.

"Of course you understand, Mr. Snow. Their bodies were disturbed—you said it yourself. Someone brought the corpses in here and snapped a picture. They're dead, and you know they're dead. They're wearing the same clothes they were buried in. You need to explain yourself, sir. Believe me. If you don't tell me what's going on, I'll bring your world down."

The undertaker brushed his white hair back with his hands and lowered his eyes to the carpet. He'd suddenly become anxious and upset.

"I'll lose my business," he said in a faint voice. "I'll lose everything."

Matt pulled a chair out from the row and positioned it so that he could face the undertaker. "Tell me what happened," he said in an even voice.

"There was a break-in. A burglary."

"How did he get in?"

The undertaker shook his head. "We don't know. Nothing was disturbed. The doors and windows were locked. There was no sign that anything happened at all. As far we could tell, whoever it was either had a key or came in during the day, found a place to hide, and waited."

"Did you call the police?"

"No," he said. "At the time there was no sign that anything had happened at all. The burglar alarm went off like a door had been opened. When our security company inspected the building, they told us that it must have been a false alarm."

"When did you know that someone had actually broken in?"

The undertaker raised his eyes off the carpet and gave Matt a long look. "When I was preparing the Strattons' bodies for their funeral service. When I was dressing them."

Matt suddenly realized that he knew what the man with blond cornrows had done here. He'd taken the picture, but there was more to it than that. Something even darker.

He leaned forward. "How were they disturbed, Mr. Snow? What did you find when you examined the older girl and her mother?"

The undertaker gazed back at him like he might vomit. He tried to swallow but couldn't, his face a bright red. When he finally spoke, his faint voice broke into a handful of pieces.

"It wasn't their bodies," he said. "It was their clothing. Their panties and bras."

"What did you find?"

"Semen," he said.

CHAPTER 48

Matt could barely keep himself together as he hit the expressway heading for Center City.

He thought about the crime scenes at both the Strattons' and the Holloways'. Neither one had revealed any sexual involvement by the killer. No one's body had been violated on the night of the murders except for the sexual intercourse that occurred between mother and son. Yet there had to be a sexual component somewhere based on their profile of the killer.

If he trusted the profile, then it had to be there, and it was.

The killer wanted a piece of himself to be with his female victims forever. It was in the photograph he'd placed on the Strattons' bedside table. And now there was a piece of him in the ground with them as well.

Matt had thought about the killer's interest in collecting trophies. But as he glanced at the family portrait in the plastic bag on the passenger seat—a photograph of five dead people smiling with their eyes open before a Christmas tree—he couldn't handle the harsh view of this new reality. He felt soiled even considering it. He felt his blood boiling over in a cataclysmic rage. He'd thought that he'd seen the worst the world could give as a soldier in Afghanistan, the worst the world could give on the streets of Los Angeles as a cop and a detective, but the man with blond cornrows was living in an entirely different universe. Somewhere past the abyss and on the other side of a black hole.

He cracked open the window and lit a Marlboro. Then he switched on the radio and dialed down to 90.1 FM. WRTI broadcast two digital channels from Temple University's campus in North Philadelphia. Growing up in New Jersey, Matt had been an avid listener since his early teens. It was the top of the hour, and the station was segueing between shows with a blues cut that Matt often listened to on his cell phone and tablet.

Buddy Guy playing "Sweet Little Angel."

Matt tried to listen. Tried to smooth away some of the sharp edges, but in the end, the effort was futile. He switched off the radio, took another drag on his smoke, and barreled toward the city. Within twenty minutes he was pulling into his parking space below the federal building.

Matt slipped the Strattons' portrait into his briefcase. But as he folded over his copy of the *Daily News* and stuffed it behind the picture frame, that stray thought resurfaced, and it couldn't wait until he reached his desk.

He pulled out his laptop and booted up the machine.

The society page. He'd seen it at the funeral home while he held the Strattons' portrait in his hand. The sight had triggered an idea. A possibility that slipped away before he could catch it.

Matt clicked open his web browser, found his bookmark to the *Philadelphia Inquirer*, and performed a search for the words *David Holloway happy at home*. When he hit the Enter key, a list of articles assembled on the screen. Matt only needed to read the first entry and clicked the link.

It was a story about the Holloways from Devon, Pennsylvania. A story from the society page that had been published in late August when the weather was nice. Apparently, Holloway was trying to reinvent his tarnished image by chairing a fundraiser for the Philadelphia Zoo. The event proved unsuccessful. But just like the piece Matt had read about Jim Stratton, the article's focus was on David Holloway, the family man. There were photographs of his Main Line mansion set on the spacious grounds behind the wrought iron fence. His collection of vintage cars, and three shots of his wife and children on the terrace by the pool.

Matt might find it difficult to prove, but the idea that the man with blond cornrows was selecting his victims from the society page of the *Philadelphia Inquirer* seemed more than worthy of any investigator's consideration.

He looked back at the screen and a short list of key words—*happy, ideal life, worry-free*—it all seemed to fit their profile.

Matt shut down the power, slid his laptop into his briefcase, and climbed out of the car. After popping a mint into his mouth, he headed for the elevators. When he reached the hallway upstairs and turned the corner, he spotted a US marshal standing before the doors to the Crisis Room.

"How can I help you?" the man said.

Matt nodded. "I need to get to my desk."

The US marshal shook his head. "Not now you don't. They're shooting video in there."

"Would you mind if I took a quick look?"

"Sure," he said, raising his finger to his lips. "But do it quietly."

Matt stepped into the room. The overhead lights had been switched off, the movie lights providing the only illumination on the entire floor. Matt stayed by the door, keeping to the shadows and darkness. He could see Kate Brown sitting at her desk, listening to the federal prosecutor talk about what he deemed "the hunt for Dr. Baylor."

"It's a fight worth fighting," Doyle said in an overly dramatic voice. "A fight for the best and brightest. We're in the hunt for a monster, and we're beginning to see light at the end of the—"

Matt stopped listening. What struck him most about the moment, what he found so absolutely devastating, was the expression on Kate Brown's face basking in the soft glow of all those movie lights.

She was buying it. She was all in. Doyle was going places, and she wanted to go, too.

Matt stepped out of the room without making any sound and started down the hallway. Rogers's door was open and he was sitting behind his desk, talking to someone on the phone. He motioned Matt into the office, pointing to a seat and beckoning him to sit down. After a few minutes, he hung up and stood.

"Doyle's going to be tied up all afternoon. My suggestion is that you come back early in the morning. We want to know what you discussed with Dr. Baylor yesterday. We plan to shoot your deposition on videotape."

"You mean I'll be under oath?"

Rogers nodded. "At this point I think it's best for everyone."

They were putting together a case against him. They were building a case.

Matt got out of the chair, stepped over to the window, and gazed at the city. It was a dark afternoon, the buildings lit up as if night would be arriving early.

He didn't know what to do. If Rogers had been a reasonable man, he would've shown him the family portrait, explained that it was taken at the funeral home, that the Strattons were dead, and that the killer had a fascination with panties and bras and dead women. If the special agent had been a reasonable man, he would've said, "Nice job, Jones. Let's get those bodies exhumed. We're finally on the right track."

But Rogers wasn't a reasonable man. And after Doyle's interviews this afternoon were aired on TV, everyone involved would be too deep in to back out. With these broadcasts, the dye would be set, the trip locked in forever.

Matt realized that he was repeating his past. He was working with people who could no longer see the truth and were forced to make up their own. He was working with people he couldn't trust or rely on.

Which was worse? The new reality of who the killer was and what he was actually doing? Or the new reality of what the FBI's task force seemed incapable of doing?

When Matt added it all up, they almost canceled each other out.

He turned away from the window and walked out of Rogers's office, feeling the emptiness imprisoning him. The pain and anguish of facing a formidable opponent with no weapons or air support. He could feel the blowback. He could feel his soul burning—black and blue and all bruised up like the face of a heavyweight prizefighter with one or two rounds to go.

CHAPTER 49

Matt didn't notice them at first. He had been sitting on a bench in the park across the street from his apartment building for more than half an hour. He had been drinking takeout coffee from Benny's Café Blue and watching the day finally give in to night. He had been trying to process what he'd learned over the past forty-eight hours and figure out what came next.

But there they were. The blond man with the knapsack standing on the corner to his left. And the woman in the business suit keeping watch on the corner to his right. It was nothing more than a curiosity. But when Matt spotted the man with the shaved head and eyeglasses walking down Pine Street, crossing at the corner on Twenty-Third, and passing the blond man with nothing more than a simple nod, Matt knew with certainty that something was going on.

Both men had keys to the apartment next to Matt's, indicating that they shared the place. Yet they hadn't spoken to each other, they hadn't said a word. Instead, they nodded the way people often do who work together.

Matt watched the man with the shaved head hurry into the brightly lit lobby and step into the elevator. He turned and checked on the man and woman posted on the corners. He didn't think that they could see him with his bench set in the darkness between two street lights. He wasn't even sure it mattered. But just in case, he pulled his scarf up to conceal the lower half of his face.

He sat back and settled into the bench. He had no idea or even the hint of an idea that what he'd picked up on had anything to do with him. He'd only seen these people once, and on three separate occasions. It was more like sitting at the bar last night and trying to decipher the relationships between the two young women drinking vodka martinis with the older man. It was an entertaining distraction. A mind game that provided a well-needed break from the harsh reality he was facing as a homicide detective on unfriendly soil.

It was completely innocent, completely pure—it was all of these things until he happened to look up and see the lights to his apartment switch on.

He felt his pulse quicken.

No doubt about it, the lights to his apartment on the fourth floor were on.

He lowered his gaze to the street as quickly as he could, eyeing the two watchers on the corners. He spent several moments sizing them up. Several moments assessing their presence. They were searching the sidewalks, picking through all those faces, their cell phones ready to warn the man with the shaved head at the first sighting. The woman in the business suit came off like a bean counter. And while the man with the blond hair appeared as if he worked out and was in decent physical shape, he looked as nervous as the woman.

Matt shook his head in disappointment, then drew his .45 and chambered a round as quietly as he could. Slipping the pistol into his jacket pocket, he lowered his scarf and walked to the other side of the square. When he reached Panama Street, he made a right, and then another, and started down the sidewalk. He was on Twenty-Third

Street, heading for his apartment building and keeping his gaze locked on the man with blond hair.

He caught the man's eyes picking him out of the crowd and watched him make a quick phone call. As Matt reached the corner and waited for the light to change, he glanced up at the sky and saw the windows to his apartment miraculously go dark. The blond man had started walking toward the building like everything was cool. The woman in the business suit had her eyes on Matt, but disappeared into the crowd heading north on Twenty-Fourth Street.

Matt picked up his pace, hitting the lobby doors just behind the man with blond hair. As he followed him inside, he pulled his gun out and knocked the man onto the marble floor. He went down hard, turned back for a look, and seemed confused and frightened. Matt aimed the .45 at his head, ready to fire.

"I'm FBI," the man said in an anxious voice. "My ID's in my pocket."

"That's the sad part," Matt said. "I figured out who you were five minutes ago. Now dig your piece out of your jacket and slide it across the floor. And be cool, pal. You do anything stupid, it'll be the last thing you do, got it?"

The man nodded, then pulled a Beretta M9 out of the holster on his belt and slid it forward. Matt picked up the pistol and jammed it into his left jacket pocket.

"Roll over onto your stomach."

The man complied, and Matt frisked him from head to toe. Then he grabbed the man's knapsack and took a step back.

"We're going upstairs," Matt said. "Here's what you need to know. If you do anything that I take as threatening, and I mean anything, I'll blow your fucking heart out of your chest. I think you know who I am. And I think you already know that I do what I say. It's not your night, pal. It's mine, got it?"

The man nodded again. "It's your show, Jones. You have no worries."

"Then get up, get in the elevator, and pretend you're the Statue of Liberty."

The man climbed to his feet and carefully stepped into the elevator. They rode up to the fourth floor where Matt beckoned the man into the hallway with the muzzle of his pistol.

"Where are we going?" the man asked.

"Your place."

Matt gave him a push. Everything about the day had become lost in the gloom.

"Unlock your door," he said. "And if there's anyone in there like the guy with the shaved head, for your sake, you might want to tell him to back off."

"I'll tell him, Jones."

Matt watched the man dig his keys out of his pocket and unlock the door. Anxiety and fear were showing on his face. Matt poked the door with the muzzle of his .45 and pushed it open slowly. The hinges creaked, and the blond man cleared his throat.

"It's me, Pat. It's Glen. You need to chill, man. You need to be cool."

Matt followed him inside, checking the kitchen behind them, then taking a single step forward. The man with the shaved head was pointing another Beretta M9 at him from the master bedroom.

Matt gave him a long look and could tell that he was as panic-stricken as his friend.

"You're shaking," Matt said. "You'll never be able to pull it off. You'll either miss or hit your friend here, and I'll put a slug in the center of your forehead. If you lower your piece to the floor, no one gets hurt tonight. If you don't, you'll miss the holidays. You'll miss the rest of your life."

The man with blond hair nodded. "Put the gun down, Pat. This is stupid. He's a cop. Put the gun down so we can talk this out."

The man in the bedroom was still trembling, and Matt doubted whether either one of these guys were anything more than techs who had been issued M9s, the federal standard. Matt watched him close his eyes and open them again. Sweat was percolating all over his face, and Matt took this as a bad sign.

"Your friend's right," Matt said. "Don't get stupid. Just lower your gun to the floor and take two steps back."

A moment passed. And then another. And then, finally, the man with the shaved head tossed the Beretta onto the carpet and stepped away.

"Thanks," Matt said. "Now lean against the wall while I frisk you."

The man did as he was told. After Matt took charge of the second pistol, he patted the man down and ushered him into the living room with his friend.

"On the couch," Matt said. "And toss your IDs on the table. Let's go. It's been a long day, and all of a sudden, I've got a busy night."

As the two agents dug their IDs out of their pockets and tossed them on the coffee table, Matt took in the room. There was a couch and a chair by a floor lamp, but that's where any resemblance to a living room ended. Matt gazed at the long worktables and desk chairs facing ten LED video monitors mounted on the main wall. The worktables were equipped with digital recording devices, along with a laptop and telephone that went with each chair. The people working here were part of a surveillance detail.

Matt scooped up the two IDs and stepped back, even though he no longer considered either one of the men a threat.

He turned and quickly glanced at the LED screens. They were switched on, and despite the fact that the lights were off in the FBI's apartment next door, the cameras were sensitive enough to pick up images in detail.

The FBI had been watching Matt since he first arrived in the City of Brotherly Love. From where he stood, every room in his apartment seemed to be covered from every angle.

It was a surveillance operation that Matt guessed the FBI used on a regular basis. This time Matt had been the fool who had trusted them.

As his situation began to settle in, as he chewed over his new, ever-changing reality, he wondered if there was a place in the human psyche beyond anger and rage. An emotion hiding somewhere deep inside a human being's soul that was so frightful, so abhorrent, so palpable, that he could taste it in his mouth.

He skimmed over the IDs. The young man with blond hair was an assistant agent in charge by the name of Glen Kerry. The man with the shaved head, Pat Richards, was forty-two years old and shared the same title.

Matt tossed the IDs back on the coffee table and gazed at them. He was curious and wanted to understand.

"You guys are techs, right?" he said finally.

Both of them nodded.

"Why are you doing this?" Matt went on in a low voice. "I don't get it. We're on the same side."

They looked at each other, but it was the man with blond hair who spoke up.

"I don't know why we're doing this," Kerry said. "It's not our job to know why. We're just following orders, Jones."

Matt turned to the man with the shaved head. "What were you doing in the apartment?"

"One of the cameras in your living room went down. I had to switch it out."

Matt nodded, still curious. "Who do you guys work for? Who's giving the orders? Who's your boss?"

Kerry shrugged. "Same as yours, Jones. Assistant US Attorney Ken Doyle from the Department of Justice. He's the one calling the shots."

CHAPTER 50

Andrew loaded his bong with another hot pinch of that weed he thought had been cut with something. He struck his lighter and took a deep hit, unable to hold his breath for more than five or six seconds.

He set the bong down and sat for a few minutes watching his bedroom walls morph into sheets on a clothesline again. Once the wind settled down, he got up to check on his mother. He'd been looking in on her at the top of every hour since he murdered her. This time he sensed a difference the minute he pushed open her bedroom door.

The odor was so foul, so dense, it almost knocked him down. He looked at her on the bed. In the first hour of her death, he had cleaned her wound, covered it with a piece of gaffer tape, and dressed her in a jogging outfit. He'd also made the bed with clean sheets, unfolded the comforter, and laid her out on the far side of the mattress next to her table. Rigor mortis had begun to set in an hour or so later. Now she was stiff as a fence post, her skin ice-cold. But what struck Andrew most was the change to her face. It almost seemed like the skin around her mouth was shrinking. Her teeth were jutting out, her expression a hideous grimace that he could hardly look at.

She moved.

Andrew nearly leaped out of his skin. When he realized that it was the weed, he turned away from her and tried to collect himself. He had work to do. It had been nearly fifteen hours, and Reggie Cook's corpse was still on the kitchen floor.

Andrew cracked open the windows, lowered the shades, and switched on his mother's fake candles. Then he returned to his room for the Glade PlugIns he'd picked up at work. He was hoping to manage the stench with three scents: Sweet Pea & Lilac, Apple Tree Picnic, and something he smelled through the plastic and particularly liked called Hit the Road. Ripping open the packages, he spaced them out using three outlets on three different walls. After giving his mother a last look, he stepped into the hall and closed the door.

He had to keep moving. He had to stop wasting time and get it done.

He grabbed his spy glasses off the worktable, switched on the wireless camera mounted in the frames, and headed downstairs to the kitchen. Fitting the glasses over his ears and nose, he gazed at the plastic shower curtain he'd ripped out of his bathroom to cover Reggie Cook's dead body and crossed the room.

The odor was abhorrent. And when he lifted the shower curtain away, he realized that he'd waited too long. Reggie was an hour or two past ripe, and the wave of stench was overwhelming.

Andrew spread the plastic curtain on the floor, then wrapped a kitchen towel around his face and tied it behind his head. When he sprayed Reggie down with a can of air freshener, it didn't seem to do any good.

The weed was playing with his head again, and he tried to keep himself together. He dragged the body across the floor and onto the shower curtain. Along the way, Reggie's boxer shorts slipped off, and the big, hairy slob was naked now. His dick was the size of a donkey's and standing on end, and Andrew tried not to look at it for too long. Thoughts about his mother seemed to come to life before his eyes, various scenarios between her and her animal boyfriend when her son wasn't around.

Andrew's mood darkened. He pulled the towel away, removed his spy glasses, and switched off the camera. There was no longer a good reason to record the event on video. After tonight he never wanted to see or think about Reggie Cook again.

He picked up his roll of gaffer tape, then wrapped and sealed the body in the plastic shower curtain. Reggie was so big and so stiff from rigor mortis it took almost a quarter of the roll to join the seams and keep everything tight.

It was late. Well after midnight.

Andrew stepped out the back door into the fresh air and casually gazed over the picket fence at Mr. Andolini's house. The windows were dark; the old man and his wife, early risers. He climbed down the steps and walked over to the gate between the two properties. He was looking for Mr. Andolini's wheelbarrow, which he usually kept by the back door. Andrew didn't see the cart and began to worry until he spotted it by the woodpile.

He paused a moment and forced himself to become aware of his surroundings. The neighborhood appeared to be quiet. He didn't see a single house with any lights on. Once he began to feel safer, he unlatched the gate, hurried through the yard, and took charge of the cart.

The wheel was squeaking and it wouldn't stop, and Andrew started hyperventilating. He rolled the wheelbarrow through the gate and over to the steps. Then he ran inside, seized the wrapped-up corpse by its feet, and yanked the dead weight out the door. He could see, even feel, Reggie's head bouncing off the steps. Somehow he managed to get the stiff corpse on the wheelbarrow, but the balance was off and the cart tipped over.

Andrew watched the body tumble onto the frozen lawn in horror. The idea that Reggie might break in half crossed his mind, and he almost screamed. He could feel his heart pounding in his chest so hard that he thought it might blow. He rolled the wheelbarrow closer, lifted the wooden body up with all his strength, and set it on the cart. After making a few adjustments, he lifted the handles and rolled the heavy load to the end of the driveway.

The squeaky wheel was absolutely unnerving. That dog barking on the next block didn't help much either.

He could feel the panic. He could feel the dread reaching out for him from behind.

He started down the street with his massive load, hurrying toward the Delaware River at the end of the block as best he could. He knew that he was vulnerable. He knew that he was out in the open. If a car happened to drive down the street, everything about his life would be tossed into the weeds.

He filled his lungs with air and tried to walk faster and faster still. Each house he passed, each new set of dark windows, seemed to increase the terror chasing him down the street. But after five long minutes, he finally made it. He was rolling down the path and onto the dock. He was watching himself again. He could see himself reaching the very end, the cart's handles rising into the air. He could hear himself grunting and groaning, and then that big splash Reggie made as he went for a last swim.

Andrew wasn't too worried about the shower curtain staying rolled up. He doubted that gaffer tape was even waterproof. At this end of the river, fish and snapping turtles were still plentiful. What the water didn't take away, the miracle of nature would.

Andrew's eyes had adjusted to the darkness, his high mellowing. There was enough light reflecting off the cloudy sky to see the corpse beginning to float downstream toward the city. The current appeared strong tonight. When the body finally sank in the frigid water, Andrew gave the city a last look with all its lights and tall buildings, then lowered the cart and wheeled it home.

CHAPTER 51

Matt sensed movement through the windshield and peeked over the dashboard. He was parked on Mount Vernon Street, halfway up the block from Kate Brown's townhouse on the corner. He had spent most of the night here. He would have preferred to confront her sooner, but when he arrived he saw a Lincoln out front with a driver behind the wheel.

The car was still there, and so was the driver. Whoever was inside Brown's place had stayed over last night.

Matt watched the front door open. He could see Kate in that robe of hers. He could see her kissing someone. When the man turned and walked down the steps, Matt got a good look at his face.

It was the assistant US attorney, Ken Doyle.

His driver got out of the car and opened the rear door, saying something amusing to Doyle as he climbed in the backseat. In spite of the distance, Matt could see the pistol on the driver's belt and guessed that he was doubling up as a driver and a bodyguard.

Matt waited for the Lincoln to make a left on Twenty-Third Street and vanish around the corner. Then he climbed out of his Crown Vic, bolted down the street, and gave Brown's front door three light taps like he might be Doyle and he'd forgotten something.

It worked. Brown popped open the door with a bright grin on her face. A bright grin that went dark and nose-dived the minute she realized who her visitor was. Matt pushed his way inside, his energy and strength all dialed up. He heard her scream, but ignored it.

He looked at her open robe and tangled hair. He looked at the anger in her eyes, all the venom. He wondered if she could see the same thing on his face—the same thing, times ten or twenty.

"You're a stupid bitch, Kate. I know all about it. I know about the bugs and cameras in the apartment you put me in. And now," he said, tossing it over. "And now I know about this."

She shook her head and took a step back. "It's not what you think it is, Jones."

He gazed at her body and the open robe. "It's exactly what I think it is. It's even worse than I think it is. You've been doing him all along."

"That's not true."

"Of course, it's true. You've been fucking him since the beginning. Whose idea was it for you to fuck me? For you to spy on me? That was your job, right? Stay close and keep an eye on me?"

She didn't say anything, but took another step back. Matt noticed a pistol on the table beside the fireplace.

"Whose idea was it, Kate? Is he paying you? Did he promise you a promotion? You're his slut, right? His man toy? His fucking FBI whore?"

Her face had turned blue, her body trembling like water in an angry pot that's just reached a boil.

"You're the one who doesn't get it, Jones. You're the one who's being played right now."

He shook his head at her. She seemed so foolish.

"What are you talking about?" he said.

"You think you're so damn smart. Doyle has it all over you, Jones. He knows something about you that even you don't know."

"I don't know a lot of things, Kate."

"He knows something about you that's personal."

The venom was still showing on her face, the nervous gleam in her eyes hot like fire. Matt shrugged, letting her play her game and thinking about his new, ever-changing reality. The idea that his life was repeating itself as if some supreme being was pulling all the strings and laughing at him as he struggled to carry on.

"Okay, Kate. Okay, I give up. What's Doyle know that I don't know?"

She paused a moment. She was measuring him. She seemed delighted with herself.

"The Department of Justice asked the FBI in LA to run a sample of Dr. Baylor's DNA against every employee in Los Angeles County. They got a hit, Jones. The day before you left LA, they got a hit."

Matt shrugged. "Oh yeah?" he said. "Who did it match up to?"

She grinned at him again, like a devil, like a bloodsucker or ghoul. "You," she said joyously. "Baylor's your uncle on your mother's side, and you're a jackal. Doyle's been using you since day one."

Her words pierced his body like a switchblade and went all the way through. He didn't move, and he didn't say anything. The weight of his new, ever-changing reality seemed almost too heavy to carry now.

His uncle. His mother's brother. The reason Dr. Baylor had saved his life, not once, but twice.

It was heavy, but it was clean.

Matt's mind surfaced as Brown took another step back. He had never hit a woman before. He had never even thought about it. And as a police officer, when confronted with domestic violence, he had always done his best to comfort female victims. When he got burned six weeks ago by a woman he'd fallen in love with, when he realized the magnitude of what she had done, physical violence had never even entered his mind. Even now, as he remembered the people she'd hurt and even ruined, he had to admit that he would never describe her as being evil.

But Kate Brown was an altogether different kind of woman.

And if she had ever succeeded in reaching her pistol on the table by the fireplace, Matt would have had no problem drawing his .45 and shooting her dead.

But she never did make it to her pistol. At least Matt never saw her reach the table.

Like most people who are vicious, or even wicked like Brown, she might be worth killing, but not punching her lights out.

He never saw her reach the pistol because he turned around and walked out on her. Within minutes she had become sordid and irrelevant and so very unimportant. He needed to find Dr. Baylor now. He needed to talk to the maniac who had brutally murdered four college girls with a box cutter. The doctor who had saved his life not once but twice. His uncle. His mother's brother. His own flesh and blood.

CHAPTER 52

Andrew heard the doorbell and cringed. Rolling over in bed, he glanced at the clock radio and sat up. It was after eleven, and he'd slept in.

He tried to clear his mind. Sleep hadn't come very easily last night, and he kept waking up after being swept away by a nightmare that seemed more vivid than most. When he caught a whiff of his mother's decomposing body mixed with the three Glade PlugIns, he realized the nightmare that had seemed so realistic wasn't a nightmare at all.

He'd shot his mother and her boyfriend yesterday, and both of them were dead.

The doorbell rang again. Andrew slipped on a pair of jeans and stepped over to the window for a look down at the front porch.

It was Avery Cooper, and she seemed anxious.

He stepped back from the window and tried to think. He didn't want her in the house. He didn't want anyone in the house. But when she rang the doorbell a third time, she seemed determined to see him.

"I know you're in there," he could hear her saying. "Your car's parked at the curb, Andrew. Now open up. It's me. Avery."

She started beating her fist on the door and rang the bell over and over again.

Andrew scanned the bedroom, checking for anything that might appear incriminating. At a glance, the place seemed okay. He straightened out the bed, then rushed downstairs before the doorbell rang again.

He found her on the front porch, peering through the window into the living room. He unlocked the door and opened it, squinting as the bright daylight struck his face.

"What are you doing here?" he said.

"That's a nice way to greet your girlfriend. *What are you doing here?* Instead of hey, it's nice to see you."

He smacked his dry lips together. "Hey, it's nice to see you, Cooper."

"Ha," she said in a loud voice. "Nice try, Andrew. It's too late now."

He watched her storm into the house, then stop and look around. He walked in and closed the door. He was hungry and needed a bowl of cereal. Avery had an odd look on her face and appeared horrified.

"What's that smell?" she said.

He shrugged it off. "What smell?"

"That awful smell, Andrew."

"Oh, that," he said, thinking on his feet. "It's mice in the walls. The exterminator said it wouldn't go away for a couple of weeks. I got used to it after a day or two."

"You mean you've got dead mice in your walls?"

He nodded. "That's what the exterminator said."

Her eyes got big and wide and she laughed. "Oh my God."

She seemed to settle down after that. Andrew was amazed by her naivety. She'd bought his off-the-wall explanation at face value, and he didn't even have to work for it.

He led her into the kitchen and offered her a bowl of Rice Krispies, but she said she'd already had something and wasn't hungry. Once he ate and rinsed his dishes in the sink, they headed up to his bedroom.

"Why is that door closed?" she said.

He turned and followed her eyes to his mother's bedroom.

"It's my mother's," he said in as casual a voice as he could find. "She likes to keep it closed."

"The smell is worse up here."

"A little bit, yeah," he said.

"Where is she? Where's your mom?"

"She's out of town. She's visiting relatives."

Why was Cooper so curious? Why all the questions? Why the third degree? He watched her check out his room, her eyes touching everything like she owned the place.

"When's your mom coming back?" she said.

Andrew picked up on her voice. She was up to something.

She gave him a look and repeated the question. "When's she coming back, Andrew?"

He shrugged. "Next week, I think. Why?"

"Because I brought something," she said excitedly.

"What?"

She had a naughty look going behind her smile. She dug a small plastic bag out of her pocket, pulled it open, and dumped two pills on the worktable. Andrew examined them for a moment.

"What are they?" he said finally.

She smiled again, then got out of her jacket and tossed it on the chair.

"Ecstasy," she said. "Want to have some fun?"

The love drug.

Andrew had never done ecstasy before. His mother had always told him that it was the kind of high that required a friend. And whenever his mother had used the word *friend*, warning beacons went off in his head.

He turned back to Avery. He looked at those eyes of hers, nodded slowly, then watched her swallow a pill and chase it down with a sip of water from the bottle he kept by his bed. Andrew hesitated to pick up the pill, worrying that he might lose control of himself and give up his secrets. He watched Avery discover his bong and the small amount of reefer already in the bowl. When she struck his lighter, took a hit, and giggled, he grabbed the water bottle and swallowed the remaining pill. Then he added more reefer to the bowl and took his first hit of the morning.

When he turned, he found Avery on his bed with Ryan Day's briefcase. She was skimming through the gossip reporter's files. She was reading them. Andrew finally noticed her clothing. She was wearing a red tube top that seemed loose and stretched out and only concealed a small portion of her black bra. Her jeans were just like the jeans his mother used to wear. Skintight and riding two inches below her hips.

She giggled at him and her eyes got big. "What are these files?"

He gave her another long look. He could tell that she was already stoned out of her mind on a single hit. He wondered what would happen in a half hour or so when the ecstasy kicked in.

She crossed her legs and giggled again. "Why are you reading this crap?"

He smiled at her. Everything would be okay. He could sense it. He could tell.

"It's my job," he said finally.

"What job?"

He paused a moment, glancing at her cleavage. When he met her eyes, it almost felt as if he were melting.

"I'm a secret agent," he said in a low voice.

She nodded at him. She was appraising him and seemed pleased. When she spoke, her voice reminded him of angels.

"You mean you're a secret agent and not an international man of mystery?" she said.

"Fuck those men of mystery."

He raised his hands and shrugged. When she started giggling again, it seemed contagious, and he tumbled onto the bed and lay down beside her.

CHAPTER 53

Matt needed to become invisible—needed to find Dr. Baylor—and as he added up everything he'd just learned from Kate Brown, the grand total staggered his mind.

He cracked open the window in the Crown Vic and lit a Marlboro. He was waiting for the light to change on Tasker Street. Once it finally turned green, he pulled forward and cruised down Sixth Street. He was touring South Philadelphia in search of a special kind of body shop. He'd spent enough time as a cop in uniform patrolling the neighborhoods south of the Santa Monica Freeway in LA to know what he wanted and why.

Snyder Avenue looked promising, and he made a right at the corner, still thinking things over, still doing the math.

The apartment he'd been given had been wired for video and sound. The woman assigned to service him had been a spy and a whore. Matt had no doubt that the Crown Vic he'd been issued came equipped with a GPS device, and perhaps even a video camera and a microphone.

They were watching, and they were listening, and it was all about survival now. Surviving this ordeal with Doyle and Rogers and the delusional Kate Brown, and absorbing the fact that a serial killer like

Dr. Baylor was his own flesh and blood. That every time he'd ever spoken with the doctor, on every occasion they had ever met from the very beginning, the doctor *knew*. He knew everything about Matt, his history with his mother, his history with his father. He knew everything.

A memory surfaced. The conversation he'd had with the doctor in the Strattons' library. Matt had asked him why, if he was singling out the greedy, he had spared his father's life. And Baylor's response had been quick and decisive.

I thought that the honor belonged to you, Matthew. The only thing that will give your father's death meaning is if it comes from you, and only you.

Matt spotted the body shop five blocks west on Snyder Avenue and pulled over. The building was set in a residential neighborhood and meticulously maintained by someone with money. But what struck Matt most about the garage and storefront was the fact that the body shop didn't have a sign.

Matt guessed that the business existed off the grid and probably didn't even have a name.

He thought about the car he was driving and the people who might be watching. He didn't want to linger too long, so he locked up the Crown Vic and entered the building through an open garage door.

"Hey, it's you," a man called out in a voice that boomed.

Matt turned and saw a man in his late thirties walking toward him from the other side of the ten-bay garage. More than a handful of mechanics and technicians looked up from their cars.

"It's really you," the man went on. "The cop from LA. The guy chasing that serial killer. He's in the papers, fellas. He's on TV."

Matt kept his eyes on the man as he approached him. He was wearing expensive clothing, a tasteful pair of slacks and a casual dress shirt. The watch on his left wrist looked like a Rolex.

"Are you the owner of this shop?" Matt said.

The man shrugged, seemed amused, and took a moment to size him up. "Maybe," he said. "And maybe not."

"What's your name?"

"Carlo Genovese," he said. "What's yours?"

"Matt Jones."

Matt took in the body shop, then turned back to Genovese. He noted his dark hair and brown eyes, his grooming meticulous. But it was his person, his overall confidence, that Matt was counting on.

"I need a favor, Mr. Genovese."

"Why me? The paper says you're FBI now."

Everyone in the shop had stopped working and moved in behind their boss. Matt tried not to be intimidated and made a point of taking a step closer and meeting Genovese's gaze.

"There's something wrong with my car, Mr. Genovese. I need someone to bring it in, put it on the lifts, and take a long look."

"How long a look are we talking about?"

Matt thought it over. "Two, maybe three hours."

Genovese nodded like he could read Matt's mind and still seemed amused, but didn't say anything.

"While my car is being inspected by one of your technicians, I'll need to rent another. A car with no history and plates that someone forgot to write down. A rental paid in cash. What you need to know is that certain people are looking for me. They may pay you a visit. They may even demonstrate some degree of enthusiasm."

"Enthusiasm," Genovese said, narrowing his brow. "Are you saying that the killer might show up in my shop?"

"No," Matt said. "The Feds."

Genovese hesitated for a moment, then began laughing. As it settled in, everyone in the garage joined in.

"You said your name's Jones, right? Detective Matt Jones?"

Matt nodded.

"This is South Philadelphia, Detective Jones. The FBI doesn't run things here. We do."

Matt nodded again. "You think it would be possible to get my car checked out? Maybe I could give you my card, and if anyone did stop by looking for me, maybe you could give me a call on my cell and let me know."

Genovese took a moment to think it over. "If you're in a jam with the FBI, Detective, then this one's on the house," he said finally. "I can't wait till they get here. I'll have Rose make a fresh pot of coffee."

Matt handed over his business card and caught Genovese's wicked smile. He'd picked the right place—the shop with no sign, the business with no name, and an owner who called himself *maybe*.

CHAPTER 54

Andrew checked his watch and realized that the nervous feeling he'd been dealing with for the past forty minutes, that feeling that reminded him of drinking too much coffee, was completely gone now. In its place was something entirely different. Something from the other side of the universe.

It had been an hour and a half since he dropped that tab of ecstasy.

For the first time in his life, his entire being was overflowing with a supreme brand of confidence. The entire world seemed to be glowing with peace and love and a certain level of contentment that went beyond anything he had ever imagined or even dreamed of. He looked over at Avery on the bed. She had pulled off her tank top and was getting out of her jeans. Her pink panties didn't match her black bra but it looked good to him. Everything he was seeing in the room and out the window looked good to him.

"It's hot in here," she was saying. "I know it's the ecstasy, but I need something to drink, Andrew. Orange juice or something."

He could see the sweat collecting on her forehead and above her full lips. He didn't want to move. He didn't want to leave her alone in the room. He was in love with her, he realized. He was in love with her being, her body, the idea of her, the fact of her, the sound of her voice. But it was more than that. Way more. He loved everything about her. The things she was touching. The things she was looking at.

"I don't think there's any orange juice," he said. "But there's a six-pack of water in the fridge."

"Bring it up," she said. "I'm really thirsty."

She tossed her jeans on the chair. Her long legs were mesmerizing; his dick, rock hard.

It took all of his strength to get out of his desk chair and leave her. And all he could think about was returning as quickly as he could. He raced down the steps and into the kitchen. Popping open the fridge, he grabbed the bottled water, then spotted two mango-extremo-flavored Gatorades and stopped. He couldn't decide which would taste better right now. After several moments, he picked the Gatorade and rushed back upstairs.

Everything was good until he reached the landing. That's when he hesitated. That's when he froze.

The foul odor of his mother's corpse had hit like a bomb and suddenly taken over the second floor. As he started down the hall, he noticed that his mother's bedroom door was standing open. He peeked inside and found Avery standing over the corpse in the candlelight.

He couldn't comprehend why he didn't feel nervous. He didn't understand why he wasn't afraid. His eyes rose from his mother's death grimace to Avery's gentle face.

"Are you okay?" he whispered.

She turned and gazed at him without saying anything. There was something different about her now. Maybe it was her wide-open eyes, or the shock he saw on her face. She seemed so beautiful in a cheap sort of way. So familiar to him. So fresh and young.

She moved closer, pushing her body into him and kissing him.

"What happened to your mom?" she whispered.

"I shot her."

"Why?"

He ran his hands beneath her arms and into the small of her back, her skin so soft and smooth. "She did things to me," he said finally.

He wasn't sure if she was even real anymore. He kissed the sweat on her forehead. He felt her body melting into his body. He felt her pulling him onto his mother's bed.

CHAPTER 55

Matt spotted the elementary school on Sugartown Road and made a right, idling by the Holloways' mansion in Devon. When he realized no one was there, he pulled up the drive and parked behind the guesthouse. He got out of his car, eyeing the property carefully, then legging his way around the mansion to the front door.

The lockbox was attached to the door handle. Brown had called the combination universal. Matt held his breath as he entered the numbers one-eight-seven, the penal code for homicide in California, then exhaled when the box swung open and he found the key. Once he was inside and felt the warm air, he became grateful no one had thought about turning the heat down.

Dr. Baylor had once said that he had eyes on him. As Matt had driven out from the city, he'd checked the rearview mirror and, just like his drive from the funeral home to the Strattons', had no sense of being followed.

He decided to give it time and headed upstairs, ignoring the odor of dried blood and all those idiotic animal heads mounted on the wall. It took a few minutes to find Mimi Holloway's dressing room, and after he did, he made a quick search of her lingerie. While he couldn't tell if anything was missing, the drawers appeared full. When he checked the hamper, the killer's future trophies were still here as well.

Matt's cell phone started vibrating. He didn't recognize the caller ID, but switched on his phone.

"This is Jones."

"And this is me," a man said. "Or should I say, maybe."

Matt recognized Carlo Genovese's voice instantly and followed his lead by not using his name.

"What's up?" he said.

He heard Genovese cover the mouthpiece on his phone and say something to someone in the background. A door closed, then Genovese came back on.

"They were just here," he said. "Your friends left a few minutes ago."

Matt walked out of Mimi Holloway's dressing room heading downstairs. "Friends," he said.

"I don't think so," Genovese said. "And they seemed disappointed that they missed you. There was a woman with them. On the hot side, but bitchy."

Bitchy didn't begin to describe Kate Brown. Matt let the thought go.

"Did they take the car?" he said.

"Yeah, they've got it. You can keep the one I gave you for as long as you need it."

"Where did you say I was?"

"John's Roast Pork, grabbing a sandwich. It's ten blocks down the street, and I said I saw you getting on a bus. By the way, we found a GPS device hidden underneath the dash. There's a built-in microphone and camera in the rearview mirror. You're better off now. Be safe, friend. You ever need another favor, don't hesitate to ask. See you when you return the car."

Genovese hung up. Matt saw a shadow move on the kitchen floor and, when he entered, found Dr. Baylor sitting at the breakfast table with a glass of water.

"I followed you from the city," the doctor said.

Matt nodded. "You're pretty good because I was looking for you and I didn't see you. How did you get in?"

"One of the goals of scouting a location is to walk away with keys."

Matt shook his head at the new, ever-changing reality that he was beginning to think might be heavy enough to kill him. He gave Dr. Baylor—his uncle, his dead mother's older brother, and a serial killer who'd murdered four coeds—he gave the doctor a long, careful, even unbelievable look. When he spoke, his voice was surprisingly steady.

"You should have turned yourself in when you had a chance in LA, Doctor. It's not safe here. Not with these people. You were right. You're the One because you're the bigger headline." Matt leaned against the counter. "It's your eyes, by the way."

"My eyes?"

"You and my mother," he said. "She had the same blue eyes."

It hung there, in the kitchen with the high ceilings, in the death house with all those animal heads on the wall. Matt's words settled into the room hot and crackling like a wildfire.

Baylor turned to him with a quiet, almost innocent expression showing on his face. But soon the intensity changed and his eyes turned inward. Matt guessed that the doctor had become lost in another time, sifting through his earliest memories. His past.

"Then you know," Baylor said.

Matt felt his heart pounding in his chest. "I know something else about you, Doctor. You murdered your mother and father. That's how this got started. You did it for exactly the same reason you murdered the three coeds in Los Angeles, and another in New Orleans. Your father was a big name on Wall Street, but he was running a Ponzi scheme with his business partner. When it fell apart and was made public, you became embarrassed. All of a sudden, you, my mother, and your entire family were living in shame. His business partner took the fall because he's the man you described to the police when they asked you what you saw. But he was only a phantom. You knew that he was as guilty as your father in the Ponzi scheme, and you wanted to see him go down, too. He took the fall for murdering your parents and died in prison. But it had to be you. You're the one who killed your parents. That's the only way any of this makes sense. How old were you?"

Baylor still seemed lost, his voice quieter now as he reflected. "I was twelve," he said. "I was called Joseph then. Your mother and your aunt and I had a sister, Eleanor, who was thirteen and died a year later in a farm accident when we moved away."

"When you moved?"

"Before our parents died, we lived on Curtis Place in Maplewood, New Jersey. We lived in a very nice house in a very nice neighborhood, and we were all very happy. It was a beautiful three-level Georgian colonial built in 1907. Lots of trees, close to the train, and an easy commute for Father, who, like your father, was the King of Wall Street in his day. Over the years I've kept an eye on our former home. No one can seem to get comfortable there anymore. It's been on and off the market ever since the murders. People in the neighborhood say it's haunted."

Matt realized that while his family history was sordid and decidedly corrupt, even murderous, hearing his uncle, a man who would always be known to him as Dr. Baylor, talk about it felt like a blessing from the heavens. A chance to get another glimpse at his family. A way to inch closer to his mother, who'd died when he was just a boy.

"Tell me what happened?" Matt said. "I want to hear you tell me."

The doctor shrugged. "You already know what happened, Matthew. We were living a storybook life, and then one day the stock market crashed and we found out that Father was responsible for all these people losing everything they had in this world. The worst part of it was that most of his investors were regular people who couldn't absorb the loss and move on. Their lives were destroyed. Their hopes and dreams, their entire world was ruined. They used to stand in the street outside our house, shouting and screaming and throwing rocks at the windows. Death threats became an everyday event. My sisters and I were picked on at school. One of my teachers had lost her pension in the crash. She thought we deserved to pay for her misery, so she overlooked the bullying that was going on. I defended my sisters with my fists as best I could. But then one day, a man grabbed your mother. We were just kids on our way home from school. We were walking down the sidewalk, and he picked her up and started shaking her as if the crash, as if what Father had done, had been all her fault. I grabbed a rock and smashed him in the face. When he ran off, I found your mother crying on the sidewalk. That's when everything began, Matthew. My war on the self-centered and my hatred for greed. That's the day I decided it had to end."

"You shot your parents after they fell asleep."

"I told my sisters that I thought I'd heard someone break into the house. I woke them up and told them to hide in the attic. Then I walked into my parents' bedroom, took the gun out of my father's top drawer, and shot them four times, just to make sure. I ran upstairs. It was dark, and no one saw the pistol. I hid it in the attic underneath some insulation. As far as I know, it's still there."

"Tell me about my mother."

Baylor's eyes were on him, the melancholy showing on his face clear and true. "We were taken away from the house in Maplewood. We moved in with relatives, a distant cousin, who owned a farm in South Jersey and grew corn, tomatoes, and peaches. Our names were changed to protect us, and no one knew our secret. Not even after Eleanor was killed."

A moment passed. Long and dark and sharp as cut glass.

Their *secret*.

Matt suddenly realized that this was all about their secret.

"What is it, Matthew? What just happened? What's wrong?"

Matt didn't say anything right away, his mind filling in his past like concrete being poured into an intricate mold of ascending stairs. His family's plight really was about his mother's secret. He could feel it in his gut now.

He met his uncle's gaze, a serial killer's gaze. "It's the reason my father walked out on me and my mother. It has to be."

"What reason could your father possibly have had to justify walking out on his wife and son, and trying to erase both of you from his past?"

Matt ignored the anger he heard in his uncle's voice. "It's the secret you kept, Doctor. My mother must have told my father about her past. She gave up her secret, and he panicked and walked out. It's the only way all the dots connect."

"But that makes him worse," the doctor said.

Matt nodded. "It means that he was a coward from the very beginning. That he left the woman he loved—I'm assuming that he loved her—he abandoned his wife and son on the off chance a secret that had been kept for decades might someday be exposed."

It seemed so clear. His father was just getting started and wanted to make a career on Wall Street. Unknowingly, he'd married the daughter of Howard Stewart, a former investment banker and scoundrel who got caught cheating and stealing people's money in what was then the biggest Ponzi scheme in the history of the New York Stock Exchange. The biggest con ever, that was, until Bernie Madoff came along and did exactly the same thing all over again.

And that's why it really was all about the secret Matt's mother had been keeping. If anyone found out about her past, M. Trevor Jones would have been blackballed. His career would have been destroyed before it even got off the ground.

If anyone found out.

Matt couldn't help thinking that his father was as much a scoundrel as any of these horrible people. He couldn't help thinking that maybe killing his father was what came next instead of chasing a madman with blond cornrows. He looked over at his uncle and caught the doctor staring at him as he sipped his glass of water.

Matt had noticed that his eyes had gone dead a few minutes ago, and his uncle had that look going. The one he shared from time to time with Adam Lanza and Dylann Roof, the mass killers in Connecticut and South Carolina. Matt was beginning to feel more anxious. He checked his watch. They'd spent more than thirty minutes here, and it felt long.

"We need to get out of here," Matt said. "Out of here, and out of the city."

Baylor nodded and got up from the table. "Give me a quick update."

Matt sensed something was wrong and thought he heard an errant noise. "We need to get out of here."

"Two sentences."

Matt got into his jacket and grabbed his scarf. "He's using the society page in the paper to pick his victims. Both Stratton and Holloway were featured stories on the first page. We know what he looks like, but there's still no way of identifying him. Nothing's changed. No one's looking for him."

The doctor nodded. "It's time to go."

Matt opened the kitchen door and watched his uncle leg his way past the pool and into the backyard, heading for the rear gate. But after just a few minutes—before the doctor even made it halfway—Matt saw the men in black uniforms carrying rifles enter the lawn from the trees. They seemed all jacked up as they shouted at him and surrounded him. He could hear the sounds of others storming the mansion and racing down the hallway toward the kitchen.

Matt shook his head. They hadn't made it. Half an hour turned out to be five minutes too long.

He raised his hands and waited, staring out the window and watching the men in black uniforms push his uncle onto the ground, their rifles pointed at his head. He heard them entering the kitchen behind him. He caught the reflection in the window of a man in a black uniform moving toward him with his rifle up and ready. He could feel three sets of different hands grab his jacket and scarf, yanking him backward and heaving him onto the kitchen floor.

The violence was unnecessary, but he didn't say anything. And he didn't look at them or try to fight them off. They seemed scared, and he didn't want to give any one of them the opportunity to shoot him in the back. He didn't want to die at the hand of an amped-up cop the way so many young men were dying these days.

He could feel them jamming their knees into his back. When one of them ripped at his hair and smashed his face into the floor, Matt kept his cool. Blood seemed to be spilling everywhere. He could hear them shouting at him. He could feel his wrists being cuffed. He could hear FBI Special Agent Wes Rogers announcing his arrest and reading him his rights.

Aiding and abetting—he stopped listening after that.

When the men in black uniforms lifted him off the floor, he looked outside and saw his uncle being herded toward the house. When two of the men inside the kitchen seized Matt's arms and shoulders and spun him around, his view changed.

Assistant US Attorney Ken Doyle was standing beside his fuck object, Assistant Agent in Charge Kate Brown. They were wearing big grins, and both seemed delighted with the way things had finally turned out.

No doubt about it, the two of them were going places.

Doyle stepped forward, still grinning as he measured Matt. "You were the media's golden boy, Jones. You could have had anything you wanted. But now your career in law enforcement is over. I'm gonna ruin your life. I'm taking you down, and I'm gonna enjoy it."

Matt met his gaze, the blood dripping off his chin onto the floor. "Baylor isn't the killer, Doyle. You've got the wrong man. You're just too full of yourself, too stupid to get it."

The federal prosecutor laughed. Kate Brown seemed to find Matt amusing as well.

Doyle glanced at the two men holding Matt up, then nodded and turned away.

"Get it him out of my sight," Doyle said. "He's an insult to anyone who carries a badge."

CHAPTER 56

Matt was sitting on a bench with Dr. Baylor in a holding cell in the Federal Detention Center across the street from the FBI's field office in the federal building. US marshals had taken them into custody. After their arrival to the underground parking garage just a few aisles down from where Matt used to park the Crown Vic, they were ferried through a tunnel that connects the two buildings below Seventh Street. They were fingerprinted and photographed and placed in this cell.

They had been waiting for twelve hours, but nothing had happened. No interrogations, no interviews, no written statements. Just a tray of food last night and another this morning.

Matt gazed through the bars at the TV mounted on the wall over the doorway. The network was breaking into their normal programming with a special report. Matt almost choked when he realized that it was Doyle, the federal prosecutor, holding a morning press conference from the Crisis Room across the street.

Even at a glance, even dulled down by the filter of television, Matt could feel the electricity in the Crisis Room. Doyle wanted a big headline, and he'd achieved a big headline. The room appeared to be jam packed with media from every market in the country. As the federal prosecutor read his opening statement, flanked on stage by Kate Brown and Wes Rogers, a barrage of strobe lights from cameras representing the newspapers and various web news services hit the room in rapid-fire succession. The video broadcast for network and cable outlets flickered and glowed from the flashing lights like a horror movie.

It seemed clear that Doyle was trying to play the role of a federal prosecutor and remain cool, calm, and collected. It seemed clear that he was playing the part of a future attorney general. But the big grin on Brown's face, the look of primal satisfaction in Rogers's eyes, had become infectious. Overnight the three of them had become conquering heroes. The city, even the country, had been saved from a madman on this cold day in December, and the media was eating it up.

Dr. George Baylor, the serial killer who had murdered three coeds in LA, another girl in New Orleans, and two entire families in Philadelphia on the Main Line, had been captured and taken into custody. But that was only where the federal prosecutor's story began.

Assistant US Attorney Ken Doyle was pushing his story into a far darker place. A soulless place with no oxygen where no candle could ever burn.

Matt looked at the media wall that was being used as a high-tech background for the sea of cameras. The three massive video screens towering over the stage were switched on. The monitors on the left and right included two images of Dr. Baylor. But the screen in the center was decidedly different.

The screen in the center was an image of LAPD Detective Matt Jones.

The photograph had been taken by a US marshal, but only after a doctor had cleaned up his face. Only after Matt's bloodstained shirt had been switched with a clean one.

Doyle finished his statement and took a question from a reporter. Matt gave Dr. Baylor a nudge and turned back to the TV. Doyle had told Matt that he would ruin his life yesterday, and apparently, the federal prosecutor was a man who kept his word.

"I'll answer that question," Doyle said, pointing at a journalist who was off camera. "I'd be happy to answer that question. I've felt for more than a month that there was no way Dr. Baylor could have escaped LA without help. The more I thought about it, the more convinced I became that he had someone on the inside helping him out. I didn't trust the LAPD, so instead of working with them, I asked the FBI to run the doctor's DNA against everyone who was employed by Los Angeles County. When we got a hit, when I realized that LAPD Detective Matt Jones was related to Dr. Baylor, that the doctor was in fact his uncle on his mother's side, it became clear that in all probability, Detective Jones had helped, even engineered Baylor's escape."

Everyone in the Crisis Room seemed to let out a gasp at the same time.

A man shouted from the audience. "If you thought Jones was a dirty cop, then why did you deputize him as a US marshal and bring him into the task force?"

Doyle covered his mouth before a smile could leak out, then pretended to give the question some degree of thought. He took a sip of water and cleared his throat.

"You have to understand who Dr. Baylor was and is to answer that question," he said as he lifted his chin and brushed back his hair. "We had been given the monumental task of hunting down a killer of unprecedented savagery and cunning. There are times when investigators have to lay it on the line and take risks. I realized that I had reached that moment in the hunt for Dr. Baylor. In order to capture this mass killer, I had to be willing to take a risk."

It almost seemed like Doyle had become an actor in a play. It looked like he was striking poses as the strobe lights continued to spray rapid-fire light his way. He seemed so full of himself. So difficult to watch.

"Could you talk about the risks you took, Mr. Doyle?" another man called out like he was planting talk points.

The federal prosecutor nodded, his voice becoming intimate. "Here's the situation," he said. "We have a dirty cop who let a serial killer off free and clear. They're related by blood. We even know that Dr. Baylor saved the dirty cop's life when he was shot. So what do we do? What would you do? In a case like this, you'd take advantage of the situation, which is exactly what we did. We exploited the relationship. We used Jones to bring the doctor out of hiding, and it worked. Once we had him out in the open, we pounced. With the two of them off the street, everyone's safer now."

A female reporter spoke up. "But what about the danger you exposed the public to?"

Doyle flashed a boyish smile and shook his head. "That was the beauty of *my* plan."

The federal prosecutor took another sip of water. If his intention was to let the words *my plan* settle into the room, Matt guessed that it worked. Everyone in the Crisis Room quieted and became still.

"No one was ever in jeopardy," Doyle went on finally. "There was no risk to the public at all. We had eyes on Detective Jones twenty-four seven. His apartment was wired and monitored by FBI agents who were right there. His car was equipped with a GPS device, cameras, and sound. When he was out and about, Assistant Agent in Charge Kate Brown, this fine member of the FBI, had Jones every step of the way. We should give her a hand, folks. Every taxpayer should be proud."

The media clapped and cheered, and Kate Brown, the FBI agent who apparently now defined the standard, smiled and lowered her eyes as she feigned humility in what had the look and feel of a command performance. When another burst of strobe lights hit the stage, Matt turned away and caught Dr. Baylor staring at him. The doctor didn't seem very pleased with Agent Brown.

"I was following you one night, Matthew. I saw you with her. I saw you go into her townhouse."

Matt nodded and held the gaze. "It was part of Doyle's plan, right?"

Baylor's eyes went dead as he thought something over. "Right," he said in a dangerously quiet voice. "Part of Ken Doyle's plan. They're an item, aren't they? They're together."

Matt nodded, wishing for a Marlboro and no longer able to listen or watch the federal prosecutor's press conference. Even though Doyle's words were false, even though the facts had been bent and broken and glued together with flour and water, it seemed to ring so true. Even worse, the media appeared to accept everything at face value and were all in.

Matt could feel it in his body and his mind. His new, ever-changing reality. The plane he was piloting losing power and hitting the treetops before bursting into flames.

No way out. No parachute. Just heat and fire.

The cell-block door opened. The man who entered was dressed in an expensive suit and wore eyeglasses. His hair was graying, his eyes dark, and Matt guessed that he was somewhere between forty-five and fifty. Nothing about the way he was dressed—the way he carried himself—looked like a US marshal. The man stopped at the door and gazed through the bars, his eyes moving from Dr. Baylor to Matt.

"Someone wants to see you, Jones."

"Who?"

"Your attorney."

Matt exchanged looks with the doctor, then turned back. "My attorney? Who's my attorney?"

"A guy who just performed a miracle."

"Is that right?" Matt said. "What's his name?"

The man paused a moment, almost reverently. "Teddy Mack," he said finally.

CHAPTER 57

The man beckoned Matt into the elevator, and they descended to street level. After passing through a series of checkpoints, they walked down a long hallway to a room at the very end. The man pointed at the closed door.

"I'll be waiting for you out here," he said.

The man turned away. As he took a position against the wall, Matt spotted the semiautomatic strapped to his shoulder and realized that he was in fact a US marshal.

That feeling in his gut came back. That feeling of facing the unknown. Something was going on that he couldn't see yet.

Matt opened the door just as a man turned from the window. Stepping around the meeting table, Matt shook his hand.

"My name's Teddy Mack, Detective Jones. I'm a defense attorney, and I've been retained by Ryan Day and the television network to represent you. Sorry it took so long."

Matt nodded, thinking about how the gossip reporter had come through for him. The surprise almost took his breath away. As the defense attorney offered him a seat, it struck Matt that Teddy Mack had been the attorney who solved the ET Killings fifteen years ago in

Philadelphia. Matt could remember his face now. He could remember reading the newspaper everyday with his aunt in New Jersey and watching Teddy Mack on TV. Mack had just graduated from law school and had gone up against the district attorney to solve the most brutal serial murder case in the city's history.

An innocent man had been set free.

Matt slid the chair out and sat down. "I thought you gave up practicing law to work with the FBI. I read that in the paper a long time ago."

Teddy Mack nodded as he returned to the window and leaned against the sill. "Just for a couple of years," he said. "Just long enough to solve a case and confirm why I always wanted to be an attorney. It looks like Ken Doyle is out to get you, Detective. Do you have any idea why?"

"It could be a lot of reasons," Matt said. "My guess is that you're probably not interested in speculation."

"If that's your guess, you'd be wrong."

Matt gave Teddy Mack a long look. He was a tall, angular man with an athletic build, no older than forty. Matt could tell the moment he met the defense attorney that he was unusually bright. But there was something about him that Matt found striking even though he couldn't put his finger on it. He had a strong chin and prominent cheekbones. His suit appeared to be Italian and handmade, his silk tie a standout. But there was something about him. Something more than that. Almost a certain darkness. Almost the look of someone who had taken a hit in life and was ready for the next one. The look of someone who knew how to get things done while swimming against the tide.

"So what's with Doyle, Detective? Why is the federal prosecutor out to get you?"

"Because he's got the wrong man," Matt said in a quiet voice. "He's doing his press conference, he's taking credit for the arrest, he's posing for the cameras—but he's got the wrong man. Dr. Baylor had nothing to do with the murders of the Strattons or the Holloways. The killer is the same man who beat up the gossip reporter the other night. The *Daily News* published a picture of him taken by the hotel's security cameras. I briefed Agent Brown repeatedly, and I warned Doyle that he had the wrong man on numerous occasions. Unfortunately, neither one of them have done anything."

Teddy Mack flashed a thoughtful smile. "I've known Ken Doyle for more than a few years. He's a man with issues."

"Many issues," Matt said.

The defense attorney moved to the head of the table and grasped the back of the chair with both hands. "He's coming after you, Detective. He'll try anyway. He's already calling for a review of the way you and the LAPD handled the homicide investigations two months ago. And not just the three young women who were murdered in LA. He's saying that you knew Baylor was your own flesh and blood all along. Let me ask you something."

"Anything."

"When you were shot six weeks ago, why didn't you go to a hospital?"

"I was shot by a dirty cop," Matt said. "I was on the run and couldn't go to a hospital. My only chance was Dr. Baylor. At the time, no one knew that he was the killer."

"Exactly," the attorney said. "But that's not what it'll look like. Doyle thinks that because Dr. Baylor's a blood relative, everything that went down is open to question. Who's to say that the detective who shot you was really dirty? Who's to say that when you shot his partner it wasn't an act of murder? You see where he's trying to go?"

"But it's ridiculous. It's worse than ridiculous. It's ignorant. There's no basis in reality. The facts, the official record, speak for themselves."

Teddy Mack nodded. "People like Doyle don't generally have much use for facts. He's not an investigator, he's not even a very good prosecutor. Ken Doyle's a politician, Detective. A politician on the move. It doesn't matter how things turn out. When it's over, he'll have everything he ever wanted."

"And what's that?"

"Name recognition."

Matt sat back in the chair, noticed his hands quivering, and realized that he was nervous. His supervisor in Hollywood, Lieutenant Howard McKensie, had called it right before he'd even left LA. McKensie had taken one look at Doyle and known.

Trouble ahead. Proceed with caution.

Matt turned back to his attorney. "What happens next?"

"I'm having a car brought around that will take you to Ryan Day's hotel."

"A what?"

"A car. Day's been released from the hospital and needs to talk to you. He said it's important and that I shouldn't be in the room."

Matt got up and stared at Teddy Mack incredulously. "You're saying that I'm out of here?"

His attorney nodded.

Matt was stunned. "How? Why?"

Teddy Mack shrugged. "Doyle doesn't have much of a case against you, not when you really think about it. He can talk to the media all he wants, but in the end he's just pontificating. They have no record of you speaking with Dr. Baylor in the past other than your initial meeting when you were held at gunpoint. When you were released, you came forward and told them everything you knew. They're aware of a second meeting but have no details other than what you may or may not have said to Agent Brown. I doubt her thoughts on the matter would be admissible. As far as yesterday goes, they have no evidence that while you were at the Holloways' you spoke with the doctor or even knew he was there. According to the statements of the US marshals who took you into custody, they walked into the kitchen and found you standing by the counter. When they looked out the window, they saw Dr. Baylor in the backyard running away. That could mean a lot of things."

"Maybe so, but I can't believe that Rogers and Doyle are signing off on this."

"To be honest, they don't know that you're about to be released. They're not in the loop right now. When they find out, I imagine that they won't be very pleased. Setbacks go with the job."

"What about Dr. Baylor?"

"He's a different story, obviously. A team of deputy DAs was put together yesterday afternoon in Los Angeles. The doctor will be returning to California later today or tomorrow to be held until the order of trials can be sorted out."

Matt shook his head and started pacing. Everything that Teddy Mack was saying seemed so overwhelming. So unreal and dreamlike. He wondered if he could trust it.

"They might not have a case against me," he said. "But they could hold me over while they put something together."

"That's true. They could hold you over, I guess."

Matt met Teddy Mack's gaze. "Then how is this happening?"

Teddy Mack opened his briefcase and pulled out an envelope with the Marriott hotel's logo printed on its face.

"You have a friend in the FBI, Detective. Someone high in the food chain who respects you. A guardian angel, so to speak, who just happens to be a friend of mine as well. The day he first met you, he gave me a call. He was excited. He was impressed."

Matt's mind had gone blank ten minutes ago. "Who?" he said, still flabbergasted.

"Dr. Stanley Westbrook. He believes in you."

CHAPTER 58

Dr. Westbrook believes in you.

He hadn't seen the FBI profiler since the Strattons' funeral at old St. David's Church. Curiously, Dr. Westbrook wasn't on stage with *the team* during the press conference. As Matt searched his memory, he didn't remember seeing the profiler when the cameras cut to members of the task force sitting in the audience as well. It had been Dr. Westbrook who had offered an alternate profile on the mass killer and confirmed Matt's earliest theories. When Rogers and Doyle scowled at Matt during the funeral service, he could still see the expression on Dr. Westbrook's face. The profiler no longer appeared to have been judging him. Instead, Matt had detected an even, measured gaze. The look of genuine curiosity.

Could Westbrook have known what Doyle and Brown were up to, and not approved? Had Westbrook been reciting the party line early on when he'd given Matt such a hard time?

The answer appeared to be a resounding *yes*.

Matt rode in the passenger seat of an unmarked black Chevy Suburban from the Federal Detention Center on Seventh Street to the Marriott Downtown at Twelfth and Filbert Streets. It was a high-speed ride by the US marshal in the business suit. Word of Matt's release had somehow been leaked to the media, and all those cameras had been waiting for them before they could exit the building. Apparently, Doyle had proffered his theory that the homicide detective from Hollywood whom Matt had shot dead might not have been guilty of anything. Like a growing number of journalists working the political beat these days, no one bothered to check the record, and the questions came in the form of vindictive and self-righteous shrieks.

Is it true that you let Dr. Baylor go because he's your uncle? Did you really help the serial killer escape? You shot an LAPD homicide detective multiple times and let another burn to death in a house fire. Were they getting too close? Is that why you killed these people? Were you secretly working for Dr. Baylor?

Followed by the blow of blows.

Why do you hate women? Are you a serial killer, too?

Matt grabbed hold of the seat as the US marshal swerved between cars with his foot on the floor. As Matt watched him roar up the street, he couldn't help noticing the intensity of his eyes and the half smile that seemed to be permanently seared on his face. The man who wouldn't introduce himself or give his name lived in a state of perpetual amusement.

He swung around the corner, then pulled in front of the hotel lobby, the tires screeching as he came to a hard stop. The man turned and shot Matt a look.

"This is as far as I go, Jones. You're on your own now. No one followed us. You know Mr. Day's suite number?"

Matt nodded. "I've got it, thanks."

"And your attorney gave you a room key?"

Matt nodded again.

"Then you're all set, Jones." The man passed over a large manila envelope. "Your piece," he said. "Everything you brought with you was packed up and moved from the apartment on Pine Street. You should find everything in your room two floors below Day's. I guess detectives get rooms and celebrities take the suites. I've gotta go. I'm late."

Matt swung the passenger door open and got out. It had started to snow, and he watched the US marshal in the business suit with no name pull the Chevy Suburban into the street and disappear in the tunnel that cuts through the Reading Terminal Market.

He opened the manila envelope and gazed inside at his .45 and holster. Then he turned to the hotel, still in shock that he was free.

The building was massive, its footprint the size of the entire block, with a walk-in entrance on Market Street as well. Matt entered the lobby and rode the elevator up to the nineteenth floor. Ryan Day's suite was down the hall on the right. He tapped on the door and, while he waited, removed his pistol from the envelope and slid it into his holster.

"Who's there?" the reporter said through the door.

"It's me, Day. It's Jones."

He heard the locks release, and then the door snapped open. Matt was so grateful to Day for hiring Teddy Mack, so surprised by his sudden release, that all he wanted to do was shake the reporter's hand. But when he got a look at Ryan Day's face, when he cut through the stitches and the bruises still tattooing his skin, he could tell that the man was terrified.

"What is it, Day? What's wrong?"

The gossip reporter checked the hallway, then ushered Matt inside, slammed the door shut, and threw the locks.

"A package was delivered to me here at the hotel this morning. Something so horrible I don't know what to do, Jones. I'm in trouble. I'm at my wit's end."

Matt felt a chill ripple up his spine. "What is it?" he said quickly. "Show me."

Day nodded, but was unable to stop shaking. Matt looked around and spotted an envelope beside the reporter's laptop on the table in the living room. Day turned and hurried over to the table.

"Take a seat," he said, trying to catch his breath. "It's video. The killer sent me a disc, Jones."

Matt grabbed a seat and watched Day click a media window open and hit Play.

"Did you touch the disc?" he said.

"Only the edges, Jones. I'm scared shitless, not scared stupid."

Day got up and switched off the lights, then returned to his seat as the video began playing. Within a second or two, Matt felt his chest tighten and his soul lock up.

He heard the screams. He saw the terror on their faces.

The killer had recorded the night he'd murdered the Strattons. He must have been wearing spy glasses, because the horrific images were shot from the killer's point of view. Every move he made, every shot he fired, every moment, including the boy having intercourse with his mother—every single detail of the night was here in living color. But even worse, cut against these images from hell on earth was the sound of the killer's voice. He was goading his victims into submission. Shooting them one by one in order to force them to obey his commands. And he was laughing at them. Whenever one of his victims would give in, whenever one of them was shot, the horrid moment was accompanied by an insane giggle.

Matt felt his blood pressure hit the ceiling and tried to calm down.

It suddenly occurred to him that he hadn't heard any gunshots. He could see the killer shooting his victims, he could see the wound, but the pistol wasn't making any sound. He remembered his initial theory that the Strattons had been murdered on the landing in order to insulate the sound of the gun shots. That may still have been true about the loud shrieks his victims were making—their pleas and cries for mercy—but the pistol was equipped with a sound suppressor. He could see a piece of it moving in and out of the shot at the bottom of the frame. Something big and bright blue that seemed too outlandish to identify.

Matt shook his head as he watched Jim Stratton, MD, take the final bullet. The killer didn't wait around to watch the man bleed out. He fired the gun, laughed as his victim collapsed against the wall and grabbed his daughters' hands. After a few minutes, the killer wiped the blood away from Stratton's chest and taped over the wound. And then the final outrage. The blow of blows. The camera shot began to jitter for several moments, and Matt realized that it was the killer scooping the blood off the floor with his hands and spraying the walls while jumping up and down in a psychotic glee. He could hear the beast cackling in the background.

The screen went black, along with Matt's spirit and being—his core burned out. No words could describe what he'd just witnessed. Time would run out before he could ever forget what he'd seen and experienced.

"It's not over yet," Day said in a shaky voice. "Keep your eyes on the screen."

Ten seconds passed before another image faded up.

It was a naked young woman. A teenager with blond hair, lying on a bed and having sex with a man. The shot was from the man's point of view—the killer's point of view—the digital video camera mounted on a pair of spy glasses again. The image included her entire body from midthigh to her face resting on a pillow. She appeared to be enjoying herself. She was sweating and moaning and gazing right into the lens. She looked wasted, and Matt guessed from the intensity of her perspiration that she might be using ecstasy.

It was a spooky shot. In some ways as haunting and grotesque as the recording of the mass killing. A shot of another kind of victim, a girl in over her head.

But that wasn't what stood out here. Not the feelings of sadness, or even despair.

Matt looked at the girl's swollen breasts and then her face just to make sure. He took a deep breath and exhaled.

It was her, he was sure of it. He recognized her and remembered seeing her naked body. He remembered seeing her on the man's cell phone at the hotel bar the other night.

The man with the wool cap pulled over his blond cornrows.

But even better, that feeling of being awestruck hit him in the belly again. That feeling that the case was about to make another huge step forward.

He pulled Day's laptop closer, his eyes glued to the video image. After a few seconds, he spotted it on the wall. The mirror on the wall above the bedside table. A man's reflection. The killer's reflection. The man with blond cornrows, wearing a pair of eyeglasses.

CHAPTER 59

Matt wasn't surprised that his access card to the federal building's underground garage still worked. He was driving the car Carlo Genovese had lent him, a Honda four-door sedan that melted into the flow of traffic and no one seemed to notice. Pulling down the ramp and first aisle, he noted Wes Rogers's car and parked in the first empty space that wasn't marked.

His cell phone was vibrating. When he checked the face, he could see his supervisor's name blinking on the screen and took the call, Lieutenant Howard McKensie.

"What the hell is going on, Jones?"

"Everything's gonna work out, Lieutenant. Everything's good."

"Everything's good?" he said in a voice so loud Matt jerked the phone away from his ear. "Are you out of your mind? A federal prosecutor just called the LAPD incompetent. You want to tell the chief how everything's good? You want to do a conference call?"

Matt checked his watch. While he understood everything that McKensie was saying and thought his lieutenant had every right to say it, he didn't have time to explain what was going on. It was already past five, and Matt wanted to head off Rogers somewhere between the elevators and his car. He checked the ceiling for security cameras, then lowered his gaze to the concrete columns spaced every twenty feet or so.

"Are you there, Jones? Are you fucking there?"

"It's going to work out, Lieutenant. We're close and I'm back."

"You're back?"

He saw Rogers step out of the elevator. He got out of the car with his briefcase strapped to his shoulder and moved in behind a column. "The monsters are gone, Lieutenant. You'll have to trust me on this. And I've gotta go."

Matt switched off the phone, drew his .45, and chambered a round. Moving to the side, he watched the special agent approaching his car. The man was sending a text message—a natural victim completely oblivious to his surroundings. When Matt heard Rogers's car chirp and saw the lights flash, he waited a beat for the special agent to turn his back and open the car door.

That's when Matt touched the back of Roger's neck with the muzzle of his gun.

The special agent froze, and the cell phone dropped out of his hand.

"Let me guess," Rogers said quietly. "Actually, it's more than a guess. I can see your reflection in the fucking window, Jones. What in the world do you think you're doing?"

"We need to talk."

Rogers lowered his gaze and shook his head as if saying anything more would be pointless.

"We're going up to your office, Rogers."

"We're what?"

"Going up to your office."

The special agent shrugged and shook his head again. "What are you doing, Jones? You get the break of a lifetime, and now you're fucking up again. It must be in your nature. You can't help being a fuckup. It's your way."

"This isn't a negotiation, Rogers. I need five more minutes of your life. Just five minutes, and then I'm gone."

"Why?"

"Because there's a mass killer, and he's still out there. I'm gonna put the gun away. You're gonna be good, and you're gonna give me five minutes. Those five minutes will end up saving your life, Rogers."

Rogers turned and gave Matt a hard look. "Save my life?"

Matt met his gaze and nodded. "Five minutes and I'm history. I promise. We'll look at a DVD, and you'll tell me what you think. And then I'm gone. Forever gone."

The severity of expression in the special agent's eyes eased some. "Okay, Jones. Put the gun away and let's go upstairs. I've got five minutes to spend on a chance."

Matt trusted Rogers because he thought he had to. But also because Ryan Day had made a copy of the DVD, and either way, the truth would eventually come to light.

They rode the elevator up to the eighth floor, and as they walked down the hall to Rogers's office, all eyes were on Matt. No one said anything, just a lot of head scratching and long looks, cut with a few groans. Matt ignored it, watching Rogers switch on the lights and following him into the office.

The computer remained on, but sleeping. Matt slipped on a pair of vinyl gloves and reached into his briefcase for the DVD. He was about to remove the disc from the paper sleeve when a man wearing a tie stepped into the doorway. Matt assumed that he was an agent but had never seen him before. He noted the semiautomatic strapped to his shoulder, his gelled hair combed straight back, the suspicion showing on his face.

The man gave Matt a look, appeared to notice the .45 beneath his jacket, then turned to Rogers.

"Everything okay?" he said in a husky voice.

Rogers nodded. "Everything's cool."

The man looked back at Matt, sized him up, and shook his head. "I don't know how you pulled it off, Jones. But I've gotta say, the world's a pretty fucked-up place when the jail door opens and an asshole like you walks out."

Matt remained expressionless. "Do me a favor."

"What's that?"

"Close the door."

The agent exchanged looks with Rogers and eventually walked away. Matt crossed the room and closed the door.

"Where's Doyle?" Matt said.

"On a train to DC."

"What about Kate Brown?"

"She went with him."

A short moment passed. Matt thought about Brown, then let go of the anger and all the images that went with it. After a deep breath, he removed the disc from its paper sleeve and inserted it into Rogers's desktop computer.

"You should probably sit down, Rogers."

"I'll decide what I do and when I do it, Jones. Play the DVD. Your five minutes is almost up."

"Suit yourself."

Matt grabbed the mouse and waited for the computer to recognize the disc. When the media player opened, he hit Play and tried to brace himself for what came next.

The screams. The shootings. The horror.

All those moving images.

After a minute or two, he turned and gazed at Rogers. The special agent was leaning on the credenza, the expression on his face broken. Matt found it extraordinarily difficult to look at the man. He could sense his pain and thought that he might be taking the hit personally.

Matt picked up the mouse and fast forwarded to the second media entry. When the image of the blond teenager having sex faded up, Matt pointed at the killer's reflection in the mirror.

"That's the killer, Rogers. That's the man we're supposed to be looking for. The one who made the front page of the *Daily News*."

It hung there . . . like waves of radiation raining down on them from a red-hot sky. Rogers sank into his desk chair, his eyes blank. After a long moment, the special agent spoke in a deep and subdued voice.

"How many people have seen this?"

"A couple. This is the original. The killer sent it to a friend of mine. It needs to be logged in as evidence, checked for fingerprints, and examined by your tech unit."

"Meaning that there are copies?"

Matt nodded without saying anything.

Rogers shook his head and exhaled. "On a bad day, the bureau is everything you think it is, Jones. On a good day, we can still hit it out of the park. This is a bad day. A real bad day."

"I just want to know if we're on the same page, sir."

Rogers met his gaze. "Westbrook was right about you. I'm sorry I didn't see it sooner. If anyone else gets hurt, it'll be on me and I'll walk with it to my grave."

Matt didn't need to repeat the question. They were reading the same book and turned to the same page. He opened his briefcase and fished out the Strattons' family portrait still sealed in the plastic freezer bag.

"The killer masturbated on Tammy's and Kaylee's underwear the night he took this picture. The image was taken at the funeral home, and everyone in it is dead. Their bodies will need to be exhumed as soon as possible."

Rogers appeared to be flabbergasted, even dazed. He leaned closer to examine the photo. After a few seconds, he seemed to get it, then shook his head again and let out a sigh. Several moments passed, the silence electric. When the special agent finally spoke, his voice was just above a whisper.

"I need you to do me a favor, Jones."

"How can I help?"

"I want you to keep this to yourself and lie low for a couple of days. I understand how difficult that will be for you, but I need to do certain things my way. Can you do that for me?"

Matt nodded.

"Who's your friend?" Rogers went on. "Who has a copy of this disc?"

"I'd rather not say, sir."

Rogers took the hit and let it go. "I deserved that. Let me ask you this. Can the person be trusted to keep it under wraps for a while?"

"It's not really in his nature, but in this case, yes. He's aware of what's at stake and has already agreed."

Rogers picked up the phone and entered three numbers on his key pad. After listening for a moment, he spoke into the handset.

"Get in here, Lee."

Rogers hung up. A few moments later the door opened and the man with the tie, the gun, and the gelled haired walked back in.

Rogers got up from his desk chair. "Lee, you need to tell Jones that you're sorry for the things you just said to him. He's a better detective than you are. He just broke open the case. If you don't apologize, then leave your badge at the front desk and get out."

CHAPTER 60

Andrew Penchant rolled his desk chair closer to the TV and waited. *Get Buzzed* had cut to a commercial break, and the acid brewing in Andrew's stomach had risen into his throat, his rage oozing out of every pore in his milky-white skin.

With only seven minutes left to go, there had been no mention of the video clips he had sent to Ryan Day at his hotel. No mention of either sequence he'd burned onto a disc. Day had signed for the package almost ten hours ago. It seemed more than disturbing that his gift to the gossip reporter hadn't led off tonight's show.

After three and half minutes of nonsense—a string of commercials targeting the brain-dead—the show switched to a *live* feed from Ryan Day himself.

Andrew took in a deep breath and exhaled in anticipation of what he believed would be his first taste of fame and fortune. Day had played it smart after all. He was saving the best for last.

Andrew moved closer to the screen. Day was leaning against a park bench, the shot wide enough that Andrew could barely tell that he'd kicked in the reporter's face just a few days ago. The Love sculpture was over Day's right shoulder, the Christmas tree over his left, with a view of the art museum in the distance.

After twenty or thirty seconds—and to Andrew's horror—he realized that the idiotic man was talking about love and forgiveness, the meaning of the holiday season for all people no matter who they were or what they believed in or prayed to. The dumb shit was saying how grateful he felt about being alive, how lucky he was to have such wonderful friends and family members in his life.

And then *Get Buzzed* ended. And then that stupid motherfucking TV show had the audacity to stop.

Just like that. The show that Andrew had been waiting all day to watch was over.

Andrew wanted to hit something. Break something. Kill it.

He had gone to all that trouble of burning the disc and paying extra for immediate delivery by a messenger service. He'd been hoping that the video would explode onto the scene and immediately "go viral." That after all this time, he would finally achieve the fame he deserved, and the media attention and wealth that went with it.

Instead, that little shit didn't play it. He didn't even mention it.

That little worm he should have killed when he had the chance.

His mother's bedroom door opened, and Avery walked out with three Glade PlugIns that looked like they'd gone dead.

"They're not working," she said. "Nothing's working anymore. And something's going on outside the house."

Andrew's eyes rocked from the TV to her face. "What's going on outside?"

"Someone has a flashlight."

Andrew's body shuddered as he leaped out of the chair and ran into his mother's bedroom. The stench had evolved over the past twenty-four hours. The foul odor had become so rich, so dense, so outrageous, that he had difficulty breathing without gagging. As he noticed the beam of light moving across the window shades and crept across the room without looking at his mother's rotting face, he couldn't understand why Avery spent so much time in here alone. It seemed so singular and so strange.

He shook it off, moved the shade slightly, and peeked through the narrow gap. It was Mr. Andolini. The old man had walked through the gate and was standing in the driveway with a flashlight in one hand and his cell phone in the other.

Andrew felt his stomach fire up. He turned and shot Avery a quick look, then knelt down to listen to the old man through the open window.

"There's a foul odor coming from the house," Mr. Andolini was saying. "No, it's not gas. It's the smell of something rotting. Something big like a dead body. The windows are cracked open and it's December. Something's wrong, I tell you. I haven't seen the woman in days."

Andrew got up, motioned Avery out of the room, and shut the door. "He's on the phone with the police."

Avery shivered. "We need to get out of here."

"You need to get dressed. I want to pack some things."

Avery stepped into her jeans, her voice all spooked out. "There's no time to pack. We need to get out of here, Andrew. Now."

Andrew shrugged. While Avery finished dressing, he tossed his gun and the STP oil filter—Dirty Diane—into his knapsack. Then he shut down his laptop, unzipped another pocket in the pack, and slid it in. He'd bought more reefer and a new lighter and fresh pack of rolling papers and tossed them into the pocket as well. As he gazed around the room, he felt the panic begin to wash through his chest and belly.

He needed more time. He needed to check on what he was leaving behind.

There was another hit of reefer in the bong. One more hit before saying good-bye. He struck the lighter and sucked the smoke into his lungs.

"Come on, Andrew," Avery said, pleading. "Let's get out of here."

He started coughing, grabbed his knapsack, and followed her as she ran downstairs and headed for the front door.

"Don't open it, Avery. Wait a minute."

She turned and looked at him, and he could tell by her wild eyes that she was way past being scared. Andrew ran over to the window and peeked outside. Mr. Andolini had just closed the gate and was walking back to his house. Once he went inside and closed the door, Andrew turned and gave Avery the nod.

"My car's parked in front of the next house up. Let's go."

He switched the lock and shut the door behind them. Leaping down the steps, he could see Avery rushing through the darkness toward his car. He could hear her gasping for air. He could hear her grunting and groaning and even sobbing as she tried to run faster and faster still, like just maybe the Grim Reaper was closing in from behind.

CHAPTER 61

Matt tapped on Ryan Day's hotel suite door. When he didn't get a response, he dug his cell phone out of his pocket and sent the gossip reporter a text. After a few moments, Day returned the message.

On location all day. Back later.

Matt returned the phone to his pocket and walked down to the elevator. Rogers's favor seemed so difficult to keep. He wanted to be part of the hunt. He wanted to be there if and when the man with blond cornrows was identified and captured. He wanted to be there if the man put up a fight.

He had ordered breakfast in and spent the first few hours of the morning following up on some of the new information Dr. Baylor had given him. He'd scoured the *New York Times*' archives and read every article he could find about the murders the doctor committed as a twelve-year-old boy. Matt had even managed to locate the house in Maplewood, New Jersey, where the homicides occurred—the house where his mother had been born and spent her early childhood.

The doctor had told him that their home had been on and off the market since the murders, and that there was a rumor among neighbors to this day that the house might be haunted. In fact, the property was on the market again at an asking price of $2.1 million. Matt had found pictures of the place, both inside and out, on the Realtor's website and had become more than curious.

He rode the elevator down to the lobby. He'd parked Genovese's Honda in the garage across the street. Within a few minutes, he was pulling onto Filbert Street and winding his way through the city toward the Ben Franklin Bridge and I-95 North. According to the car's navigation system, depending on traffic, the drive to Maplewood wouldn't take much more than an hour and a half. At eighty-five miles per hour, the trip only took sixty-five minutes.

He toured the neighborhood briefly, then made a right turn onto Curtis Place, searching out house numbers and trying to bridle his memories of his mother. His love for her and the pitch-dark sadness at losing her when he was a boy. That feeling of being abandoned by his father and turned into an orphan until his aunt reached out and saved the day.

He could still see himself sitting on his mother's lap. He could still smell the fragrances of her clothing, her skin, and the shampoo she used to wash her beautiful hair. He spotted the house and slowed down. A Realtor's sign was in the front yard, along with information leaflets about the property. Matt pulled over and let his eyes wander up and down the street. It was late morning on a weekday. Everything seemed quiet, so he turned into the drive and got out.

He spent a few moments thinking about what this might look like to a neighbor and decided to walk onto the front lawn and take a leaflet. As he gazed at the house, he could hear his uncle's voice describing the home he so obviously cherished as a boy.

It was smaller than Matt expected. But it was also nicer. He felt the same way about the neighborhood and imagined it a near-perfect place to grow up.

He walked around to the back, climbing the steps to the rear porch and gazing through the window. Then he stepped over to the back door and looked through the glass.

No one was living here. The house was up for sale, the rooms completely empty of furniture. Even better, the burglar alarm on the wall by the door had been shut down.

He turned and checked the neighbors' houses. Both were set closer to the street and not visible from here. Behind him were the garage, a pool, and a privacy hedge blocking the houses on the next street. He thought it over. If he could get in without breaking a window, if he could—

He dug his key ring out of his pocket, examining the deadbolt and wondering if one of his jiggler keys would work. He carried three, and decided to try the last one on his key ring first. It took less than two minutes to hear that telltale click and feel the deadbolt slide back into the lock.

He pushed the door open and entered the kitchen. He felt his pulse quicken. He didn't want to spend too much time here. Just long enough to feed his imagination and get a feel for how his mother had lived the first ten years of her life when things were still good.

He made a sweep through the first floor, noting the high ceilings and ornate moldings and the wood floors that looked and smelled like they'd just been sanded and refinished. After stepping into the sun porch and gazing out the windows at the street and front yard, he hit the stairs and found the master bedroom. He played the murders back in his head. The things he'd read online and what the doctor had told him. The wall where the bed would've been placed seemed obvious. His grandfather's chest of drawers, the place where he kept his piece, felt like it might have stood beside the large walk-in closet.

Just thinking about the idea that he had a *grandfather*, that he'd used the word in his mind, blew him away. It didn't matter that the man turned out to be a scoundrel just like his father. That in the end, he needed to be shot and killed just like his old man.

Matt tried to shrug it off, but the task of processing everything he was learning about himself and his family seemed overwhelming.

As he found the stairs to the attic, he couldn't help remembering what he'd told his supervisor in Hollywood. The monsters swimming inside his head were gone. Really? He smiled as he chewed it over. Maybe they were just hiding yesterday.

But the smile only lasted until he reached the third floor.

Baylor had claimed that he'd hidden the murder weapon underneath the insulation between two joists, and Matt assumed that he was describing an unfinished attic. The rooms here had been finished with plaster and moldings, and he couldn't believe how disappointed he felt. Matt had wanted to see the attic as it had been on the night of the murders. He'd wanted to see the place where his mother and her siblings had hidden all night until daybreak.

The ceilings were vaulted here, matching the slope of the roof. He examined the woodwork and smoothed his hand over the plaster. Nothing about these rooms appeared newer than what he'd already seen on the first two floors.

And then he noticed it. A small door placed just above the baseboard in the room farthest from the stairs. He knelt down, grabbed the handle, and pulled the door open. It had the look and feel of a secret room. Matt pointed his cell phone into the darkness, switched on the flashlight, and crawled inside. There were blankets here, pillows, an old radio, and a stack of children's books. He spotted the bare lightbulb and pulled the cord. As his eyes drifted over the space—his imagination all lit up—he couldn't remember a time when he felt more alive. He had never experienced such joy.

He crawled across the boards until he reached the exposed joists and insulation. Working his way toward the roof, he lifted away the insulation until he reached the end, and there it was.

The murder weapon.

Placed exactly where his uncle had said it would be.

A Smith & Wesson .38 Special. Matt wrapped his hands around the handle and held it to the light. It was a big gun for a twelve-year-old boy to fire. Big and awkward. Matt knew that in its day, a .38 Special like this one was the weapon of choice and would have been carried by almost everyone in law enforcement.

Matt checked the cylinder and found four spent shell casings. He could feel his heart going. He could see his uncle as a boy standing in the darkness of his parents' bedroom. He could see him pointing the gun, struggling to hold the weapon steady, and probably shocked and frightened by how loud the first shot would have sounded.

Four spent shell casings. The gun that killed the man who had stolen everybody's money and ruined so many lives. A man who had fed off others until there was nothing left to eat.

Another King of Wall Street. Another bloodsucker like his father—dear old Dad.

Matt switched off the light and crawled out of the secret room. As he gazed at the pistol in daylight, it looked like an antique.

It looked like a family heirloom with a unique history that no one would ever know or remember. A vague story from a long time ago. Something about a secret room in a house that used to be haunted, but no longer was because the murder weapon had finally been located and removed.

He slipped the gun into his jacket and headed back down to the kitchen. The leaflet with information about the house was on the counter. Matt took it with him as he walked out the door and down the driveway to his car. It was still before noon, and he had all day to deal with keeping his favor to Special Agent Rogers. Try as he might, he didn't think he'd make it.

CHAPTER 62

Matt ordered two bagels with lox spread to go, along with a large coffee and two sugars. He was standing at the counter, watching TV at one of his old haunts, Deli on a Bagel, in Pennington, New Jersey, about an hour south of Maplewood. He'd just driven by his aunt's old house. As he cruised down Route 31, heading for I-95 just a few miles south, he spotted the sandwich shop and decided to stop in.

The news channel had just interrupted their broadcast with a special report, and Matt braced himself for news that the FBI had made progress and he wasn't with them.

But it was something else. The body of a thirty-five-year-old woman had been found in her home in the Northeast last night. Sarah Penchant had been shot and killed, her body not discovered for several days. The police were looking for her boyfriend, Reggie Cook, an ex-con with a history of sexual abuse. Matt looked at Cook's mug shot on the screen and lost interest. The ex-con looked like a slob. If he'd been on the run for a couple of days, Matt guessed that he was long gone.

The woman behind the counter set down his coffee and a paper bag with his order. Matt walked over, then heard something on the TV and stopped.

"She had a twenty-one-year-old son," a man was saying. "And they were unusually close. He's missing, too."

Matt looked up at the TV, sensing something. A reporter was interviewing the dead woman's neighbor on the sidewalk—an old man standing before the death house. And he was repeating himself.

"She had a twenty-one-year-old son, and they were unusually close. He's missing, too."

The mug shot of Reggie Cook had been replaced with a new one. Matt heard himself let out a groan. His entire body lit up and shivered as he swallowed the image on the screen without chewing it over. The dead eyes that he'd missed at the hotel bar and those blond cornrows.

The face of a mass killer. A mass killer who now had a name.

Andrew Penchant.

Matt bolted out of the deli to his car. When he tried to get his keys out of his pocket, he realized that he had the bagels and coffee in his hands. He pulled himself together. Once he got everything in the car and climbed behind the wheel, he fired up the engine and entered Wes Rogers's number into his cell phone. Rogers picked up after the first ring.

"Where are you, Jones?"

"About a half hour north of the city. I need the address."

"What address?"

Matt pulled out of the lot, felt the front wheels grip the road, and brought the car up to speed. I-95 was only a minute or two away.

"His name's Andrew Penchant, Rogers. The woman who was murdered in the Northeast is his mother. He's our guy. Turn on your TV."

The special agent cleared his throat, his voice pressing. "I need to know where you've been today, Jones. It's important."

Matt paused a moment to think it over. He couldn't get a read on what was going on in Rogers's mind. It didn't make any sense.

"I drove up to Maplewood, New Jersey," he said slowly. "Now I'm in Pennington. I'm on my way back."

"Maplewood, New Jersey? Stop messing around, Jones. I told you it's important."

"I'm not fooling around. You need to tell me what's going on, Rogers. I want the address, and I want it now."

"Baylor escaped," Rogers said in a low voice. "About an hour ago. It hasn't been released to the press yet."

Matt settled into his seat as he tossed it over. "How?"

"Two US marshals were escorting him back to LA. They were driving to the airport when Baylor complained of chest pain."

Matt didn't really need to hear the details. He could guess the rest. Baylor would have been examined by a cardiologist. The cardiologist would have ordered an MRI. Because Baylor was a doctor, a surgeon, he would've known that all metal objects, including handcuffs, would have to be removed in order to perform the scan. And it would have occurred in a room where he would have found himself alone.

Magnetic resonance imaging. MRI.

Matt saw the entrance to I-95 South. Once he cleared the ramp, he kicked the car up to ninety miles per hour.

"Did he hurt anyone?" he said.

"No," Rogers said. "Once the technician prepared him for the procedure, everyone walked out to watch a video feed in the control room. Apparently, the MRI facility at South Crest Hospital has a rear exit. For thirty seconds, no one was home. Security cameras picked him up running out of the lobby and taking off in a cab."

For a split second, Matt wasn't sure how to feel or even what to think. But only for a split second. After that, his mind was flooded with images of Dr. Baylor's victims. The three innocent coeds in LA and the twenty-year-old in New Orleans—Kim Bachman, a girl who weighed less than a hundred pounds. Matt had always wished that he hadn't been told the girl's weight. Somehow Bachman's small size made her more vulnerable in his mind. It made her murder seem darker in some fundamental way, and Matt always had a hard time dealing with it.

"I'm sorry he got away, Rogers."

The special agent didn't say anything, but Matt could guess what he was thinking. Rogers wasn't going to survive the blowback. Baylor's escape was just the last nail in a long series of nails buried in his coffin. Once the world caught up to this new, ever-changing reality, once Andrew Penchant was identified as the real killer, anyone who had stood on stage with Assistant US Attorney Ken Doyle would be circling the drain. Everybody who didn't get this one right would go down as roadkill.

Matt heard Rogers sigh. When the special agent spoke finally, his voice had weakened.

"I'll call Philly PD, Jones. I'll get you that address."

CHAPTER 63

Matt entered Sarah Penchant's address on Walnut Avenue into the car's navigation system and realized that it was close. No more than twenty-five minutes and only a couple of blocks off I-95.

Rogers had called with the information from Philly PD, but still wanted Matt to stand down and not act in an official capacity. His reasoning sounded suspicious, particularly after Matt switched on KYW radio and realized that the story of Baylor's escape had broken wide-open. By the time he reached Walnut Avenue and got a first look at the rundown house, he decided to meet Rogers halfway.

He didn't see any patrol units parked at the curb or anywhere on the street. When he gazed up the driveway, he found it empty. Matt imagined that the crime scene had been fairly straightforward and would have been processed sometime last night.

A lockbox was attached to the front door, but it wasn't an FBI investigation, and Matt doubted that the combination would match the universal one-eight-seven like the others.

He checked the clock on the dash. He had decided to meet Rogers halfway, meaning that he wouldn't break into the house until darkness fell around four thirty. He cruised down to the end of the block, saw the river, and pulled over before a small park. Adjusting the mirrors so that he had a clean view of Penchant's house, he settled in behind the wheel, switched the radio back on, and waited.

After listening to the news station for twenty minutes—the length of an entire news cycle—it became clear that Dr. Baylor's escape was a PR disaster for both the FBI and the Department of Justice. And while Matt understood that Rogers had his hands full, it didn't excuse the fact that there was still no mention of the break in the Stratton/Holloway murder cases. No mention of Andrew Penchant or warnings to the public. But far worse, there was no mention of any progress that could be considered a matter of public record.

Matt remembered his conversation with Rogers last night. The special agent had asked him how many people had seen the DVD of the Strattons' murder, then asked Matt to lie low and keep a lid on everything. As he tossed it over now, Rogers's request sounded like a con in a bad Hollywood movie.

It was starting to get dark. He squinted as a pair of headlights struck the rearview mirror and hit him in the eyes. He noted the lights on the roof and realized that it was a patrol unit. The car slowed down before the death house, then continued to the end of the street, passing Matt's Honda and making a turn at the corner. After a minute or two, Matt saw the patrol unit round the block on the other side of the death house and vanish up Walnut Avenue, heading toward I-95.

Matt took a sip of the coffee that had turned ice-cold, then got out of the car and walked up the street. Most of the windows in the houses he passed were still dark. He kept his eyes on the house with the picket fence that shared a property line with Sarah and Andrew Penchant's home. The old man he'd seen being interviewed on TV was in the kitchen with his wife. They were seated at a table and appeared to be eating an early supper.

Matt walked up the steps to the front porch and tried the lockbox. One-eight-seven didn't work, nor did any combination of these three numbers. When he tried his jiggler keys, he couldn't seem to get them to work either. He began to feel uncomfortable. He was spending way too much time at the front door. After checking on the neighbors, he hurried down the drive and up the steps to the back door.

He stared through the glass into the dark house as he gave his jiggler keys another try. When he couldn't get any of them to work, he knew what he had to do. He grit his teeth, took a step back, and drove his heel into the door just above the deadbolt. It was a hard kick. A drive so solid and loud that the wood frame tore loose and the door crashed open. He checked on that old couple again. They hadn't heard anything and were still seated at their breakfast table. But a dog on the next street over started barking, and it sounded old and mean.

Matt entered the kitchen, closed the door, and listened in the gloom. It was a quiet house, just the sound of the refrigerator and a slow drip from the sink. When the wind blew, he could hear the windows rattling. He dug his cell phone out of his pocket and switched on the flashlight. There were no signs that a murder had occurred here, just the strong smell of Clorox and an air freshener.

Matt moved through the first floor and up the stairs, unable to find anything that would have indicated that Sarah Penchant was shot here. He entered the master bedroom. That foul odor from an air freshener was stronger here, almost overwhelming. But still no smell of death. The bed had been stripped. Matt checked the floors and the bathroom, and didn't see any blood.

He walked out of the room and stepped into the second bedroom. From the way it was furnished, this had to be Andrew's room. He spotted an expensive briefcase that seemed out of place on the floor by the window. When he opened it, he found three files and realized that they belonged to Ryan Day.

He set the briefcase aside and moved over to the table by the bed. While he didn't find a copy of the photo Penchant took of the Strattons at the funeral home, he noticed a book and opened it.

The words were handwritten, the first page dated seven years ago. Penchant had purchased a blank book and written a story that went on for about ten pages or so. Pictures had been sketched in, pictures that appeared crudely drawn and devoid of any technique even for a child.

Matt skimmed through the words. Penchant had written a story about a family who lived down the block. He called them *the happy family*. One night after the happy family had a barbecue in the backyard and went to bed, the Grim Reaper's son, Andy, paid them a friendly visit with a sword in his hand.

"You're too happy," Andy proclaimed. "And your neighbors don't like it. Your neighbors hate you. They hate every one of you. Your happiness must end, and it must end tonight!"

Matt shook his head. Andrew Penchant had written a story about killing a family seven years ago. He would have been around fourteen at the time. Dr. Westbrook's profile was spot on.

Matt noticed a knapsack on the bed and set the book down. Moving to the desk chair, he propped his cell phone with the flashlight against the lamp and zipped open the bag. There was a laptop computer here, a small bag of reefer with papers and a lighter. When he opened the main pocket, his heart fluttered in his chest.

He was staring at a Glock .40 caliber semiautomatic with a bright-blue STP oil filter fitted to the muzzle. Matt felt the sudden rush of adrenaline washing through him like a tidal wave. It was a fascinating homemade sound suppressor, but that's not why he was having difficulty catching his breath.

Andrew Penchant was here.

He was in the house.

He had to be.

If this knapsack had been on the bed last night when detectives processed the crime scene, they would have logged it in as evidence and taken it away.

Matt switched off the flashlight and picked up the pistol with the oil filter. The balance was off, the gun front heavy. He checked the mag, held it to the dim light feeding in through window, and counted fifteen bullets. Chambering a round as quietly as he could, he stood up, moved to the door, and listened.

A minute went by, and then another.

Matt eased through the doorway and into the master bedroom. All he could hear was his own breathing. Short, shallow breaths. The bathroom seemed particularly dark.

Still, he knew that Penchant was here. He could smell him. Somewhere lost in the horrific odor of the air fresheners was something new. It was the smell of reefer. Penchant had been here, probably watching Matt from the doorway as he went through his things.

But he was gone now. The room was clear.

Matt moved down the hallway, checked the second bathroom, and returned to the first floor. As he stepped into the kitchen, his cell phone started vibrating in his pocket. The ringer was switched off, yet it seemed so loud. He read the caller's name on the face, then quickly looked for a corner beside the doorway and backed in with the Glock .40 up and ready.

He was standing in the last place anyone would check if they entered the room. Matt was about to give up his position, but he had Penchant's gun and thought he still had the upper hand.

As he mulled it over, he realized that he didn't have a choice. He had to take the call because it was Wes Rogers. He needed to do it in as few words as possible.

Matt switched on the phone and remained silent.

"Are you there, Jones? Are you there?"

"Yes," he whispered.

"What's wrong with your voice?"

Matt ignored the question. "What do you want?"

"We exhumed the bodies, Jones. A preliminary exam seems to back up the undertaker's story. We brought him in, and he's talking. I realize that things aren't moving as fast as you'd like, but we have to do this my way."

Matt remained quiet, listening to the silence in the house.

"We're working with Philly PD," Rogers went on. "They have DNA samples from the son of the murder victim in the Northeast, this kid with the cornrows, Andrew Penchant. If we get a match with the semen found on Tammy Stratton and her daughter's underwear, we go public. What you need to know is that Sarah Penchant's boyfriend, Reggie Cook, washed up on shore this afternoon near the airport. He'd been shot in the head and neck. The investigator from the coroner's office said it's possible both were killed around the same time. Philly PD thinks that Andrew Penchant shot Cook and murdered his mother."

Matt switched off the cell phone. He heard a board on the stairs creak, and stepped out of the kitchen. As he passed the dining room, his eyes moved to the window just as a figure dropped from the second floor onto the driveway.

Matt raced through the kitchen and ripped open the door. He could see Andrew Penchant running through the backyard. He had his knapsack and was heading for the next street over. Matt chased him across the lawn and through the trees. But as he started around a fence toward a neighbor's driveway, he took a hard blow to the chest and collapsed onto the ground. Penchant had a baseball bat and took another full swing at his lower back. He was all juiced up and screaming at him from above.

"What the fuck is wrong with you, man? You were supposed to be my friend."

It sounded like Penchant had freaked out. Matt saw him raising the bat and reached out to block the hit. It was a blind move with Matt protecting his head and face and rising to his knees.

But Andrew Penchant had faked him out by pulling back. By the time Matt got to his feet, the man with blond cornrows was running off with his gun and the oil filter and to a car waiting for him in the shadows at the end of the driveway.

Matt gazed at the blond-haired girl behind the wheel as Penchant jumped in. She couldn't have been more than eighteen. She was staring back at him like a black widow with a baby face. Her gray eyes were smoldering, her expression sullen and pouty and evil, just like her man's. Her soul mate.

Matt drew his .45, jacked back the slide, and emptied all eight rounds into the car as it sped off. When the last shot had fired, when the flashing stopped and all the noise, the baby-faced blonde gave the car horn a double tap like she was laughing at him.

Like she thought it was a game, and she wanted him to know that everything was okay.

CHAPTER 64

Andrew Penchant traded looks with Avery, still behind the wheel, then turned back and gazed through the windshield. Ryan Day had just climbed out of the van and was sliding the side door shut. He could see Mr. Hollywood waving at his friend and walking across Filbert Street toward the hotel as the van drove off. The little shithead seemed so happy with himself Andrew wished that they could run him down and get it over with.

Unfortunately, he needed to talk to the slob.

It was day 2 in "let's see if *Get Buzzed* plays the DVD Andrew had made of the Stratton murders." Day 2 in the big contest, and Day still hadn't mentioned that he'd received such a wonderful gift.

Andrew opened his knapsack, made sure that the oil filter was fixed tight to the muzzle of his pistol, then zipped up the pocket and passed the bag over to Avery.

"Are you sure you can do this?" he said. "We could wait. We could try to figure out another way."

She smiled. "I'm ready," she said. "Ready to party."

Andrew watched her light a half-smoked joint from the ashtray and take a hit. No doubt about it, she looked stoned.

"Let's talk about this," he said.

"I'm gonna ride up to the nineteenth floor with him."

Andrew nodded. "Open your jacket. Let him see your tits. He'll dig it."

She unzipped her jacket and tossed her scarf on the backseat. "I'll let him have a good look. Then I'll make small talk like I'm staying in the next room. Once he pulls out his key card, I'll take the gun out of the pack and force him into his room."

Andrew was in love with her. "Exactly," he said. "And then you call me on my cell."

She kissed him deep and wet and then smiled. "Gotta go, baby."

Andrew watched her run across the street, catch up to Day, and follow him into the hotel. Pulling the keys out of the ignition, he waited a few moments, then locked up the car and walked toward the lobby doors. After five minutes of waiting outside, he started to get nervous. But ten minutes later, his cell phone rang out and he saw Avery's name blinking on and off the face.

"You okay?" he asked.

"Room nineteen twenty-seven," she said in a playful voice. "You were right. He liked me, and he liked the view. He asked me out for a drink later. What a perv."

Andrew entered the lobby with his face down. When he stepped into the elevator, he pulled a tissue out of his pocket and pretended to use it while blocking his face from the security camera. He reached the nineteenth floor, found the room, and tapped on the door. A moment later, Avery opened up and struck a pose with Dirty Diane in her right hand. Andrew noted the excitement in her glazed eyes, then looked past her at Ryan Day hunched over and sitting on the floor.

Andrew entered the suite and locked the door. Stepping into the bathroom, he grabbed two hand towels and used the first to tie Day's wrists behind his back. Then he removed the man's eyeglasses, ground them into the carpet, and gagged him with the second towel.

Andrew laughed as he tied the man up. The celebrity gossip reporter, the Hollywood big shot with the bruised face, had succumbed to his power and appeared to be terrified.

"Look," he said to Avery. "He's trembling like a little baby boy."

Ryan Day let out a groan.

Andrew spoke through clenched teeth. "Why didn't you use the DVD I sent you, Day? It was a gift. It cost me money. It would've made me rich and famous and given me the life I deserve."

Day tried to speak through the gag, but started weeping. A muffled "Please, don't hurt me" came out.

Andrew noticed the laptop in Day's briefcase, set it on the table, and switched on the power.

"Where were you today, Mr. Hollywood? I looked for you all over town but couldn't find you."

Day muttered something.

Andrew slapped him on the side of his head. "You want to get kicked again, you shithead? You want to get beaten and smacked and go to the fucking hospital like you did the other night? Tell me where you were?"

Day shook his head. "On location," he managed through the towel.

"On location," Andrew repeated with delight. "You hear that, Avery? Mr. Hollywood over here was *on location*."

Avery burst out in laughter.

Andrew glanced over at her as she sat down on the couch, her eyes bloodshot and wild and still all tripped out. Her hair needed to be washed and combed, and as he thought it over, both of them could have used a hot shower and a clean change of clothes.

He turned back to the computer. On the start page, he saw a handful of media files. The one with today's date stood out, and Andrew clicked it.

After a beat, the media player opened and a copy of today's broadcast of *Get Buzzed* began playing in the window. It had the feel of a hidden camera with Day standing behind a bush at the front gate of an enormous mansion. The kind of mansion Andrew had always dreamed of living in. The kind of home Andrew had always thought his life as a man of mystery, a headline, and a living legend, maybe even a secret agent, demanded. The building was set on an open body of water with a massive yacht anchored just offshore. There was an Olympic-sized pool and a private beach. The entire property was showy and flashy and reminded Andrew of the way rich people lived in Las Vegas.

It came down to a matter of lifestyle for Andrew—getting back to the basics. Andrew had always liked his steak overdone, or as they say in fancy French restaurants, *well done*. Why should his home be any different?

He pulled himself together and tried to focus.

A man in a business suit had just exited the mansion and was being ushered by two bodyguards into a long black limo. The camera had zoomed in for the shot, the editor slowing the speed down so that the TV audience would be able to get a good look at the important man's face.

Andrew leaned closer to the screen.

The man looked just like Detective Matt Jones. A grown-up version of Matt Jones. A rich-guy version.

Andrew turned to the reporter. "Who is this, Day?"

Day closed his eyes and shook his head again, refusing to speak. Andrew walked over and slapped him on the side of his head again.

"It's who I think it is, isn't it? It's Jones's rich old man. The freak who won't even admit that he's got a fucking kid. You shot this in Connecticut, didn't you? That's where he lives, right? *On location* in Connecticut?"

He slapped him with an open hand again, then turned to Avery. "How's your high?"

She shrugged, then nodded and looked up in confusion.

"You feel like having sex with this slob? He's a TV star. It might be good to shoot it."

She didn't get where he was going. He turned back to the reporter.

"Hey, Day, you feel like fucking my girlfriend?"

Day appeared to wither. Andrew got up and waved Avery over.

"Let's get him out of his clothes," he said. "Pull his pants down and get his boxer shorts off. I'll get my phone out and shoot it."

She smiled back at him. Andrew could see Day cringing as Avery loosened his belt, got him out of his shoes and socks, and pulled his pants down. When she unbuttoned his shirt, he started weeping again, shaking more violently, his eyes losing their focus.

"What about his shirt?" she said. "His wrists are tied."

Andrew knelt down, aiming the camera on his phone at them. "Do the best you can," he said. "And take off your top."

Ryan Day appeared to flinch and shrink back as Avery removed her tank top and pulled his shirt over his shoulders.

"Do you really want me to take off his boxer shorts?"

Andrew pulled the phone away from his eye and gave the reporter a good look as he thought it over. He could feel the sweaty man's sorrow and humiliation and was sickened by him. He could hear him whimpering and pleading like a coward through the hand towel.

"Forget it, Day. You're a creep. I don't want you touching my girlfriend. I've got a better idea. Avery, I want to show you something. Go get the gun."

Avery ran back over to the couch and picked up the Glock .40 fixed to the STP oil filter.

"Did you bring that joint with you?" Andrew said.

She nodded and met his eyes. "Yes."

"Better take another hit."

"I'm wasted. I don't think I need it."

"Take one just for me."

As Avery lit the joint and drew the smoke into her lungs, Andrew moved closer to Day and lowered his voice. "I want to know where Jones's father lives in Connecticut. You tell me, Day, and we go away. You don't, and things could get out of control. My guess is that I could probably look it up on the Internet, so it's not like it's a big deal. Know what I mean? There's no reason to not give it up."

Avery started coughing and appeared dizzy. She stumbled, reached out for the coffee table, and sat down. Andrew picked up the semiautomatic pistol and put it in her hands.

"You okay?" he asked.

She nodded, then wiped her nose with the back of her hand and started giggling. "The room's spinning. I'm hallucinating."

Andrew smiled at her. He was in love with her. All the way in love with her.

"Isn't she perfect, Day? Isn't she a knockout? When this is all over, you should fly her out to Hollywood and put her on your show." He gave the reporter another slap. "Now what's the address in Connecticut?"

Day lowered his head and stared at the carpet like he'd just figured out that he didn't stand a chance.

"What's his address, Day?" Andrew repeated.

Day didn't respond or even try to respond.

Andrew pulled Avery over and pointed at Day's right thigh. "I want you to aim the gun here and pull the trigger. You think you can do that?"

She was still giggling, still wiping her nose with the back of her hand. Andrew watched her stand up, struggle to find her balance, and move closer to Mr. Hollywood. After a moment, she aimed the pistol at his thigh, but her hands were shaking so violently Andrew had to steady them for her.

"It's okay, beautiful," Andrew said in a gentle voice. "Nothing's gonna happen. You're not even gonna hurt him. In the spy business, they call this a warning shot. Right, Day? You're a reporter and you won't tell me what I want to know. We need a warning shot, right, Mr. Hollywood?"

Day recoiled and became small. "Please," he kept saying through the gag. "Please don't hurt me."

Andrew raised his cell phone and switched on the video. "Okay, beautiful. You're up and we're rolling. Action."

"It's a warning shot, right?" she said, still unable to stop giggling.

"You got it," Andrew said. "Take your shot."

Avery stepped even closer, the gun still bouncing up and down in her shaky hands. Andrew watched Day's eyes rise up from the carpet, pass over her black bra until they reached her face, and then, finally, her glazed eyes.

"No, no, no," he pleaded through the gag. "No, no, no."

Avery pulled the trigger, and the Glock .40, fixed with an STP oil filter to suppress the sound, clicked fifteen times until the mag ran out. She dropped the pistol on the carpet and turned to Andrew.

"What happened?" she said in a panicky voice. "I didn't hear anything."

Andrew smiled and beckoned her to take a look at what was left of Ryan Day, the celebrity gossip reporter, Mr. Hollywood, laid out before her in a pool of blood.

She started to giggle again, then stopped and took another hit off the joint.

"I'm so dizzy," she said.

CHAPTER 65

Matt saw the director of hotel security cross the lobby, heading for his office down the hall. He recognized him from the news clip he'd seen on television a few mornings ago.

Matt had been trying to get in touch with Ryan Day all night and had become concerned. The reporter wasn't answering his cell phone or returning text messages. When he knocked on his door, Day didn't answer and all Matt heard from the other side was silence.

Still, Matt didn't start to really worry until he decided to have a drink and saw Day's camera operator sitting at the bar. Apparently, they had spent the day in New York and Connecticut and returned a couple of hours ago. Day was supposed to meet him for a drink before dinner, but never showed up. When Matt asked what they were doing in Connecticut, he wouldn't say.

Matt followed the security director through the door and into his office. The nameplate pinned to his suit jacket read "Mr. Harvey." Matt guessed that he was in his midfifties and probably didn't spend too much time at the gym.

"May I help you?" the man said.

Matt could see recognition showing on his face. He seemed spooked and a little jumpy.

"I think something's happened to my friend in nineteen twenty-seven. We need to check on him. You need to bring your master key and open the door for me."

Harvey sized Matt up, then shook his head and winced. "I know who you are, Jones. I saw it on TV. I don't have to do anything."

Matt grabbed him by the shoulder. "We can talk about it in the elevator. I'm in a hurry."

The security director gave Matt a push and pulled away. "You helped a serial killer escape, for Christ's sake. I don't care who's paying for your room. I don't like you. I'm gonna have you thrown out of the hotel."

The man made a mistake and pulled a walkie-talkie out of his jacket pocket. Before he could bring the device to his mouth and press the Talk button, Matt batted it onto the floor and grabbed him by the collar. Mr. Harvey struggled, but it was pointless. Matt moved in closer, nose to nose, his voice low and dead.

"There's no time for this, Mr. Harvey. Believe me—wrong guy, wrong night. Do I need to frighten you? Do I need to threaten you or scare you? Do I need to arrest you? Is that what it's going to take for you to do your job? I can do all of the above, but we're wasting time. Now let's go."

Matt released him. After a few moments, the security director picked up his walkie-talkie, pulled himself together, and nodded with a frown.

"Okay," he said. "Let's go."

They walked out and rode the elevator up to the nineteenth floor without exchanging a single word. That troubled feeling in Matt's gut had become overwhelming. Day was a reporter. Reporters returned calls. It was in their nature to return calls.

They started down the hallway. He noticed the security director's eyes get big as he drew his .45 and chambered a round from a fresh mag.

"Give me the key card, Mr. Harvey. And you'll need to stand back."

"What's going on?"

"I wish I knew."

They reached the door, and the security director handed over the master key card. Matt slipped it into the reader, heard the lock click, and pushed open the door an inch at a time.

His eyes raced across the room, then screeched to a stop when they landed on Ryan Day's bullet-ridden body. He drew the door closed to block the view and closed his eyes. He'd sensed it, but wasn't ready to see it.

"Do you have your walkie-talkie, Mr. Harvey?"

The man stammered nervously. "Yeah, what is it? What's in the room?"

"Call the police," Matt said. "Tell them Ryan Day's been murdered. And do yourself a favor. Step away from the door and don't look inside."

Matt heard the security director make the call over his walkie-talkie, then opened the door and entered the suite. He took in the crime scene, cataloging the details in rapid succession. The spent joint on the coffee table, and the burn mark it left on the wood. Papers dumped all over the floor. The refrigerator door standing open, the drinks and snacks looted. It looked like Day had been stripped down to his boxer shorts in order to humiliate him as a man and as a human being. He'd been bound and gagged and shot so many times that he was barely recognizable, his wholeness, his person, chopped into body parts.

Images surfaced. Pictures in his mind of the baby-faced psycho bitch behind the wheel of her car, and Andrew Penchant with his blond cornrows, sitting at the bar the other night, making some sort of deviant play. Matt could feel the clouds moving in over his soul. His emotions dragging him into the thunderstorm.

He knelt down, kissed the first two fingers on his right hand, and touched Day's forehead. The reporter had helped him when he needed it most. But it was more than that. Ryan Day had given him back his family. His history. His roots.

Matt sensed movement and turned to the doorway. Mr. Harvey was staring at Day's corpse and appeared to be panic-stricken.

Matt walked over to the laptop, slipped on a pair of vinyl gloves from his pocket, and touched a key. When the computer woke up, he saw the media player on the screen and pressed Play.

For several moments his mind remained numb like he was just going through the motions. He saw the mansion, the yacht, and the limo waiting before the front entrance, but nothing seemed to connect or register. And then the door opened, and a man who looked quite like himself walked out and climbed into the limo.

His father was exiting his mansion on the Sound.

Ryan Day had found him. A big thought with an even bigger ending.

Matt felt his skin flush as he worked his way through the idea and its possible consequences. Then he bolted out the door and sprinted down the hall to the elevators. He had a chance, he kept telling himself. He had a chance because when he touched Day on the forehead, when he'd given him his blessing, the reporter's body was still warm.

CHAPTER 66

It wasn't that Matt forgave his father as much as he had reached a point where he was finally beginning to understand him.

The idea that his father in all probability had walked out on his wife because she told him her secret was unforgivable. The fact that his father refused to even acknowledge the existence of his son after his wife died of cancer was unforgivable. But for Matt the worst of all was yet to come. The idea that his father would try to keep what he'd done to both Matt and his mother a secret, the idea that he would hire a man like Billy Casper to gun down his own son and make his entire past go away, was beyond the pale.

Yet as Matt crossed over the Ben Franklin Bridge and hit I-95 North bound for Greenwich, Connecticut, none of it seemed to matter.

He didn't need to forgive the man in order to understand him. And he couldn't sit on the sidelines and let his father and his second wife and their two sons become Andrew Penchant's next mass killing.

M. Trevor Jones, the King of Wall Street, deserved better. It sounded so strange to play those words in his mind. He deserved to be outed in public. He deserved to be incarcerated for attempted homicide, to be living with the population in a federal prison.

His father deserved to be shunned and disgraced.

But not killed.

Matt had sensed this change in his attitude when he first set eyes on the .38 Special hidden between the joists on the third floor of his mother's former home. He'd sensed it, but he hadn't been able to bring it to the surface.

He'd pulled the insulation away to reveal the murder weapon. The gun that his uncle had used to kill his parents at the age of twelve so many years ago.

But Matt knew in his heart—knew it then—that he wasn't built like Dr. Baylor. Repeating what the doctor had done, killing his own father, wasn't the right answer anymore.

He reached in and felt the .38 Special still jammed into his jacket pocket. He ran his fingers over the muzzle, and then the cylinder and handle.

Killing his father wasn't the answer here.

His cell phone started ringing. Matt checked the face, saw Rogers's name, and took the call.

"I hope you've got good news," Matt said.

"Greenwich PD sent two units over to the man's house. They said the place is clear, but they'll stay until everything gets sorted out. The man has a pair of bodyguards, and both are licensed to carry firearms."

"So I've heard," Matt said. "Thanks, Rogers."

The special agent paused a moment. When he came back, his voice had changed and sounded more subdued.

"He told Greenwich PD that you're not related, Jones. He told them that he's not your father."

Matt didn't say anything. He was just grateful that Greenwich PD had been willing to help.

"I'll be there in ninety minutes."

Rogers cleared his throat. "It doesn't sound like he wants you to come. He might not let you on the property."

Matt let it pass. "What's going on?"

"I'm at the hotel with Philly PD," he said. "But you've got enough on your plate. Turn on your radio. And call me when you get to Greenwich."

Rogers hung up. Matt switched off his cell phone, cracked the window open, and lit a smoke. It was starting to snow, and he switched on the radio. He'd lost the signal out of Philly and switched to KYW's sister station WCBS 880 radio in New York.

There were only two stories. The snowstorm that had become a nor'easter and was expected to hit the East Coast with a vengeance tonight. Hurricane-force winds, flooding with high tide, and two or three feet of snow were only part of the good news. But the big story was Ryan Day's murder in Philadelphia, the host of the popular TV show *Get Buzzed*, and the manhunt for Andrew Penchant, a twenty-one-year-old who allegedly murdered his mother and her boyfriend and was believed to be traveling with a younger woman who still hadn't been identified.

The baby-faced blonde with those smoldering gray eyes.

Matt reached the New Jersey Turnpike and took another drag on the cigarette. The snow was blowing sideways now, and traffic heading north reduced to two lanes and moving at only forty-five miles per hour.

His stomach started going again. He tried to keep cool.

CHAPTER 67

Indian Field Road hadn't been plowed yet, the snow almost a foot deep. As Matt slid through a curve, he spotted his father's mansion and the lights from two patrol units in the drive.

He pulled down the road and through the gate and parked underneath the front entrance. The wind was howling, the nor'easter brutal. Zipping up his jacket, he got out of the car and ran over to the patrol unit idling by the steps. He knocked on the driver's side window. When no one responded, he brushed the snow off the glass and peered inside.

And then he flinched.

The car was running, the lights were on, and the two cops in the front seat were dead.

The cop behind the wheel had been shot in the face, his partner in the forehead.

Matt drew his .45, eyeing the house and property, then ran over to the second unit backed into the mansion's parking area. Like the first patrol car, the engine was idling and the lights were on.

But Matt could feel it in his bones before he even got within ten feet of the car. He saw the snow accumulating on the windshield and did the math. He ran around to the driver's side, wiped the snow away, and gazed inside.

Two more cops shot in the head.

Matt shivered as he took a deep breath and tried to focus. He noted the footprints in the snow, and did a quick inventory of the cars parked in the lot. The Range Rover, the Bentley Continental GT, the Jaguar F-Type coupe, and MX-5 Miata roadster hadn't moved since the snow began falling. But the rundown Toyota Corolla with Pennsylvania plates had and, from the tire tracks, appeared to have been here for at least an hour.

Matt spotted the footprints by the Corolla and followed them with his eyes to a door that he guessed opened to the kitchen. Like the tire tracks, the footprints didn't appear fresh.

He needed to work quickly. He opened the car door, took the cop's radio mike, and pressed Talk.

"Officers down," he said in as calm a voice as he could manage. "Officers down."

The dispatcher came on, a female who sounded concerned. "You're not Sergeant Murphy," she said. "Please identify yourself."

A hard gust of wind blew snow into Matt's face. He didn't have time to get into a conversation.

"This is LAPD Detective Matt Jones. Four of your people were sent to a home off Indian Field Road. All four are down, and the two shooters are still here. Andrew Penchant and a young female. I need your help."

Matt dropped the radio mike, popped open the trunk, and ran to the back of the car. When he looked inside, he spotted a twelve-gauge pump gun, picked it up, and checked the mag tube. It was a shotgun designed specifically for law enforcement that Matt had used in the past. A Remington 870P with a short fourteen-inch barrel and an extended mag that held two additional three-inch shells. One shell had already been chambered. Five more had been loaded into the tube.

He spotted a box of shells in a nylon pack and ripped it open, grabbing two handfuls and stuffing them into his pockets. Then he ran up the steps and tried the front door. When he found it locked, he stepped back and, without hesitation, pulled the trigger.

The sound of the 870P was deafening. The three-inch load blew open the door and knocked it onto the floor. Matt grimaced as he chambered another shell and entered the mansion.

It was all about speed now and not wasting time. He spotted the wide staircase and raced up the steps. His first thought was that Penchant would repeat himself and commit the murders on the second-floor landing. But when he reached the top and prepared to fire the shotgun, no one was here.

Matt began to worry. He found the master bedroom, but no one was here as well. The house was dead quiet.

He raced back downstairs and stormed through the first floor—room by room—completely focused on his mission. This was no longer about making an arrest. As he turned the corner, he saw two bodies at the other end of the hallway and burst forward. It was the two bodyguards he'd seen with his father on the news, laid out on the floor beside a set of doors that were closed. Both men had been stripped of their weapons and shot in the back. Matt moved over to the doors and listened.

Silence. Stillness. None of it good.

He readied the shotgun, grit his teeth, and kicked open the doors. And that's where he found them. His father, his stepmother, and their two sons. The sight carried so much weight to it that Matt had to take a moment before he could enter. He noted the books on the shelves, a library table, and his father's desk—everything gathered in quick glimpses, everything playing like a nightmare. The room had the feel of being private—a space where his father could work and read without being disturbed.

Matt's eyes drifted back to the four murder victims and the pools of blood collecting on the Oriental rug and hardwood floor. His stepmother and her two sons had been stripped of their clothing. Like Tammy Stratton and Mimi Holloway, one of her sons had been draped over her naked body. Matt guessed that both sons were in their midtwenties. After his return from Afghanistan, he had driven up from New Jersey to take a look at things. At the time he had wanted to confront his father, but in the end, decided against it. He could remember spying on them while they drank wine and cocktails on the terrace. He could remember his stepbrothers dressed as if they were twins. They would've been twenty, and the way they were dressed had seemed so odd and disconcerting.

Matt walked over to his second stepbrother and knelt down for a look at his face. As he lowered his gaze, he noticed semen on the floor beside a second pair of panties. They were pink and way too small to fit his stepmother.

What the hell were these people into? How could anyone start out fresh and become an Andrew Penchant? And how could anyone like Penchant find someone to be with who was apparently a kindred spirit?

Matt glanced at his father, noting all the papers on the floor and the gunshot wound to his chest. Even though his father remained clothed, he found the sight of his dead body too painful to look at. There was too much going on. Too many dark clouds racing over his being, and Andrew Penchant and his psychotic getaway driver were still free, still living and breathing in the real world.

He jumped to his feet, rushing for the doors, when something in the room moved. Matt took a deep breath and turned back to his father.

His eyes were open. He was staring at him.

Matt ran back into the room, knelt down, and felt his father take his hand. He could see the man appraising him, measuring him—his eyes big and wide and filled with a certain kind of wonder and curiosity. As he held Matt's right hand with his own, he raised his free hand and felt Matt's face almost as if he couldn't believe that his firstborn son was real. He smoothed his fingers over Matt's forehead and down the bridge of his nose. He touched his cheeks and felt his chin. Then he gave Matt's hand a light squeeze. He was trying to say something, but didn't seem to have the strength to speak.

He lowered his gaze, and Matt followed his eyes over to his wife and two sons. Matt could tell that he was replaying his horrific evening in his mind. The nightmare and the terror.

After a long moment, his father looked back at him, and a tear dripped down his cheek. And then another. When he gave Matt's hand another squeeze, everything inside Matt seemed to stop. He could feel that flock of blackbirds flying through his soul again. Wave after wave coming from a full moon.

"I'm here, Father," he whispered. "I'm sorry I was too late."

His father gazed back at him. After he gave Matt's hand another squeeze, his eyes lost their focus and he became still.

"I'm sorry I was too late."

CHAPTER 68

Matt ripped through three rooms until he reached the living room and a wall of glass.

The blackbirds were still migrating through his soul from a full moon.

Everything inside him was coagulating into a hardened mass of rage. Everything he'd seen since he left LA, everything he'd experienced, all of it burning up inside him like a wildfire that could never be contained.

Something caught his eye. Lights through the heavy snow.

He tried to focus. It couldn't be Greenwich PD. He was standing before a window that faced the terrace and the Sound.

He moved over to the set of French doors. The snow was still blowing sideways in a hard wind. Throwing the locks, he pushed open the doors and stepped outside into the storm.

It was his father's yacht, the *Greedy Bastard*. He could see Penchant and the blonde scrambling across the deck. Penchant had just made it into the bridge and switched on the lights. It looked like the girl was trying to free the line lashed to the rear cleat. Like they were thinking about taking the yacht out for a ride in the storm.

Matt didn't know anything about boats. The *Greedy Bastard* could be a large boat or a small ship. He didn't know what to call it or what words to use. All he knew was that the yacht stretched past eighty or ninety feet and obviously required a crew.

He sprinted across the terrace and down to the dock. The tide was up, the rough swells steep and ocean-like. Climbing into one of the three dinghies, he untied the line and pulled the cord on the motor. After three tries, the engine lit up and he began to cut through the choppy water. The spray was ice-cold and stung when it smacked his face. For a brief moment, he thought about what might happen if he fell overboard in water this cold. He guessed that he might last for a minute or two, but not much longer than that. Hypothermia would come so quickly he probably wouldn't even realize his own death.

He shook it off. He was closing in on the yacht, less than fifty yards out now. The blonde had untied the first line and was running from stern to bow. But then she stopped and turned and looked right at him. Her eyes got big and crazy and she rushed into the bridge and started shouting something at Penchant.

Then both of them ran onto the deck, each with a pistol in their hand. They were looking for him in the snow. They were listening to the motor and searching for him in the darkness.

Matt couldn't afford to cut the engine. Not in water this choppy or this cold. All he could do was brace himself.

Penchant seemed to locate him, raised his pistol, and fired a single round. When the girl followed his lead, Matt thought that he heard the slug hit the water about ten yards off to his right.

They fired two more gunshots—the sound of the pops identical and way too clean to come from a Glock .40 semiautomatic. Matt guessed that they were using the weapons they'd pulled off the bodyguards before shooting both men in the back.

Before shooting his father.

Matt let it go. He was closing in now and guessed that every inch forward made him more visible. He raised the shotgun and waited. When it looked like Penchant had located him in the darkness and was ready to take a third shot, he pulled the trigger, rocked the slide back, and fired another shell.

It worked. The girl slipped, but rushed toward the bow to release the line from the buoy, and Penchant scrambled across the deck into the bridge. Matt killed the motor as he glided into the stern. After lashing the dinghy up, he took a moment to load three more shells into the mag tube, then started up the ladder. The *Greedy Bastard*'s engines turned over, the sound deep and throaty before they cut out. Penchant tried a second time, but the engines still wouldn't catch.

Matt peered over the rail and up the deck. The girl had released the second line and vanished. The *Greedy Bastard* was floating away from its mooring buoys and beginning to toss up and down in the wind and big waves.

Penchant tried the engines again. This time both of them turned over and lit up. When Matt heard Penchant adjusting the throttle, he climbed over the rail and ran toward the bridge. He looked through the window and could see Penchant standing before the wheel. He raised the shotgun. From a distance of twenty feet, he couldn't miss.

And that's when the blonde decided to swing the boat hook down and strike Matt on the head. He lost his footing on the ice and fell, the shotgun sliding across the deck and out of reach. It had been a hard blow, and his heart started pounding as panic set in. He could see her standing before him with a wicked grin on her face. He tried to scramble to his feet, but she took another swing with the boat hook and knocked him down again. She tossed the pole aside and reached for the semiautomatic stuffed in her jeans.

Matt lunged for the shotgun, rolled over as fast as he could, and pulled the trigger. The heavy blast missed, but she lost her balance and slipped on the ice. As she tried to recover, she started screeching almost like she'd snapped and lost all control. Matt was afraid to look at her too closely. Afraid she might have snakes in her hair. Afraid he might turn to stone. He drove the butt of the shotgun into her face, then watched her shudder and go down. She mumbled something, and Matt grit his teeth. When she snatched her gun off the deck and got to her knees, when she turned and raised the pistol in the air, when her eyes seemed to widen and glow and met Matt's gaze, he pulled the trigger and watched her take a three-inch shell in the gut. Then he chambered another shell, raised the barrel to her face, and pulled the trigger again.

The sweet smell of spent gunpowder permeated the air. He could see the girl's mangled body snap backward, hit the railing, and vault upward in the heavy winds. Matt ran over to the rail fast enough to see her hit the water and vanish. But as he looked at the splash, he saw the boat's wake and realized that the *Greedy Bastard* was underway.

He turned, but not fast enough.

Penchant was standing in the doorway with his semiautomatic raised. From the expression on his face, he had witnessed the shooting and seen his girlfriend get blown overboard into the void. Matt pulled the trigger and dove sideways onto the deck. The shotgun hadn't been aimed anywhere near Penchant, but seemed to shake him up enough to throw off his timing. Matt heard the pistol fire, chambered another shell, poked the muzzle up and out, and pulled the trigger.

The blast missed Penchant, but the shards of glass from the bridge window didn't. Matt heard him let out a scream and watched as he rushed back into the bridge, throttled the engines all the way up, and cackled like a madman.

The *Greedy Bastard* picked up speed, the large vessel slicing through the whitecaps. Matt turned back to the bridge and saw Penchant spinning the wheel in a violent motion. As the yacht changed course, Matt looked over the bow and knew that they were doomed. He could see a dark mass through the snow. An island made with piles and piles of large black rocks. Penchant was steering the *Greedy Bastard* straight ahead.

Matt aimed the shotgun at him and fired his last two shells. Penchant was hit, but from a distance, and roared with laughter in spite of the blood streaming down his jacket. He fired his pistol into the air, shrieking and shouting over the wind.

"I told you we were brothers, Jones. I told you we were friends."

He turned to Matt and flashed a grin. But all Matt saw were his light-brown eyes. Finally, those dead eyes.

The same hollow look that he shared with Adam Lanza and Dylann Roof. The eyes of a beast. A devil.

Matt watched Penchant turn away and gaze over the bow. He listened as the man with blond cornrows let out another shriek and emptied his pistol into the ceiling of the bridge. One deafening shot after the next.

Matt's eyes snapped back to the rocks. He calculated the amount of diesel fuel it took to run a luxury yacht this size and could see the explosion in his mind. Five, maybe ten seconds—no time to think. He tossed the shotgun onto the deck, then climbed over the rail and dove into the ice-cold water. His only chance at survival was to shut everything down and swim toward shore as fast as he could swim.

He heard Penchant howl with laughter as the *Greedy Bastard* skidded out of the water and crashed into the rocks. A split second ticked off before the air cracked and the explosion billowed upward. Matt took a quick look over his shoulder—the snow burning up in the fireball before it could reach the water. The wind dying out as all the air seemed to be drawn into the massive flames. The dark December sky lighting up bright as noon. The sound of debris flying out of the fireball and hitting the water close by.

Matt turned back and started to swim toward shore. And then he felt the pain ricocheting through his body. The gunshot wounds in his chest and gut that had been healing for seven weeks had come alive in the ice-cold water. It was a stabbing pain, almost as if the knife had been red-hot. As if the knife wouldn't stop penetrating his flesh.

He realized that he was becoming light-headed and could no longer feel his arms and legs, just the four gunshot wounds.

He started to sink, then pulled himself back up. The water looked as black as ink. He tried to pull himself together and started swimming. He concentrated on moving his arms and legs even though he couldn't be sure they were even there.

Over and over again he played a fantasy in his head. A series of simple images. Quiet images. A man taking a swim on a hot summer day. A man who looked quite like him. Over and over again, until finally, he pulled himself onto the beach and heard himself let out a series of tortured gasps. As he fell to his knees in the snow and sand, unable to stop shivering, he looked up and saw them coming. Men and women in uniform carrying flashlights and brandishing guns. They were running across the lawn. They were running toward him. He could see them coming in the night.

CHAPTER 69

Matt went through his meds, zipped up the pocket, and slid his shaving kit into his briefcase. After checking the time, he took a sip of coffee and started folding clothes and tossing them into the duffel bag. His flight to LA was about three hours off, and Rogers had promised to swing by the hotel and give him a lift to the airport.

The TV was switched to a cable news channel, which Matt found difficult to watch because of the subject matter.

As it turned out, Kate Brown's take on Assistant US Attorney Ken Doyle didn't work out as she had hoped. The federal prosecutor *wasn't* going places, and probably would never become the nation's next attorney general.

Instead, Ken Doyle had become the Department of Justice's latest fall guy.

Matt watched the federal prosecutor trying to push his way through the media gathered on the sidewalk outside the Trump Hotel on Pennsylvania Avenue in Washington, DC. Most of the audio was garbled as microphones and cameras were knocked together or pushed away. It looked like Doyle was trying to exit the hotel and walk down the sidewalk to his office in the DOJ Building on the other side of Tenth Street. But he was on his own and seriously outnumbered.

Someone knocked on the door. Matt looked at the pack of cigarettes on the table and, without hesitating, tossed them into the trash—over and done. Then he crossed the room and opened the door. It was Special Agent in Charge Wes Rogers, wearing a grin on his face.

"This is the day I've been looking forward to since you first got here, Jones."

Matt gave him a look and laughed. "You mean because you're driving me to the airport."

Rogers nodded and seemed delighted by the idea.

Matt walked back to the bed and finished packing up his clothing. Rogers had come through when he needed to come through, and Matt had decided that he liked him. The feeling was mutual, as Rogers had offered him a job twice since he returned to Philadelphia from Greenwich.

"You got any news?" Matt said.

Rogers's eyes widened. "It's not public yet, but the word from Justice is that if Doyle had done his job as a prosecutor and stayed out of our way, the road to Andrew Penchant would have been—look, she's saying it for me."

He stopped talking, and Matt followed his gaze over to the TV. A journalist had stepped away from the crowd and was using it as background for her update and summation of the story.

"According to three sources in the Department of Justice, Assistant US Attorney Ken Doyle stepped out of bounds and got in the way of the FBI's investigation. One source close to the attorney general said, and this is a quote, 'Mr. Doyle should have known that he was being paid as a prosecutor, not an investigator, and he ended up leading the task force off the cliff.' Another source told me that the FBI's Behavioral Analysis Unit had offered a profile matching Andrew Penchant early in the game. If Mr. Doyle had let the FBI do their job, they told me, M. Trevor Jones, one of the most celebrated men in the world of finance and often regarded with affection as the King of Wall Street, would almost certainly be alive today. And so would his wife and two sons. The FBI has also confirmed through DNA analysis—the rumors now official—that LAPD Detective Matt Jones is indeed Mr. Jones's firstborn son and only known survivor."

Matt switched the power off and tossed the remote on the desk. It was all out in the open now. Out in the open and very hard to look at all at once, and in the light of day.

Rogers protested, but seemed amused. "Why did you shut it off?"

Matt didn't say anything, and shrugged his shoulders like he'd had enough.

"I can guarantee you what her next sentence would have been, Jones."

Matt zipped up his duffel bag. "Yeah, what's that?"

Rogers laughed. "Have you looked outside? Do you see what's going on out there?"

Matt knew what Rogers was talking about. Doyle may have had twenty-five cameras following him around in Washington. But since Matt's new, ever-changing reality made another change and word got out on TV and the Internet, since the producers of *Get Buzzed* broke the story wide-open in Ryan Day's name, hundreds of news outlets had begun assembling outside the Marriott Downtown in Philadelphia. Filbert Street had been shut down between Twelfth and Thirteenth Streets to accommodate the crowds.

They had their story finally. Matt was the firstborn son of the King of Wall Street, the only surviving member of the family, and, on his mother's side, the nephew of Dr. George Baylor, a serial killer and a fiend still on the run and living in the free world. But even more, Matt was the grandson of Howard Stewart, who, until Bernie Madoff came along, was the biggest scoundrel Wall Street had ever known.

As if his bloodline wasn't enough, the story had a finish.

Jones, a rookie homicide detective from Los Angeles, had come to Philadelphia to assist the FBI in the investigation of the Stratton murders, and then the Holloway murders. And he hadn't just solved the case. He had tracked down the monsters, risked his life to go into battle with them, and, on his own, taken both of them out. Andrew Penchant and Avery Cooper would never hurt anyone again. Both of them were dead.

Matt's new, ever-changing reality. It was all out in the open now. Out in the open and still very hard to look at.

He grabbed his bags and turned to Rogers. "Let's get out of here."

Two US marshals were waiting for them down the hall, the elevator doors open. They stepped in and rode down to the first floor. Once the doors opened in the lobby, hundreds of strobe lights started flashing and everything went electric. Ten more US marshals were here, ushering them through the sea of cameras to a black Chevy Suburban parked at the entrance. People were shouting questions at him. They were asking Matt to smile, give a high five or even a fist bump. People were cheering and clapping, some even holding signs. When Matt waved at the crowd, the intensity of light from the flash units almost blinded him. He climbed into the backseat behind Rogers. After shutting the door, he glanced at the driver and saw a familiar face.

It was the US marshal in the business suit. The man with no name who liked to drive fast. He had a smile on his face and he nodded.

"Looks like you're goin' to Disneyland, Jones."

CHAPTER 70

Matt cracked open a beer and walked out onto the deck. It was Christmas Eve. The sun had set about an hour ago. It was a clear night, a quiet night, and he could see the entire basin from Venice Beach and Santa Monica to the tall buildings downtown.

He took a swig from the bottle. None of the homes on the south side of the canyon had survived the wildfire. In spite of the darkness, he counted fifteen black spots on the south rim. Fifteen families who had lost everything. He knew that there were five more, he just couldn't see them in the night. He also knew that the wind had carried the firestorm over to the north side, but only two houses had burned down.

He heard a pair of coyotes yipping and howling from the canyon floor and wondered if they'd climb the hill tonight to sleep underneath his deck. He'd seen them the day after his return, and somehow all four pups had survived.

His hand reached for his shirt pocket before he realized what was going on. It had been an automatic response to what he was thinking. He'd reached into his pocket for a pack of cigarettes.

He laughed and took another sip of beer. He'd tossed the pack out before leaving Philadelphia for a reason. He'd tossed the pack out because it was time.

His cell phone started vibrating. Digging it out of his pocket, he read the caller ID on the face and felt his stomach begin churning.

The caller was Ken Doyle.

Matt stared at the federal prosecutor's name, letting the phone ring three more times before finally taking the call.

"This is Jones," he said.

Doyle didn't say anything, and Matt could hear him breathing.

"What is it, Doyle? Why the hell would you call me?"

"Hello, Matthew. Merry Christmas."

Matt recoiled. It wasn't the federal prosecutor. It was Dr. Baylor, using Doyle's phone.

"What have you done, Doctor?"

"Nothing much," Baylor said in a voice too casual to trust. "Just trying to get in a little R and R after a few hectic weeks. I've been reading the papers and watching the news. It seems you're a conquering hero these days."

"Until they check out the family tree."

Baylor hesitated again, then came back. "You were, of course, hoping to bring levity to the conversation, and I was supposed to laugh, but didn't. It must be difficult for you, Matthew. Dear old Dad didn't make it, did he? The man who abandoned you and your mother is finally dead."

Matt didn't say anything, everything in his world turning bleak and ominous.

"It's official," the doctor went on. "The monkey's off your back, but it means that you're an orphan now, so I'll bet it stings."

Everything in his world was slipping back into the gloom. Matt didn't take the bait and wasn't thinking about his father or himself right now. He was thinking about Doyle's caller ID.

"What have you done, Doctor?"

"Not much, really."

"What have you done?"

"How should I put it? I've tidied up a few loose ends."

Loose ends. Matt could picture the two loose ends as if he had been standing in the same room with Baylor.

"You're in Doyle's house in Washington, aren't you?"

"I think I am, Matthew. I think I'm using his phone. You must have noticed the caller ID."

Matt pricked up his ears, concentrating on what he was hearing in the background. There was a creaking noise, and it seemed to be repeating itself.

"Is Kate Brown there?" he said.

Baylor took another moment, almost as if he needed to think it over.

"Is she there, Doctor?"

"At some level, yes," Baylor said. "Not in spirit anymore, but yes, she's here."

Matt's heart skipped a beat and started pounding. "You cut her, didn't you? The Glasgow smile. The Chelsea grin. You did it again. You couldn't help yourself. You killed her."

"She does look happy. I'd have to agree with you on that, Matthew. Good old Kate's sporting one hell of a smile these days."

Matt leaned forward and took the blow. He could see Kate's face just as he could still see the faces of Baylor's first three victims in Los Angeles—Millie Brown, Faith Novakoff, and Brooke Anderson. He could see the doctor drugging Kate and slicing her face from ear to lips and lips to ear. He could see him waiting for her to wake up and look at what he'd done to her. He could see the madman waiting for her to scream so that the cuts on her skin would break open and all the blood would flow.

He could hear her cry out. He could hear her weeping.

Several moments passed, the horrific images in Matt's mind blowing through him in a series of hard and twisted waves.

He could see Kate's hideous face. Her corpse.

He looked out at the sea of lights that helped make the City of Angels so peaceful. So beautiful. He looked up at the stars in the sky and a new moon.

"What about Doyle, Baylor?" he said quietly. "Has he got a smile on his face, too?"

"Actually, poor Ken here has had a couple of rough days watching his career go down the tubes. He got fired this afternoon, and he didn't take it very well."

Matt shivered, the hairs on the back of his neck standing on end. "What's that noise, Doctor? That creaking sound?"

"Why that's Ken, Matthew. Your good friend. The former prosecutor who's been disgraced."

"What's he doing?"

"Not much, really. Just sort of . . . hanging around."

New images surfaced before Matt's eyes. One after the next.

Baylor cleared his throat. "Isn't it wonderful that you solved your murder cases and I'm still a free man? A nephew and his uncle. A detective and a plastic surgeon. Isn't it remarkable that the two of us can coexist in the same world, Matthew? That we can coexist and thrive in our professions?"

Matt stood up, turned to the east, and looked at the tall buildings downtown. "But we can't coexist, Doctor."

"And why is that?"

Matt couldn't really find the words and settled for the obvious.

"Because you're insane," he said finally.

ACKNOWLEDGMENTS

Many thanks go to my editors, Kjersti Egerdahl, Charlotte Herscher, and Jacque Ben-Zekry, and to the entire team at Thomas & Mercer. I'd also like to thank my agent, Scott Miller, and Charlotte Conway for their advice and support. This novel wouldn't feel authentic and true without the help of many friends and professionals working in law enforcement. Any technical deviation from facts or procedures is my responsibility alone.

ABOUT THE AUTHOR

Photo © 2015 Robert Ellis

Robert Ellis is the international bestselling author of *Access to Power*, *The Dead Room*, the critically acclaimed Lena Gamble novels—*City of Fire*, *The Lost Witness*, and *Murder Season*—and the Detective Matt Jones series, which includes *City of Echoes* and *The Love Killings*. His books have been translated into more than ten languages and selected as top reads by *Booklist*, *Publishers Weekly*, National Public Radio, the *Chicago Tribune*, the *Toronto Sun*, the *Guardian* (UK), *People* magazine, *USA Today*, and the *New York Times*. Born in Philadelphia, Ellis moved to Los Angeles to work as a writer, producer, and director in film, television, and advertising. For more information about the author, visit him online at www.robertellis.net.